MISSIO EARTH

FIL MUNAS

A NEW AUTHORS PRESS

Paperback ISBN: 978-0-578-14333-0
Hardback ISBN: 978-0-578-14334-7

A NEW AUTHORS PRESS

PRINTED IN THE UNITED STATES OF AMERICA

MISSION TO
EARTH

CONTENTS

PROLOGUE

𝕿 his is the account of a mission I undertook from Galymon to a small rocky planet in a quiet quadrant of our present Universe. My original report on this matter was delivered to the Most High Tribunal of Galymon which is our Supreme Authority on my home planet. I wish to acknowledge my deep gratitude to our High Tribunal for this opportunity.

The following is meant to acquaint my esteemed readers not from Galymon to our way of thinking:

Truth and Fairness are the arrows
Rolling down the stream of life,
All through the vistas of tomorrows,
Yesterday's struggle, today's strife.

So come with me beloved people
Traveling in this Space and Time;
All soaring higher than the eagle,
Searching for that Mystic Rhyme.

Like living gods with wondrous vision
Boldly scanning cosmoscapes;
Allied in Life we too shall mission,
Through those ageless, timeless shapes.

Sword of Fairness, Shield of Truth,
Our sherpas for this wondrous time;
And fired by the flame of youth,
We'll seek and find that Mystic Rhyme!

Mac

CHAPTER I:
ARRIVAL

Galymon is my home planet. It is one of six major planets of a binary star system in our present Universe. Our stellar family is nestled in the third spiral arm of the venerable Meon galaxy, a large face-on spiral galaxy known on planet Earth as the Pinwheel galaxy. Galymon has approximately twice Earth's mass and three times its diameter.

Galymon was once a nomad planet meandering in interstellar space for a bit more than six billion years when we were entrained by the gravitational well of two newly minted binary stars, Mo and Po. That happened about 2 billion years ago. The word "planet" itself comes from the Greek word for "wanderer" or "nomad." Humans had noted how a few starry light-points moved across the night sky in relation to the countless other stars that remained fixed. These wanderers they called planets. Nomad planets are objects of planetary size that are ejected from their formative stellar systems. Our own astral parent was a single B-type star called Boo, now demised. B-type stars are about ten times as massive as the Earth's star, the Sun, and live for just 100 million years. But during their brief existence, they shine a thousand times brighter than the Sun. Luckily, Galymon was ejected from our planetary nursery before Boo flamed out. We then drifted in interstellar space until gravitational capture by Po and Mo.

There are countless nomad planets in the cosmos. Some of these wandering planets may be later captured by the gravity of new stars, like Mo and Po did Galymon. Most galaxies are literally teeming with these roaming planets. Galaxies may harbor hundreds of such nomads for every star they contain, thus potentially hosting many trillions of them. Many nomad planets have their own native sources of energy, and some have advanced lifeforms on them. Life was established on Galymon when our planet was still nomadic, long before entrainment by our present pair of step-stars.

Our two luminaries Mo and Po, are quite near each other, hardly 77 million miles[1] apart at perigee or closest approach; at apogee they are 318 million miles apart. These two stars are much alike, having approximately similar masses and luminosities. They are both F-type main sequence stars rotating around a common center of gravity. Po and Mo are fourth generation stars of high metallicity and well past middle age. Almost two-thirds of their stellar lifespan is now behind them, though they

---

1   Two systems of units are commonly used on Earth for mensuration, though alternate systems do exist. One is the imperial, or foot-pound-second (FPS) system, the other is the metric, or meter-kilogram-second (MKS) system. The MKS system is the one usually used for scientific measurements, and for common usage in many regions of Earth. However, the narrator prefers to employ the FPS system in this accounting because it was the one commonly used for measurement by most of the population in the narrator's neighborhood during this visit. For conversion, one meter is 3.28 feet, and one kilogram is 2.2 pounds. A mile is 1.61 kilometers. Though the French sought to metricize time in units of ten as well, a second still represents similar bits of time in both systems.

still have enough hydrogen left in their stellar cores to continue fusing that element to generate energy for another 1.02 billion years in the case of Po, and 1.13 billion years for Mo.

The main sequence is a distinctive distribution of stars that forms on a scatter-graph called the Hertzsprung-Russell diagram. Stellar sequences are obtained by plotting the color of a star on one axis of this graph, against its brightness on the other axis. When plotted in this way, several continuous bands of stars appear on the graph. Stars along one distinct band are called main sequence stars. The vast majority of stars shining today are still on the main sequence. Most stars on the main sequence are stable for long periods of time. They all produce energy by fusing hydrogen into helium in their stellar cores. The rate at which they do this depends on the mass of the star itself. The larger the mass, the faster they burn out and die, and the shorter their presence on the main sequence of the Hertzsprung-Russell diagram. These main sequence stars are classed into seven types depending on their mass. On Earth, by convention, each type is identified with an alphabet character, noted here from the most massive to the least massive stars—the average life expectancy of each star type, in billions of years, is shown in parenthesis after each letter: O(0.01), B(0.1), A(1), F(3), G(10), K(50), and M(200)[2].

Populations of stars are birthed in successive generations. First generation stars were condensed from matter which was present in the primordial Universe. This primal matter consisted

---

2   Upwards of 90 percent of all stars in this Universe lie on the main sequence. The bulk of them consist of the least massive M-type stars, each one averaging just one-fifth of the Sun's mass (the Sun itself is a G-type star). By contrast, the most massive stars, the O-type, average 50 times the Sun's mass. The abundance in the Universe of each star-type on the main sequence is as follows: O(0.00001%), B(0.1%), A(0.7%), F(2%), G(3.5%), K(8%), and M(80%).

mainly of just two elements—almost three-quarters of it was hydrogen and one-quarter helium. By atomic nuclear fusion, in a
process called stellar nucleosynthesis, these first generation stars
eventually forged heavier elements such as carbon, nitrogen,
and oxygen from this primordial matter. Still heavier elements
were manufactured by stars, particularly at the very end of their
life cycles, by further fusion of lighter elements produced earlier. As the dying star repeatedly expands and contracts during
its death throes, it successively fuses heavier elements during
each contraction. The star may eventually shatter in a supernova
explosion, dispersing this enriched material and seeding the surrounding region with heavier elements. New second generation
stars condense from this enriched medium and are technically described as having higher "metallicity," a reference to the
heavier elements present in these new stars—the term does not
refer to "metal" in the commonly understood sense. As these
second generation stars in turn die and disperse their material
once again, they endow the interstellar medium with even greater metallicity to input into the next generation of stars. The cycle
repeats from generation to generation. Po and Mo were born in
the fourth generation of this process.

The Universe we occupy today has a beginning in space
and time. Of course, before this Universe itself was born, the
concept of space and time was meaningless, because space and
time are merely properties of the existing Universe we inhabit;
others are different. This particular Universe emerged 13.798
± 0.037 billion years ago from a quantum fluctuation in the
perennial Ocean of Eternity—universes are forever appearing

in this way. From an infinitely small and infinitely dense point dubbed a singularity, far smaller in dimension than the nucleus of an atom, a sudden efflux of matter, and its mirror image antimatter, were produced in copious amounts. This particular event is called the Big Bang.

Now, matter and antimatter usually appear in precisely equal quantities during these random quantum fluctuations in the Ocean of Eternity, only to instantly annihilate each other and disappear completely from independent existence. That, then, would be the end of this astonishing tale with nobody here to hear about it. But in this unusual instance, for every 1,000,000,000 (one billion) parts of antimatter formed, there were 1,000,000,001 parts of matter produced in the Big Bang. That single extra part per billion of matter, left over after the matter/antimatter annihilation at the beginning of this event, makes up the entire contents of the cosmos we know. But for that tiniest of asymmetries, nothing at all would be here in this Universe, which itself would not exist.

At its commencement the Universe was a hot, formless "soup" of the most elementary particles: quarks and leptons. Then as it expanded and cooled, layer upon layer of structure developed— protons and neutrons and electrons, atomic nuclei, atoms, stars, galaxies, clusters of galaxies, and superclusters of galaxies. In the first fraction of a second after emerging from the singularity, our Universe experienced a momentary burst of exponential expansion called inflation, before settling down to a more leisurely rate of growth. Inflation commenced when the Universe was a billionth of a billionth of a second old. The inflationary epoch ended in a flash, between 10^{-33} and 10^{-32} seconds after it began. During this inflationary period the Universe expanded at superluminal velocity, meaning a growth spurt faster than the speed of light.

From its initial subnuclear size, it swelled during inflation to a macroscopic size of a few yards or meters across.

Following this brief inflationary period, the Universe continued to expand at a much more relaxed pace. As it expanded of course, the Universe cooled as a consequence of the expansion. Once the temperature dropped to approximately 3000°C (5432°F) in about 400,000 years, atomic nuclei formed. These first nuclei were individual protons, the basic form of matter. Different numbers of protons stuck together make up the various elements in nature. At this point now, protons were able to combine with free electrons to form neutral atoms—first hydrogen and then helium—in a 3:1 ratio. This event allowed the energetic photons, then bound up in the foggy plasma of the primitive Universe, to split off from that plasma and stream away into surrounding space. The Universe thereupon became clear and transparent, and there was light for the first time in its history. This original appearance of light in this Universe is called the Cosmic Dawn. That initial propagation of energy can be detected even today as the Cosmic Microwave Background (CMB) radiation. The first generation of stars were then born from the neutral matter thus formed. That was how our Universe came into being and then evolved during the very early stages of its development. Even though the condensed version of events described here may lack specific details, it faithfully outlines the genesis story of the present cosmos that we find ourselves in. This Big Bang formulation of cosmogenesis is the currently prevailing consensus for the origin of this Universe. The model itself is fortified by the corroborative evidence provided for it by the CMB radiation.

Like our own beloved Mo and Po, many stars in our Universe belong to binary, or even multiple star systems. Stars harbor planets around them more often than not. Galymon travels in a stable orbit averaging 227 million miles from the center of mass, or gravity, of both our stars. Planets in binary star systems may orbit around one or both stars; those that orbit both stars are called circumbinary planets, and Galymon belongs in that category. As could be imagined from this description, our planet's revolution around its two stars, which in turn orbit each other, along with Galymon's own axial rotation around itself, makes the sequence of days and nights quite remarkable on my home planet.

Even more complex planetary systems are common in our Universe, many with multiple stars gravitationally linked to each other in elaborate orbits. For example, one such system in my home galaxy is a close neighbor to Galymon. It harbors a small life bearing planet within a stellar formation of four large stars. The four stars of this particular system are paired into two sets of binaries. The two stars in each binary pair orbit their own respective centers of mass. Then, the two binary sets in turn orbit a second center of mass between the sets themselves. The life bearing planet mentioned here revolves around a particular star in one of the binary pairs. All four stars in the system illuminate that planet's gorgeous landscape. They do this over various time sequences corresponding to the respective motions of these celestial bodies in this intricate cosmic ballet. Successive days and nights on this planet are magnificently orchestrated in mesmerizing rhythms.

Our Universe today subsumes a vast ocean of matter and energy. Some of this is concentrated into countless stars and myriad planets organized in local collections called galaxies. There are billions of these starry galaxies throughout our current Universe— current only because universes themselves have finite life cycles. An average sized galaxy in our Universe could contain over 400 billion stars. Stars frequently have swarms of planets and other objects swirling around them. As noted already for Galymon, planets may be ejected from their stellar systems and wander around interstellar space as nomad planets.

What follows in this narrative is an account of my visit from Galymon to a small planet called Earth. The Earth, along with companion objects, orbits a solitary main sequence G-type star called the Sun. The Sun, now in the middle of its stellar life-cycle, is a third generation star located in a galaxy called the Milky Way which contains over 300 billion stars. Viewed from Earth's present location in its galaxy, my own Meon or Pinwheel galaxy could be found in the constellation Ursa Major (Great Bear) and is identified in the standard Earth-based publication called the *New General Catalogue of Nebulae and Clusters of Stars*, as NGC 5457. Our galaxy is a face-on spiral galaxy like the Milky Way, about two-thirds larger in diameter. It contains approximately 1,000 billion, or 1 trillion stars.

Galymon is about 6.5 megaparsecs from Earth. A parsec, short for parallax of one arc second, is a geometric measure of distance and is equal to 3.26 light years in length. As a megaparsec is one million parsecs, then 6.5 megaparsecs is a little more than 21 million light years away. A light year, also a unit of length, is the distance that a photon of light will travel in one full Earth year. Since light advances at a constant speed of 186,282 miles a second in a vacuum (299,791 kilometers per second), it will complete about six trillion miles in one Earth year. Therefore, calculating for 21 million light years, Galymon is approximately 126 quintillion miles from Earth. This distance, though immense in human terms, is just the blink of an eye on the scale of the Universe.

Our Universe is indeed an exquisite expanse of endless wonders spread in a magnificent array across every imaginable panorama of time and space. It is filled with enchantment and breathtaking visions. It is also full of menace and violence. This Universe nourishes utopian expanses of idyllic peace and serenity, randomly interspersed with dreadful cataclysms of deconstruction and renewal. We are, ourselves, a constituting feature of that Universe—not apart from it, but a part of it— completely integrated into its very fabric and function. We are the Universe scrutinizing ourselves, and therefore the Universe is scrutinizing us. On Galymon we believe that in this realization rests the reconciliation between the extremes of nothing and everything, from existing in a state of "being" to its opposite state of "non-being." My dear reader, our Universe is a cornucopia of wonders. I will describe to you in the pages that follow some of the marvels I have witnessed.

At this point in my narrative, a general observation regarding the degree of exactitude and precision in the numbers attached to the data presented here would surely be in order. It is certainly obvious that a measuring device must be sensitive to the magnitude of the measurement being taken. For example, quantifying the mass of a proton requires infinitely greater precision and accuracy to be meaningful, than if measuring the mass of a planet. The Law of Appropriate Proportions applies just the same to measurements and to measuring devices as well. For instance, the age of the present Universe we inhabit is about 13.8 billion current Earth years; a few dozen million years on either side of this figure will not significantly alter the conceptual validity or relevance of that number. Yet, a few months imprecisely added or subtracted from the five year life expectancy of a guinea-pig would make that figure inaccurate and quite misleading.

So come with me my esteemed reader as I describe my mission to Earth, and kindly join me as I explore my host planet and examine the characteristics of the life it nurtures. We shall also soon meet with the dominant lifeform that inhabits its space today.

꧁꧂

My name is Mac. I was commissioned by the Most High Tribunal of Galymon to journey to a small rocky planet selected from among several dozen other life bearing planets we detected during a systematic scan of space in a narrow wedge of the Orion Arm in the Milky Way galaxy. The Orion Arm lies between the Sagittarius and Perseus Arms of that galaxy. I was ordered by our High Tribunal to conduct a mission to the selected planet because it held an unusual population of matter based beings. These creatures referred to their terrestrial[3] home as Earth, and to themselves as Humans or People. What attracted our attention to their planet and focused our interest on them was that these beings who called themselves humans, were sapient as well. Sapience means the possession of self-consciousness or self-awareness, a more developed and elaborate form of consciousness than sentience is. Sentience is merely the ability to sense and become aware of the external environment, a feature common to all life everywhere, since any lifeform requires this property to survive in its own environment. Sapience, on the other hand, characterizes the ability of creatures to be *aware of being aware*, an attribute far less common in our Universe.

---

3   A terrestrial, telluric, or rocky planet, belongs to one of two classes of common planets. The first class of planets, to which Earth belongs, is composed primarily of silicate rocks and metals. The Latin words *terra* and *tellus* refer to "Earth" and indicate that these planets are similar to planet Earth in structure. All rocky planets have a central metallic core mostly of iron, surrounded by a mantle of silicates. These planets differ in structure from a second class of much larger gas planets formed mostly of hydrogen, helium, and water.

What additionally attracted our attention to Earth as a possible target for further exploration, was that these sapient humans who lived on its rocky surface had only quite recently acquired the ability to navigate space outside their own planet's gravitational confines. Understandably, at this time in their brief cosmological history, they knew only how to use the rather primitive technology of controlled chemical combustion to propel their rockets to the escape velocity needed to exit their planet's gravitational clutches. Even so, these astonishing humans had fairly recently succeeded in placing a miniscule satellite[4] they had fabricated entirely by themselves into low Earth orbit only a little more than fifty years ago. Then hardly a decade later, they successfully transported a few humans across a brief distance of 1.3 light seconds to the surface of their single natural satellite, the Moon. They were then able to bring those individuals safely back to Earth after walking on the Moon.

Humans seemed to be filled with curiosity and adventure. Upon loosening the gravitational chains that bound them until so very recently to the surface of their own planet, these people proceeded to send complex probes and measuring devices to land or fly-by all the known major objects in their stellar system which they call the solar system. In this way they obtained the most spectacular images from space of their local neighborhood, and much further beyond.

About forty years ago these humans lobbed their first physical message destined for interstellar space in the form of a

---

4   Sputnik I, the first satellite ever launched by humans into outer space, was a 184-pound capsule placed there through rocket propulsion by the now defunct Soviet Union. Sputnik achieved an Earth orbit with an apogee (farthest point from Earth) of 584 miles and a perigee (nearest point from Earth) of 143 miles. It circled their planet every 96 minutes and remained in orbit for several months until it fell back and flamed out in the Earth's atmosphere.

gold-anodized aluminum plaque identifying themselves and their location in the Universe. We were informed on Galymon while still pondering suitable planets for direct exploration, that a vessel called Pioneer 10 carrying this golden plaque had crossed the outer limits of their solar system's heliosphere. The heliosphere is the circumscribed region of space dominated by their star and extends for about 10 billion miles in every direction around the Sun. Its edge is often regarded as the interface between the solar system itself and the rest of interstellar space. At the time that we noted their plaque at the edge of the solar system, humans themselves had lost radio contact with Pioneer 10 for approximately ten years previously, because the craft had run out of power to broadcast signals back to them on Earth.

While still on Galymon, as we were carefully appraising planets that were identified as potential candidates for exploration, our team was fortunate to acquire and read an extraordinary book published on Earth some 44 years ago. The book titled, *The Naked Ape: A Zoologist's Study of the Human Animal*, written by a most gifted zoologist and fabulous author named Desmond Morris, played a significant role in Earth being selected as the subject planet for further investigation by us. This book, a bestseller on Earth when it was first published, represented a popular attempt by humans to accurately and comprehensively portray themselves, not as exceptional or unique objects created by an exclusive and closed process, but as a natural extension of the biological world itself, thus putting them on the same plane as all other lifeforms on their planet. This remarkable burst of candid sapience on their part certainly cued us positively in their direction.

Yet another factor influencing us on Galymon that favored

exploration of Earth rather than other candidate planets, was the recently burgeoning cognitive resonance of humans. This extraordinary flowering of complex ideas and concepts among these inhabitants of Earth—creatures that had appeared only so recently in their planet's history—was very meaningful to us on Galymon as we continued to finalize our list of planets to explore. It alerted us to a paradigmatic shift in the developmental trajectory of this lifeform. For us on Galymon, it seemed exceptional that much of this cognitive blossoming had occurred in hardly the last two centuries of this curious creature's chronology. In fact, only fairly recently had humans arrived at an elegantly comprehensive explanation, based on universally acknowledged evolutionary principles, to account for the provenance of life on their planet. In the physical realm of existence as well, these astonishing people had begun to conceptualize space and time as a single composite entity, sculpted locally by aggregations of matter within that matrix. This, they correctly figured, produced gravity-wells around those objects in proportion to the object's mass. These are only two examples of the accelerated cognitive processing these humans were displaying recently.

The final cut, certainly, was not easy to make. Other planets located in that narrow wedge of special interest to us in the Orion Arm of the Milky Way, also had promising features to offer, laying legitimate claims to our affections. One such notable planet was home to creatures routinely using teleportation, which was indeed quite impressive, but also rather common in our Universe today. These beings with teleportation had already begun their own missions to nearby life anchoring planets or moons that were inside a circumscribed area they called their Near Abroad.

Another stellar system harboring life that we detected

from Galymon lay almost next door to Earth and its own solar system. Humans know this object as Alpha Centauri AB,
a binary star system only 4.37 light years from their Sun. It
is their second closest stellar neighbor after the red dwarf
star Proxima Centauri—sometimes called Alpha Centauri
C—which is a little nearer at 4.24 light years away. Alpha
Centauri A and B are stars hospitable to life in their neighborhood. Alpha Centauri A is a G-type main sequence star
(yellow colored) just like the Sun, but 10% more massive
than Earth's star. Alpha Centauri B is a K-type main sequence
star (orange colored) about 10% less massive than the Sun.
These twin stars orbit a common center of mass approximately every 80 Earth years, with the stars approaching as close
as one billion miles to each other, and then receding back to
3.3 billion miles apart. Those distances are greater than the
average separation of 77 million miles between our own twin
stars, Po and Mo.

K-type stars or orange dwarfs, because they are relatively
cooler and burn slower and therefore have longer life expec-
tancies, are more likely to host matter-centered life on their
planets and moons, than would G-type stars or yellow dwarfs
like the Sun which are hotter and shorter lived. A typical habitable planet orbiting a K-type star, on average, would be older
than Earth, and about two to three times larger. The larger size
ensures the dependable retention of an atmosphere. It also gives
the planet a smoother surface with shallower oceans that are
fragmented by more numerous land masses for life to evolve,
and it provides more magnetic shielding against cosmic and
stellar high-energy radiation.

Only very recently did humans themselves become aware
of an Earth sized planet orbiting Alpha Centauri B at about 4

million miles from that star. Now, that particular planet does not support Earthlike life because of extreme daytime surface temperatures due to proximity to its star. However, within that same stellar system, we had earlier detected from our location on Galymon, a planet called Odissa orbiting Alpha Centauri B from about 183 million miles out. This planet is home to three different types of carbon based sapient lifeforms, one of them more technologically advanced than humans are. It was thus extraordinarily challenging for our High Tribunal to choose a designated planet for an exploratory mission.

After much thought and deliberation, a senior guild of Tribunes made the final decision to direct the proposed mission to Earth, rather than those other planets, many of them though possessing quite astonishing features.

A note regarding the probable intentions of extraterrestrial visitors may be appropriate here.

Most unsolicited extraterrestrial contacts are usually intended to secure territory and strip resources from stars and planets. The hunt for copious oxygen bearing atmospheres to expropriate and use for the benefit of the invaders is especially common in certain parts of the Universe. These oxygen hunting species, frequently fleeing oxygen depleting worlds, confiscate oxygen rich ones like Earth, often decimating preexisting lifeforms on captured territory. So too is the mining for carbon and carboniferous compounds, especially oil or tar sands, the latter more correctly called bituminous sands. These are deposits of silica or sand, saturated with an extremely dense and viscous petroleum residue called bitumen. Humans themselves

are already extracting hydrocarbons to burn for energy from
tar sands on their own planet without evincing much concern
for the environment. Extraterrestrial armies, of course, are not
seeking out bituminous sands for their raw energy content—
advanced civilizations capable of such raids can generate as
much energy as they need from other sources. Instead, they
are looking for these carbon compounds as root stock for
manufacture of a host of higher order products like plastics,
fertilizers, and pharmaceuticals. Advanced extraterrestrial species have been mining their nearby moons and asteroids for
eons already, and are simply searching for new supply sources
from further afield to replenish their depleting resources. They
usually teleport the seized material back to their home bases or
use wormholes for transportation, unless of course they decide
to settle on the new territory themselves. Such physical colonization leading to permanent settlement in remote locations by
alien civilizations is by and large less frequent than temporary
incursions for plundering resources for themselves.

The element calcium is still another valuable substance in
high demand across the Universe. Calcium makes up hardly 0.007% of matter in the cosmos. It is used for numerous
structural applications by matter-centered lifeforms, all the
way from external shells and internal skeletons of soft-bodied
animals, to limestone and cement for construction. When calcium is deficient in a galactic neighborhood, competition for
the element can be brutal and intense. The notorious Calcium
Wars of the Baby Boom galaxy almost 9.8 billion years ago is
a classic case in point. Other important heavier elements too
may be lacking or deficient in certain regions of the Universe,
depending on the metallicity of stars in that neighborhood, thus
provoking raids and incursions for those valuable resources.

Water is always at a special premium for many lifeforms in our Universe, and has been the basis for the demise of many transgalactic civilizations when their water resources evaporated. The hunt for new water can be never ending; whole oceans have been stolen. These materials are sought after by extraterrestrials when their environments are deficient in them. Such celestial colonization is not any different from expansion and colonization of local space by resident creatures already *in situ.* Their own documented example should direly inform humans about this matter. Their wholesale invasions and depredations across their own planet in search for more territory and resources, is a matter of undisputed historical record.

Most invasive species, whether local or celestial, are unlikely to be tourists. Their intent is certainly not sightseeing, but occupation and control of the space they enter, exploiting and profiting from its animate and inanimate resources. The unending orgy of war, genocide and species extermination by humans, a matter of open historical record, may provide a sobering template for the possible outcome of these extraterrestrial encounters. In just the last 500 years alone, native human populations on three continents on their planet—South America, North America, and Australia—were almost wiped out by other humans who encountered these unfamiliar civilizations. Galymonians also experienced a similar phase when we first encountered other civilizations. The number of species wiped out and the incalculable harm done to ourselves and others were incomprehensibly monumental. We surely would have continued on this path of mutual destruction until we had all perished, but for the advent of our Great Sage Wonda, who taught us how to live and let live.

An interesting example of extraterrestrial colonization

occurred on a galaxy near Earth. Mac knows of a sapient lifeform called Ruints living in the Triangulum galaxy (NGC 598), a close neighbor to the Milky Way. These two galaxies are just three million light years apart. Ruints are extraordinarily complex boron based creatures that flourish by zombifying prolific carbon based lifeforms called Erins, on many star systems in their galaxy.

A zombie, in Earth mythology, is a dead person given the semblance of life by an external agent that controls the zombie's behavior and actions. Zombies remain under control of the external agent because they do not have a will of their own. As a matter of fact, there exist several lifeforms in the Universe where the behavior of one creature is possessed and controlled by another for the sole benefit of the possessor. This type of meta-parasitism is also seen on Earth. For instance, we had noted on Galymon, from data gathered when screening for planet candidates, that humans themselves had reported several cases of zombiism on their own planet.

Certain wasps on Earth commandeer caterpillars to stand guard over their young. The wasp first lays its eggs on the caterpillar. The eggs hatch and the wasp larvae enter the caterpillar, feeding on the caterpillar's body fluids. When ready to pupate, the wasp larvae emerge from the caterpillar by eating through its skin without killing the host. The larvae then attach themselves to a nearby twig and spin their cocoons. The nutrifacient host caterpillar, still alive, now becomes a zombie, faithfully guarding the wasp-cocoons until the adult wasps emerge. Only after that event does the caterpillar finally die. Then there is the peculiar case of the zombie spider and the sorceress wasp. The wasp lays her eggs on the spider's abdomen. Just before the wasp larvae hatch, the enchanted spider compulsively spins a curious looking net, nothing like the web these spiders normally construct. Yet this strange new platform is perfectly designed to support the cocoons of the wasp larvae.

In another reported case by humans, a tiny roundworm can turn an ant into a zombie. The black ant in this story lives in tropical forest canopies and blends imperceptibly into its surroundings, camouflaged from birds that would otherwise devour it in a hurry. In this way, the ant remains safe from habitual predators, until it become enchanted by a tiny worm. Ants infected with this roundworm develop strikingly red berry-colored abdomens and are propelled to venture further away from their colonies than they normally do. These infected zombie ants, scurrying from their homes and looking much like juicy red berries, are readily noticed by birds that eat them. After digesting the ant, the birds pass the parasitic roundworms in their droppings to infect other unsuspecting ants that in turn become zombies.

There are many other instances of zombiism on Earth. Yet another example is *Toxoplasma gondii*, a brain-dwelling protozoan that lives by cycling through both cat and mouse hosts. Infected mice become surprisingly daring and unafraid of cats. These fearless mice, therefore, get eaten more frequently by cats. The parasite can thus more readily enter the cat and complete the feline phase of its life cycle, to be excreted in cat feces that is ingested by other mice who thereby become infected by the parasite. Some people speculate that *T. gondii*, which infects humans as well, can induce behavioral changes in their human hosts too, who may then demonstrate a higher incidence for risky behavior, like the infected mice hosts do.

A peculiar form of collective zombiism was once reported from a stellar neighborhood of the Comet galaxy. This spiral galaxy sporting a comet-like tail is some 3.2 billion light years from Earth. Dwelling in a region of this galaxy are creatures that use tantalum in superconducting composites, allowing them to transmit electricity in a network across their region with almost 100% efficiency. The element tantalum was named by humans after the starving Tantalus of Greek mythology who was forever being "tantalized" by food and drink placed just outside his reach. Tantalum makes up only 0.00000008% of all matter presently in the cosmos. It was even harder to come by in the low-metallicity milieu of the second generation galactic neighborhood those creatures inhabited, thus requiring much time and effort on their part to acquire the metal. So these tantalum using creatures zombified another lifeform to perpetually seek and hoard tantalum for them. Tantalum was practically useless for these zombie hoarders except as body ornaments, much like gold is for humans, but these zombies continued to treasure and horde that lustrous transition metal tantalum for their masters, who came by periodically to collect the stockpiled tantalum.

Back here on Earth again, certain snails infected by an endoparasitic worm go through a monstrous physical transformation and eventually commit suicide in loyal service to their zombifying masters. This hideous chain of events proceeds this way: a susceptible snail species first eats bird feces containing the zombifying worm's eggs. The eggs hatch inside the snail's gut forming motile cysts that migrate into the unfortunate snail's eyestalks. There they transform the slender eyestalks into plump, pulsating, and striped cones that look much like juicy, delicious caterpillars. The snail's behavior now changes dramatically. Whereas unaffected snails prefer the shade and a low profile, the infected ones sprouting gruesome eyestalks that look like plump and succulent larvae, begin to suicidally venture out into the bright sunshine where they become inviting targets for birds. The bird devours the zombie snail and the master parasite thereby enters the bird's digestive tract where it develops into adulthood. The adult worm goes on to lay eggs in the bird's rectum that are released in its feces to infect new snails.

Now, in the matter of ruints mentioned earlier, their zombification of erins served a priceless proliferative goal for them. The element boron, their primary structural constituent, is quite sparse in our Universe. Unlike carbon and other elements which are liberally produced by stellar nucleosynthesis in the cores of stars, boron is not manufactured that way. It is made only in meager quantities by a process called cosmic ray spallation, a mechanism for producing certain elements by the impact of cosmic rays on ordinary matter. Cosmic rays are very high energy particles zapping around in space, mostly hydrogen and helium nuclei, emitted across the Universe by supernova remnants of dead stars. When cosmic rays bump into ordinary matter, those high energy particles occasionally strike and split heavier nuclei present in the impacted matter, thus generating by nuclear fission trace amounts of certain elements not produced in stars by nuclear fusion. Boron is made in this way. Therefore, since there is always a scarcity of boron in the cosmos, boron based life is rare in the Universe. When it does occur, such lifeforms are extremely sparse and tenuous.

Ruints, the boron based lifeform that Mac encountered in the Triangulum galaxy, overcame this limitation by evolving the ability to inject a suite of boron based molecules into their hosts, the erins, and thereby possess the bodies of these extremely prolific carbon based erins living on planetary ecosystems in their galactic neighborhood. Ruints thus usurp the biology and behavior of these erins, controlling and turning them into zombies for their own existential purposes. In this way, though their core substance, boron, remains rare in the

Universe, these ruints are able to achieve widespread distribution in their quadrant of the Triangulum galaxy by introducing bits of themselves into and zombifying the prolific carbon based erins living alongside them.

Before leaving this curious topic of zombies, Mac must certainly mention a species of peculiar Earth based creatures called *Sacculina*. These organisms, related to barnacles, are parasites of both male and female crabs. If a female *Sacculina* enters a male crab, it will interfere with the male's hormonal balance, castrating and sterilizing the male crab, and changing its bodily layout to resemble a female crab. The female *Sacculina* has even been known to cause male crabs to perform mating actions typical of female crabs. Male crabs carrying *Sacculina* in them develop nurturing behaviors typical of female crabs. Female crabs, of course, maintain their feminine character when infected by *Sacculina*. The natural ability of crabs to re-grow a severed claw is lost after *Sacculina* infestation—all the energy the crab would have expended on its own growth and reproduction is now directed to the zombifying *Sacculina* possessing the crab. A male *Sacculina* then looks for a female *Sacculina* attached to the underside of a crab. He implants himself in her, and starts fertilizing her eggs. The crab, whether male or female, then cares for the *Sacculina's* eggs as if they were its own, having been zombified and rendered infertile and compliant by the parasite.

For the benefit of my many friends on Earth who I had the greatest honor and privilege of meeting during this mission to their planet, I have herein rendered into one of their indigenous languages called English, portions of the report I delivered to our High Tribunal in my own native "speech." The reader should kindly note that this report is addressed to the Tribunal and was therefore written with that objective in mind. Many of the concepts, metrics and thought processes familiar to my own kind on Galymon would be incomprehensible to my dear friends on Earth due to the structure and functioning of human and galymonian minds respectively. Because of these limitations, the translation of the report from my native tongue to an Earth dialect required the careful rendering of its contents into a form and style that would be reasonably acceptable to people on my host planet. Regrettably in that case, the narrative itself becomes restricted by the vocabulary, idioms, thoughts and images that humans themselves are comfortable with. I am reminded here of Plato, one of Earth's most revered philosophers, born 2,440 years before Mac visited his planet. Plato encapsulated this problem in an episode of his book, *The Republic*—a dialogue much admired by humans even today. Plato illustrated this limitation in the famous Allegory of the Cave described therein.

In this allegory, presented as a dialogue between Plato's older brother Glaucon and Plato's mentor Socrates, the narrator, channeling Socrates, compares uninitiated people to prisoners who are chained and confined to a cave. The prisoners' movements are so restricted that they can look only in a single direction, which is the one straight ahead of them. Gazing forever in that single direction, the prisoners see shadows projected onto the cave wall before them. These shadows seem to move around, and some to speak. The prisoners carefully observe, discuss, and remember what these shadows are doing, assigning great honor and status to those prisoners among them who could quickly remember these intricate and seemingly important details.

But in fact it is not as it seems to the prisoners. In reality, there is a fire burning at the back of the cave. In front of the fire is a pathway alongside which is a low wall. Behind that wall are real people walking along the pathway, but hidden by the wall. They carry aloft figures of people, animals, and other objects made of many different materials. These are the puppets that cast the shadows projected by the fire—shadows the prisoners see on the cave wall before them. The sounds, incorrectly attributed to these shadows, are actually being made by the people carrying the puppets. This then is the illusion the prisoners experience every day in the cave, unaware that behind the illusion lurks actual reality.

Then one day a prisoner is released from his chains. He stands up, looks around the enclosure and sees the fire at the back of the cave. He quickly notices how the shadows and the sounds are produced. The freed prisoner suddenly realizes that everything he had ever known in his life inside the cave was an illusion, merely shadows cast before him, though based on a reality he was unaware of. He next follows an exit leading outside the cave.

The former prisoner is first blinded by the daylight he encounters outdoors. After his eyes accustom to this sudden influx of photons, he begins to clearly see trees, animals, people, and other objects which were only represented by puppets in the cave whose shadows he had seen projected onto the cave wall. He realizes then that all those things do indeed exist and are knowable to him now only because light from the Sun provided him a brand new perspective. Returning to the cave he is blinded again, this time by the darkness inside. As his eyes adjust to the dark, he once more sees the old shadows on the cave wall. He tells the other prisoners, still shackled and confined, all the marvelous things he saw and learned upon his release from imprisonment. His startled comrades are incredulous and unbelieving, summarily rejecting his narrative, certain that their old friend had gone mad.

This famous parable delineates the communication issues that must always be considered by any alien entity wishing to transfer special understanding of a subject to another lifeform possessing different perceptual and cognitive abilities. A primary hurdle here is that these attempts may fall entirely on deaf ears, the recipient lifeform not even perceiving or recognizing the presence of the alien lifeform. A more alarming outcome is that the recipient may become terrified by the contact and consider the whole business as some sort of dangerous or harmful magic. Or, as in the case of Plato's prisoners, the informant may be considered completely insane.

Take the electromagnetic force for example. This force is one of four fundamental forces of nature—the other three are gravity, the weak nuclear force, and the strong nuclear force. The electromagnetic force is carried in a spectrum, as a wave that has both amplitude and frequency; the amplitude is inversely related to the frequency. The electromagnetic spectrum proceeds from the infinitely small to the infinitely large, all the way from gamma rays to radio waves, spreading freely throughout space as it propagates. Along this infinite continuum, visible light, the tiny band of the electromagnetic spectrum that humans can see, spans a mere 1,280 billionth of a foot to 2,300 billionth foot (390 billionth meter to 700 billionth meter). Obviously therefore, this minuscule slice of the electromagnetic spectrum that humans perceive can only reveal a mere spangle of reality.

Now, perception by any organism is strictly limited by the structure and functioning of its sensory systems. In human vision for example, the organ of sight called the eye contains specialized tissue known as the retina. The receptivity of the retina is rigorously limited to information carried on that narrow band of the electromagnetic spectrum, and none else. Humans call that band visible light. The bulk of the spectrum to them, therefore, would be "invisible" light which they cannot monitor with their natural senses. When wavelengths contained in that tiny band of visible light fall on specialized cells in the retina called rods and cones, electrical currents encrypting the information carried in those wavelengths are correspondingly generated. These electrical currents are then relayed by nerve fibers to the visual cortex of the brain where they are decoded and interpreted as sight. Since these retinal cells are completely insensitive to the infinite spectrum of wavelength lying outside that narrowly circumscribed range, natural human vision is extremely bridled and strictly limited to just that tiny window of the spectrum. Galymonians, in contrast, can visually detect or "see" wavelengths way beyond that shred of electromagnetic spectrum directly perceived by humans, thus expanding our natural vision to cover a huge chunk of the spectrum. We can, accordingly, see far beyond the upper infrared and lower ultraviolet boundaries that limit the natural vision of humans. Consequently, our surroundings are bathed in colors and visions that humans cannot even imagine. Therefore, taking just this one sensory modality as an illustration, galymonians perceive a vastly more elaborate universe than do the inhabitants of Earth. As in Plato's allegory of the cave, this knowledge is difficult to communicate to creatures unable to appreciate the phenomenon.

The noted German philosopher Arthur Schopenhauer observed 160 years ago that, "every person takes the limits of their own field of vision for the limits of the world." Only in recent decades have humans tried to push their observational envelope beyond their own optical limits by engineering instruments that can detect and record information carried on other wavelengths of the electromagnetic spectrum, and have used this new ability to scan and observe the astonishing nature of the world around them.

Galymonians have other capabilities as well, adaptations not yet present or fully evolved among the inhabitants of Earth at this moment in their cosmic history. Mac will briefly allude to some of these as well.

Déjà vu, a word directly borrowed from French, literally means "already seen." It is the strong sensation humans feel that an event currently being experienced is already known to them from the past. Just on face value alone it seems to suggest an acquired knowledge of the future. Déjà vu is reported to occur in about 80% of humans, at least occasionally, decreasing in prevalence with age. Humans tend to offer simple neuropsychological explanations for the phenomenon, but its very existence alone is significant. Déjà vu among galymonians is an intrinsic and evolved part of their nature, allowing instant mental access to the future without the need to physically travel there.

Humans have only lately come to realize that all the visible matter and energy they can directly detect in the cosmos, when bundled altogether, is less than 5 percent of the entire physical contents of the Universe. The bulk of the Universe then, more than 95 percent of it, consists of something else that humans refer to as "exotic" or "dark" matter and energy[5]. The presence

---

5   The Dutch astronomer Jan Oort was the first human to demonstrate the presence of dark matter in the Universe some 78 years ago. Oort noted a discrepancy between the observed orbital velocities of stars in the Milky Way, when compared to the orbital velocities that would be expected from the gravitational effects of all the ordinary matter in the galaxy together. Oort's results indicated the presence of more matter in the galaxy than was actually being observed. That unobserved substance was named dark matter. Dark energy, for its part, was proposed as a repelling, anti-gravity force to explain the expansion of the Universe observed by the American astronomer Edwin Hubble 81 years ago.

of these exotic substances are implicitly assumed by them in order to explain the gravitational dynamics of their Universe as they observe it today. The adjective "dark" or "exotic" is used because humans cannot directly detect or currently manipulate this material; their existence is only inferred by people because of the effects they produce on ordinary matter and energy, much like jinns or angels do. Remarkably therefore, people cannot yet interact with most of the Universe they inhabit. Unlike humans who cannot relate to these actors at this stage of their cosmic development, galymonians fully possess the ability to manipulate and interact with all forms of matter and energy in the Universe, exotic or not. On Galymon we distill dark energy from space and use it as an antigravity force to propel our vehicles around, like humans use gasoline on Earth for the same purpose. Quite unlike gasoline however, dark energy is completely nonpolluting and is virtually an unlimited resource.

Galymonians can also instantaneously transfer information and execute actions over unbounded distances by using a process called quantum entanglement. Quantum entanglement is very mystifying to those who do not fully comprehend its provenance. By using quantum entanglement, one can perform any desired action at a remote location by sculpting reality locally. This "spooky action at a distance" as one of humankind's greatest physicists, Albert Einstein[6] once called it, would seem like magic to the uninitiated.

The core requirement for action through quantum

---

6   Professor Albert Einstein who lived in the last century was a German-born American theoretical physicist and mathematician whose extraordinary genius and intellect elucidated the nature of Space and Time for modern humans. His astonishing insights and equations transformed the field of physics in his time and space.

entanglement is that the interacting components, wherever they may be located in the Universe now, should have once been in physical contact with each other at some point in their history. Since everything in the contemporary Universe was once all bound together in the primordial singularity at its inception, this core requirement is fully satisfied. Using quantum entanglement therefore, we can perform a desired action at any location in the Universe from any other location in that same Universe, wherever those different locations may now be positioned in space and time. By this remarkable process, action is instantly transmitted and accomplished immediately at the remote location.

Humans are only now beginning to grasp this astonishing phenomenon they call "non-locality." For instance, just barely a few years ago, some people noticed that the rate of radioactive decay of certain atoms on their planet, which they had always presumed to be an established and immutable physical constant for any particular breed of atom, varied minutely—but measurably—in exact synchrony with certain energetic activity on their Sun. The Sun, of course, is located relatively a world away, about eight light minutes from their home planet where the radioactive decay was being monitored. Astonishingly, this decay effect was found to instantly and precisely synchronize to the solar event, with no lagging time delay of 8 minutes present.

Another unusual feature of galymonians compared to humans, is our ability to enter and experience other combinations of time and space anywhere in the Universe. To do this, we first fix our desired coordinates with a device that may be imagined as somewhat analogous to a satellite-based global positioning system that my human friends are quite familiar with on Earth.

We use naturally occurring pulsars, known also as neutron stars, to triangulate reference points for our devices, rather than the geostationary satellites that humans use for their GPS. In our unique positioning system, obviously, the time dimension is simultaneously figured into the calculus as a coordinate. We then produce an exact doppelgänger[7] of ourselves in that designated space and time location using quantum entanglement for this purpose. After the desired out-of-area experience is completed through the doppelgänger, we project that whole encounter back to our permanent selves, subsequently vacating the doppelgänger in the remote location. This special technology allows Mac and other beings with this unusual ability to "travel" vicariously around the Universe, both in space and in time.

Among the many differences between humans and galymonians, one especially is quite remarkable and very significant. That difference has to do with how reality itself is experienced and perceived. The issue comes down to a singular question: is reality digital, or is reality analog? Is it a particle, or a wave? Is reality like a television image formed by innumerable but individually discrete particles called pixels continuously arranged and rearranged to form moving pictures, or is reality instead like a perpetually flowing stream of images that morph into each other imperceptibly, and are devoid of any boundary demarcations? To galymonians, reality is clearly analog in format and informs us through a continuous wave-function. It therefore has infinite manifestations since it is non-particulate by nature. Humans, instead, seem to experience reality primarily as a cross section of the unending reality-wave function, thus

---

7   Doppelgänger is a German word literally meaning "double walker." In its
    modern sense the word refers to any duplicate, or look-alike, of the original.

compartmentalizing reality itself into past, present, and future.
Reality to them is digital or particulate in nature.

Therefore, due to these and other structural and functional differences between humans and galymonians, the task of
credibly transposing my observations into a coherent account
that could be appreciated by my gracious hosts on Earth is a
formidable task indeed. I have devoted much time and great
effort to this difficult endeavor, but continue to feel that even
more could be done in this regard. Especially for that reason,
I most humbly implore my worthy readers on Earth to kindly
forgive any deficiencies or limitations they may encounter, as
they proceed to critically examine the narrative I have respect-
fully submitted here.

As for my beloved galymonian cohorts, I have the great
honor and distinct privilege to introduce them to another astonishing lifeform in our Universe.

I embarked on this mission to Earth as my permanent and
continuous image, not as a duplicate doppelgänger projection.
The Most High Tribunal of Galymon had always mandated in
its published rules and regulations that all critically important
missions of exploration originating from our particular location be conducted by the designated individuals only as their
permanent selves. The premise and justification for this special
directive was that doppelgängers may not be sufficiently sensitive to the innumerable nuances and subtleties that are always
present during any expedition whatsoever, and is therefore
expressly prohibited in an undertaking considered especially
important and significant. Because of this special requirement,

quantum entanglement was not an option for my mission to Earth—Mac had to physically travel to the designated planet.

Before the actual voyage began though, numerous meetings were held between myself and our senior mission control personnel on Galymon to review every imaginable detail of the current assignment prior to departure on this mission. A tiny, but faithfully representative sample of Mac was compiled and securely stored for future reference, just in case an unexpected accident destroyed me and I must be reconstructed from scratch. All contingencies were anticipated, acknowledged, and accounted for. That is standard operating procedure for us on Galymon.

Moments before departure, I was subject to a thorough physical and mental decontamination. Because of the great danger of polluting host territory with piggybacking alien lifeforms, particularly microscopic ones or other difficult to detect types, a meticulous cleansing is mandatory before embarking on a mission—not just a physical scrubbing down, but also psychological disinfection to remove every prejudice and bias that may exist in overt or covert form. Prejudice means "pre-judgment." Therefore prejudice, or bias, of any kind is invariably lethal to the goal of uncompromising objectivity and will always guarantee a failed mission. This common anomaly among lifeforms is one of the hardest deviations to extinguish during pre-mission decontamination protocols. Any inclination, however slight, to identify and root for a desired outcome will bring subjectivity into the process and make any data collected utterly useless. Therefore, all principal missionaries are steadfastly advised never to take sides on any issue—to have no dog in the fight. These procedures, of course, are not required for doppelgängers.

My journey from Galymon to Earth was entirely uneventful. I glided through the designated wormhole[8] and reached my target planet where I landed upon a body of water called the Sargasso Sea near the coast of an island known as Bermuda. There I assumed the form of an adult male human inhabitant of my host planet—humans were the dominant creatures at the time of my visit. Unlike galymonians, humans come in two distinct prototypes called genders, one male and one female. The two are quite dissimilar in physical size, body contour, and their reproductive roles and functions. There are also certain anatomical, physiological, and cognitive differences between them as well. These gender differences are collectively referred to as sexual dimorphism.

Once established, I then proceeded to explore my host planet and its lifeforms for a fraction of a tikun. A tikun is a common unit of time duration for us on Galymon, somewhat like an hour would be for humans on Earth. Converting this construct to the way people experience time, a full tikun would last approximately a century, or 100 revolutions of Earth around its star. My sojourn on Earth lasted 0.033 (recurring) tikun. That would be three full Earth orbits and a bit more—precisely 3 years, 3 months, and 18 days on my host planet.

The Sun and its satellite system of visible matter, known to humans as the solar system, has eight named major planetary bodies. The Earth is the third one out from their star. In order of increasing distance from the Sun, humans have named these eight major planets, Mercury, Venus, Earth, Mars, Jupiter, Saturn, Uranus, and Neptune. By order of increasing mass instead, the eight planets would line up as, Mercury, Mars,

---

8   A wormhole is a link in the topology of space and time, connecting two widely separated locations in our Universe.

Venus, Earth, Uranus, Neptune, Saturn, and Jupiter. There are also several dwarf planets in the solar system, such as Eris, Pluto, Ceres, and numerous others. Pluto, once recognized a major planet by humans, was recently removed by them from this special designation and reclassified as a dwarf planet. As would be expected in stellar systems everywhere, there are numerous other objects smaller than planets in the solar system, such as comets, centaurs, and asteroids.

As I relate this story about my mission to Earth and record for your kind attention my discoveries, impressions and experiences on that small rocky planet, I would like to take a moment and recall to your imagination the larger vision of our Universe itself. In its ultimate structure, the physical picture of the Universe appears much like a web—a syncytium or net—made up of voids surrounded by filaments that crisscross, meet, and interconnect with each other throughout its enormous expanse. Ordinary matter that humans can perceive, progressively aggregates into larger and larger units of itself to form this cosmic network of filaments. As we zoom out on the Universe, we see planets and stars aggregating to form galaxies, galaxies forming galaxy groups, groups of galaxies forming galaxy clusters, and clusters of galaxies forming galaxy superclusters. The whole composite picture appears like one single interconnected entity. The renowned poet and philosopher, the great Alla-guru, who once lived on Galymon before emigrating to another planet in a different galaxy, was so moved by this tantalizing image upon first seeing a photograph of our Universe that the famous bard was inspired to pen a short evocative verse about the physical Universe he saw:

While gazing on our Universe
By way of inner Eyes,
I see a mighty Cosmic Nurse
Embracing all that lies:
Around the realm of Space, its Course,
And Time unbound and free;
I see a self-sustaining Force:
I see both You and Me!

Once again, my esteemed readers should please bear in mind that I have significantly re-worked this narrative in both style and structure, from the format in which it was originally presented to Galymon's High Tribunal. I have done this by re-formulating my earlier presentation in a way that allows me to communicate with the many valued friends I know from Earth. As you study this account, please bear in mind that my narrative was especially concerned with the fascinating history and behavior of humans as I understood them during a very brief visit to their planet. Imagine, for a galymonian with an indefinite lifespan, a little more than three years is indeed but a hiccup in time. Therefore, it is possible that some of the observations and conclusions recorded in this narrative are merely the flitting impressions of a hurried extraterrestrial.

For that, I earnestly hope my generous hosts on Earth will forgive me.

CHAPTER II:
METRIC

As already noted in my narrative, all life has sentience or consciousness, which simply means the ability to sense and respond to the surrounding environment. A striking feature in humans, extending beyond sentience, is a special quality called sapience, that uncommon ability to project knowledge and experience into the future and thereby anticipate events still to come.

Humans are aware and sensitive to the future and to the relentless passage of time. They feel the onward rush of temporal events, not only in their own personal lives, but also observe it in others around them. They follow time's implacable effects on everything they know. Humans, accordingly, had to devise a way to record and document this phenomenon called time. To that end, they invented the calendar.

My beloved friend and esteemed colleague Professor Tao[9], offers a popular lecture for acolytes about the configuration

---

9   Professor Tao is a venerated galymonian whose monumental work, *A Classification of Cosmic Life*, is renowned throughout our galaxy.

of space and time, delivered at seminars in our Institute back home on Galymon. Time and space make up the contours of everything humans know in this Universe. For them, space is experienced in three dimensions—length, breadth, and depth. Time comes in just one dimension, flowing inexorably from the past into the future. The boundary where the past transforms into the future is called the present, the place where humans reside. Of course, other cosmic lifeforms may, and often do, experience these dimensions differently. More than a century ago, Edwin Abbott an English schoolmaster, in a dimensionally revealing novella called *Flatland: A Romance of Many Dimensions*, described a world where individuals lived in just two spatial dimensions—length and breadth— a place called Flatland. They lacked a height dimension and therefore could not construct upright walls or spanning bridges between locations. Abbott recounts the story of the Flatlander, Mr. Square, visiting a no-dimensional world (Pointland) and a one-dimensional world (Lineland), thereby illustrating the topography of those domains. For example, in Lineland, people could not overtake or pass each other. Square later visits a three-dimensional world (Spaceland) where humans live, but he cannot quite imagine it. For humans, the three dimensions of space and the one of time are woven into a matrix called spacetime, distributed uniformly throughout the Universe by the Big Bang. Matter exists within this spacetime. Concentrations of matter, proportional to their mass, mold and shape this fabric of spacetime around themselves. The three dimensions of space are measured with a measuring-rod or tape. Time is measured with a clock or calendar.

The Persians were among the very first human cultures to

devise and use a solar calendar. Iranian calendars were a succession of calendars used for more than 2,000 years by that civilization. The great Iranian astronomer, mathematician and poet, Omar Khayyam, produced an extremely precise solar calendar more than 900 years ago. Khayyam measured the length of the solar year as equal to 365.24219858156 days, an amazingly accurate figure. Khayyam's Persian calendar was even more precise than today's widely used Gregorian or Western calendar, developed 503 years later. In a much beloved quatrain from *The Rubaiyat of Omar Khayyam*, translated many centuries later from the Persian by the English poet Edward FitzGerald, the great sage Omar muses:

Ah, but my Computations, People say,
Reduced the Year to better reckoning?—Nay
'Twas only striking from the Calendar
Unborn To-morrow, and dead Yesterday.

In order to establish a suitable scale to measure and record the passage of time, humans have subdivided its course into convenient intervals of their basic time unit, an Earth day. A day is defined by them as the time taken by their planet to complete one full rotation on its axis. They then reckon one full revolution of their planet around the Sun as an Earth year, containing 365.25 days. A day is divided into 24 hours, an hour into 60 minutes, and a minute into 60 seconds. A second is 1/86,400 Earth day. The year is divided into 12 months of 30 or 31 days each, except for one month with 28 days normally. A month has a bit over 4 weeks, with 7 days to a week. The Earth day is gradually getting longer. As the rotation of the planet is slowed by its Moon's gravitational drag, the Earth day correspondingly increases in length. Though this change has been miniscule over their own short history, humans may correct for this discrepancy by tacking on extra "leap-seconds" as necessary. In about 140 million years from today, a day will have a full 25 hours in it. People can now keep time very accurately with instruments called "atomic" clocks that measure time to within a third of a second over a million years. They do this by measuring the movement of electrons in selected atoms such as cesium-133, when those electrons vibrate between two energy states.

Humans experience time as a river, flowing implacably from the past to the future, never the other way around, though there is nothing inherent in the nature of this Universe or the fundamental laws of its physics that forbids this from happening. In contrast to humans, galymonians experience time as a swirling lake with no pre-set direction of flow, and so we can channel time along any pathway we please. Humans, quite unlike galymonians, are compelled to behaviorally divide their perception of time into past, present, and future, since they can only experience this function unidirectionally. That is a limitation they endure even though the laws of physics do not require it. Humans are consequently enmeshed and forced to reside inviolably in the present—their past is history and their future a mystery.

Such being the case, in order to record chronological events relative to each other, these humans had to first establish an inflection point in their perennial river of time that they would then designate as the "beginning" for this archival purpose. An especially important and momentous event in their history, real or imagined, is usually chosen to designate that starting point in their calendar and to set as a marker for "zero-time." Time is then counted as occurring before that inflexion point, or after it. Mutual agreement among all humans as to which memorable event in their history should be recognized as zero-time for this calibration has yet to be achieved by them. A parochial event acknowledged as extraordinary and very significant by one human culture may be considered nonexistent or trivial by another. Therefore several such calendars, sporting different start dates, have been used on Earth to record events. Some are more widely employed than others; some are extinct or used only to date festivals and celebratory events. This lack of common agreement with respect to the starting year for their calendar makes it rather cumbersome to compare historical dates between the different calendar systems without first crunching numbers to translate one system's dates to another.

To avoid this cultural parochialism in timekeeping, it was proposed by nonsectarian scientists on my host planet that the year when reliable radiocarbon dating first became available to determine the antiquity of organic samples, be designated as the new zero-time reference. Radiocarbon dating is a technique to estimate the age of a sample of organic material, which by proxy tells the age of the organism that produced it. The method depends on carbon-14, a radioactive isotope of carbon that decays at a known steady rate. This carbon isotope has a half-life of 5,730 years and is useful to determine origins back to about 60,000 years—for dating more remote antiquities, other radioactive isotopes with longer half-lives are available. Organisms incorporate carbon-14 atoms when alive, in the same ratio the isotope was present in their environment alongside other carbon isotopes they ingested. By carefully measuring the ratio of carbon-14 to non-radioactive carbon in the sample, the extent of carbon-14 decay since its incorporation into the sample can be calculated, thus providing an age for the specimen in question. The assumption here, of course, is that atmospheric carbon-14 levels had remained constant throughout the period of incorporation, which is unconfirmed. Thus ages of antiquities derived from such dating are only estimates.

Radiocarbon dating as an analytic tool was firmly established 60 years before Mac visited Earth. So that particular year, when the technique became commonly available, was set as the kickoff point for this new secular calendar, and was designated the Present. The years preceding the availability of radiocarbon dating would then be called Before the Present (BP) and is used today for dating in geology. The years following the availability of radiocarbon dating, though not official yet, would then be After the Present (AP). For comparison purposes across culturally determined calendars, listed according to their own self-described antiquity, here are the corresponding years when radiocarbon dating became available: 5,710 for the Jewish[10] calendar, 5,051 for the Hindu calendar, 2,494 for the Buddhist calendar, 1,950 for the Christian calendar, and 1,369 for the Muslim calendar.

Mac will employ the designations BP and AP to reference specific points in time for the purposes of this narrative.

---

10 Jewish, Hindu, etc. are examples of faith-based belief systems humans use to conjure their origin, purpose, and destiny. Such systems are called Religions. Humans have witnessed numerous religions come and go on Earth thus far. Some religions had only a few followers, others hundreds of millions. Most religions consist of a set of core beliefs purporting to explain human advent and destiny—and the Universe itself—as the purposeful activity of a supernatural agency. Religions usually involve devotional and ritualistic observances by adherents. Many human cultures use a pivotal moment in their religious history as the starting point for their calendars.

I will now begin my account with a brief summary of the location, geological history, physical description, and spatial orientation of Earth, my designated host planet. This outline is included here to provide an overview of the topography and developmental history of the subject matter under consideration. The data, though superfluous for some, could be relevant for others who may not reside in the region described here, or are unfamiliar with this particular coordinate in the Milky Way galaxy—the material is therefore specially intended for their benefit. Mac has transmitted a full and complete version of this data to Alka, our quantum supercomputer at the Tribunal's main offices on Galymon. Those desirous of accessing the complete file may kindly do so by logging on to Alka using the appropriate protocol.

Earth, as noted before, is a member of the solar system. This stellar configuration consists of just one star that humans call the Sun. The Earth, together with its single star and the other components of its stellar family, is located in the Milky Way galaxy. The Milky Way is a spiral galaxy shaped like a discus whose star filled interior is approximately 100,000 light years in diameter and averages about 1,000 light years in thickness—it bulges at the center and tapers toward the circumference. It has over 300 billion stars and is close to 13.6 billion years old, just a tad younger than our common 13.8 billion year old Universe.

Like most spiral galaxies, the Milky Way has a central bulge harboring a supermassive black hole of about 3.7 million solar masses. The black hole at the center of my own Meon galaxy is smaller. These two supermassive black holes are not particularly large as galaxies go: some galaxies host enormous central black holes of many billions of solar masses. A black hole is a region of spacetime where a sufficiently large and compact mass of ordinary matter collapses and implodes into itself due to its own massive gravity, a process called gravitational collapse. The collapsing mass is crushed and vanishes into a singularity from which nothing, not even light, can escape the extreme distortion of spacetime caused by the black hole's extraordinary gravity. Black holes can grow by devouring matter in their neighborhood, including other black holes they encounter, to become supermassive ones like those found at the center of galaxies. These supermassive black holes at their centers influence the development and evolution of galaxies.

The Sun with its solar system is about 28,000 light years from the center of its galaxy, just over half way out from the galactic hub. Earth's yellow star is located on the minor Orion Arm of the Milky Way, between the major Sagittarius and Perseus Arms. The Sun is about 4.6 billion years old and contains more than 99 percent of the entire visible mass of its stellar system.

The Earth, along with its single natural satellite the Moon, is approximately 93 million miles distant from the Sun. Humans refer to this distance as an Astronomical Unit (AU), a natural scale for them to imagine and correlate distances within their own solar system. When Mac visited Earth, the Moon was just about a quarter million miles away from my host planet. Yet, when Earth's moons were first born—there were two moons to start with—the primary and secondary moons were much closer to Earth, a mere 15,000 miles away, and obscured most of the night sky as viewed from Earth at that time. The two moons eventually joined up to form the single silvery Moon visible today. The Moon continues to recede from Earth, currently at a rate of about 1.6 inches (4 cm) every year. Also, since its formation, the Moon has been slowly braking the Earth's rotational speed due to the drag of lunar gravity called tidal forces, acting on the planet and gradually slowing the Earth down, making each day last just a little bit longer. When the Moon first formed, an Earth day was only about six hours long, just a quarter of what it is today.

The Earth formed 4.56 billion years ago with the solar system's other components—the remaining planets, comets, centaurs and asteroids. All these objects individually coalesced by gravitational accretion from the remnant of the solar nebula. This remnant of the solar nebula was the disc shaped cloud of residual gas and dust swirling around the newly formed star, the leftovers from the gravitational collapse of a molecular cloud that birthed the Sun. Molecular clouds are composed of molecular hydrogen and helium, with small amounts of heavier elements depending on the local metallicity[11]. They are the birth places of new stars and planets. Molecular clouds that exceed a mass of 100,000 stars are called giant molecular clouds. Giant molecular clouds are the largest denizens of galaxies and may reach up to 600 light years in diameter. They contain enough gas and dust to form hundreds of thousands of stars.

The trigger for the collapse of the solar system's molecular

---

11   Segue 1 is a tiny satellite galaxy orbiting the Milky Way and has the lowest metallicity known to humans anywhere in this Universe. It is a fossil galaxy of just a few hundred stars that died and stopped evolving and went extinct about 13 billion years ago, not long after the Universe itself was born. Stars in Segue 1 have negligible metallicity, being composed almost entirely of primordial hydrogen and helium with hardly a trace of heavier elements present.

cloud was the shockwave from a nearby supernova explosion that had just preceded the collapse. Humans became aware of this fact from analyzing two primitive meteorites collected in Antarctica that were found to contain grains of silica forged in that supernova explosion predating the birth of the Sun and the solar system. Pre-solar grains of silica stand out from the rest because of their unusual mix of chemical isotopes which cannot be explained by processes known to operate in the solar system itself. Their isotopic composition can only be accounted for by nucleosynthesis in a supernova environment.

A quick overview of comets, asteroids, and centaurs may be of interest here. These objects are aggregates of matter remaining after the solar system's planets had formed.

A comet is a relatively small and icy solar system body that orbits the Sun. It has a nucleus of frozen water-ice, gas, and dust. An atmosphere of water vapor, carbon dioxide and other gases surrounds the nucleus, and a tail of dust and ionized gases trails the comet. The tail develops when the comet is close to the Sun and always points away from the Sun because of outward pressure exerted by the solar wind[12]. Comets by the billions orbit the Sun from way beyond the major planets, in the Kuiper Belt and Oort Cloud. The Kuiper Belt extends out for 1.85 billion miles from the orbit of Neptune (between 30 AU and 50 AU), and the Oort Cloud is roughly 50,000 AU, nearly a light year from the Sun. Comets residing in these locations are occasionally nudged toward the Sun by gravitational perturbations caused by the giant outer solar system planets

---

12 The solar wind is a steady efflux of matter ejected from the Sun at supersonic speeds, streaming outward from the upper atmosphere of the Sun to the far ends of the solar system. It is a plasma of charged particles composed mostly of protons and electrons.

or nearby stars, and are thus driven into the inner solar system where they could intercept planets and collide with them. Comets often display periodic orbits separating them into two classical types—the short-period comets arising in the Kuiper Belt with frequencies less than 200 years, and the long-period comets from the Oort Cloud with frequencies longer than 200 years.

Asteroids belong to a class of small solar system bodies that orbit the Sun. The term has come increasingly to specify small rock-ice and metallic bodies of the inner solar system reaching to the orbit of Jupiter. Most asteroids are located in the main asteroid belt between the orbits of Mars and Jupiter. Asteroids vary greatly in size, from a few hundred miles in diameter, to as little as a few yards across. Millions of asteroids inhabit the solar system, many believed to be the shattered remnants of planetesimals, bodies from the young Sun's nebula that never grew large enough to become planets. Asteroids, too, may become dislodged from their orbits and destructively slam into unsuspecting planets in their path. Earth has been hit innumerable times by asteroids, and so too has the Moon. Impact craters produced by these collisions are testimony to those events. These impact craters are far more pristine and visible on the Moon than on Earth, because the Moon's quiescent geological profile arising from lack of surface water and air, tend to preserve these impact craters on its surface—on Earth they simply erode and weather away.

Centaurs are small solar system bodies that share features of both asteroids and comets, hence the name centaur from a mythical half-horse, half-human creature. Centaurs revolve around the Sun mainly between the orbits of Jupiter and Neptune. They are compact bodies of different sizes and colors consisting of various ices, silicates, and organic compounds. Gravitational perturbations caused by the giant planets occasionally fling centaurs into the inner solar system, risking impact with planets.

The centrally located Sun accreted most of the matter in the collapsing solar nebula, ending up with almost 99% of the entire solar system's mass. The Sun, through this accumulative process, grew massive enough to trigger nuclear fusion reactions in its compressed and superheated core. Transmutation of hydrogen into helium by this fusion process releases huge quantities of energy. That nuclear energy produced in the stellar core first appears as very energetic, short wave radiation trapped in the bowels of the star. As this energy battles to the star's surface from deep within the core where it was generated, the energy becomes gradually degraded in strength by interactions with matter, and its wavelength correspondingly increases toward that of visible light. In the Sun's case for instance, it takes a full one million years for the high-energy nuclear radiation produced at the core to slowly work its way through the star's convective zone to the surface as visible light; the photon then zoom away into space. The concentrated matter which is the star, thereupon lights up and shines. Thus is a star born.

Most of the remaining 1% of the solar system's mass left over from formation of the Sun was distributed among the planets and their moons. A tiny fraction not used up for this purpose, became asteroids, centaurs, and comets.

The planets of this stellar system can be sorted into two principal groups: the small rocky planets, and the giant gas planets. The small rocky planets consist of the four inner ones: Mercury, Venus, Earth, and Mars. The giant gas planets are the four outer ones: Jupiter, Saturn, Uranus, and Neptune. The inner and outer planets are separated by a gap between the orbits of Mars and Jupiter called the asteroid belt filled with asteroids as already noted. Although some asteroids, such as Ceres and Pallas, are spherical and a few hundred miles in diameter, the majority of asteroids are irregular chunks of rock and metal measuring less than a few yards across. The total mass of all asteroids combined is less than the mass of Earth's Moon alone.

The rocky planets lie between 0.39 and 1.52 astronomical units from the Sun. All four rocky planets are relatively small, less than 8,000 miles in diameter. They all have hard rocky surfaces. These planets possess relatively thin or even negligible atmospheres: the heat from the young Sun prevented gases in the parent solar nebula from condensing on planets that were closer to the Sun. Earth's atmosphere was formed later, mostly by gases vented from inside the planet by volcanism.

The gas planets lie between 5.2 and 30.4 AU. At these distances, the nebula was cool enough for gases to condense, allowing these outer planets to grow massively and retain huge atmospheres. The gas giants are made predominantly of hydrogen, helium, and water-ice. Jupiter, the largest gas giant, has a diameter of nearly 89,000 miles. Neptune, the smallest, has a diameter of 30,775 miles.

The new Earth, molten at first, cooled to form a thin outer crust. As the Earth cooled further, heavier elements like iron and nickel sank to its center, and lighter ones like silicon, aluminum, and magnesium rose to the top. This process of sedimentation settled the Earth into three main layers based on the chemical composition and density of the materials in play. Going from the surface to the center, the three layers are crust, mantle, and core. The crust, 3 miles to 25 miles in thickness, is composed mainly of aluminum silicates. The mantle is 1,800 miles in thickness and is largely made up of oxides of silicon, magnesium, and iron. The bulk of Earth's internal heat is located in the mantle. The mantle is plastic and fluid in consistency, like tar, separated into upper and lower mantles. The topmost surface of the upper mantle which is solid, fuses with the solid crust above it to form the lithosphere. The lithosphere is fractured into plates called tectonic plates that are fused to the surface of the underlying hot, fluid mantle. The Earth's core consists of a liquid nickel-iron outer core 1,430 miles thick, and a solid pure-iron inner core extending another 750 miles from below the outer core to the planet's center. Though the inner core is hotter than the outer one, it remains solid because of the vastly higher pressure at the center. The temperature there can reach 6,000°C (10,800°F), as hot as the Sun itself.

Earth's magnetic field, an indispensable shield which single-handedly deflects the solar wind, is generated by motion in the liquid outer core caused by the planet's rotation, exactly as in a dynamo. Without this remarkable magnetic field, the solar wind would simply strip away the planet's thin atmosphere and expose its raw surface to lethal radiation. But for this magnetic shield, carbon based life could not exist on Earth. Both the Moon and the planet Mars, for instance, which are significantly smaller than Earth and therefore cooled much faster, lost their liquid metallic cores which solidified due to the cooling. As a result, they could no longer generate the magnetic field required to deflect the solar wind streaming past them. Thus their nurturing atmospheres were gradually stripped away by the solar wind, turning them into dry, desolate and inhospitable places for carbon based life to exist.

Two virgin moons formed around Earth 4.53 billion years ago, soon after the planet itself appeared. The moons were the result of a glancing impact between the primordial Earth and a smaller protoplanetary body called Theia that was the same size then as Mars is today. That glancing encounter gouged out a huge depression across one hemisphere of the growing Earth, forming an enormous basin that subsequently filled with water to become the Pacific Ocean. That is why almost all the surface land on my host planet is found in the hemisphere opposite to that ocean. Some of Theia's mass became part of Earth, and some, together with some of Earth's mass, was ejected out into space as a nebula around the newly formed Earth. This ejecta then re-aggregated into a major and minor moon, each one in the exact same orbital path around their planet as the other one was. Earth had two moons then. The minor moon, with a diameter of about 625 miles, gradually sidled up to the major moon over tens of millions of years, finally merging with it to form a single Moon. Because they were both in the same orbit and moving in the same direction, the collision itself was in slow motion, the minor moon becoming gravitationally plastered onto the major one to form Earth's single Moon with a diameter of 2,159 miles. This explains why the Moon's two hemispheres are so different today. The Moon is tidally locked to Earth. The hemisphere forever facing Earth, the one familiar to humans, is covered by low lava-filled plains. On the contrary, the far side of the Moon which is never visible from Earth is entirely different in its physical features. It is a landscape of rugged and mountainous highlands, the remains of the smaller companion moon that was appended there. The secondary moon's impact was slow enough to pancake its material across that hemisphere, rather than crashing into it and carving out a gargantuan crater instead.

Impacts during the formative stages of a stellar system are extremely common and very spectacular. The planets themselves carry scars from those events. One such impact reversed the rotational spin of Venus, the second planet out from their star. Looking down on this planetary system from the north pole of their Sun, all the planets, including Venus, are seen to revolve around that star in a counterclockwise direction. That would certainly be expected if the collapsing solar nebula was also rotating in that same direction. Surprisingly though, while all the other planets also rotate axially in the same counterclockwise direction, as one would expect from the existing angular momentum at their formation, Venus alone rotates in a clockwise or retrograde direction. This was the result of an early impact on that planet, reversing its rotational spin. The Sun rises in the west on Venus.

Earth, like most other planetary bodies in space, is spherical in shape, a smidgen flatter at the poles than at the equator. Its equatorial diameter is 7,926 miles, the polar diameter 7,900 miles. Its circumference at the equator is 24,902 miles, at the poles 24,860 miles. Earth has a volume of 260 billion cubic miles. It has a surface area of 197 million square miles, 70 percent of which is covered with liquid water held predominantly in oceans, and about 30 percent by dry land. Even though 70% of its surface may be covered with water, the average depth of water in the oceans is only a little more than two miles. Water also exists in big pockets deep inside Earth, 250 miles or more under the planet's surface, still liquid even at the higher temperatures found there because of the greater pressure at those depths. The volume of this subterranean ocean of water may rival the amount contained in the oceans on the surface of my host planet.

The Earth rotates on an axis presently tilted at 23.45° away from a line perpendicular to its orbital plane. Its rotational speed is approximately 1,038 miles an hour at the equator, the planet completing one full axial rotation in 24 hours. As noted before, humans call this interval of time, a day. Each day consists of alternating light and dark photoperiods, depending on which hemisphere of their planet is facing the Sun. These photoperiods, of course, are different in sequence from the ones on Galymon, since my home planet orbits two stars.

It should be noted here that the precise time it takes Earth to complete one full rotation around its axis at its current rotating speed, is 23.9344 hours, or 23-hours, 56-minutes, and 4-seconds. This figure would therefore result in an obvious deficit of 3-minutes and 56-seconds (0.0655 hours) for a 24-hour day. The discrepancy would accumulate over each rotation to reach a value of almost 24 hours—or one full day—lost in the course of an entire year of 365.25 days. That lost day each year is recouped by the single extra rotation around its axis that the Earth passively experiences simply as a result of completing one full revolution around the Sun. To illustrate this point imagine, dear reader, that you are the Earth; now place a chair in the center of the room to represent the Sun; revolve around it, facing the chair at all times. In that revolution around the chair you have passively rotated once around yourself, since you faced all four sides of the room during that revolution. Therefore, because of this single passive extra rotation each year, the average day for Earth is 24 hours. This bit of arithmetic, though, is different from a leap year. In a leap year, an additional whole day is added to the year on the last day of February every quadrennial or fourth year, to compensate for the quarter day not counted in the 365.25 days of the preceding three common years. Thus humans count 365 days for common years, and 366 days for leap years.

As noted before, Earth revolves around its solitary star, the Sun. Earth's orbital speed is approximately 66,660 miles an hour, completing a full revolution around its star in 365.25 days—or a year. Directionally, the Earth's revolution is counterclockwise around its star as viewed from above the planet's orbital plane, and is oriented in the same direction as the rotation of the Sun on its own solar axis[13]. The Earth's rotation or axial spin is also in the same counterclockwise direction. Because the planet's axis is tilted from the orbital plane, its surface at any given latitude, except at the equator, receives the energy from its star in a cyclical pattern over the year, thereby resulting in cold and warm seasons, and producing corresponding wind movements and monsoonal activity.

In addition to my host planet's primary motions of rotation and revolution, the Earth and the entire solar system travel at a speed of 515,000 miles an hour around the Milky Way galaxy. The Earth completes one galactic orbit, called a Galactic Year, in approximately 240 million Earth years. In a galactic year then, the Sun and its family traverse a great circle of 181,000 light years around the Milky Way. Therefore, reminiscing back to this same time last galactic year, it was the early Triassic on Earth and dinosaurs were just beginning to make an appearance on their planet.

---

13 The solar rotational period depends on the latitude where the measurement is taken because stars are composed of gaseous matter (plasma) and therefore less rigid in their structure. The rate of rotation is fastest at the Sun's equator and slows as the latitudes increase toward its poles. The Sun's surface rotational period is about 25 Earth days at the equator, 35 at the poles.

My exemplary human hosts have only lately configured this galactic geography. Their star's Great Circle has an average radius of about 28,000 light years from the galactic center. As the Sun and the solar system circle the Milky Way, they periodically drift back and forth, toward and away from the galaxy's center. The Sun and the solar system also move up and down across the galactic plane like a carousel; one complete up-and-down cycle takes about 60 million Earth years to complete.

These cyclical displacements in the position of the Sun and its retinue, relative to the orientation of other stars and massive objects in the vicinity, cause gravitational perturbations that displace and catapult objects within the solar system itself. These dislodged objects—comets, centaurs, and asteroids—periodically crash into planets causing massive and widespread destruction. Such cosmic events have powerfully impacted life on Earth, just as they have on other life bearing planets in the Universe. On my host planet, humans have identified at least four major impact craters from these displaced objects in just the past 70 million years alone. These craters are: Chesapeake Bay Crater (USA)—53 miles wide in 35 million BP; Popigai Crater (Russia)—62 miles wide in 35.7 million BP; Chicxulub Crater (Mexico)—110 miles wide in 66 million BP; and Kara Crater (Russia)—40 miles wide in 70.3 million BP. Many millions of bolides have smashed into Earth ever since my host planet formed 4.56 billion years ago.

With your kind permission now, Mac will digress here momentarily and draw the attention of my esteemed readers to the practical effects of these different empyrean motions.

The cyclic phenomena described here, produced by these celestial mechanics, come with various frequencies. Some may even appear random to observers looking at it from a limited time frame. These phenomena have profoundly influenced the rhythm and order of life on my host planet, as they do everywhere else in the Universe. These cosmic happenings have shaped and molded the history of life itself as it unfolded here on planet Earth.

First notice that the Earth spinning around on its axis causes alternating photoperiods of brightness and darkness that humans call day and night. Clearly, these photoperiods profoundly influence the biology and behavior of every lifeform on the planet—from mating to feeding, and everything else across the board. Similarly, the seasonal cycle of winter and summer produced by the planet's revolution around its star on an inclined axis, along with related global weather patterns and monsoons, also greatly impact the biology and behavior of its biosphere. Likewise, the galactic cycle has equally profound and consequential effects. However, the impact of the galactic cycle on Earth and its lifeforms, unlike that of night and day, or winter and summer, occurs on a much longer time scale that cannot be directly perceived by humans because of their limited lifespan. Yet unsurprisingly, cyclically connected phenomena appear like clockwork during the "seasons" of the galactic year. The Earth has witnessed close to twenty such galactic cycles so far. In another twenty the Earth itself will be gone, devoured by the very star that birthed it. The Sun, in its dying throes then, would have ballooned into a red giant to encompass and devour its Earth-child, before shrinking eventually into a white dwarf star.

In this regard, let me draw the attention of my honored readers to the cosmic catastrophe that happened to my host planet approximately 66 million years ago. The ghostly signature of that celestial tribulation can still be detected in a huge scar on the Earth's surface buried under the Yucatan Peninsula in the modern country of Mexico. Humans call it Chicxulub Crater, the impact site of a huge extraterrestrial projectile that capriciously careened onto the planet's orbital trajectory. And upon that impact, literally out of the blue, the Cretaceous geologic period abruptly ended on Earth—with a bang that was heard around the world.

Humans have carefully studied the Earth's crust along the junction where the Cretaceous ends and the next period, the Paleogene, begins. This crustal boundary is called the Cretaceous-Paleogene boundary, or K-P boundary (Cretaceous is abbreviated "K" from its German, *Kreide*, meaning "chalk"). Examination of this boundary at different locations on Earth's surface revealed that along the K-P junction there was a high concentration of the metallic element iridium. This iridium concentration was tens of times greater than normal for the Earth's crust generally. That concentration of iridium along the K-P boundary, and the ratio of its different isotopes at this location, closely matched the levels that are found in certain types of asteroids and centaurs, leading humans to the conclusion that a giant bolide, either an asteroid or a centaur, had smashed into Earth around 66 million years ago, covering the planet's surface with a fine coating of iridium rich dust. Much of the credit for this exceptional piece of detective work goes to the Alvarez duo, the brilliant father and son team from the United States of America. *Père* Luis Alvarez a physicist, and *fils* Walter Alvarez a geologist, first proposed this possibility, and confirmed the iridium anomaly in 30 AP.

The K-P boundary revealed a further startling fact. Below

the boundary, corresponding to the Cretaceous Period, fossils of dinosaurs and other organisms that lived at that time were found as expected. But immediately above the boundary, just where the Paleogene began, these previous fossils had abruptly vanished. The conclusion was evident—dinosaurs were wiped out in a geologic instant by that monster bolide. A celestial body from space, measuring about six miles wide, had smashed onto the planet's surface like a cosmic tsunami, spewing doom and mass extinction for creatures on Earth that day.

This earth-shattering event from circa 66 million BP, represents one of the recurring annihilations of living organisms that periodically plague my host planet's biosphere. There have been five such major mass extinctions, and at least fifteen less extensive ones, in the previous 500 million years of Earth's history. This is after multicellular organisms had evolved on Earth to suffer mass extinctions in the first place and leave fossil evidence behind for study by humans later—no fossil records of mass extinctions are clearly visible before multicellularity. The five major mass extinctions since 500 million BP were, successively, the Ordovician, Devonian, Permian, Triassic, and Cretaceous mass extinctions. In the last one, the catastrophic Cretaceous extinction, dinosaur species, the dominant life-forms on Earth then, as humans are today, were completely wiped out, along with numerous other creatures of that period. In that particular conflagration, approximately 85% of all living species on Earth perished.

These recurrent, cyclical mass extinctions—both the major and the minor ones detected by humans in their fossil record—appear to occur about every 26–30 million years or so. Retrospective scrutiny of a number of these extinctions show evidence of severe environmental disturbances and mass mortality, some quite consistent with catastrophic impacts. The Shiva hypothesis, named after the Hindu god of destruction, attempts to connect the apparent periodicity of mass extinctions on Earth to an astronomical pacemaker. This hypothesis proposes that these periodic bolide impacts may be due to the motions of the solar system through the Milky Way galaxy. Noted already before, as the solar system revolves around its galaxy, it also oscillates up and down across the galactic plane, as well as back and forth from the galactic center. These motions lead to quasi-periodic encounters with interstellar objects causing fluxes in gravitational forces. This galactic carrousel effect may be the cyclical perturber of Oort Cloud comets and Kuiper Belt objects, leading to periodic showers of these bodies directed at the Sun and the inner solar system.

Each vertical oscillation of the solar system during its grand sweep around the Milky Way takes about 60 million years from peak to trough. Therefore, approximately every 30 million years, the Sun and its retinue will cross the dense central plane of the galaxy which is always heavily packed with countless stars and stellar black holes. Passage through this highly populated galactic neighborhood alarmingly increases the risk for close encounters with other massive objects there that could gravitationally shake up some of the trillions of comets in the Sun's Oort Cloud. This may periodically drive showers of these comets toward the central star and the inner solar system. Studies now looking at more cases of mass extinctions on my host planet in the past, seem to point to evidence of large asteroid or comet impacts—complete with dateable impact craters, layers rich in iridium, shocked minerals, and micro-tektites (tektites are gravel-sized objects of colored natural glass that are formed from terrestrial material ejected during extraterrestrial impacts). Quite revealingly, an underlying periodicity of about 30 million years appears to mark the paleontological record uncovered by these studies. Assuming this periodicity constant from the beginning, then in the 4.6 billion years of its existence so far, the Sun should have transited the galactic plane more than 150 times. Bolide impacts on Earth are pretty common.

Many of these periodic mass extinctions, therefore, point to the catastrophic impacts of large comets or asteroids upon my host planet. They appear in discreet pulses, characterized by sudden mass mortality of animals on land, air, and sea. There is extensive decimation of plant life across the planet. Major environmental shredding is demonstrated by changes in carbon isotopes, and severe climatic disruption is revealed by oxygen isotope shifts. These mass extinctions are frequently succeeded by rapid evolution of surviving species filling the vacated niches abandoned by victims of the preceding disaster.

This deadly cycle of doom has great relevance to any possible contemporary impact hazards to Earth. The up-and-down oscillation of the solar system in the course of its galactic orbit just passed through the Milky Way's densely populated central galactic plane. That notable event occurred only within the last few million years. According to some credible scenarios, a barrage of comets was dislodged from the solar system's Oort Cloud around that time. These far away objects should be approaching the inner solar system in the relatively near future. Only time will tell if Earth sustains a hit again tomorrow. Alternatively, some extinction events appear as if from nowhere, out of sync with this ominous astronomical pacemaker. It is fully expected that at least some comet and asteroid impacts will occur independently of the periodic perturbation of Oort Cloud comets predicted by the Shiva hypothesis.

In the brief lifetime of any single human which rarely, if ever, exceeds 100 years, a 30 million year cycle may appear unimportant to their individual futures. Yet one well-placed impact, certain to happen sometime, can wipe them all out of existence in an instant. This contingency has been the fate of numerous successful species on Earth in the past. Of course, for a lifeform living beyond tens of millions of years, such events would be commonplace. Time is relative.

⁂

Dinosaurs are an extinct group of animals now. Their name comes from the Greek words *deinos* and *sauros*, meaning "terrible lizard." At one time, these fabulous creatures made up a diverse passel of animals on their planet, becoming the dominant lifeforms on Earth in their heyday. Some of them, like the titanosaur sauropod *Argentinosaurus huinculensis*, were up to half as big as modern jumbo jetliners. They thrived and flourished for more than 160 million years, spanning the Late Triassic Period circa 230 million BP, right till the end of the Cretaceous Period in 66 million BP. Then, at a fateful moment, these highly successful creatures suddenly vanished in the blink of a geologic eye, as that rogue bolide gone wild hit their home planet. During the mass extinction that followed, closing out the Cretaceous Period, the once dominant dinosaurs disappeared from the face of their planet, never to be seen or heard from again. They left behind a most remarkable offshoot that survived the holocaust to appear today as modern birds.

Mac visited the area now in modern Mexico's Yucatan Peninsula, late of a summer morning on that stormy Wednesday circa 66 million BP when that monster bolide hit. An enormous 110-mile wide circular depression, known to humans as the Chicxulub crater, extending out from the northern edge of the present Yucatan Peninsula into the adjacent ocean, silently marks the spot today. The isthmus connecting the two Americas had still to appear when Mac visited the area—there was no Gulf of Mexico when that asteroid or centaur struck. The Atlantic Ocean was then confluent with the Pacific between the Americas. A huge torpedo-shaped land mass, about the size of present day Madagascar, and home to a cornucopia of creatures, projected out from the northern coastline of South America. That landmass would be violently stricken and its surface incinerated by the bolide strike about to happen. The Earth's crust in the region would be severely stressed, causing seabed fissures, and uncorking fiery volcanoes that eventually created the lovely islands of the Caribbean.

Another 63 million years would pass after that deadly bolide hit, and further to the west, the Isthmus of Panama would appear and bisect the great ocean, thereby connecting the two separate continents together. This new land bridge—that appeared about 3 million BP—would then allow for a vigorous interchange of species between the two Americas. That grand dispersal transferred and mixed an eclectic assortment of creatures that had evolved separately on the two continents. Humans would come along much later, in 36 BP, and reconnect the oceans with a narrow shipping channel called the Panama Canal. With the construction of the Panama Canal, humans once more severed the free exchange of land animals between the two American continents.

I will return now to my personal observations on that fateful day when the deadly bolide struck.

An unbroken and menacing layer of dark clouds in the sky

completely blotted out the Sun when Mac arrived on the peninsula that day. The time was approaching high noon and a cold steady drizzle was oozing from the overcast firmament above. Suddenly, a loud sound blasted the air from about 200 yards away. It began abruptly, starting as a high-pitched whine, then increased rapidly in volume and intensity to virtually shatter the listener's ear, before fading quickly into a series of dwindling honks. This pattern was repeated every 22 seconds. Presently, similar sound producers joined that fatidic chorus, the ensuing cacophony having an eerily apocalyptic quality to it.

Mac looked in the direction of the sound. A herd of hungry herbivores was feeding in a lush thicket of cycads growing on a slope along an engorged stream. There were fifteen of these creatures, posthumously christened by humans *Ankylosaurus magniventris*, both adults and calves, browsing in the cycad thicket. These armored dinosaurs were first recognized by humans from fossil footprints found in the South American country of Bolivia in 103 BP. Unlike bipedal, meat-eating dinosaurs, these herbivores moved on all four feet. The largest of them was more than 20 feet long, nearly 6 feet in height, and weighed upwards of 4 tons. They were armored on the outside with massive knobs and plates of bone embedded in the skin. Their underbellies, in contrast, had no armor and remained soft and vulnerable. A stout tail, held perpetually raised and parallel to the ground, ended in a spiked knob, a lethal club-like structure handy for defense. Adult males were multicolored with bright red plates along their neck and tail, and purple, blue and green ones along the sides. The females and calves were a solid purplish-black. Those sounds Mac had just heard were the mating calls of the males.

Overhead, framed by the dreary gray skies, a band of

Quetzalcoatlus northropi gracefully rode the buoyant air currents on offer, tirelessly scanning the landscape below for potential prey. These elegantly flying creatures were reptiles, though not in the dinosaur family. These animals were huge, with wingspans greater than 30 feet and weighing more than 400 pounds, probably the largest flying creatures of all time the Earth has ever seen. Their wings were formed by a membrane of skin with no feathers attached. They randomly emitted shrill screams that ominously pierced the air and could be heard from miles away.

Not far off on a low hill overlooking the feeding ankylosauri, a pack of shiny *Velocisaurus unicus* was hungrily eyeing the browsing herbivores. There were six of these creatures altogether. Velocisauri were obligate carnivores. This particular species, *V. unicus*, had been slowly migrating north from southern Argentina over the previous 9,000 years because of adverse climatic changes in their far southern habitat. Adults of this hardy species stood approximately 2 feet tall by 4 feet long, weighing about 25 pounds. Though small, they had powerful beak-like mouthparts with razor sharp teeth, and were exceptionally fleet of foot. Their bodies gleamed in vivid technicolor, like something quite out of this world. Their sleek skins were completely covered with transparent dermal scales that could instantly assume the exact shade and coloration of their immediate surroundings. These astonishing velocisauri performed this remarkable feat by rapidly priming chromatophores in their skin, just like modern chameleons do, but many magnitudes better. They were so adept at camouflaging themselves in this way that they could just magically vanish into their surroundings and remain completely undetected except to the most discerning eye, seemingly covered by an invisibility cloak.

These unusual creatures showed little sexual dimorphism,

both males and females appearing quite alike. Velocisauri were bipedal and fast sprinters, hunting in compact packs of four to eight individuals. Those on the hill that summer day when the bolide struck were plotting to slink stealthily over toward the browsing ankylosauri. They had spotted a juvenile that had moved a little away from the main herd, browsing deeper into the cycad thicket and heading toward the stream. Once within striking distance, the *Velocisaurus* pack would leap and cling onto the unarmored underbelly of the doomed *Ankylosaurus*, rapidly eviscerating the victim and buckling the huge beast, crashing it to the ground. Just one successful strike could feed the pack for weeks.

The velocisauri on the hill finalized their moves before trotting off toward the browsing ankylosauri in the cycad thicket.

Right about then, a whistling sound could be heard approaching from the north. Within moments it had become an earsplitting boom. A brilliant light appeared in the sky, slicing violently through the cloud cover, heralding the end of that world. A huge object from space traveling at 12.5 miles a second was about to strike the planet. Exactly at 12:08:02 PM, an enormous fireball brighter than a thousand suns smashed into Earth's lower atmosphere, releasing more energy upon impact than five billion Hiroshima sized atom bombs. The payload comparison here is to the atomic bomb dropped by the United States of America in 5 BP on the city of Hiroshima in Japan. The Hiroshima bomb was a small uranium fuelled nuclear fission bomb with a yield of 15 kilotons, the explosive equivalent of 15,000 metric tons of trinitrotoluene (TNT), a chemical explosive. That single atomic bomb leveled an area of about 2 miles in diameter around the point of impact. Between 60,000 to 80,000 people were killed instantly. In just 150 days, close to half the city's human population of 340,000 were dead. More died later from delayed radiation effects. My gentle reader can imagine what an asteroid or centaur packing the punch of 5 billion such bombs would do.

Everything on the Earth's surface within a radius of 150 miles from the impact site was vaporized. The pack of hungry velocisauri and the browsing herd of ankylosauri that Mac had been keenly observing only a moment ago were now instantly incinerated. Many trillions of tons of dust, gases, and water vapor spewed into the atmosphere, ushering midnight at noon. Monstrous fires, started by the intense shock wave of the bolide's impact, propagated rapidly for thousands of miles in all directions. Enormous tsunamis rose from the oceans, causing unimaginable destruction. A chain reaction of earthquakes and erupting volcanoes, compounded by hot, gale-force winds, devastated the face of my host planet. When it was all finally over, fully 85 percent of living species then on Earth had perished.

❧❧❧

These cosmic hurricanes are commonplace to life in the Universe. Some are seasonal and predictable, linked to galactic and other celestial cycles, just as meteorological hurricanes on Earth are seasonally linked to the planet's orbital swing around its star. Others of this ilk are apparently random and unpredictable. They are all truly titanic energy discharges of unimaginable power and intensity, packing so monstrous a punch that they impact the very fabric of spacetime itself. These are indeed cosmic slayers, yet they officiate as midwives to usher in a brand new order after they destroy the existing regime.

Mac once explored a recently devastated planet called Kalpa that occasionally hosts sapient life on its surface. Kalpa is located in a dwarf spheroidal galaxy about 7,400 light years in diameter. This dwarf galaxy itself is only about 17,000 light years from the edge of a much larger spiral galaxy around which the dwarf orbits. Now, the planet Kalpa revolves around the star Ketu near the outer rim of the dwarf galaxy. Ketu in turn, with Kalpa and its other planets in tow, completes one revolution around its own galaxy every 42 million years. Therefore, predictably like clockwork, every 42 million years, Ketu and its planets must transit their closest point to the huge gravitational powerhouse that is the giant spiral galaxy. Every time that happens, just as Ketu is at its perigee to the spiral, a vortex of violent gravitational forces perturbs the Oort Cloud harboring comets around Ketu. This gravitational disturbance nudges a veritable shower of comets toward the star. Because of the plethora of comets discharged, since Ketu's Oort Clout is supersaturated with them, some of these comets almost always seem to collide with Ketu's planets, including Kalpa, destroying most Kalpan life every 42 million years.

Now, subsequent proliferation and evolution of life on Kalpa occurs quite rapidly from the remnants left behind after these periodic cosmic catastrophes happen. The accelerated pace of biologic evolution on Kalpa compared to Earth, is facilitated by physical and chemical factors unique to that planet, like temperature, gravity, radiation levels, and available catalytic surfaces. On rare occasions, Kalpa escapes bolide impact during its 42 million year cosmic cycle, thus providing sufficient time for sapient life to emerge and flourish on the planet until the next cosmic bombardment comes along. The last time sapient creatures appeared on Kalpa was 212 million years ago. These were autotrophic—or self-nourishing—sessile beings, grounded to the surface by a rooting structure. The underground roots of each organism synapsed with those of others, forming a planet-wide neural network for exchange of information and community organization. They thrived nearly 15 million years before being wiped out by Kalpa's next mass extinction.

Another striking and instructive example of mass extinction occurred recently in a quadrant of spacetime about 240 million light years from Earth in the direction of the Southern Cross, a constellation visible in the night sky of my host planet's southern hemisphere. This extinction event is memorable because it was self-inflicted. A population of sapient creatures called Parwins, several trillion in number, lived in a volume of interstellar space about as large as that occupied by the red-giant star Aldebaran which has a diameter the distance from Mercury to the Sun. Parwins were composite energy beings and had lived quite successfully for many billions of years in the stillness of space between the stars. Energy to sustain and nourish all their life functions was derived from a nearby white dwarf star. The parwins would concentrate and channel matter—which they wrung out of empty space by separating virtual particles—into the white dwarf that in turn radiated energy from that matter. The parwins collected and metabolized that energy for their living functions. Unfortunately for them, a profligate new generation driven by insatiable greed to extract more and more of this energy, flooded the white dwarf with so much matter that the star eventually exceeded its critical Chandrasekhar[14] limit and exploded in a supernova, taking along every single parwin with it.

---

14 Subrahmanyan Chandrasekhar (40 BP–45 AP) was an Indian-American astrophysicist, renowned for his research on the structure and evolution of stars. The Chandra X-ray Observatory, a premier space telescope launched into high Earth orbit by the United States of America in 49 AP, was named after him.

For annotation purposes, a supernova is an acute and extreme-ly luminous stellar explosion that produces an extraordinary burst of radiation, often briefly outshining an entire galaxy, be-fore eventually fading from view over several weeks to months. During this short time, a supernova can radiate more energy than the Earth's Sun would emit over its entire lifetime. The explo-sion ejects a good portion of the star's outer layers into space at a velocity approaching a tenth of light-speed, driving an immense shock wave into the surrounding interstellar medium. This shock wave propagates an expanding shell of gas and dust from the ex-ploding star. In fact, the Sun and the solar system, as mentioned earlier in this narrative, were born when just such a supernova shockwave collapsed a molecular cloud.

Supernovas occur at the end of stellar life-cycles and rep-resent the death throes of stars whose cores exceed a certain critical mass that humans call the Chandrasekhar limit. This critical core mass, after the star's outer envelope is shed, is approximately equal to 1.4 solar masses. Stars below this core limit like the Sun—after losing their outer layers during the ter-minal red giant stage—do not explode as supernovas but exit quietly as white dwarfs. Because of the smaller mass, gravity is not strong enough, and therefore gravitational core collapse stops at a certain point. An object as big as the Sun may com-pact to a volume the size of Earth to become a white dwarf. If a quiescent white dwarf has mass added to it afterwards, like the parwins did to theirs, and the star eventually reaches the Chandrasekhar limit, it would belatedly go supernova like the parwins' white dwarf did.

For dying stars with cores exceeding the Chandrasekhar limit, their demise is dramatic and different—they go out as supernovas. If the star's core weighed between 1.4 and 3 solar masses after losing its outer layers, for which the original star itself must be between 8 to 20 solar masses, gravity is now strong enough to squash the supernova remnant into a plasma of pure neutrons called a neutron star. In this case, each solar mass may compact to just 5 miles in diameter. If the dying star's core was greater than 3 solar masses, for which the original star must weigh more than 20 Suns, then gravity would be so strong that the remnant implodes out of sight and vanishes into space as a black hole. Compress an object like Earth to the size of a marble and voilà, gravity would turn it to a black hole.

Mass extinctions caused by either natural or self-inflicted events happen repeatedly in every corner of spacetime. Mac used the word hurricane, a common weather term for humans, to allude to the End Cretaceous mass extinction on Earth. On Galymon we call it a Pissassi.

Mass extinction of lifeforms inhabiting celestial bodies or living in interstellar space is indeed a common occurrence. As can be readily imagined from the immensity of the Universe we occupy, somewhere out there on the highways and byways of the cosmos, mass disappearances of once dominant lifeforms are happening at this very moment. Just on Earth itself, in the last 500 million years of multicellularity, there have been at least five major mass extinction events that have devastated life on my host planet. In each of these five cases, more than half of all species inhabiting Earth at the time of the event died in a relatively short period. Local factors such as climate effects, volcanism, and change in ambient oxygen levels; and cosmic events like bolide impacts and supernova explosions, have been responsible for these cataclysms. These events, by and large, can occur anytime. They have happened on Earth in the past and will certainly happen again in the future, either tomorrow or in many million years to come. In most cases it is difficult to predict exactly when that would be, unless the prognosticators have the ability to travel into the future and back.

Mac was intrigued to learn in 61 AP while still on Earth, that humans had just recognized a supernova explosion in my own Meon galaxy back home. The supernova in question was observed in the Pinwheel galaxy by astronomers on Earth just as the designated star was beginning to explode as seen from my host planet. They called the supernova SN 2011fe. The event was discovered by humans using high resolution instruments since it is not visible to the naked human eye from their planet. Of course, at the moment when Earth astronomers recorded supernova SN 2011fe, the event had already taken place in my galaxy 21 million years earlier—that is how long the signal from the supernova, traveling at the speed of light, took to reach my host planet. Back then, here on Earth, it was the early Miocene Epoch of geologic time and the ancestors of future humans were tailless monkey-like apes called *Proconsul* living in Africa.

That supernova explosion in my home galaxy caused more than a dozen different mass extinctions of susceptible lifeforms living less than 20 light years from the source of the explosion. In that unfortunate mix, two sapient populations were also exterminated. Fortunately for galymonians, our planet was spared this catastrophe since Galymon is located more than 3,000 light years away from SN 2011fe. It may be of interest to note here that one of the five major mass extinctions known to have happened on Earth, the one from approximately 445 million years ago and called the Ordovician mass extinction, may have had a similar origin. At that time in Earth's history, all multicellular life on the planet was still confined to the seas and the oceans. As a result of the Ordovician event, more than 60 percent of all marine lifeforms were wiped out. Some Earth scientists believe that a supernova explosion similar to the one reported in our galaxy, could have been responsible for that mass extinction. It would certainly be instructive to return to that time and check the hypothesis out.

The ravaged biospheres in that regional mass extinction on my home galaxy some 21 million years ago due to SN 2011fe, have now recovered. The overall impact of mass extinction events are quite variable. Generally speaking, following the initial impact, only "weedy species" survive—these are the plants and animals which can live in diverse environments and reproduce quickly. Later on, new species evolve and diversify to occupy empty niches. As a rule, biodiversity recovers within 5 to 10 million years of the extinction event. In the most severe cases of mass extinctions, like the End Permian one here on Earth that killed off 96% of species, full recovery may take as long as 15 to 30 million years.

Life in our Universe is a vulnerable phenomenon, yet it is adaptive and versatile. The seeds of life are everywhere you look, dispersed throughout the cosmos. Life is an integral part of the constitution of nature and will manifest whenever conditions are right for it to appear and flourish. It thrives against great odds in the most unusual of habitats, changing and adapting to prevailing conditions. Mass extinctions may wipe out whole biospheres in a relative instant, but life goes on.

CHAPTER III:

LIFE

L ife on Earth is typically centered in matter and is carbon based. The internal organization and behavior of this kind of life can be surmised from the nature of the element carbon itself. Carbon is often the substrate for matter-centered life in many neighborhoods of our Universe, and therefore most astute extraterrestrial travelers are quite familiar with its remarkable properties and attributes.

Carbon atoms are made in dying stars exceeding a certain mass. Stars shine as their hydrogen is converted to helium by nuclear fusion which releases energy as a byproduct. As the star ages and continues to shine, its supply of hydrogen becomes used up and its outer layers cool down and change color, the star itself expanding to become a red giant. As the red giant expands, its core experiences reciprocal collapse, compressing the center even as the star's outer shell dilates. This recompressed core now begins to fuse helium nuclei—known as alpha particles—in a reaction called the triple alpha process to forge carbon atoms. This triple alpha process can only naturally occur in the central cores of stars containing very dense and very hot matter.

The name "carbon" comes from the Latin *carbo* for "coal." Carbon is a nonmetallic chemical element assigned the symbol "C" by humans. It has many allotropic or physical forms, of which the three best known on Earth are amorphous carbon, graphite, and diamond. In these different allotropes, the same element carbon appears to be either brilliantly transparent as in diamond, or completely opaque as in charcoal or graphite. All allotropes have the same chemical properties but appear physically very different only because of the spatial orientation of individual atoms in them. Carbon has a melting point of 6,332°F (3,500°C) and boils at 8,721°F (4,827°C).

Carbon has the atomic number 6, indicating the element has six protons or positively charged particles in its nucleus. Neutral carbon atoms have six electrons or negatively charged particles as well, orbiting the nucleus and balancing the net positive proton charge. Carbon is tetravalent, meaning four of its six electrons are available to form bonds with other elements, including other carbon atoms, thus allowing carbon to form many chemical compounds which is dandy for the business of life—the numerous carbon compounds will make up a more cosmopolitan menu for life to select from.

It should be mentioned here that the chemical properties of an element are determined by its atomic number, or the number of protons in its nucleus. These chemical properties are unaffected by the number of neutrons it has. Neutrons are proton-sized particles with no electrical charge. They occur together with protons in the nucleus of atoms. Unlike protons, the number of neutrons in an element can vary, thereby producing different isotopes of the same element. Carbon has three naturally occurring isotopes with 6, 7, and 8 neutrons respectively in their nuclei. This is in addition to the six protons that all carbon atoms possess, thus giving rise to carbon-12, carbon-13, and carbon-14 as isotopes. Of these three isotopic forms of carbon, carbon-12 and carbon-13 are stable isotopes. Carbon-14 is radioactive with a half-life of 5,730 years.

The two simplest elements, hydrogen (75 percent) and helium (23 percent), together account for 98 percent of all ordinary matter in our present Universe. Yet notably, the element carbon (0.5 percent) is the fourth most abundant one around, just after the element oxygen (1 percent). All the other elements[15] in the Universe combined make up only the remaining 0.5 percent. Carbon is the first element on that list to be solid at terrestrial temperatures. It readily combines with oxygen, the element just ahead of it in abundance, releasing copious amounts of energy that can be used to fuel life processes. Carbon possesses enormous chemical versatility, creating numerous bonds with a number of nonmetallic atoms, including itself, and also—most importantly for life—with nitrogen, oxygen, and hydrogen.

With carbon as primary scaffolding, other significant elements in life on Earth are hydrogen, nitrogen, oxygen, phosphorus, and sulfur. Carbon's capacity to combine with many different elements is superlative, and its ability to form long polymeric chains is unsurpassed. But carbon is certainly not the only foundation element employed by matter based lifeforms in our Universe.

---

15   There are 92 naturally occurring elements in the present Universe, ranging from atomic number 1 (hydrogen) through atomic number 92 (uranium). Humans have synthesized several transuranium elements, now reaching to atomic number 118 (ununoctium). Transuranium elements to atomic number 98 also occur naturally, but in extremely trace quantities. The great Russian chemist Dmitri Mendeleev in 81 BP published the Periodic Table wherein the elements, when arranged serially by their atomic number and electron structure, show a periodic recurrence of congruent properties.

Life that is centered on other elements, besides carbon, exists in the cosmos as well. Silicon lies just below carbon in the carbon family of the Periodic Table of Elements, and shares some of its periodic partner's chemical signature. Silicon, with nitrogen and oxygen, forms a variety of polymeric macromolecules stable in high ultraviolet habitations. This property is invaluable on planets with solidified metallic cores and thus unprotected by magnetic shields, or those located around certain classes of stars emitting high energy radiation. Silicon, however, forms fewer compounds overall than does carbon. It is also less common that carbon is, though silicon itself ended up more abundant than carbon in the Earth's crust. Silicon based life, though less widespread than carbon endowed ones, occurs in regions of the Universe where carbon chemistry may be unfeasible due to the prevailing physical environment in such locations. Germanium, another element in the carbon family of the Periodic Table, and boron and arsenic not in the carbon family, occasionally participate as the primary element in matter-centered life in our Universe. Ruints, encountered earlier in the Triangulum galaxy, are known to be sapient boron based creatures that zombify prolific carbon based ones.

The word chauvinism is derived from the name of a French soldier, Nicolas Chauvin, who reportedly had undying fealty to his Emperor Napoleon. It was originally a term used by humans to describe excessive nationalistic fervor. The word's meaning was later expanded to refer to any form of bigotry or bias. No greater chauvinism exists on Earth than chauvinism about life. The "lifeform" concept is much broader than is usually allowed by traditional human views that stem from Earth's matter-centered life. Since humans themselves are composed of matter, they tend to be very chauvinistic about it.

All life manifests itself through metabolism, which is essentially the systematic manipulation and processing of information. This information processing is certainly not limited to chemistry and matter-based metabolism alone, as found here on Earth. Since information manipulation requires the application and use of force, any of the four fundamental forces of nature can independently accomplish this objective and easily qualify as potential lifeforms. There are thus four broad categories of living metabolic entities in our Universe—electromagnetic, strong-force, weak-force, and gravity lifeforms—all of them able to manipulate and process information bits, each corresponding to one of the four fundamental forces of nature that split from a unified force at the Big Bang. Humans and all other native lifeforms on my host planet, are evidently electromagnetic creatures. Any creature using electromagnetic bonding of atoms, electron flows, or electrical and magnetic fields, is a member of this class. Thusly, all biochemical life anywhere would qualify as electromagnetic lifeforms. Of course, in this regard, there exist numerous other forms of non-chemical life as well throughout the Universe.

For example, gravitational lifeforms employ the most abundant and efficient form of free and unrestricted energy available in this Universe, namely, gravity. They often derive their energy by manipulating encounters around stars, black holes, or even entire galaxies. Some of these lifeforms are truly humongous, being fashioned from spacetime itself, and occupying cubic light-years of volume. The relatively smaller entities in this class of beings use the rotational and orbital motions of planets and moons as sources of gravitational power. Even still smaller gravitational lifeforms may metabolize energy directly from falling liquids such as waterfalls, harness wind power from persistent cyclonic storms as in

Jupiter's Great Red Spot, mine ocean currents, or utilize planetary and stellar seismic activity in their biology.

On the other hand, lifeforms based on the strong nuclear force arise in different environments from that of gravitational beings. The strong-force is the strongest in nature, but is effective only over miniscule subatomic distances. Chromodynamics is a quantum field theory that describes subatomic particles such as quarks and gluons and their respective interactions, with the "color" of the quarks playing a role similar to that of an electric charge for the electromagnetic force. Color, in this instance, is different from visual color, and describes a property of the quark. These chromodynamic creatures are subatomic beings often inhabiting neutron stars where the existing conditions are most favorable for their appearance and evolution.

Now back to carbon based lifeforms on my host planet. They could be loosely described as self-contained biological systems that strive to maintain their distinct compositions by actively reprocessing and recycling the matter and energy that goes to form them. This traffic in energy and matter occurs both within the system itself, as well as across its borders with the outside environment. That intrinsic and spontaneous process of self-organization is called homeostasis, or self-sustenance. The concept of homeostasis was first described by the famous French physiologist Claude Bernard in 85 BP, and the word homeostasis itself was later coined by the American physiologist Walter Cannon in 24 BP.

The word homeostasis is derived from the Greek words *homoios* meaning "of the same kind" and *stasis* for "standing still." It is the ability of a living system to preserve and maintain (stasis) its essential composition and structure (homoios) by the coordinated responses of its parts that block or neutralize any influences tending to disturb its customary organization. It is the tendency of cells and organisms to regulate themselves by a system of feedback controls that stabilizes and preserves their structure and viability, thereby opposing changing environmental conditions trying to disrupt this pristine state. Life thus attempts to sustain itself against the ravages of time and space through homeostasis. Homeostasis, then, is that indispensable biologic process that continuously aims to renew and sustain the system's integrity. A dynamic network of equilibration and adjustment mechanisms makes homeostasis possible.

When everything else is kept constant, all organized systems in nature become progressively more disorganized and chaotic with the flow of time. This time dependent increase in disorganization and chaos within closed systems is called Entropy, a key construct derived from the Second Law of Thermodynamics. Thermodynamics, a branch of the physical sciences, deals with the relationships between heat and other forms of energy—such as mechanical, electrical, or chemical energy—and, by extension, the relationships between all forms of energy. The Second Law simply states that the entropy of a closed system always increases. The entropy of an isolated system never decreases because isolated systems spontaneously evolve toward thermodynamic equilibrium, a state of maximum entropy (disorganization, randomness) within the system. Therefore entropy increases over time in all closed systems. The Universe itself, taken as a whole, has been steadily increasing in entropy ever since the Big Bang.

The Second Law, first formulated by humans in 126 BP, simply postulates that heat cannot spontaneously flow from a colder region to a hotter one. Heat only flows from hot to cold, never the other way around. The law is therefore an expression of the direction of energy flow and its dissipation in the natural world. As a corollary, the Second Law acknowledges the observation that over time, differences in temperature, pressure, chemical, and other gradients tend to even out inside a closed physical system that is kept isolated from the exterior. The measure of entropy determines how much this process has progressed. Systems flow from low entropy states with high organization, to high entropy states with low organization. Stated differently, the entropy of a closed system that is not in equilibrium will increase over time until its entropy attains a maximum value, at which point the system reaches full equilibrium and shows the greatest disorganization and randomness.

Life, then, is evidently a process that countermands and reverses this ubiquitous trend toward entropy within closed systems. Life strives, through homeostasis, to maintain its various internal gradients and organizational structure by performing biologic work using energy, thereby resisting the ravages of entropy. This energy to battle entropy is derived either by capturing it chemically from an external energy source such as sunlight, or by ingesting appropriate matter already containing preformed energy such as plants and animals. The former systems are called autotrophic (from the Greek *auto* for "self" and *trophic* for "feeding"), the latter heterotrophic (Greek *hetero* for "other"). Autotrophs obtain their reduced carbon for subsequent oxidation and energy extraction from inorganic carbon dioxide, whereas heterotrophs get this carbon from feeding on other life-forms containing it.

Water, chemically dihydrogen monoxide, is a compound

widely distributed on the surface of my host planet. It is the essential solvent for carbon based life on Earth.

In order for matter-centered life to exist and thrive anywhere in the Universe, such as on Earth, participating atoms and their molecules must be physically able to encounter each other closely enough to react chemically and thereby manifest the numerous properties distinctive to this form of life. That is hard to do within a solid matrix. A gaseous matrix certainly would be the most efficient for such atomic and molecular interchange to occur, but because of my host planet's geophysical properties such as its gravity, atmospheric pressure, ambient temperature and so on, a gaseous organism would be hard-pressed to maintain its structural boundaries and integrity on Earth—though such organisms do occur in other habitats possessing different physical properties. A liquid matrix then, given these limitations, would be most suitable for carbon based life on my host planet, and to accomplish this all important purpose, water served as the vehicle for lifeforms on Earth.

In order to serve as a solvent for matter based life, the prospective agent must possesses certain important qualities. First of all, it should be widely available in the area, preferably a thalassogen. In cosmogeology, a thalassogen is a substance capable of forming a planetary ocean. If the intended solvent is extremely rare in an area, there may not be enough of it around to sustain an ecology[16]. Furthermore, the proposed substance should be an effective solvent for both inorganic and organic compounds, and a suitable medium for ionization of these solutes so they could

16   There are some notable exceptions to this rule of abundance. In the arid desert areas of southwestern North America where water is extremely scarce, the desert kangaroo rat *Dipodomys deserti*, a large rodent, can survive simply on water molecules conserved from the normal metabolism of dry food, without having to drink a drop of water during its entire lifetime if necessary.

interact and form ionic chemical bonds among themselves. The solvent must also have a broad liquidity range within its operating habitat so that organisms may remain biochemically active over a wider span of temperatures. The optimal solvent should have a high enough dielectric constant or the ability to provide electrical insulation from external electrical currents to solutes dissolved in it. The solvent's specific heat or the amount of heat energy needed to raise its temperature by a standard unit, should be relatively high so that organisms can enjoy thermal stability. Typically, the solvent should also possess a low enough viscosity to flow easily.

Water fulfills all these requirements for life on my host planet; no other substance is a comparable candidate to replace water as the solvent for carbon based life on Earth. But certainly, in other domains, away from Earth, where chemical and physical conditions are vastly different, other solvents may perform the same function for matter-centered life there, as water does for life on Earth.

Ammonia, chemically trihydrogen nitride, is a common alternative to water as a solvent for many matter-centered life-forms in our Universe. Ammonia exists in large quantities on gas giants and nomad planets, and is a thalassogen present in sufficient amounts to act as a life-fluid in many extraterrestrial locations. Chemically, liquid ammonia is homologous to water, with an entire bailiwick of organic and inorganic chemistries occurring in ammoniacal solution comparable to what happens in aqueous solution. Ammonia's liquidity range on Earth is between -108°F to -28°F, but as the atmospheric pressure rises, that range increases correspondingly. At just 60 atmospheres which is less than the pressure on Jupiter or Venus in the solar system, ammonia will boil at 208°F which is close to the boiling point of water on Earth. Ammonia-life is therefore not necessarily "low temperature" life. Ammonia dissolves organic compounds better than water does, and has the extraordinary ability to directly dissolve several metallic and nonmetallic elements such as sodium, potassium, phosphorous, iodine, and sulfur. Ammonia, however, possesses only a quarter of the dielectric constant of water, but it has a slightly higher specific heat. It is less viscous and therefore freer flowing than water. Ammonia is a common solvent for lifeforms on many gas giant planets. Other solvents for matter-centered life around the Universe are hydrogen fluoride, hydrogen cyanide, sulfuric acid, and methanol. There are still more solvents on that list.

The laws of life are universal principles of nature, similar to the laws of electromagnetism, radioactivity, or gravity. Life itself is not an extraordinary or supernatural phenomenon as some human belief systems seem to espouse. Just as the laws of gravity organize matter and energy on a vast scale to form stars and galaxies and thus decrease the entropy of such systems, the laws of life likewise, under the right conditions, organize matter and energy on a more diminutive scale to form organisms in this instance and decrease the entropy of these smaller systems in an analogous fashion.

Vitalism, a much discredited doctrine these days, once seriously proposed that living entities were different from non-living ones because they possessed an exclusive nonphysical attribute within themselves and were governed by principles different from inanimate objects. Modern humans have now clearly rejected this assertion. Vitalists believed that living organisms contained an *élan vital* or "vital spirit" which they described as a discrete essence that infiltrated the entire body and imparted life to it. Some equated this essence to the soul, an insubstantial and nonphysical presence that was believed to have its own individual existence separate and distinct from the material body.

Since the emergence, approximately 500 years ago, of formal scientific thinking based on direct observations and experimental methods, people began to seriously challenge the whimsical notions of vitalism. As a consequence of this trend, natural explanations already offered for physical and chemical phenomena were now extended to biological systems as well. The renowned French philosopher Rene Descartes (354 BP–300 BP) and the scientific tradition that he sponsored, embraced this concept wholeheartedly and maintained that animals and humans are *automata* or just mechanical devices, differing from artificial ones only in their degree of complexity. The difference, according to this new scientific viewpoint, was only a quantitative one, not a qualitative feature. Under vitalism, humans had believed that organic compounds required a "vital force" for their synthesis and could therefore only be made within living organisms. Friedrich Wohler, a German chemist who had earlier trained as a physician, entirely disproved this contention in 122 BP by synthesizing the organic compound urea from inorganic chemicals for the very first time in the laboratory.

In broad terms, life on Earth is a condition that characterizes objects possessing intrinsic signaling capabilities, from those that do not. Objects possessing this signaling function are called "animate" in contrast to all others which are designated "inanimate" and devoid of this signaling capacity. For definitional purposes, a contiguous and circumscribed living system is an organism. A signal in biology is any information-encoded message that is transmitted from one organism to another, or from one location inside an organism to another location within it. Organisms typically perform chemical metabolism, maintain homeostasis, possess a capacity to grow and reproduce, react to stimuli, and adapt to their environment over succeeding generations through natural selection.

Living systems exist in nature by actively exporting the accumulating entropy within their borders to the outside. Therefore, in this fundamental equation of life, the entropy of the environment outside the organism will increase by the same quantity that entropy inside the organism decreases. Entropy is hence exported by living organisms to enable them to maintain or modify their internal organization and execute necessary biological activity. This entropy exchange process for carbon based life on my host planet is accomplished through catalyzed chemical reactions using electromagnetic forces.

Life on Earth is a chemical formulation and should be understood essentially in terms of chemistry. It rapidly appeared very early on Earth, soon after the planet had gravitationally accreted from the residual matter in the solar nebula. Life resulted from the ubiquitous presence and continuous interactions of small organic molecules which are widely distributed across the present Universe. Under the physical and chemical conditions prevailing in the early prebiotic Earth, these molecules became engaged in a growing spiral of chemical reactions that soon gave rise to nucleic acids, proteins, and other organic macromolecules that make the platform for matter based life on Earth. First brought together almost four billion years ago, these same chemical reactions continue to provide the coherence for life on my host planet to this very day.

Life can be extinguished by a condition called Death. For Earth based creatures, death is the cessation of homeostasis which was the process that hitherto kept the organism alive by exporting its entropy to the outside world using energy produced by chemical reactions. Death, by this reckoning, is a passive process marking the cessation of these reactions and the end to homeostasis. Homeostasis, as was already noted for organisms on Earth, requires the consumption of energy in order to do work to move those gradients around. Therefore, when death occurs, this energy consumption ceases and the gradients are lost. Death can be reversed by resumption of homeostasis. There are lifeforms, even on Earth, that at times appear dead by objective criteria, but can resume homeostasis and active functioning when environmental conditions change and become more favorable for living.

Growth or increase in size, and reproduction or self-replication, though often included in the definition of life, are not inevitably required for it to exist. Certain microbes on Earth living deep below-ground endure without seemingly growing or dividing for millions or even tens of millions of years. My dear comrades on Earth were astonished when Mac told them of a race of beings living on the surface of a brown dwarf in the great Comet galaxy—home to the zombie tantalum collectors—a spiral galaxy about 3.2 billion light years away in a cluster of galaxies humans identify as Abell 2667. Brown dwarfs are substellar objects tens of times larger than the largest planets, yet not quite large enough to ignite as stars. These beings on that brown dwarf in the Comet galaxy, known as Datu to friends in their neighborhood, are predominantly deuterium based creatures that also incorporate other atoms and molecules—like the element palladium and the compound zirconium oxide—as

catalysts in their internal structure. Deuterium is a stable heavier isotope of hydrogen with a nucleus containing one proton
like hydrogen, but with an extra neutron as well. Deuterium
has the same atomic number and chemical properties as ordinary hydrogen, since only protons in the nucleus determine the
chemical properties of an element. Datus generate energy for
all their biologic activity by controlled "slow" nuclear fusion.
As noted previously in this narrative, nuclear fusion is also
the process stars use for energy production, a fact that became
known to humans hardly a century ago. Slow nuclear fusion is
a catalyst assisted process occurring at much lower temperatures than regular stellar nuclear fusion.

Mac would describe datus as adorable little creatures that
have about the mass of a large hippopotamus and the volume and
sentience of a small oyster. Datus emerge fully formed from the
brown dwarf's plasma lagoons when these lagoons are periodically churned every eighteen hours by ripples in the surrounding
spacetime fabric caused by gravitational waves from two nearby
neutron stars orbiting each other. Among their many unusual
properties, datus remain unchanged in size, showing no growth
after they spontaneously emerge from their plasma lagoons. They
never multiply or reproduce. They perish rapidly by dehiscence
after six weeks of life, merging their contents back into the exact plasma lagoon of their origin where they return to die, like
salmon on my host planet flocking to their natal lakes from far
out at sea to spawn and perish at the end of their own life cycles.

Life on Earth is ubiquitous and pervasive, exactly as it is
elsewhere in our Universe. This comports with the observation
that the Universe, on average, is homogenous and isotropic.
Homogenous implies uniform consistency; isotropic means
similar properties when measured in any direction.

Humans have frequently discovered life flourishing on Earth in the most extraordinary places. Nearly two miles under the surface of their planet where temperatures are a toasty 140°F (60°C), colonies of bacteria are known to thrive on energy derived from external nuclear fission. These astonishing creatures had been living unsuspected by humans deep under Earth's surface for millions of years, and were only discovered by people hardly five years before Mac arrived on the scene. As uranium atoms in the bacteria's deep underground habitat spontaneously undergo natural decay and emit their energy as radiation into the neighborhood, that radiation then splits water molecules by radiolysis, releasing free hydrogen into the environment. The clever bacteria then combine this free hydrogen with sulfate ions from the surrounding rock, thereby producing biologic energy to sustain life in a place where humans once imagined no life could ever exist. The laws of life, like all natural laws, are universal. They are permanently inscribed into the fabric of the cosmos itself. Given accessibility to necessary preconditions, these laws of life will unfailingly assemble living organisms from appropriate substrates, not only here on Earth, but everywhere else in the Universe as well.

These fascinating creatures come in countless avatars and occupy every available niche in the cosmos. They arrive in all shapes and sizes, from garishly explicit to quietly sedate, filling every dimension of space and time. They are all over the place. At times their paths intersect and leave marks of the rendezvous. Many human civilizations have kept legendry accounts of these seemingly extraordinary encounters. Whether these accounts are real or imagined however, it is now impossible to tell.

Viruses, more correctly called Virions, thriving in prolific numbers right here on Earth, are arresting examples from this fabulous smorgasbord of life. These creatures are widely distributed across the planet in every possible ecosystem on Earth. They are likely the most abundant type of biological life in this part of the Universe, tending to proliferate across space.

Virions were completely unknown to humans before 58 BP. In that year, the Tobacco Mosaic Virus was identified by the noted Russian botanist Dmitri Ivanovsky, who isolated an unusual form of matter from affected tobacco plants. His extract from infected plants produced a transmissible disease in healthy, uninfected tobacco plants.

This uncanny infective agent had inexplicable qualities. It appeared utterly inert and lifeless when located outside its tobacco host cell. Alongside matter considered living by the human standards of that time, these unusual fragments appeared entirely dead. The extract described by Ivanovsky dissolved in water like any other solute, could be crystallized out of solution again, and passed unimpeded through a porcelain bacterial filter. From all reasonable criteria of that period, this exotic form of matter was certainly not alive.

Ivanovsky was puzzled. He had never before seen something as strange as this. Amazingly, once inside its host cell, this inscrutable substance came alive and proceeded to reproduce mirror images of itself. Though humans only came to appreciate the reality of virions in this way barely a hundred years ago, thanks to the elegant work of Ivanovsky, viral particles themselves were not actually visualized until some forty years later. That had to wait for electron microscopy to arrive, a technique that uses an electron beam instead of visible light to examine submicroscopic objects. These electron beams had wavelengths 100,000 times smaller than visible light, thus enormously enhancing resolution and producing magnifications up to ten million times larger than the original object. This is so because in order to image an object, the wavelength of the incident radiation has to be smaller than the targeted object itself, so that the rays will strike the object and be reflected back to the observer, rather than just pass forward around the object.

This discovery of virions by humans hardly a century ago challenged them to fundamentally reconsider the definition of living matter, and of life itself.

Virions are carbon based lifeforms constructed on the same biologic principles like the other creatures on Earth are. They are very basic in their organization and function with just two primary goals in mind—capture of appropriate host cells, and multiplication of viral particles. Their toolkit consists of only a few molecules. They cannot store any free energy and remain alive only inside a host cell. Once inside the host, a lifeless virion would resurrect itself and became alive. It would then commandeer the biologic machinery of the host cell and force that cell to replicate more viral particles precisely like itself. After the host cell produces countless viral replicas, the new population of daughter virions destroy and exit the host. Outside the host cell they again become inert and play dead until they reenter a fresh host and are then resurrected anew. Are virions dead matter, or are they living entities? The answer clearly seems to be both, as virions can oscillate between dead and alive. Professor Tao has written extensively on this subject.

In the year 7 AP on Earth, a distinguished British author and cosmologist named Fred Hoyle (35 BP–51 AP) published a popular novel called, *The Black Cloud*. In this fabulous and riveting tale, Hoyle describes an encounter between humans on Earth and an enormous molecular cloud which is in fact a sapient creature half a billion years old. The Cloud, an electromagnetic lifeform, operates on the principles of plasma physics, not molecular biochemistry. Memory and intelligence are stored in panels of solid-state material. Currents of ionized gases carry nutrients to wherever they are needed within the Cloud and are distributed by electromagnetic forces.

The Cloud occupies a huge volume of space. It has a diameter larger than the distance from the Earth to the Sun. Its density is sufficient to give it a mass equal to two-thirds that of Jupiter, the largest solar system planet. It is an intrepid, solitary, interstellar voyager that deliberately moves from one star to another, replenishing its stores of nourishment from these stellar sources. Now heading toward the Sun to feast on that star's hydrogen reserves, the Cloud is poised to destroy life on Earth in this feeding frenzy. It is unaware the planet harbors living beings. The human protagonists in this adventure finally succeed in establishing radio communication with the Cloud and inform it of their predicament. The Cloud graciously offers to exit the solar system. Before departing, the creature transfers personal information about itself. It indicates that its lifespan is undetermined and could presumably last forever unless it perished from an accident or took its own life. Clouds have no gender. They occasionally reproduce vegetatively, transplanting a zoetic, or living module of themselves, onto a suitably lifeless molecular formation they might encounter on their interstellar journeys.

This fabulous tale spun by a famous cosmologist from Earth conjures up all that is possible in the amazing cosmos we inhabit. The potential is immeasurable and boundless. We have a proverb on Galymon we tell our babies, reminding them that in a Universe of infinite probability endowed with countless possibilities, nothing is improbable since anything is possible.

Just a few years ago, in 57 AP, an international team of scientists on my host planet using a computer model of molecular dynamics, discovered that particles of inorganic dust can become organized into spiral structures that interact with each other in ways usually associated with life. Not only do these helical strands attract similarly configured ones in the surrounding plasma, but they also undergo changes usually associated with biological molecules like proteins and DNA. For instance, these helicals can divide to form duplicates of themselves, or induce mirror-image changes in their neighbors. Furthermore, they can evolve into yet more complex structures as less stable ones break down, leaving only the fittest helicals to survive in the plasma. Thus these simple self-organizing structures exhibit all the obligatory properties needed to qualify them as "inorganic" living matter—they are autonomous, they influence their neighbors, they reproduce, and they evolve.

About thirty years ago, in 32 AP, an even more unusual form of real life, more fabulous than Hoyle's mythical Cloud, was discovered by humans on their very own planet. They called it a Prion.

Prions produce certain rare diseases in animals, such as scrapie in sheep and goats, or mad cow disease in cattle and humans. Prions contain no genetic material. A prion is a single protein—a chain of amino acids—normally present in tissue in a benign or non-prion form. By simply folding itself physically into an aberrant shape, the legitimate protein transforms itself into a rogue agent now called a prion. The newly minted prion then actively recruits other normally configured protein molecules in the victim to also fold aberrantly like itself, and thus convert themselves into the lethal prion-protein form. Prions demonstrate how easily life can manifest itself even within simple molecular formulations such as an uncomplicated chain of amino acids.

Prions bring to mind another form of life Mac encountered while on a mission to a galaxy sporting more than the usual number of supernovas. The galaxy in question is identified by humans in their *New General Catalogue of Nebulae and Clusters of Stars* as NGC 1316. It is a radio galaxy about seventy million light years from Earth in the Fornax constellation. This one is a lenticular galaxy and is the fourth brightest radio source in the sky from Earth. Radio galaxies are active galaxies that are very luminous at radio wavelengths. While large galaxies typically host three supernovas per century, NGC 1316 has blasted four supernovas in just 26 years, two of them in less than a span of five months.

Stars in NGC 1316 can become afflicted with a lethal stellar condition called primary stellar dysnucleosynthesis or starpox, caused by a parasitic lifeform known as Poochi. Poochis are aberrant hydrogen atoms made from mutant protons carrying a "color" imbalance in their quarks. Quarks are components of subatomic particles and are among the fundamental constituents of matter. Now poochis, these mutant hydrogen atoms, infiltrate susceptible stars where they actively recruit and induce standard-issue hydrogen atoms to join their fraternity and become poochis as well. The transfigured hydrogen atoms then enter the doomed star's energy cycle, disrupting stellar nucleosynthesis by speeding up the rate of nuclear fusion. Stars thus infected with poochis therefore age prematurely and die faster. If these stars possess sufficient mass to exceed the Chandrasekhar limit, they go out as supernovas, thus accounting for the excessive supernova activity detected by humans in NGC 1316. Mac has pondered long and hard about which of these creatures is the more unusual lifeform: prions or poochis?

Lichens are strange creatures living on Earth. They are composed of not just one, but two separate organisms bound in a single body. One is a fungal component called the mycobiont that attaches to a surface and gathers water and nutrients for the couple. The other lichen component is the photobiont made up of green algal or bacterial cells. By capturing sunlight as an energy source, the photobiont uses photosynthesis to elaborate energy rich compounds for the lichen pair, using the accumulated water and nutrients absorbed by the mycobiont. The organisms in lichen—sometimes there are more than just one photobiont—live together in a single collaborative body structure called the thallus. Lichens are extremely hardy creatures and can latch on to all types of surfaces. They are found living in scorching deserts on Earth, as well as deep in the frigid polar regions of my host planet. Humans have sent lichens in open containers into outer space and brought them back to Earth alive and well.

The diversity and extreme adaptations of carbon based life just on Earth alone are startling in their manifestations, and are indeed quite astonishing in their extent and distribution. Deep under the solid crust of Earth, as far down as humans have been able to sample, real life exists and even thrives. A tiny worm makes its home 2.24 miles underground in an environment of intense pressure and heat with hardly any organic molecules around to feed on. Yet those worms make a decent living under these uttermost circumstances. There are microbes that metabolize energy so slowly that they live for millions of years. Strange creatures exist seven miles under the ocean's surface, thriving around hot vents on the floors of the deepest seas.

Life is everywhere. There are no sterile surfaces in the Universe.

The capacity for life as found on Earth, for example, is a fundamental property of the matter/energy conjugate distributed isotropically—that is, nonpreferentially—throughout the cosmos. On Galymon, we refer to this conjugate as Metta, a general term we apply to all quasi-biotic substrates. The four principle laws that determine how metta is enlivened, known as Mensa's[17] Laws, are fully described in that exhaustive encyclopedic compilation, *The Universal Compendium of Natural Laws and Edicts*. The four Laws of Life can be referenced in the said compendium under *Mensa—Laws Of*. This famous compendium, reviewed and revised periodically, was first compiled almost 3.4 billion years ago by a select committee of sapient beings from the Virgo Supercluster of galaxies, to which both my own galaxy and the Milky Way belong. Today, this supercluster encompasses a diameter of 110 million light years and contains about 50,000 galaxies of various sizes, one of countless such superclusters in our Universe.

---

17 Mensa was the illustrious Dorgonon who first experimentally confirmed the Laws of Life on Tven, an anomalous antimatter galaxy now extinct. The eminent Mensa employed a newly discovered "time-retraction" technique, making it possible to retrospectively conduct experiments in a different era when the Universe was young.

The Laws of Mensa are well known to Mac and our folks back home on Galymon. We consider them fundamental to the form and functioning of our Universe. Given appropriate conditions, these laws generate life across time and space. The appearance of life in all its complex manifestations is a constant feature of the cosmos, shepherded onto stage by these laws. Yet it is difficult and challenging for a galymonian to deconstruct Mensa's Laws to the satisfaction of my esteemed friends on Earth. This problem arises from the transactional difficulties of exchanging information with an alien lifeform, a constraint Mac had indicated at the beginning of this narrative.

I shall try to approach this impasse by firstly explaining to my human interlocutors that the phenomenon they call "life" is not simply the product of an enlivened metta's physiochemical functions such as cognition or thermoregulation, but is a founding principle of its very nature and constitution—like magnetism or radioactivity. Secondly, I strongly suspect the reservations my human friends may have with Mensa's Laws arise from the distraction of anthropomorphism.

Anthropomorphism is chauvinism. It is the overriding compulsion to view everything from a purely human platform. Mac makes this assertion with the greatest of humility, without intending any offense to the sensitivity of my dear and valued companions on Earth. The problem with anthropomorphism is that it not only bestows human characteristics and attributes—such as modes of thinking, feeling, and motivation—to non-human beings, but it also tries to understand the intrinsic nature and behavior of such non-human creatures in purely human terms. By this fatal fallacy, all manner of mettas are viewed by humans through the prism of their own metta.

A major obstacle preventing my esteemed human friends

from recognizing the nature of life from a broader perspective evidently arises from their own natural inclination to separate all matter surrounding them into "living" and "nonliving" types. This instant division of every object into "dead" or "alive" is conducted reflexively, without conscious thought or premeditation by the individual making that determination. Clearly, from a survival perspective, it is quite necessary to make that distinction quickly, firmly, and continuously, so as to evaluate if a piece of matter is suitable for consumption—or to avoid being consumed by it; the goal here is whether to eat, mate, or flee from another lifeform. This inherent ability to instantly recognize all visible carbon based life on their planet is a fundamental property of life on Earth. Regrettably, this fixation on just their distinctive form of life makes them blind to the numerous other prototypes that exist.

Hylozoism, from the Greek *hyle* for "matter" and *zoos* for "alive," is the term used by humans for the proposition that all matter possesses life and that life by itself is inseparable from matter. Although the concept of hylozoism correctly discards the fallacy of anthropomorphism, it fails to recognize that matter—or to use the broader galymonian term, metta—just by itself is not alive; it merely has the capacity and proclivity for life. Life is produced only when metta is entrained to express that property by forces described in Mensa's Laws acting within the purview of a passel of prescribed conditions. These conditions can appear in very diverse locations on our Universe. Just as carbon based life here on Earth is ubiquitous and can exist in unusual places, so too does life elsewhere in the cosmos appear in many manifestations, thriving in the most exotic of neighborhoods. Once life becomes overt and gains a foothold anywhere, it evolves into more complex forms. That particular principle is enunciated in Mensa's Fourth Law.

It is important to distinguish here between hylozoism and the spurious doctrine of vitalism. Vitalism, described earlier, decouples matter from life. It postulates an "essence" or "vital spirit" that must uniquely infuse matter for it to manifest life and perform biological functions. Vitalism contends that death extinguishes this essence from matter, returning the matter to a nonliving form. It therefore posits a dualism for the natural world, arguing that mind/soul versus body/matter are independent and separate constructs. In contrast to vitalism, hylozoism is an unitarianism and asserts that substance and spirit are one. Life is a property of matter and intrinsic to it. The mind or spirit does not exist apart from the body or matter.

Hylozoism should also be clearly distinguished from animism. Unlike hylozoism, animism is a belief in the existence of individual spirits that inhabit natural objects. Each spirit has its own unique way of thinking and feeling, and possesses its own willpower. Likewise, hylozoism should be differentiated from panpsychism. Panpsychism is a concept that attributes awareness to all matter and is unrelated to hylozoism, though some people erroneously conflate the two.

The earliest theories of life proposed by humans were all materialistic or matter-dependent. They all postulated that only matter existed and that life arose in matter from a complex arrangement of elements constituting that matter. Empedocles (2,440 BP–2,380 BP), a prominent Greek philosopher from the ancient city of Akragas in Sicily, made the case that everything in the Universe is formed by combinations of four everlasting elements, or "roots of all" as he called them. Empedocles named these four elements, Earth,

Water, Air, and Fire. The different forms of life, he believed, were caused by various admixtures of these four root elements. This view is now defunct.

It is notable that throughout the history of human thought, a hylozoistic view of nature has been very common. More than 2,500 years ago the legendary Thales of Miletus from the eponymous city in ancient Anatolia, and hailed by the great Aristotle[18] himself as the first genuine philosopher in the hallowed Greek tradition, attempted to explain natural phenomena without reference to mythology or the gods. He was enormously influential in this respect. Thales' rejection of mythological explanations became the foundation for the subsequent scientific revolution some 2,000 years later. For this reason, Thales has been nominated by modern humans as the "Father of Science." He was a dedicated hylozoist, and ever since his time there have been many other renowned philosophers and scientists who have been proponents of hylozoism.

Given the primitive nature of human knowledge in his time, Thales's hylozoism was rather naïve and simplistic. He proposed that "water" was the "alivening" principle in all forms of matter. All things originated from this water and all things ended in it, the water being neither created nor destroyed. The water that Thales described was not the common inorganic compound of hydrogen and oxygen that humans routinely recognize as water. In Thales' water, life was intrinsic

---

18   Aristotle (2,334 BP–2,272 BP) was a brilliant Greek philosopher and prolific author who wrote highly influential tracts on logic, ethics, natural sciences, medicine, and politics. He had a profound influence on the style and formalities of human thinking. Although some of his major pronouncements were later shown to be incorrect, Aristotle is considered a seminal figure in human intellectual history. He advocated deductive reasoning, where theory followed observation and logic, not faith or wishful thinking.

and inherent to it, with matter and life both combined into one substance. Thales held that every manifestation of matter, including life, arose from this substance. There were others as well who championed classical hylozoism. The brilliant and prolific German physician and biologist, Ernst Haeckel, who died in 31 BP and was criticized for his ideologically racialist views, insisted that matter must contain life since life derives from matter. Fundamentally then, do atoms possess an intrinsic property—like their mass, resonance, spin, etc—to naturally organize as lifeforms? It evidently appears that way, a priori.

These views of hylozoism may be quite unsophisticated and rather misleading by today's standards. They ignore the premise that matter by itself is not alive. Matter simply has the components and potential for life. Life itself has to be cultivated in matter through the proper application of natural laws and the availability of suitable prevailing conditions.

The phenomenal growth of modern science in the past two centuries demolished the notion of dualism in nature. The new discipline of biology revealed the physicochemical character of living organisms by experimentation—attributable knowledge only comes through the Experimental Process. Scientists and secular philosophers on my host planet today soundly reject any notion of duality between matter and life, or body and soul, at least within their own domains. Instead, they subscribe to the modern unitary view of nature, recognizing substance and essence as confluent and indivisible. Every characteristic of life on Earth resides in the properties of matter and has no provenance apart and separate from it. The majority of scientists and well informed humans today readily accept this proposition which directly derives from the principle of hylozoism. Of course, many so-called "matterless" lifeforms, such as pure force-beings and thoughtbots, exist in the Universe without breaching this principle of unitarianism.

Abiogenesis is the technical term humans use to refer to the emergence of biologic life from nonliving matter.

Fred Hoyle, author of *The Black Cloud*, introduced earlier in this narrative, was skeptical of abiogenesis and dismissed the probability of biologic life ever starting on Earth from scratch. Hoyle himself was a proponent of Panspermia. Panspermia is the notion that life arrived on Earth from outer space carried on falling cosmic debris, thereby inoculating the planet's surface and seeding Earth with primary life which evolved into more complex organisms. In advancing the concept of panspermia, Hoyle used clever statistical arguments to show that the probability of cellular life arising de novo on Earth was as unlikely as a "tornado sweeping through a junkyard" and producing a fully equipped "Boeing 747" aircraft. This erroneous analogy predictably applies the fallacy of irreducible complexity to the phenomenon of life. In making this spurious comparison, Hoyle naively overlooked important biological principles familiar to most practicing biologists—the argument has therefore been called Hoyle's Fallacy. The full fallacy arises from disregarding everything about the system except for its size and complexity, leaving the remaining variables unaccounted for. This fact is clearly illustrated by Hoyle's flawed reference to the myoglobin molecule in his fallacy.

Myoglobin is an oxygen-binding protein found in the muscle tissue of animals. Hoyle argued that with 20 possible amino acids to choose from, myoglobin, with a sequence of 153 amino acids, has a probability of only 20^{-153} to form in a single step inside a "random-amino-acid" machine. What Hoyle failed to note was that myoglobin's function is a property of the folded protein, not the amino acid sequence itself. Other amino acid sequences may fold with similar functional effects. Even an imperfect arrangement may be superior to its predecessor, evolution then channeling these processes along pathways to optimization. Myoglobin was simply the molecule finally put into place by evolution, not the first one to suddenly pop up from the passel of amino acids available for its formation.

The earlier misbegotten notion of spontaneous generation, which held that fully formed creatures arose intact from inert matter, has a long and ancient pedigree going back to remote times. Holding sway from before the time of Aristotle who is reputed to have formally given this now discredited doctrine affirmation and credibility more than 2,300 years ago, this erroneous belief persisted and endured until only a few hundred years ago. Many eminent philosophers and scientists along the way were among those who believed that maggots formed from putrid matter, mice from dirty hay, and crocodiles from rotting logs. These assumptions were later disproved with simple experiments and were subsequently discarded. For example, the first experimental evidence against spontaneous generation came in 282 BP when the Italian physician and poet, Francesco Redi, showed conclusively that no maggots appeared in meat when flies were prevented from laying eggs on it.

The spectacular advances that humans achieved in the physical and chemical sciences starting some 250 years ago, produced theories of abiogenesis that were based more firmly on credible scientific foundations. In 26 BP, the Russian biochemist Alexander Oparin proposed a hypothesis for the origin of life on Earth which became the basis for future models of abiogenesis. He postulated that life arose in nonliving matter through progressive chemical evolution of carbon based molecules in a suitable molecular environment. Over time, increasingly more complex molecular aggregates were formed and picked by natural selection from among competing candidates. The system eventually acquired the ability to maintain its internal structure and stability through homeostasis, and also to replicate itself. Thus did the first living matter appear on Earth. Further evolution of this ancestral form produced the parade of life that flourishes on Earth today.

Curiously enough, most of my valued human friends will only identify certain forms of carbon based matter as being alive. They are usually unaware or insensitive to other forms of living beings, some of which contain no matter at all. Such matterless organisms are found inhabiting numerous cosmic domains. An example of this type, made entirely by gravitational forces, occupies an unusual region of a bizarre galaxy. Those creatures are tailored from the void by gravitational sculpting of spacetime around them. The galaxy in question is the Black Eye galaxy (NGC 4826), located some 20 million light years from Earth. It has a dark band of light-absorbing dust in front of its bright galactic nucleus, giving rise to its earthly name Black Eye, meaning "Evil Eye." It is a spiral galaxy located in the Coma Berenices constellation when viewed from the present galactic location of my host planet.

A peculiar feature of this galaxy is that the stars and gas in the outer region of the structure rotate in the opposite direction to the stars and gas in the inner region. The inner region has a radius of about 3,000 light years, the outer region extending for another 40,000 light years further. There is a distinct boundary established where the inner and outer rings, rotating in opposite directions, face each other. The unusual form of gravitational life reported in this galaxy inhabits the space separating the inner and outer regions. Called Jivans, these creatures are best described as disembodied and nonmaterial thought beings or thoughtbots. Numerous other creatures that would be even stranger than jivans to humans, tailored from a variety of exotic cosmic substrates, exist in every dimension of our Universe, and may even interact with Earth's own space-time coordinates. Some of these beings are able to spectrally transit in and out of my host planet's landscape.

Across the plains of Sard in the Pelican nebula of the Milky Way galaxy, lives a most fabulous and legendary creature. Called Sardons by galactic neighbors, their "aliveness" is obligatorily glued to their physical state. Sardons are elaborately complex three-celled organisms. Each cell has roughly the mass of a large house on Earth and the volume of a small suitcase. The outer limit of each cell—the presumptive cell membrane—is bounded by a magnetic field rather than by molecules of ordinary matter as in terrestrial life.

Below a certain temperature, where they can maintain a solid structure, sardons remain intelligent and friendly creatures able to understand and replicate the mysteries of the Universe. Hydrogen fusion is their preferred method for energy generation. They use proton beams successfully for teleportation, and are even now mastering the more advanced technology of cognokinesis, or the movement of matter by thought.

At higher ambient temperatures, sardons rapidly undergo phase shift and transform quickly from a solid to a liquid state. In the liquid phase, their homeostatic mechanisms shut down and their energy fields and various molecular aggregations lose their gradients and rapidly equilibrate. They now appear entirely non-alive and exhibit the expected properties of a viscous liquid like tomato soup. When temperatures fall again and the solid phase returns, homeostasis and living gradients are quickly reestablished and sardons expeditiously resume their sapient and friendly personalities once more. Each time they transit from solid to liquid and back to solid again, they exchange unique information-bits among themselves, so that when they reconstitute after each cycle, they are similar yet different from their former selves.

Sard has about the combined mass of all the planets in Earth's solar system. It orbits the rim of a spinning black hole, staying at the very edge of the black hole's event horizon. Consequently, time becomes dilated on Sard by the black hole's gravitational effect, and therefore each orbit around the black hole takes about four million years to complete in Earth time. Now, there is a gravitationally locked companion star to the black hole that continually ejects matter into the accretion disc, always onto just one hemisphere of the black hole because of the gravitational lock between the two. When Sard enters this "lit" side, it is warmed by the falling material, thereby switching sardons into the liquid phase where they naturally cannot remain alive. They appear to vanish, only to reappear two million years later when Sard nips around the corner to the "dark" side of the black hole, and temperatures cool down enough for these astonishing creatures to return. Remarkably, when they do return, they carry on exactly where they had left off, acting as if nothing had happened.

Sardons cycle between dead and alive approximately every two million years. Though vastly different in size, complexity, sapience, and the nature of their deaths and reincarnations, sardons, in Mac's view, recall the recurring dead-and-alive existence of virions on Earth.

The first major attempt by humans to classify the life found on my host planet into distinct categories and groups in a rational and systematic way, was undertaken by the great Aristotle himself, that most uncommon Greek philosopher and thinker. Aristotle was a "natural philosopher" as scientists[19] were known in his day. He classified all living organisms believed to exist then, into two broad categories—based on their ability to move—as plants or animals. In his book *Historia Animalium*, or History of Animals, issued circa 2,300 BP, Aristotle grouped animals according to their similarities. For instance, he divided his animals into those "with blood" and those "without blood" corresponding roughly to vertebrates and invertebrates. The "blooded" animals he divided into five groups: quadrupeds that gave live birth (mammals), quadrupeds that laid eggs (amphibians and reptiles), birds, fishes, and whales. The "bloodless" animals were also divided into five groups: gastropods, crustaceans, insects, shelled animals, and zoophytes or animals that look like plants. Aristotle's system of classification remained the authoritative dogma right until the Modern Era. His classification was clearly not evolutionary, and different "species" had no specific genetic relationship to each other. Aristotle regarded species as fixed and unchanging.

The modern system for classification of all life on Earth

---

19 "Science" comes from the Latin *scientia*, meaning "knowledge." The term "scientist" was coined much later in 117 BP by William Whewell, the English philosopher and historian of science.

was introduced by the Swedish physician and naturalist, Carolus Linnaeus, in a major work he first published in 215 BP called *Systema Naturae*, or System of Nature. All organisms were henceforth classified by a unique two-name, or binomial designation. Evolutionary biology, later to be expounded by the brilliant Charles Darwin and others, had not yet appeared on the human knowledge radar when Linnaeus practiced. This latter grand new insight into biology profoundly changed the way humans viewed life on their planet, and greatly influenced the manner in which they classified lifeforms using Linnaeus' binomial system.

When humans develop a speech disorder called aphasia after a stroke to the brain, they may employ singing and rhythmicity to better communicate their thoughts to others. Expressive aphasia is a neurologic disorder caused by damage to certain neurons in the brain that physically connect thought to speech. When these neurons are damaged or die, thoughts can no longer be fluidly articulated as speech; individuals may know what they want to say but cannot quite say it. The words become blocked, withdrawn, transposed or substituted. Uttering those thoughts in song, musically with rhyme and rhythm, may facilitate the flow of speech and lead to the freer exchange of ideas and information with others. With this in mind, here is a bit of poetry about life and the Universe, written by the renowned poet Oom who is more than a billion years old and resides on the surface of a white dwarf star way out in the great Sunflower galaxy (NGC 5055):

Now once upon a time when nothing stirred
And all was formless silence, spake the Word:
"An act of self-awareness now I stage"

And lo! The Universe began to rage;
Across all space and time did Being spawn,
And from that presence everything was born
In countless guises, boundless in design,
All emanating from that splendid shrine!
And there was Reason distributed rife,
All bursting with the properties of Life,
And urging on to understand its trend,
Its beginning, its middle, and its end!

CHAPTER IV

EVOLUTION

arbon based life appeared on Earth almost as soon as the planet cooled enough not to cook it. It was indeed a *fait accompli*. The short journey from simple molecules to nucleo-bases and proteins, and from there to the first biological cells took less than 1 billion years after the planet formed. The rapid emergence of life on Earth surely endorses and validates the inference that the phenomenon of life itself must be ubiquitous in our Universe. Since the Universe, on average, is homog-enous and isotropic in every direction as far as anyone can tell, then, if life is plainly here on Earth for everyone to see, it must indeed be so elsewhere in the Universe as well. Wherever you may turn to look on my host planet, whether on land, sea, or air, matter-centered lifeforms abound. There are simply no sterile places on Earth, exactly the same as elsewhere in the Universe.

Not that very long ago, these humans who inhabit Earth today collectively believed—though with some notable excep-tions—that their planet was unique and sacrosanct, the only place in the entire Universe with life on it. Now as they study their monumental cosmic home all around them with their elite and increasingly sophisticated instruments and devices, they have quickly begun to notice for themselves how amazingly congruent and similar in structure and function the whole Universe is, anywhere they care to look, in whatever direction they please. Trillions upon trillions of planets like theirs are scattered across this vast expanse of space. If there is evidently life on their own planet, why then would these other worlds be collectively any different from their own? A torrential flood of celestial data pouring in from their space telescopes and listening devices in just the last two decades, has now thoroughly inundated their curious minds and made them seriously doubt their previous cosmic assumptions. This has already began to erode and transform that unreasonable assumption humans had always nurtured about themselves since they appeared on Earth—the conviction in their own cosmic exceptionalism.

This new realization for them underwrites a universal doctrine commonly called the Cosmological Principle. This key tenet categorically asserts that when viewed on a sufficiently large scale, the distribution of matter in the Universe is homogeneous and isotropic, since forces shaping this matter should have acted uniformly throughout the Universe since the moment of the Big Bang. Therefore, there can be no significant irregularity or discontinuity in the structure and evolution of matter that was initially laid down in the Big Bang. Because of this fact, when viewed on sufficiently large distance scales, there are no preferred directions or favored places in the Universe. Simply stated, the Cosmological Principle means that averaged over sufficient space, one part of the Universe looks exactly like any other part of the Universe. Astronomers on Earth are now quite confident that physics and chemistry are no different in other cosmic locations than on their own planet. They see the same types of stars and galaxies wherever they look in the skies, and detect spectral lines emitted from the same elements in stars billions of light years away as they do from nearby ones. The Universe does indeed have a uniform consistency throughout, in every direction there is. On average, therefore, the Universe is built and functions much the same everywhere. These observations by contemporary humans are entirely congruent with the ancient Greek idea that the same uniform order governs the whole Universe.

The Cosmological Principle in its orthodox form was intended to address only the physical and chemical properties of the Universe which are the same for all observers, since observers anywhere in the Universe, including on Earth, do not occupy an unusual or privileged position within the cosmos. Since carbon-centered biologic life on Earth is a clear manifestation of the very same matter that is homogeneously and isotropically distributed across the Universe, it would seem to follow as a corollary to the Cosmological Principle, that at least carbon based life, without needing to acknowledge the other forms of life mentioned in this narrative, should be rather common and widespread across the Universe at large. And that is certainly the case.

***

The first biologic cells that appeared promptly on the young Earth in less than a billion years of its formation—and their present descendants—are named Prokaryotes by humans, a word derived from the Greek root *karyon* for "nucleus" and thus, prokaryote, or "before nucleus." This term is applied to cells lacking a visible nucleus, and contrasts with the term Eukaryotes, from the Greek *eu* for "true" or "true nucleus," used for cells that display a visible nucleus in their cytoplasm.

Humans presently classify all cellular life on their planet into three distinct Domains. These three domains are named Archaea, Bacteria, and Eukarya. Archaea and bacteria, both with no visible nuclei, are prokaryotes. They were previously lumped into a single domain of prokaryotes, but were later separated into two domains because of their different evolutionary lineages. The third domain, eukarya, includes all the eukaryotic organisms on my host planet and is subdivided into four different Kingdoms. The four kingdoms of the domain eukarya are Protista[20], Fungi, Plantae (plants), and Animalia (animals).

Prokaryotes are unicellular organisms belonging to the two domains of archaea and bacteria—a few bacteria may live in colonial groups, though all archaea and bacteria are unicellular prokaryotes. Prokaryotes have a cell wall enclosing their cytoplasm, but no discrete nucleus or other specialized intracellular structures such as mitochondria, chloroplasts and other plastids, as is present in eukaryotes. In prokaryotic cells, all intracellular structures are unbound and free-floating in the cell's cytoplasm and not circumscribed by individual membranes. In contrast to prokaryotes, eukaryotes are much larger, usually about ten times or greater in size. All cells of multicellular organisms such as fungi, plants and animals, as well as both unicellular and multicellular protists, are eukaryotes.

Avowedly, given the very early appearance of prokaryotes

---

20 Protista or protists are an assorted and diverse kingdom of both unicellular and colonial eukaryotic organisms that do not quite fit into the other kingdoms of the domain eukarya. In the kingdom of protists are plant-like protists (algae), fungi-like protists (slime molds), and animal-like protists (protozoa).

on the young Earth, carbon based life as humans today would recognize it has been flourishing on their planet for more than 3.6 billion years, which is about four-fifths of the entire existence of Earth and the solar system up until now. Life is ancient. Much before the first prokaryotes even emerged on my host planet, prebiotic molecules had already begun to cohere together to achieve this goal. It is as if the module for life was already in place when Earth began.

The word Evolution is derived from the Latin root word for "unfolding." The term may be used generally to describe the inevitable process of unfolding and transformation that occurs over time to all objects and systems within the Universe, including the aggregate Universe itself taken as a single unit. Evolution is both universal and inevitable. It is a fixed principle, embedded in the fabric of the cosmos, applying equally to people, places, planets, and pulsars. Everything, even matter, is subject to evolution. Matter's evolutionary trail for instance, advances from the singularity at its inception to its primordial form in the primitive Universe, and from there through the matter/antimatter plasma of the germinating cosmos to nucleons, and then to atoms of hydrogen, helium, and later to lighter elements by stellar nucleosynthesis, and from there to heavier elements in dying stars, to arrive at the multitude of forms recognized as matter today. This illustrates the core principle of evolution faithfully at work, and it will continue to do so forever.

More specifically however, for discussion in this narrative, the term evolution is used primarily in the context of biologic evolution. To understand this concept as it applies to themselves and the natural world around them, humans must learn to think in wider units of time than they would normally do when considering events during their own brief lifetimes. Biologic evolution is change that occurs across succeeding generations of living organisms. It operates by modifying the genetic pool—the inherited attributes of an existing population—from one generation to the next. It produces changes in descendant generations compared to their ancestral ones.

It is essential to recognize at the outset that biologic evolution is not goal oriented or mission driven. It is never imposed or tactically directed toward a predetermined outcome by any known or unknown principality or power. Evolution is completely indifferent to the consequences, or the outcome, of its operation. Doctrinally, it espouses no particular partisan or philosophical orientation and is subjectively neutral. Evolution makes no moral or ethical judgments. In the idealistic sense, the resulting product of evolution is not any better, nor is it any worse, than what came before or may come after it. The product is just different and better adapted to its current circumstances. That is the only objective of evolution, a purely utilitarian one. Those set circumstances will change with time, and evolution must follow. It is an endless process.

Nothing in the cosmos is static. All systems change, including the very Universe itself, as my dear friends on Earth have speculated ever since the great Heraclitus of Ephesus suggested that possibility. Heraclitus, hailing from the ancient Greek city of Ephesus on the western border of what is now modern Turkey, lived on my host planet about 2,500 years ago. He actively sought a universal explanation for nature and for humankind's role in it, all without the need to invoke a ruling deity or supernatural being to elucidate his observations. He believed that things were not as people saw them and described a Universe of constant change where the interaction of "opposites" as he called the process, was a constant creative force acting to produce endless transformations. Heraclitus stoutly emphasized that the only permanent reality that existed was change itself. He was indeed prescient, but in an unexpected way. Humans now know from their spectral-shift measurements of light from other galaxies that the Universe itself is changing and undergoing accelerated expansion in all directions, and that galaxies across the dimensions of space are constantly shifting in orientation to each other.

Astronomers on Earth were quite surprised by a new cosmological discovery published only recently, in 62 AP. It was noted then that individual galaxies themselves were physically evolving and changing over time. This fact was rather astonishing because people had always previously believed that galaxies were eternal and unchanging. But by literally looking back into the Universe's past with modern telescopic technology, human astronomers discovered that individual galaxies systematically evolved and became more compact and organized over time.

In a very physically real way, everything humans see around them is in the past. Information requires a finite amount of time to reach an observer and cannot be transmitted faster than the speed of light—except of course in special circumstances such as quantum entanglement. An object from a foot away appears as it did an instant in the past, equal to the time taken by light to travel a distance of one foot. Although this time interval is insignificant for nearby observations, it assumes increasing magnitude with distance from the observer.

In this way, humans can directly peer into their past. The Sun, as seen by them this instant, is how it was about 8 minutes ago; and the star Proxima Centauri when observed from Earth is already 4.24 years in the past—that is how long light from these two sources will respectively take to reach an observer on Earth. So by looking at objects further and further away, the observer is seeing them as they were earlier and earlier in their past. Thus galaxies closer to the observer are older in age at the time of observation than those further away when observed. The surprising discovery in 62 AP revealed that older, and hence closer galaxies to Earth, like Andromeda, had contents more organized and appeared as compact and orderly disc-shaped structures; in these older galaxies, rotation was the primary motion. On the other hand, younger and therefore more distant galaxies, show greater disorganization with increased chaotic motion in all directions. Revealingly in this panorama, as the view is panned from more distant to nearer galaxies, there is a steady shift to greater organization toward present time, as the disorganized motions dissipate and rotation speeds increase and the galaxies settle into well-behaved discs. Thus galaxies actively evolve over time.

Evolution, possibly best defined as change over time, is a universal actor. Biologic evolution is simply another illustration of this cosmopolitan process, in this instance affecting lifeforms on Earth rather than matter, or galaxies, or some other object in our Universe. The aim of biologic evolution is to constantly modify and reposition organisms so they optimally function in whatever environment they happen to occupy. Said differently, as the environment changes, creatures change to adapt to it. Evolution increases diversity at every level of biologic organization, from the individual organism down to the molecular level of nucleic acids and proteins. Everything evolves.

The hard evidence for biologic evolution on Earth is everywhere one cares to look in the paleontological record of the planet. Paleontology is the study of lifeforms that existed in former geologic periods of Earth's history, as represented now by their fossils. Even more recently, humans have employed the new technologies of molecular biology and genomic science to further explore and extend these observations—the genome is the sum of an organism's hereditary information. Biologic evolution, or the evolution of life, is a law of nature here on Earth, just as it is throughout the cosmos. This inviolable principle has been acknowledged by sapient beings for billions of years, or just as soon as they acquired the ability to recognize it. Yet this powerful insight that brilliantly illuminates and explains the history of all life on Earth, is only a very recent milestone in human understanding.

It was barely 150 years ago when one of Earth's most gifted naturalists, Charles Darwin, formally identified this principle in modern times and postulated his theory of Natural Selection to explain the mechanism by which evolution operated in the biologic world of his own planet. Charles Robert Darwin (141 BP–68 BP) and Alfred Russel Wallace (127 BP–37 BP), both English naturalists, are now credited with independently discovering the theory of evolution through natural selection. The senior Darwin is accorded precedence for the discovery.

Darwin described the process of biologic evolution in a book he first published in 91 BP called, *On the Origin of Species by Means of Natural Selection, or the Preservation of Favored Races in the Struggle for Life*. Darwin used the word "Races" in the book's title to refer to variations that may appear in local populations of a species. For the sixth edition of this famous book, reissued in 78 BP, the short title became, *The Origin of Species*.

Darwin's great opus fundamentally changed humankind's view of itself and its provenance, at a magnitude equal to the Copernican revolution which had rejected Earth as the center of the Universe. Darwin's book, written by the great naturalist for the scientific reader of his time, appealed to an influential audience upon publication. As Darwin himself was a very distinguished and eminent scientist of that period, his findings were taken seriously by his peers and the intellectual community living both at home and abroad. The astonishing evidence he presented so meticulously ignited widespread scientific, philosophical, and religious debate on the subject of biologic evolution. Darwin's premise of evolutionary adaptation through natural selection later became the unifying concept of biology, or the life sciences. At the very end of his famous book, Darwin concluded his paradigm shattering exposition with the charming observation that, "[from] so simple a beginning endless forms most beautiful and most wonderful have been, and are being, evolved."

There still remains bewilderment among the uninitiated regarding biologic evolution. Two observations here may help to clarify the matter. Firstly, biologic evolution is not simply a hypothesis ever vulnerable to refutation. It has been extensively vetted and endorsed by credible human scientists to a high degree of certainty. Species evolution is recognized as a fundamental law of biology now. Secondly, Darwin's theory of natural selection was simply his way to explain the mechanism by which this universal law of evolution operated to modify living organisms on his own planet. Darwin called this process "descent with modification." The fact that change happens to organisms is an observation based on paleontological evidence preceding Darwin. Going way back further—more than 2,500 years into the past—the Greek philosopher Anaximander had suggested that humans were not created as such, but evolved from fish. Darwin merely tried to explain how this change occurred within Earth's biosphere, for which he postulated his theory of natural selection.

Fifty years before Darwin published his theory of evolution by natural selection, the French naturalist Jean-Baptiste Lamarck advanced his own formulation of biologic evolution in a book titled *Philosophie Zoologique* (Zoological Philosophy), issued in 141 BP. Therein Lamarck postulated that somatic characteristics acquired by an organism during its individual lifetime, such as muscular hypertrophy due to exercise for instance, could be passed on to offspring and thus guide evolution. This model of inheritance of acquired characteristics was soon shown to be incorrect and discarded in favor of Darwin's theory of natural selection.

According to Darwin, natural selection is the machinery of evolution, the vehicle that carries organisms along the biologic road to their futures. Who gets to populate that future? How is that journey accomplished? Those are the questions Darwin addressed with his theory. Natural selection elegantly explains the progression of life—how organized complexity can emerge from simple beginnings and without any deliberate guidance. It is the special key to understanding the history of life on my host planet.

Preceding Darwin, Thomas Malthus, a British cleric and political economist, in a book first published in 152 BP called, *An*

Essay on the Principle of Population, noted that a population's growth always tended to outpace its food supply. The population would continue to multiply without regard to available food resources, overshooting its numbers beyond sustainable levels, before eventually crashing to a population commensurate with the food supply. This observation, which came to be known as the Malthusian Principle, was familiar to both Darwin and Wallace.

In Darwin's autobiography, edited and published by his son Francis five years after Darwin died, the great naturalist notes, "In October 1838 [112 BP], that is, fifteen months after I had begun my systematic inquiry, I happened to read for amusement Malthus on Population, and being well prepared to appreciate the struggle for existence which everywhere goes on from long-continued observation of the habits of animals and plants, it at once struck me that under these circumstances favorable variations would tend to be preserved, and unfavorable ones to be destroyed. The results of this would be the formation of a new species."

Darwin observed that all organisms he knew tended to outpace their resources. This in turn led to competition among individual organisms for the available goodies, a condition he aptly termed "struggle for existence." He further recognized that within groups, some individuals were inherently more successful at obtaining those resources than others. These differences between individuals were established by random variation in their inherited endowments. Those more efficient at acquiring resources, or escaping predators, or possessing some other desirable characteristic, would clearly be more successful in attracting mates. They thereby secured increased reproductive access and thus had more offspring. In this way, more of their progeny passed into the future. If those offspring in turn inherited the same "successful" trait of their parent, and so on down the line, the descendants of the original individual would eventually come to represent the group as a whole and therefore populate its future. The ancestral being has thus been transformed over time into the contemporary one, now more adapted to its changed milieu. This adaptation is clearly not static; the milieu continues to change and the organism changes along with it. The adaptation is therefore active and dynamic, and continues forever. Evolution has no destination. It is an open-ended process with no set goal.

Variations among members of a species occur randomly and unpredictably. A giraffe endowed with a slightly longer neck than its contemporaries would be a little more successful at browsing for food along tops of trees. An antelope born with a faster stride may be rather more effective at escaping from predators. In Darwin's time, the reasons for these variations were not understood, though they did know then that variations are inherited. Humans now recognize that gene mutations, copying errors during chromosome replication, and the random mixing of genes between chromosome pairs called "crossing-over" during egg and sperm formation, are factors responsible for random variation among individuals of the same species.

Humans have now satisfactorily confirmed for themselves that traits are indeed transmitted from parent to offspring through the agency of genetic material made of nucleic acids. The laws governing the inheritance of these traits were first discovered by a celebrated Austrian monk named Gregor Mendel who published his famous results in 85 BP. Before Mendel, humans simply had no idea how biological traits were transmitted from generation to generation. In a common pre-Mendelian formulation they had proposed in the matter of their own reproduction, the mother simply served as an incubator for a homunculus[21] ejaculated into her womb by the father during sexual intercourse. Mendel demonstrated, by his laborious and systematic experiments with garden peas, that traits were passed to offspring in equal proportion by both parents, through discrete quanta he called "factors" and known today to people as genes. These genes were later shown to encode specific inheritance information, passed on to offspring by a molecule called deoxyribonucleic acid (DNA). The precise molecular structure of DNA was later discovered and published about sixty years ago by a pair of molecular biologists, the American James Watson and the Englishman Francis Crick.

Genes are aggregated into structures called chromosomes, located in the nucleus of eukaryotic cells. Prokaryotes, having no nucleus, host most of their genes on a single chromosome floating in their cytoplasm. Eukaryotic species possess a predetermined and specified number of chromosomes in every one of their constituent cells—except in mature reproductive cells which would naturally contain exactly half that number since they are intended to fuse with their corresponding partner. Consequently, every gene in a chromosome has its duplicate, one copy donated by each parent. These gene pairs are called alleles. Chromosome numbers are species specific. Humans usually possess a full complement of 46 chromosomes, pigeons 80, cabbages 18, and so on. The great apes all carry 48 chromosomes grouped in 24 pairs. Humans have only 46 chromosomes in 23 pairs. That difference arose because after splitting from a common ancestor, two separate ape-chromosomes combined to form chromosome-2 in humans. Half of each chromosomal

---

21 Homunculus refers here to a miniature, but fully formed human person, believed to be contained within the male gamete or spermatozoon.

complement is contributed by one parent and half by the other, except in parthenogenesis. Parthenogenesis, or virgin birth, is a form of asexual reproduction where the offspring derive all their chromosomes from a single reproductive parent.

Alleles, acting by themselves or in groups, interact with the environment and determine every imaginable characteristic of the individual, from hair color to altruism, from nose length to intelligence. Cast in technical terms, evolution is accomplished by change in allele frequencies in a population over successive generations. Alleles with positive qualities are favored in the population by natural selection and increased in frequency; those with negative qualities are winnowed and weeded out. Therefore genes, in their chemical form as deoxyribonucleic acid or DNA, constitute the *nature* of the organism. Genes interact with the environment, or *nurture*, to build the organism encountered in the real world. This singular nature-nurture interplay is the sole designer of all creatures great or small.

My dearly beloved friend and splendid colleague, the esteemed Professor Tao, celebrated author of the renowned tome, *A Classification of Cosmic Life*, once remarked ironically to Mac at a seminar on Galymon, that the sole purpose of life on Earth seemed to be only to copulate and produce still more life. The good professor, in a rare unguarded moment, used a common expletive word to describe the act of copulation itself. Genes, which represent the molecular embodiment of carbon based life here on Earth, are thus forever driven to replicate and compete against other genes to endlessly propagate themselves. Darwin's "struggle for existence" becomes ultimately a struggle among genes themselves to proliferate preferentially at the molecular level, the organism seemingly serving only as a vehicle for the replicating genes.

Fitness is an important concept in evolutionary theory. The term Darwinian fitness is often used in this context to make a clear distinction from regular physical fitness. Fitness is defined in evolutionary biology as the ability of an organism to survive and reproduce itself. It is measured by the average contribution of genes made by an average individual to the next generation's gene pool. If differences between alleles of a given gene affect Darwinian fitness, then the frequencies of the alleles will change across generations. By modifying the allele frequency of genes as they affect fitness, fitness itself will thereby be enhanced. Alleles with higher "fitness coefficients" become more common in the population. This evolutionary sorting of genes is done by natural selection. Darwinian fitness, therefore, describes how good a particular organism is at leaving offspring in the next generation, relative to how good others in that group are at doing the same thing. Thus, if brown chickens consistently leave more offspring than purple chickens because of some selective advantage provided by their brown coloration, then brown chickens would be said to have a higher fitness, and eventually, in the fullness of time, the whole flock would turn brown. Certainly, fitness is relative, and depends on the environment in which the organism lives: the fittest during an epoch of drought may not be the fittest once that drought epoch is over. Darwinian fitness is a useful concept because it lumps everything that matters to natural selection into one condominium. Finally, it must be noted here that the fittest individual is not necessarily the biggest, strongest, fastest, or brightest kid on the block; it is the individual that ultimately leaves the most genes to the next generation that is considered the fittest.

Kin selection is a form of natural selection that includes a role for biologic relatives in the genetic fitness of individuals. It marshals the principle of inclusive fitness, combining both direct fitness (individual survival and reproduction) and indirect fitness (survival and reproduction of genetic relatives). Kin selection occurs when an organism engages in self-sacrificial behavior that benefits the genetic fitness of biologic relatives possessing genes in common with the martyr. The principles of kin selection are instrumental in the evolution of altruism, cooperation, and sociality among humans and other social creatures

Ostensibly it may appear that a behavior like altruism which favors the group at the expense of the individual, would be extinguished by natural selection because such behavior diminishes individual fitness, and natural selection works through individuals and not through groups. Yet this is not the case because the beneficiaries of altruistic behavior are usually close biologic relatives who carry the same genes as the altruist does, including the genes that promoted the altruism in the first place, thus enhancing indirect fitness. Though genes may be transmitted by direct parenting, they are also transmitted by assisting the reproduction of close relatives who would carry those same genes. It is by this logic that worker honeybees launch suicide attacks by stinging hive intruders so that others in the hive, carrying genes in common with them, may be defended from those intruders. A similar reasoning explains the alarm calls of ground squirrels that warn other group members of a predator's approach, but thereby also attract the predator's attention onto themselves. Likewise for caring by uncles and aunts, and their commitment to siblings' offspring which is readily explained by the concept of kin selection. The principle of kin selection has similarly been proposed by evolutionary biologists on my host planet to account for the preservation of homosexuality among humans. Homosexuality, like other human traits, has a genetic component. Since most homosexual individuals do not reproduce offspring, it is reasonable to assume that the genes promoting homosexuality would therefore be extinguished in a population over time. Yet this behavior remains at about the same level in humans from generation to generation. The persistence of this trait is attributed to indirect fitness through kin selection. Because of gay and lesbian altruism and solicitude toward heterosexually reproducing relatives who may themselves carry familial genes for homosexuality, the homosexual trait is thereby maintained and preserved in the population.

Genes are information carriers. They contain the genetic blueprint for the organism they will assemble. Genes achieve this end by being the source code for the different molecules making up that organism. This code is carried in DNA by four compounds called nucleobases, part of the DNA molecule. These four nucleobases are adenine, guanine, cytosine, and thymine. A set of three nucleobases from among these four, arranged in a particular sequence called a codon, then codes for each of the 20 amino acids found in biologic proteins.

This protein synthesis is accomplished by two chemical processes called transcription and translation. A segment of DNA containing codons for a desired protein is first copied (transcription) from the nucleus of the cell onto a RNA molecule—RNA, or ribonucleic acid, is much like DNA in structure. This RNA, called messenger RNA, now carrying the codon sequence for the specified protein, migrates out of the nucleus to cellular structures called ribosomes where the required protein is assembled (translation) from the information carried in the messenger RNA molecule. In this remarkable way, beginning at conception, the entire organism is built and maintained by the encrypted information in chromosomal DNA.

Epigenetics, a relatively new science to humans, seeks to

understand how the identical DNA sequences found in every
cell of an organism, express themselves differently in the same
individual.

All organisms follow a specified blueprint transmitted from
generation to generation. For this reason, hummingbirds reproduce only hummingbirds, and humans nothing but humans.
This genetic blueprint for each type of organism consists of
an agglomeration of all those individual units called genes.
Together, these genes make up the "genotype" of the organism.
Genes, copied faithfully and passed on to the next generation,
ensure that the offspring will resemble the parent. Thus every
cell in a given organism has the same genotype.

Genes are expressed as physical characteristics of the
organism, called the "phenotype." Now, if all cells in an organism possessed the same genotype, why then do these cells
manifest different phenotypes? Why are some cells neurons,
while others assume the form and function of liver, kidney,
muscle or some other cell, even though they all contain the
same genotype? Only fairly recently did humans discover that
this variation in cellular form and function was accomplished
epigenetically.

The term epi-genetics means around-genetics. It refers to
the many mechanisms by which gene expression is modified
to produce different phenotypes. One way to achieve this objective is to eclipse segments of DNA in selected cells using
special proteins, thus hiding those segments of genomic DNA.
This prevents the masked segments from becoming activated
in such cells, modifying the form and function the cell then assumes. Another way for epigenetics to modify gene expression
and thus phenotype, is by selectively adding a methyl chemical
group of atoms at specific positions in the DNA molecule, a

process called methylation. The typical consequence of methylation in a genomic region is to modify the expression of nearby genes. Chromosomes also contain "regulatory genes" that are involved in controlling the expression of other genes in the genome. These regulatory genes carry codes for proteins that selectively either inhibit or facilitate gene expression. Thus different phenotypes can appear from the same genotype.

⁂

Darwinian natural selection operates on individuals and not on groups. Biologic evolution works its magic by selecting favorable genes to pass on to succeeding generations. Since only individual organisms possess genes and groups do not, natural selection must evidently operate on individuals and not collectively on groups of them.

The effects of natural selection may take from thousands to millions of years to be noticed, far longer than the short lifetimes available for humans to directly observe full speciation in populations of organisms. Even all of recorded human history, approximately 6,000 years so far, is much too brief for that. Therefore, as a guide to illustrate this process and demonstrate the principles of natural selection over much shorter time scales, the examples that follow may prove helpful to my valued readers. None of the cases described here have yet completely produced distinct species with full reproductive separation; that would of course take much longer to happen and exceed many human lifetimes. But the trend toward that goal, and the underlying principles of biologic evolution, will be quite clear in the examples provided below.

Staphylococcus aureus is a spherical, golden-yellow

bacterium that proliferates in bunches, and appears like clusters of grapes when viewed through a microscope. The predominantly native form of this bacterium is killed by the antibiotic penicillin produced by a fungus. Yet, within a colony of susceptible *Staphylococci* are found a few unusual individuals that, by random genetic mutation, happen to produce a substance called penicillinase. Penicillinase is an enzyme that destroys penicillin and prevents the antibiotic molecule from killing the penicillinase-producing *Staphylococci*. Normally, since no penicillin is present in their natural environment and therefore does not threaten any of them, the penicillinase-producing ones are at a clear disadvantage because they are using up much needed energy to manufacture the useless product penicillinase, rather than applying that energy to growth and reproduction. Hence their numbers remain swamped by their regular brethren. However, when penicillin is introduced into their environment, the regular ones are killed off by the antibiotic, while the rare penicillinase-producing *Staphylococci* survive and multiply with no competition from their now dead comrades. The mutant forms have successfully adapted to a changed environment and become heirs to the future in this new penicillin-tainted world. This example also illustrates how antibiotic-resistance develops among previously susceptible microorganisms, a major challenge for modern medicine.

Another example of natural selection tending toward rapid species formation can be observed in modern *Heliconius* butterflies. These very colorful butterflies, found in tropical and subtropical regions of the New World, rely on bright wing-color patterns to signal their distastefulness to potential predators. The gene for wing-color in *Heliconius* is always inherited together with the gene for mate-selection, a link that accounts for the instant preference of these butterflies for mates with similar wing-color. This relationship provides a mechanism by which rapid speciation could occur in these colorful creatures. Consider a population of *Heliconius* butterflies where a mutation leading to a beneficial new wing-color resulted in even less predation of its owners. Certainly, this mutation will spread rapidly in the population because these mutants prefer to mate with similar mutants that also possess the favorable wing color, given that the genes for wing-color and mate-selection are inherited together. Over enough time, two distinct groups of *Heliconius* butterflies with different wing-colors will emerge, that, though they could still interbreed with each other, prefer not to do so. Eventually, these two groups will accumulate still other genetic variations that ultimately brings about speciation and the development of a reproductive barrier between them. Individual butterflies of different wing-colors will no longer be able to mate and reproduce with each other, or if they still could, the offspring produced by these inter-color unions would be sterile. Their reproductive isolation would now be complete and two species would exist where once there was only one.

Yet another striking example of natural selection in rapid action is the well-publicized case of the famous English gypsy moth, *Lymantria dispar*. The ancestral gypsy moth of England was a light gray colored insect that dwelled inconspicuously on the trees of its neighborhood. Their lighter coloration allowed these moths to blend harmoniously with the pale bark of their host trees in that pristine environment, camouflaging the moths from birds and other hungry predators. An occasional darker colored genetic variant, found among the lighter colored gipsy moths, would be conspicuous and therefore easier prey for predators. This kept the population of the darker ones at a bare minimum. These conditions shifted dramatically during the Great Industrial Revolution. Starting around 190 BP in England, humans began burning vast quantities of coal to operate their newly invented machinery. As time went on, the smoke, soot and pollution generated from this massive fossil fuel consumption, stained and darkened the previously pale bark of the trees, turning the tables on the lighter colored gypsy moths who were now the ones more conspicuous and susceptible to predators. The formerly rare and struggling darker gypsy moths, being better camouflaged in this unexpected new world, proceeded to inherit it and thus replaced the lighter population of gypsy moths. Here again we see evolutionary change in action, working its magic through the celebrated mechanism of natural selection.

The Central European blackcap, *Sylvia atricapilla*, is a small grey warbler measuring about 5 inches long and weighing a bit less than an ounce. The adult male in this species has a neat black cap-mark on his head, hence the name blackcap. These songbirds live and breed during the summers in Germany, and up until about 10 AP, they all over-wintered in sunny Spain. Then, about 50 years ago, backyard bird feeding by humans became popular in Britain. Consequently, some of these birds then stayed in Britain during winter because of the abundant food supply, and did not migrate on to their usual winter feeding grounds in Spain. Around 10% of these blackcaps went on to make Britain their permanent winter feeding grounds. Both populations of blackcaps, whether over-wintering in Britain or in Spain, return to Germany to breed during summer in that country. The ones from Britain, being closer to Germany, return earlier than the ones from Spain. Breeding pairs form as soon as these birds arrive in Germany, so the ones from Britain tended to breed among themselves, forming a distinct breeding population. The later-returning Spanish blackcaps, likewise, formed a breeding population with their own cohorts. In the 50 years since this reproductive separation occurred, clear physical differences have appeared in the two different breeding populations. The ones over-wintering in Britain have evolved rounder wings and longer, narrower beaks as adaptations to their shorter flying distance and to a change in their diet from fruit in Spain, to suet and seeds in Britain. Given enough time, these changes will eventually lead to full speciation.

These vignettes of accelerated evolution in population sets are, of course, not examples of full speciation—that would require a much longer time span to process, way beyond the scope of humans to witness. The examples given here are just for illustrative purposes, since they are easily comprehended and visualized because of their much shorter time frames. In the main, biologic evolution occurs at a much more leisurely pace. The evolution of the modern horse *Equus* from the ancestral *Eohippus*, a small forest dwelling mammal about the size of a fox, took all of 52 million years. Humans have carefully and accurately documented this evolutionary saga by inspecting and dating the many fossil remains found of intermediate forms that emerged during this lengthy progression of *Eohippus* to *Equus*. As the habitat of the equine ancestor, *Eohippus*, changed sequentially from forests to steppes and then to grasslands, the ancestral animal changed along with it, assuming many incarnations along the way to eventually become the modern horse, *Equus*.

Still another way of appreciating the reality of biologic evolution is to look for vestigial traces from presumptive ancestors in their modern descendants. An example here is the coccyx in humans. The coccyx, also called the tailbone, is the terminal segment of the vertebral column in tailless primates such as the great apes. It consists of a few vertebral segments below the sacrum, with limited movement between the sacrum and the coccyx. In tailed primates, a long coccyx was the spine of a fully functional tail. In such primates, the tail had an important function in their arboreal habitat, serving as an appendage for clinging to branches. When those primates, ancestral to humans, became terrestrial apes and took to the ground, they no longer needed a tail and subsequently lost it through natural selection. The tail's remnant today is the coccyx in humans and other great apes, pointing to their tailed evolutionary ancestors. If not, why on earth would humans have a coccyx?

The cecum with the attached vermiform appendix, is a blind sac-like structure at the beginning of the large intestine, or colon. The contents of the small intestine enters the colon through a valve at its junction with the caecum. The cecum in humans is a vestigial structure, and is a remnant of the large ceca found in most mammalian herbivores. In these herbivores, the large cecum hosts a huge number of bacteria which aid in the enzymatic digestion of plant material such as cellulose which is broken down into simple sugars like glucose by the resident bacteria for absorption by the host herbivore. Since humans are not obligatory herbivores and do not rely on fibrous plant tissue for their nutritional needs, the cecum and appendix have atrophied to vestigial structures in them. Again, like the coccyx, the vestigial cecum and appendix demonstrate the evolutionary link of humans to other mammals.

The auricular or ear muscles in humans are three vestigial muscles surrounding the outer ear and serve no functional purpose for them. A rare individual may assiduously practice to wriggle their ears using these vestigial muscles. These same muscles, in their fully developed form, are used by other mammals, including most monkeys, to rotate their ears in the direction of sounds for better hearing purposes. Since humans can rapidly rotate their entire heads on the horizontal plane to focus on sounds, these auricular muscles became redundant for them and were transformed into vestigial structures by natural selection. Yet the persistence of these muscles in humans clearly indicates a solid evolutionary link.

There are many other vestigial structures in humans supporting the principle of biologic evolution. An interesting behavioral and physiological vestige is goose-bumps, technically known as *cutis anserinea*. These are tiny bumps at the base of body hairs on a person's skin that may involuntarily appear in response to cold temperatures or strong emotions. This phenomenon is a vestigial reflex in humans, recalling a once robust function in their formerly hirsute ancestors to erect their body hair—called piloerection—in order to entrap an insulating layer of air for warmth, or to appear larger and more threatening to their enemies.

In science, the word "theory" has a quite rigorous meaning and is never used casually. Those humans dismissing evolution as "just another theory" reveal a regrettable misunderstanding of the word "theory" and the nature of science itself. Today, the theory of biologic evolution by natural selection is well substantiated by objective evidence, as much as the theory of universal gravitation is supported by solid observations. The principle of evolution has rapidly emerged as the foundational basis of modern biology. It provides an overarching explanation for the astonishing diversity of life on Earth. It explains why marine mammals have hip bones without hind legs, and why humans have wisdom teeth though they do not routinely grind down plant tissue or chew the cud. It makes sense of the physical similarities between a tiger and a housecat. Evolution clarifies why carnivores have bigger brains and better vision than herbivores, and why animals that swim are streamlined. Evolution explains why all biologic life, from virions to humans, have the same nucleobases and identical DNA and RNA platforms.

⁂

Biologic evolution of carbon based life on Earth is an extremely slow and deliberate process. Recognizable change in a species proceeds at a glacial pace. The winnowing of traits by natural selection, and the transmission of favorable genetic variation to subsequent generations, may take numerous progenitors to accomplish. Encoding new information in DNA and dispersing that information through genetic mechanisms is an enormously time consuming and tedious process that may require millions of years to reach fruition. At the heart of this process is the fact that genes within ancestral organisms mutate and these mutations, if favorable, are then chosen by natural selection and incorporated into descendant organisms. Often these mutations may be deleterious and will be removed by natural selection in the same way that advantageous mutations are preserved and propagated. Sometimes mutations may silently linger in the genome for generations as genotype, not presenting in physical form or phenotype, until environmental changes promote their expression. Such environmental triggers for gene expression are difficult to foresee and often unpredictable.

Remarkably, in the case of humans, biologic evolution

itself created an extraordinary mechanism to expedite this slow plodding pace of organic change. This was accomplished by developing an innovative way to accelerate the process of information exchange between individuals. That mechanism is called Speech. Speech elegantly allows for the immediate transmission of new adaptive information through extra-genomic means.

Speech, to the extent and complexity seen today on Earth, is unique to humans. It is an extraordinary mechanism for communicating cognitive information instantly to fellow members of their own species. Speech promptly grafts thoughts from one brain onto another, thereby permitting survival methodologies and useful techniques for resource exploitation to be immediately disseminated across the targeted group. This exquisite device overrides the grinding process of organic evolution which is driven entirely by the leisurely pace of genetic change through natural selection. Instead, by employing the mechanism of speech, thoughts inside the donor's brain are transformed into sounds broadcast by the vocal cords of the speaker. These sound waves are picked up by a unique auditory apparatus in the recipient's ear and then reformulated back to the speaker's thought inside the receiver's brain.

The sound sequences of speech are produced in a highly stylized format known as Language. There are many different languages among people on my host planet, estimated today at about 6,500 spoken ones. Some languages are more popular and widespread than others, yet the structure and purpose of all languages are similar—they are the vehicles for the transmission of thought.

Through biologic evolution, humans have now genetically acquired the ability to execute speech shortly after birth.

To accomplish this end, two specialized areas in the cerebral cortex of the brain begin to organize and differentiate right from birth, just as soon as the human infant is exposed to the ambient speech of others around the new baby. Speech and language will not develop if the infant is born deaf or unable to hear sounds. Brain hemispheric dominance is correlated to these speech centers as well as to handedness in humans. In right-handed people, the left hemisphere is usually dominant for speech. In most people though, regardless of their handedness, the left hemisphere of the brain remains dominant for speech and language. In comparison, only 4% of right-handers, 15% of ambidextrous persons, and 27% of left-handers have their speech centers in the right hemisphere.

Both speech centers tend to be located in the dominant hemisphere of the brain. One of them, called Broca's Area and also known as the expressive or motor speech center, deals with the conversion of thought into its motorized equivalent known as speech that can be propagated as sound waves. The other, called Wernicke's Area and also known as the receptive or sensory speech center, handles the reception of speech produced by another individual, and its conversion back into thought again in the brain of the recipient.

This ability for speech using language as its vehicle appears spontaneously in human infants without conscious effort or any need for formal instruction—it is genetically programmed into the infant's brain. Writing is the manual equivalent of spoken language and uses the same brain centers for both its production and comprehension. The fingers do the writing in this case, just as the larynx does the sounds for speech. The eyes are receptors for written language, the ears serve for the spoken form.

Once humans had discovered a reliable method to fossilize and preserve speech as writing approximately 6,000 years ago, they were able to collate and store enormous troves of thoughts, ideas, and other invaluable information in the form of papyri, tablets, books, and documents which could be readily passed on to future generations. Books were saved as hard copy—or later stored in electronic format when that option became available many centuries later. This method for transmitting novel information is not only just light years faster than biologic evolution, but is also exceedingly more economical and efficient than the old-fashioned gene-centered way of sharing information. This new "information-genome" could be instantly adapted to external changes, unlike the old "biologic-genome" that took ages to transform.

This novel information-genome has been proposed as the agent for social and cultural evolution in humans. Sociocultural evolution can be modeled on the same basic principles of variation and natural selection that also underlie Darwinian biologic evolution. Whereas genes are the replicating units for genetic information, Memes are the proposed replicating units for sociocultural information.

The notion of memes—or the *meme* of memes—was launched broadly by the noted British evolutionary biologist and acclaimed author, Richard Dawkins, in his book *The Selfish Gene*, published in 26 AP. A meme is an idea, style, or behavior that spreads from person to person, and across cultures. It is an information pattern retained in one person's mind that can be copied to another person's mind. It includes anything that can be learned and remembered, such as applications, ideas, skills, beliefs and similar mental constructs. Memetics is the study of the replication, dissemination, and evolution of memes, just like genetics for genes. Like genes, memes mutate and change, and are therefore subject to variation. Memes are chosen by

Market Selection with survival of the fittest, quite reminiscent of natural selection of genes in biologic evolution. Menes therefore adapt and evolve like genes, except of course at expressly faster speeds. Memes can be readily spliced from one human brain to another, facilitating their rapid infiltration and spread in the meme-pool, similar in notion to the gene-pool. In this manner, the ability to manufacture computers or perform brain surgery, can be acquired by a human living in Timbuktu who has done no previous work or research on the subject, by simply acquiring and mastering the appropriate meme.

Access to this exponentially growing mountain of information would expand dramatically. The person credited with this development was the talented German entrepreneur, Johannes Gutenberg, who invented the printing press in 510 BP. This remarkable invention quickly led to the mechanized mass duplication of books, allowing for the widespread dissemination of their contents. Until then, each written work had to be laboriously re-copied by hand, one book at a time. It now became possible to print them in bulk. Printed material became increasingly accessible to ordinary individuals during the years after the printing press was invented.

Books and periodicals were gathered and stored in huge centralized libraries and made conveniently available to individual humans. This extraordinary Information Revolution, starting with the printing press, mutated in 32 AP from the circumscribed domain of physical libraries to the freely accessible electronic World Wide Web (www). Logging onto www from an appropriate terminal lets any human with the required user technology and connections, living anywhere on their planet, to electronically tap into a globally interconnected network called the Internet[22] and instantly access a cornucopia of information and applications inputted into the system by countless other people. The search for information on any subject known to humans is now done at lightning speed on the internet using computer programs called Web Search Engines. Web encyclopedias, such as the popular Wikipedia among others, hosting enormous knowledge bases and offering instant access to all humans on their planet, soon appeared on the World Wide Web. Reference to Wikipedia, for instance, is free and unrestricted. Mac has consulted such web pages during this mission to Earth and can acknowledge their value in sparing many a laborious doppelgänger visit instead. The explosive growth of information and communication technologies for this species in barely the past two decades has been truly mind-boggling. People now write on word processors and communicate with web browsers.

The famous Indian poet and dramatist, Rabindranath Tagore (89 BP–9 BP), imagined a world with free and unrestricted access to knowledge for anyone seeking it. Over vast stretches of this Universe, that indeed is the norm. Humans are now tantalizingly close to that goal. An excerpt from a poem Tagore wrote in his native Bengali which he then translated into English himself, evokes just such a world:

Where the mind is without fear and the head is held high
Where knowledge is free

---

22   In 32 AP the Internet Protocol Suite was standardized and the notion of a world-wide grid of fully interconnected, information-bearing networks called the Internet was introduced. The term "internet" to label this system is very fitting. It derives from its ancestor, the intranet, where information is shared only within local networks. The internet weaves these local networks into an interconnected whole, now called the World Wide Web.

Where the world has not been broken up into fragments
By narrow domestic walls
Where words come out from the depth of truth . . .

Humans, without a trace of irony, refer to their own species as *Homo sapiens.* That label, used in a comprehensive system for classifying organisms on their planet, means "Wise Person" in Latin.

People have so far documented less than two million multicellular species on Earth. An enumeration by them in 60 AP catalogued 1,740,330 in all. Of those, roughly 1,000,000 were insects, another 150,000 were non-insect arthropods, and 156,000 were non-arthropod invertebrates. There were just 62,305 known vertebrate species, of which only 5,490 were mammals. Plants made up an additional 321,200 species, and there were about 50,000 other species such as lichens and fungi. The counting continues to this day. When all the figuring is finally over and the results tallied, humans project there may be about nine million species on their books. This tally, of course, will not count most archaea, bacteria, and protists. Imagine including all the virions and prions as well. Mac beamed a representative sample from Earth to a lab on Galymon for an accurate estimate of lifeforms on my host planet. When counting every unique organism in that sample, including all protists, bacteria, archaea, virions, and prions, there were nearly 900 million distinct lifeforms in that sample. The relative density of life on Earth is high as far as terrestrial planets go.

Carolus Linnaeus (243 BP–172 BP) was a renowned Swedish taxonomist and physician. He was among the first humans to propose a classification system for Earth's plants and animals which is still in use 275 years later. Briefly, all creatures on Earth, except for virions and prions, are filtered through eight successive categories, to be uniquely identified at the end of the process by a novel genus-species binomial name. Those eight categories, from broadest to narrowest, are: Domain, Kingdom, Phylum, Class, Order, Family, Genus, and Species. At the time of this narrative, there were three Domains defined by humans (archaea, bacteria, and eukarya); five Kingdoms (prokaryota or monera, protista, fungi, plantae, and animalia); eighty-seven Phyla; and onward up that ladder. As would be expected, as this classificatory ladder is ascended, the branches of the Tree of Life rapidly proliferate and spread out. To make it more commodious, additional categories and subcategories have been inserted between the main ones.

So, *Homo sapiens* classifies itself in the following way:

Domain: Eukarya
Kingdom: Animalia
Phylum: Chordata
Class: Mammalia
Order: Primates
Family: Hominidae ("hominids")
[orangutans, gorillas, chimpanzees/bonobos, Australopithecus, and Homo]
    Subfamily: Homininae ("hominines")
    [chimpanzees/bonobos, Australopithecus, and Homo]
    Tribe: Hominini ("hominins")
    [Australopithecus, and Homo]
    Subtribe: Hominina ("hominans")
    [Homo only]

Genus: Homo
Species: Sapiens
   (Subspecies)?

The subtribe hominina ("hominans") currently lists just one genus, *Homo*. Many species belonging to this genus once coexisted and shared the Earth together. They are now all extinct except for *Homo sapiens*. The last hominan standing with *Homo sapiens* was *Homo floresiensis*, which gave up the ghost circa 12,000 BP.

In common English usage, the word "human" is reserved for the only existing species of the genus *Homo*, and exclusively refers to anatomically modern *Homo sapiens*. In anthropological usage however, the term has expanded with the discovery of fossil ancestors of modern humans, to include those extinct species as well. Mac will adopt the common usage here, and employ the term "human" only for *Homo sapiens*. In this narrative also, the term "hominan" will be used to refer to humans—the only living representative of that group—as well as to reference now extinct members of the genus *Homo*. The terms hominin, hominine, and hominid will also be used when appropriate, to include correspondingly larger subsets of the Hominidae family. Readers should kindly familiarize themselves with these designations.

This finally brings Mac to the non-issue of subspecies. In their passion to sort out and discriminate between various objects in their environment, humans tend to group these objects into smaller and smaller categories, assorted by presumably similar characteristics. By a related logic, even within a single identified species, some taxonomists have proposed including an additional category they call subspecies, to account for real or imagined variation within the original species, especially geographic or racial ones. The putative subspecies name is added after the binomial species designation, to make up a trinomial name. By established tradition, the first named subspecies gets the honor to duplicate the species name for its subspecies name as well. An example would be the several subspecies of the iconic and threatened tiger, *Panthera tigris*. This majestic animal is divvied up into six barely surviving geographic subspecies. Those tiger subspecies would be the original Indian (*Panthera tigris tigris*), Siberian (*P. tigris altaica*), South-Chinese (*P. tigris amoyensis*), Indo-Chinese (*P. tigris corbetti*), Malayan (*P. tigris jacksoni*), and Sumatran (*P. tigris sumatrae*). This apparent tiger racialism seems to vitiate against the conventional meaning of species.

Homo sapiens has also been subjected to similar racialism. The great taxonomist Linnaeus himself, who first named the species, had suggested four geographical subspecies for *Homo sapiens*, namely, *H. sapiens europaeus* (Europeans), *H. sapiens asiaticus* (Asians), *H. sapiens afer* (Africans), and *H. sapiens americanus* (Native Americans). Unlike for tigers, Linnaeus' classification of human subspecies did not catch on, and no one has since seriously suggested that contemporary geographic and racial variants of humans be designated as subspecies. However, some paleoanthropologists have proposed the inclusion of other candidates, now extinct, for this purpose. Among those offered for inclusion as subspecies of *Homo sapiens* are Idaltu Man (*H. sapiens idaltu*) and Neanderthal Man (*H. sapiens neanderthalensis*). Under this convention, modern humans would be called *Homo sapiens sapiens*. That is one *sapiens* too many for Mac.

At the present time, there are three clearly recognizable human racial variants on my host planet, although other putative races have been proposed. Humans themselves can effortlessly view any member of their species and instantly identify that other individual's specific racial group, something an intergalactic visitor like Mac would not have immediately noticed about them.

It is usually acknowledged that the three primary human racial types emerged in different geographic locations after the spread of *Homo sapiens* from Africa. As commonly specified now, the three primary human races are Africoid (the original African prototype arising in East Africa), Caucasoid (arising in the Caucasus of Eurasia between the Black and Caspian Seas), and Mongoloid (arising in the Altai of Central Asia between Mongolia and China). There has, of course, been significant racial mixing over large areas of my host planet. The three primary racial archetypes are clearly more obvious to humans themselves, than the subspecies of tigers would be to them. If a similar classificatory logic was used for humans as for tigers, then *Homo sapiens* would be further classified into three subspecies: *Homo sapiens sapiens* (Africoid), *Homo sapiens caucasii* (Caucasoid), and *Homo sapiens mongolensis* (Mongoloid). This, of course, is not done. Subspecies classification has little biological validity.

Mac will next address the formation of Earth and the subsequent genesis and evolution of living matter on my host planet, eventually leading to humans. Professor Tao back home on Galymon will find this compelling.

CHAPTER V:
ORIGIN

It is now necessary to establish a timeline for Earth, from its inception to the present moment. This will serve as a marquee to highlight relevant observations and bring them to the attention of my dear readers.

The planet Earth is all of 4.54 billion years old. Humans accurately calculated this figure from careful radiometric dating of meteorite material they found in their planetary neighborhood. These meteorites are credible indicators of the planet's age today, since they formed in the primordial solar system at the same time as Earth itself formed. The stated age for the planet matches the antiquity of the oldest known samples from both the Earth and the Moon. Earth, then, as a planet has been a permanent resident in its local neighborhood since the formation of the solar system, or a third of the entire life of our present Universe.

The developmental history of Earth is much like that of comparably sized rocky planets in other regions of the cosmos. Since identical natural laws operate throughout the Universe, their outcomes should then be equivalent. That is the famous Cosmological Principle encountered earlier in this narrative. The Cosmological Principle is, however, a new concept among humans. They had never before heard of such a proposition. For their entire history since sapience first emerged in them, these hominans had believed they were specially created as extraordinary beings and gifted with a most exclusive home in a cosmos that was made intentionally for them. They had conjured up a geocentric Universe, literally believing that every celestial body in space moved around their anointed Earth. Intuitively it appeared that way to them.

Then hardly 450 years ago, this geocentric view was fatally challenged by the brilliant Polish astronomer, Nicolaus Copernicus, who determined that the Earth, and the other known planets at that time, in fact revolved around the Sun. This heliocentric view later came to be known as the Copernican Principle, implying Earth did not have a central, specially favored position in the solar system. Stiff resistance to this paradigm-shattering Copernican model continued for centuries thereafter. The Cosmological Principle is just a natural extension of the Copernican Principle, reiterated in 263 BP by one of Earth's grandest scientists, the renowned English physicist and mathematician, Sir Isaac Newton.

Humans classify their planet's chronological history into four principal divisions called Eons. This separation into eons is made on the basis of major geologic and biologic transitions that characterized each individual eon in the planet's history. The four eons are designated, Hadean, Archean, Proterozoic, and Phanerozoic. The first three eons make up a supereon called the Precambrian, a lengthy interval of almost 4 billion years after the Earth was formed. Visible unicellular life appeared 3.94

billion years ago in the Precambrian, then proceeded to colonize the entire planet. The fourth eon, the Phanerozoic, still in place today, began with the Cambrian Period that started out with an enormous big bang, when within the span of a relatively brief geologic instant in time, multicellular organisms rapidly evolved from the unicellular lifeforms that had existed until then on my host planet. These brand new multicellular creatures proliferated profusely and energetically tethered themselves to Earth's biosphere.

Some details of these eons will follow.

The sequence of events observed for Earth is fairly commonplace for rocky planets situated at comparable distances from G-type, main sequence, yellow dwarf stars such as the Sun. G-type stars make up about 3.5% of all stars in the Universe. Yellow dwarfs range from 0.8 to 1.2 solar masses and have surface temperatures between 9,000°F and 10,500°F. Like all main sequence stars, they radiate energy by fusing hydrogen to helium in their cores. The Sun, for example, fuses approximately 600 million tons of hydrogen to helium every single second, converting about 4 million tons of matter into energy just in that one brief second. A G-type star in the main sequence will fuse hydrogen for about 10 billion years from birth, until the hydrogen in its core is all used up. At this point, the star expands to many times its former size to become a red giant star, just like the star Aldebaran is now. The red giant then sheds its outer layers of gas during its dying throes, forming an enormous ring—confusingly named a planetary nebula—while its core cools and contracts into a small, dense object called a white dwarf star about as small as Earth, yet so dense that just a cubic inch of matter from a white dwarf would weigh 18 tons on my host planet. When the Sun becomes a red giant in approximately another 5 billion years from now, it will swell to a circumference as large as the orbit of Earth is today, engulfing and vaporizing its three proximal planets—Mercury, Venus, and Earth—before shrinking into a white dwarf. So will end the eventful history of Planet Earth.

※

The Hadean Eon derives its name from Hades, a subterranean canton for the dead in Greek mythology. Hades was the underworld where expired humans were believed to migrate after completing their allotted lifespan aboveground. It was eponymously named after the mythical king who was said to preside there. The entrance to the underworld was thought to be guarded by a ferocious three-headed dog named Cerberus, sporting a mane of snakes, a serpent's tail, and the claws of a lion. Cerberus was assigned the endless task of preventing the dead from escaping Hades, or the living from entering it. The dog's three heads represented the past, the present, and the future. An ever-obliging person called Charon, the boatman to Hades, ferried all freshly deceased arrivals across the River Styx separating the world of the living from the world of the dead. A monetized silver coin called an obol was placed by ancient Greeks on the lips of their dead kin before burial, to pay Charon for his transportation services across the River Styx. Over time however, people embellished this image of Hades into a miserable place called *Jahannam* or Hell, where errant humans were consigned upon death to be punished by roasting in a sulfurous fire for the duration of eternity.

The Hadean Eon commenced 4.54 billion years ago at the birth of my host planet. It lasted 540 million years, ending in 4 billion BP. This hellish eon began the day the Earth was born. That was when the very first accretion of material from the protoplanetary disc of the solar nebula began to form the planets. The solar nebula theory, more generally called the nebula hypothesis, explains the formation and evolution of the Sun and its solar system. Under the Cosmological Principle, this theory applies to stellar systems throughout the Universe.

Stars are formed inside massive clouds of molecular hydrogen known as Giant Molecular Clouds. These giant clouds are gravitationally unstable and matter tends to aggregate into clumps inside them. When an appropriate stimulus—like a nearby supernova explosion—strikes such a cloud, the cloud gravitationally collapses around these clumps to form dense objects that cohere together by gravity and form protostars. Upon further accreting sufficient mass to reach a critical point, a protostar begins to fuse hydrogen atoms in its core and lights up. Thus is a star born.

Remnants of the collapsed molecular cloud that remain around the newly minted star continue to swirl around the baby star in the form of a disc called the protoplanetary disc. Material from this disc then agglomerates to form planets and other objects around the star. This planet forming process starts with matter as tiny as grains of dust. These dust grains grow by accretion to become objects as big as pebbles, then boulders, then as large as asteroids, and from there to planets. Planets are inevitable once objects the size of asteroids appear. This planet forming process usually takes about 100 million years to complete after a star is born.

The Hadean Eon ended when the new planet that humans would later call Earth, congealed enough to produce the earliest known rocks. During this eon, Earth cooled, solidified, and formed its continental and oceanic crusts. From an earth-ly biological standpoint, prevailing conditions on the young Earth were absolutely hellish during the Hadean—after which, of course, humans had named the eon. A baby planet had just debuted and was hotter than hell because of intense volcanism. Its surface was molten. There were frequent collisions with the numerous other bodies then present in the solar system. Much, if not all the water currently on my host planet came from these extraterrestrial sources.

This period of frequent bolide strikes on the young Earth is called the Late Heavy Bombardment. It began around 4.1 billion BP, close to the very end of the Hadean, and continued briskly until 3.8 billion BP into the early Archean, the next eon on tap. Modern human planetary scientists reckon that the new solar system's gas giant planets—Jupiter, Saturn, Uranus, and Neptune—underwent major orbital migrations during this period and gravitationally scattered objects located in the asteroid and Kuiper belts, into wild eccentric orbits that inter-sected with the inner rocky planets—Mercury, Venus, Earth, and Mars—thus producing the Late Heavy Bombardment of that period. These displaced objects rained down heavily on the young Earth. One such major impact, eventually creat-ing Earth's own Moon, vaporized large areas of the planet's surface, spewing rocky material skyward to instantly forge a rock-vapor atmosphere around the newly formed planet. The vaporized rock condensed in about 2,000 years, leaving behind two moons in its wake that joined together later into one. The Hadean atmosphere was heavy in carbon-dioxide, mixed with hydrogen, nitrogen, methane, ammonia, and water-vapor.

Liquid water started to condense on the newly formed Earth's Hadean surface almost as early as 4.4 billion BP, hardly

100 million years after the planet itself formed, even though temperatures were still above 400°F. This early condensation of water was made possible because the heavy atmospheric pressure existing at that time increased the boiling point of water, since evaporation of a liquid depends not only on temperature but also on pressure. As the molten Earth continued to cool and form a tentative crust, subduction or sinking of these fragile crustal sections, and the accumulating oceans of water being formed on the planet's surface, absorbed much of the carbon-dioxide and water-vapor from the early atmosphere, forestalling a disastrous runaway greenhouse effect and leading to a much cooler surface temperature.

The greenhouse effect, a heating process named after the heat retention observed in horticultural greenhouses used by humans, is a planetary temperature phenomenon encountered often in stellar systems. Visible light—that electromagnetic wavelength humans can see—issuing from a stellar source like the Sun and striking a planet, is absorbed by material on the planet's surface and converted to heat. The heat thus produced is released as radiant heat in infrared wavelengths invisible to humans. Now, because light, or "visible" solar radiation, has shorter wavelengths, it is poorly absorbed by atmospheric greenhouse gases such as carbon-dioxide and water-vapor, and is therefore quite readily transmitted inward through the planet's atmosphere. On the other hand, "invisible" infrared heat radiation has longer wavelengths and therefore less efficiently transmitted back out into space because longer wavelengths tend to be absorbed and retained more completely by atmospheric greenhouse gases. This equation thus delivers a net surplus of energy in the form of heat to the planet, thereby producing the greenhouse effect and raising the planet's ambient temperature. The greenhouse effect is then able to further multiply itself through a feedback loop: as the planet's temperature increases, more greenhouse gases such as water-vapor from evaporating oceans, are added to the atmosphere, exacerbating the original greenhouse effect. The cycle reinforces itself through this feedback loop, leading to what is called a "runaway" greenhouse effect.

Venus, a similarly sized planet to Earth in their solar system but approximately 25 million miles closer to their star, suffered just such an inglorious fate. Due to the initially higher temperatures on Venus arising from its greater proximity to the Sun, water could not condense soon enough on Venus to forestall a runaway greenhouse effect. Venus soon became, and still remains, a horrible world for earthlike lifeforms to exist. On Earth however, the temperature and pressure prevailing on the young planet allowed water to condense out of the atmosphere and fall as rain onto its surface, thus limiting the extent of water-vapor as a greenhouse gas. This cleansing rain also dissolved and brought down with it the other greenhouse gas, carbon-dioxide, thus further scrubbing the atmosphere of greenhouse gases. Living photosynthetic bacteria in the next eon, that appeared early on the young Earth, further extracted huge quantities of carbon-dioxide from the air, using the gas to produce food for themselves, and releasing oxygen into the atmosphere as a byproduct.

Solid rock on the surface of the planet began to form at the end of the Hadean. The re-liquefying sections of this primitive crust, together with metamorphism and the massive melting of sediments, progressively produced magmas composed of granites which were lighter and able to float on top of the underlying basalt. Bit by bit in this way, the continental crust was born and land cover appeared on my host planet. This new type of crust had a very important feature: its low density kept it riding on the surface of the molten magma beneath it.

The Hadean Eon ended at this time, setting the stage for carbon based life to emerge in the Archean Eon which was the next act in the play.

❧

The term Archean comes from the Greek root word *arkhaios* which means "ancient." This eon is especially remembered as the time when visibly living matter first appeared on my host planet. The inordinate speed and swiftness that accompanied the process whereby inanimate matter came alive on the primordial Earth is resounding testament to the extreme ubiquitousness and obligatory presence of life throughout the Universe. The Cosmological Principle would surely support this assertion.

The Archean Eon dominated Earth for approximately 1.5 billion years. It extended from about 4 billion BP after the Hadean ended, to 2.5 billion BP when the Proterozoic began. The initial Hadean atmosphere of hydrogen and helium from the protoplanetary disc, both being very light and buoyant gases, could not be retained by the gravity of the small and still hot Earth; they soon escaped into space. The Archean atmosphere replacing this air was produced by widespread volcanic out-gassing injecting carbon dioxide, carbon monoxide, water-vapor, sulfur dioxide, and nitrogen into the new atmosphere, which also contained large quantities of mostly non-volcanic gases like ammonia and methane. Methane droplets in the air shrouded the young Earth in a global haze. During much of this time, my host planet had a "reducing" atmosphere, toxic to most organisms living on Earth today. There was little or no free oxygen available in the air. Much of the oxygen was bound to carbon, or combined as oxides with other elements such as silicon, iron, magnesium, and aluminum. In those ancient days, the Archean sky glowed orange from methane, its oceans painted green with iron, and its bristling surface pockmarked red by fiery silicates.

The surface of the new planet had already begun to solidify toward the end of the Hadean, liquid water appearing within 100 million years of its birth. The fragile Hadean crust as earlier noted was unstable, constantly breaking down, re-melting, and re-forming. The Archean would now witness land areas increase in both size and stability. Proto-continent sized landmasses appeared on Earth around the middle of the Archean. The first lifeforms that humans today would unambiguously recognize as living matter arose very early during this crucial eon. Those single-celled creatures, the prokaryotes, were the first living organisms on Earth.

Very predictably, as Mac has observed in many other locations on our Universe, matter based life arose mechanically in the murky substrates of the Archean world of my host planet. It did not take long at all for this to happen, in fact almost immediately after the Hadean ended. The precursor forms of living matter emerged rapidly once the planet's surface had cooled enough to avoid the intense thermal energy of the primordial Earth from disrupting the orderly chemical processes necessary for carbon based planetary life to emerge. This cooling of the young Earth by radiating heat back into space, enough for visible life to emerge on my host planet, took about 600 million years following its birth.

Prebiotic molecules to make carbon based life are both very common and widely distributed across the Universe. Amino acids and nucleobases are found everywhere one looks for them in outer space. Thus, a meteorite that fell to Earth in 19 AP on the village of Murchison in Australia, was found to contain 52 different amino acids and a diverse suite of nucleobases. Prebiotic molecules have been detected by humans in the spectra of interstellar gas and in circumstellar shells around stars. Some humans have speculated that the precursors of life, or even fully formed microorganisms with all the bells and whistles in place, first arrived on Earth from outer space to seed life on the planet, a hypothesis called panspermia. A newer version of panspermia, known as strong panspermia, posits that these cosmic incursions have continued to occur repeatedly, introducing new genes to the biosphere which become incorporated into existing organisms, thus facilitating and directing evolution. It has additionally been proposed by some advocates of panspermia that certain viruses may infiltrate the planet this way from outer space from time to time and cause the recurrent epidemics of influenza that conspicuously afflict humans on Earth. Mechanisms for panspermia include the deflection of interstellar dust containing biologic precursors by stellar radiation pressure, or by extremophile microorganisms—lifeforms able to withstand or even thrive under extreme physical conditions—traveling through space within meteors, asteroids, or comets. A variant of this panspermia hypothesis, called directed panspermia, envisages the intentional spreading of life by advanced extraterrestrial civilizations to other regions of this Universe. In fact, humans are themselves already contemplating the planet Mars in their own solar system as a possible site to extend their own Earth centered biology, by terraforming the red planet to make it more Earth-like.

Whether prebiotic molecules were already present on the

primitive Earth, or arrived later from outside its territory riding on cosmic debris, is inconsequential to the subsequent emergence of visible life on my host planet. Life, as humans would know and recognize it, promptly appeared in the early Archean, almost immediately after the planet's temperature had dropped sufficiently to arrest the disruptive thermal agitation on pools of these prebiotic molecules. Inherently repeating chemical cycles were soon established on mineral surfaces of iron pyrite and similar material dispersed around the Archean landscape. These substances acted as catalysts[23] for the naturally repeating chemical cycles that thermodynamically arose in the prebiotic molecular soup. Some of these cycles spun off by-products that hung around to maintain and further enhance the original cycle. Other catalysts helped assemble more complex molecules from simpler compounds like inorganic phosphates, simple sugars, nucleobases, and amino acids that were present in the prebiotic milieu, forming elaborate biochemical building blocks from these simpler substances. Soon the cycle began acquiring a momentum of its own. A cocoon of insulating lipid molecules formed around these chemical reactions, enclosing them inside a protocell from any unrelated activity occurring outside. When this envelope eventually grew to completely encase the now complex amphitheater of biochemical cycles, and ultimately broke free of its mineral attachment, the first prokaryotic cell was born. That first cell membrane—a water-repellant or hydrophobic lipid bi-layer—is found in every

---

23 A catalyst is a substance that increases the rate of a chemical reaction by reducing the amount of activation energy required for that specific reaction to occur. The activation energy is the minimum amount of energy necessary to initiate the chemical reaction. Unlike other reagents, catalysts are not consumed by the reaction itself, and can re-enter the chemical process again and again to facilitate it.

descendant of that ancestral Archean cell today, meaning every living biologic cell on Earth.

These first prokaryotes in due course incorporated other mutually beneficial prokaryotes—called endosymbionts—into their cellular space, to form intracellular organelles such as mitochondria and chloroplasts, thus giving rise to eukaryotic cells. Dr. Christian de Duve, a Belgian physician and eminent cell biologist who gracefully exited his long and productive 95 years on Earth by euthanasia in 63 AP, is widely recognized for his pioneering work on organelles in cells. He published a remarkable book called *Vital Dust* in 45 AP. This cogently written volume elegantly traces the origin of life on his planet from nonliving matter to the myriads of living incarnations found today. Mac urges correspondents interested in this important subject to review Professor de Duve's notable book, a physical copy of which was teleported to Professor Tao back home on Galymon. Professor Tao possesses a rather unusual habit for most galymonians—he is a keen collector of iconic books and documents in their pristine and original format.

The great naturalist Charles Darwin, co-discoverer of the principle of natural selection, in a letter to a friend in 79 BP, imagined the following scenario of overt life emerging de novo from nonliving molecules in the remote past. Besides speculating on the phenomenon of abiogenesis itself, Darwin makes the important observation in the letter, that emergent life on the prebiotic Earth would have been all alone by itself and therefore safe from other creatures that might have eaten it before life could fully evolve. This isolation secured the necessary time and opportunity for incipient life to completely emerge, something that would not be possible today. Darwin thoughtfully observes in the letter to his friend that, "[if] we could conceive in some warm little pond, with all sorts of ammonia and phosphoric salts, light, heat, electricity, etc., present, that a protein compound was chemically formed ready to undergo still more complex changes, at the present day such matter would be instantly devoured or absorbed, which would not have been the case before living creatures were formed."

It is quite remarkable how quickly ordinary matter begins to manifest patterns of life even when only the barest conditions for life's emergence are met. No external "creator" with a parochial and self-serving design needs to be invoked for this to happen. That is because life is an inherent property of metta, mentioned earlier in this narrative. Matter based life, in its overt form, has been present on my host planet for almost 80% of its history. The only reason it did not appear even earlier in the context of Earth is because of the limitations imposed on carbon based creatures by extreme environmental conditions prevailing on the infant Earth before then. Certainly, there are other lifeforms in our Universe not constrained by these limitations.

<hr />

The Proterozoic Eon followed the Archean and spanned almost 2 billion years, extending from 2.5 billion BP to 542 million BP, before it ended in the Phanerozoic. The term Proterozoic comes from the Greek root words *proteros* meaning "earlier" and *zoon* meaning "life," thus "Earlier Life." Although prokaryotes—those first organisms that would certainly have been recognized as truly alive by humans living today—had already fully appeared in the Archean, this new eon now witnessed those ancestral creatures proliferate and expand their domain to all the empty niches on their planet, both on water and on land. And then, the Proterozoic Eon witnessed a truly novel and distinct form of life appear on Earth. These enhanced lifeforms, streaming along in novel directions, were the newfangled eukaryotes, those vastly more complex organisms that would eventually evolve to produce really advanced multicellular life such as hummingbirds and humans. For a grand finale, the last 93 million years of the Proterozoic, known today as the Ediacaran Period, was the magnificent stage for the evolution of numerous soft-bodied multicellular organisms to unfold.

Humans have now credibly established that recurring glaciations spreading ice-sheets around their planet first visited Earth during the Proterozoic. In fact, the very first global ice-age, called the Huronian glaciation, appeared shortly after the Proterozoic began. There were four other glaciations during that eon, which began and ended in two Snowball Earths. The Snowball Earth hypothesis is the theory that Earth's surface, including its oceans, was frozen solid and covered with ice, first during the initial Huronian glaciation, and then again around 650 million BP during the Late Sturtian or Early Marinoan glaciations, all in the Proterozoic Eon. These two Snowball Earths (I and II) tantalizingly overlap in timing with two major paradigm shifts in the existing organization of unicellular lifeforms on Earth, possibly even triggering them—firstly the evolution of eukaryotic cells from prokaryotes, and secondly the emergence of multicellular lifeforms from those eukaryotes.

Snowball Earths are initiated by global cooling due to the removal of greenhouse gases such as carbon-dioxide and methane from the atmosphere. They are thus the result of a reverse greenhouse effect. Greenhouse gases may be removed by weathering processes or through carbon fixation. Once the cooling trend sets in, it is propelled by positive feedback from the accumulating snow and ice reflecting still more heat into space and cooling the planet even further. This is known as Ice-Albedo feedback. The intense stressors imposed on existing lifeforms by a Snowball Earth may have been the engine driving major evolutionary changes during the Proterozoic. The stressors of Snowball Earth I could have been responsible for sparking the emergence of more complex eukaryotes from simple prokaryotes as a means of surviving this new emergency, just as Snowball Earth II may have prompted the emergence of multicellular eukaryotic lifeforms on Earth. Back home on Galymon we know that a good hard freeze on a planet-wide scale may provide the necessary stimulus for carbon based life to evolve into more complex forms. That is a corollary to one of Mensa's Laws.

The commencement of the Proterozoic Eon coincided with the transition from a geologic phase dominated by extensive recycling of the Earth's continental crust that was a hallmark of the previous Archean Eon, to a period characterized by the preservation of this crust as stable continental platforms. In fact, geologic eons themselves are designated by humans based on these milestones.

The two billion years of the Proterozoic were characterized by the rapid buildup of free oxygen molecules in the atmosphere by a process known as photosynthesis performed by early prokaryotic blue-green cyanobacteria. Eukaryotic cells soon evolved in the Early Proterozoic, followed by the appearance of multicellular eukaryotic organisms such as sponges and colonial-algae. The supremely eventful and momentous transition from unicellular prokaryotes to multicellular eukaryotes was a

watershed event in the evolution of life on Earth. This historic
change was precipitated by removal of greenhouse gases and
the corresponding accumulation of atmospheric oxygen due to
photosynthesis. The ensuing oxygen crisis, global cooling, and
Snowball Earths were triggers for this remarkable evolutionary
outcome.

Photosynthesis transformed the earlier reducing atmosphere of the planet into an oxidizing one, and dramatically
changed the composition of lifeforms on Earth by fostering
biodiversity. Photosynthesis, of course, also resulted in the
near-extinction of oxygen-intolerant organisms on the planet at
that time, thereby precipitating an environmental crisis requiring rapid evolutionary adaptation by existing lifeforms. Before
photosynthesis, all life on Earth was anaerobic or oxygen-intolerant. The great Proterozoic oxygen crisis, brought on by
photosynthesis, caused a pandemic of mass extinction among
unicellular organisms then inhabiting the planet. Some sought
refuge in oxygen excluded spaces such as deep underground
or in underwater sediments. Those organisms continued little
changed right into the present. Others adapted to this cataclysm
through evolution, proliferating into the plethora of organisms,
including *Homo sapiens*, inhabiting my host planet today.

Photosynthesis is a crucial biochemical process now widely distributed on Earth and found in all green plants, as well
as certain bacteria and protists. Organisms endowed with this
remarkable ability can capture and covert energy radiating
from their star into chemical energy that they store in their tissues for later use. As noted before, such organisms are called
autotrophic or self-nourishing. Photosynthesis is facilitated
by a remarkable molecule called Chlorophyll that can absorb
energy from sunlight. Photosynthesis transforms Sun power

into energy-rich carbohydrates by using atmospheric carbon-dioxide and ground water as substrates. Carbon is captured from atmospheric carbon-dioxide and fixated as carbohydrates for subsequent feeding purposes by the photosynthesizer. Photosynthesis therefore actively tends to remove this potent greenhouse gas from the atmosphere. Elemental oxygen is a byproduct of this process and is released back into the atmosphere. The solar energy that is transduced into chemical energy by photosynthesis is stored and accessed as needed for performance of work and biological activity by the organisms that produce it. Those that cannot perform photosynthesis obtain their energy by consuming those that can, and are therefore called heterotrophic instead of autotrophic.

The use of energy by organisms to fuel biologic activity is a defining characteristic of life, including carbon based creatures on my host planet. The bulk of this energy for Earth centered life is obtained from photons in solar radiation through photosynthesis. However, since life is so ubiquitous on Earth as it is elsewhere in the Universe, and proliferates so readily in any available niche on my host planet, including the bottom of its deepest oceans where the Sun never shines, there had to be other ways, besides photosynthesis, for life to mine the energy it requires to exist.

Where no photons are available for photosynthesis, bacteria and other putative lifeforms have evolved around hot hydrothermal vents in the inky darkness of ocean floors, to harvest energy from inorganic molecules like hydrogen sulfide and methane that are blasted from Earth's interior through those selfsame vents. The mechanism of energy harvesting by these organisms, analogous to photosynthesis, is called Chemosynthesis. The vents they colonize on dark ocean floors are holes in the Earth's thin crust belching superheated volcanic gas from the planet's flatulent bowels. The chemosynthetic bacteria gathered around these hydrothermal vents support a vast menagerie of diverse species in their midst—such as giant tubeworms, clams, limpets, and shrimp. Not surprisingly, humans were unaware of this active biosphere until quite recently. That discovery had to wait till 27 AP when reliable deep-water submersibles became available to them.

The Phanerozoic Eon began in 542 million BP and continues to the present day. The word Phanerozoic is derived from the Greek root words *phaneros* meaning "visible" and *zoon* meaning "life," thus "Visible Life." Although the Phanerozoic makes up only 12% of Earth's timeline so far, it is the eon where life in the form that humans are mostly familiar with today, evolved and blanketed their planet. Before that time, only unicellular organisms existed—though briefly at the very end of the Proterozoic itself, a few enigmatic multicellular creatures called Ediacaran biota appeared and then promptly went incognito in the fossil record.

The Phanerozoic started with a supernova-like eruption of multicellular life during the so-called Cambrian Explosion when a veritable panoply of diverse soft-bodied and hard-shelled animals first appeared, and most major phyla that would subsequently be known to humans emerged in a relatively short period of geologic time. The very first vertebrates—the jawless fishes—appeared at this time. Until close to the end of the Proterozoic, organisms on my host planet had remained quite simple and uncomplicated, composed mostly of single cells, but occasionally organized into loosely cooperating colonies. For more than three billion years, except for the emergence of nucleated unicellular eukaryotes in the Proterozoic, and a few multicellular marine plants such as kelp, they had quietly remained this way, showing no significant entrepreneurship for change. Then, within a fleeting instant of geologic time, hardly accounting for 75 million years[24] in all, the rate of evolution and diversity of these organisms accelerated by a full order of magnitude, and the medley of life on Earth took off like a rocket and began to resemble the picture seen today. Humans remain quite puzzled about the causes for the Cambrian Explosion to this very day, and Mac did not send a doppelgänger back to that time to investigate the event.

Though the causes for the Cambrian Explosion still remain murky and unidentified by humans, it should be pointed out here that evolution is not necessarily a gradual or incremental process as may be imagined. Evolution often proceeds in spurts, interspersed with lengthy periods of dormancy. Organisms strive to preserve their identity and internal stability against accumulating external changes. When this balance is finally overwhelmed by the gathering severity and magnitude of those external factors, then either major adaptive evolutionary transformations occur rapidly, or those organisms perish. Humans call this model of evolution the Punctuated Equilibrium model. It is similar to a model for earthquakes in seismology where stressor forces accumulate steadily along underground fault lines. These forces are buffered within the system, thus producing no apparent movement on the

---

24 Biologic evolution can sometimes proceed at breakneck speed given appropriate environmental conditions. For example, it took humans less than 66 million years to emerge on their planet after the dinosaurs and much of Earth's lifeforms were annihilated in the catastrophic mass extinction at the end of the Cretaceous Period.

surface. This buffering could not simply go on forever. Eventually, the whole system is overwhelmed by the accumulated stressors and the buffered equilibrium abruptly collapses. The ground then quakes violently, swiftly releasing all that bottled up energy—a possible model for the Cambrian explosion.

Long before the Phanerozoic, Earth had witnessed large landmasses or continents continually form on its surface, drift around, aggregate, break up, and reassemble in cycles. This geologic model of Continental Drift was first proposed back in 354 BP by the Belgian cartographer, Abraham Ortelius. Continents sometimes join up as a supercontinent during these cycles. More than half a dozen such supercontinents have formed and then broken apart in the history of my host planet. The first one, called Vaalbara, appeared around 3.6 billion BP during the Archean. Now, in the Phanerozoic, continents continued drifting, and then collected once more about 300 million years ago into a single landmass called Pangaea. Pangaea was surrounded by that unbroken global ocean, Panthalassa. The massive Pangaean supercontinent again split up, starting about 200 million years ago, and slowly drifted apart to become the existing continental landforms of today. The process of continental drift, revised and renamed Plate Tectonics in 17 AP, is responsible for this phenomenon.

The word "tectonics" is derived from the Greek word *tektonikos*, meaning "carpentry" or "construction." Plate tectonics is a geological theory that describes the large scale movements of the Earth's outer crust, by building on the earlier concept of continental drift. My modern human friends, treading their Earth today, discovered that the ground on which they walk is really composed of extremely thin and irregular plates "floating" on the surface of a hot, fluid, plastic material. This thin, rigid outer shell is called the lithosphere and is broken up into irregular plates. The oceanic plates are much thinner than the continental ones. These plates, called tectonic plates, vary in thickness from less than 5 miles at some mid-ocean sites, to around 150 miles at some continental locations. Relative to the planet's diameter of about 8000 miles, these surface tectonic plates are eggshell thin. Unknown to most humans, the Earth's seemingly solid surface is a paper-thin structure fused onto a fluid base. The ground on which they had always walked, and long believed was solid to the core, was in fact an illusion. Presently there are seven major plates and several minor ones adrift on Earth's molten interior, locked in place like a jigsaw puzzle along their borders. These plates actively interact at these lines of contact, pushing together, pulling apart, or gliding past each other. Therefore, along these seams, the Earth's surface often quakes as the plates move alongside each other. Molten material from beneath the plates can gush out of vents in the seam and erupt as volcanoes on the surface.

The major African Plate has been in the process of ripping apart into two new plates since about 30 million BP. These new plates, the incipient Nubian and Somali Plates, are moving away from each other, thus pulling Africa apart along a line from the Arabian Peninsula southwards, and opening up a gash on the planet's surface about 4000 miles long, running from Israel in the north to Mozambique in the south. The dehiscing lithosphere along this line has been the source of massive volcanism over the past several million years, producing volcanic behemoths like Mount Kenya, Mount Kilimanjaro, and the Ngorongoro Crater. This widening valley—or chasm—eventually to be deluged by the ocean, is in fact the Great Rift Valley where humans first emerged on their planet 200,000 years ago.

The exact location of that emergence was the Great Rift's East African range. It is indeed ironic to note that within the next few moments of geologic time, the northern gate of the Great Rift will finally crack open, allowing the Indian Ocean to rush into the existing trough and create the new African Sea, burying the ancestral home of humanity in a watery grave.

❧⳾⳾❧

Humans divide Eons into Eras, Eras into Periods, Periods into Epochs, and Epochs into Ages. The last three epochs of Earth's history, ending in the present one, are the Pliocene, Pleistocene, and Holocene Epochs—in that order. These epochs are particularly relevant to the history of *Homo sapiens* because the gathering of evolutionary forces that propelled the appearance of this species on their planet, all came together during this time.

The Pliocene Epoch started 5.3 million years ago and ended circa 2.6 million BP. It lasted approximately 2.7 million years. During this epoch, the Earth's climate became cooler, drier and more seasonal, reminiscent of climatic conditions existing today on my host planet. The first hominin, *Australopithecus*, emerged from ancestral apes in Africa and thrived in the Pliocene. These unusual creatures were using primitive stone tools by the end of that epoch.

The Pleistocene Epoch followed the Pliocene and lasted 2.57 million years, ending around 11,700 BP. Humankind's ancestral genus *Australopithecus* disappeared during the early Pleistocene after delivering that amazingly innovative successor genus *Homo*, dubbed hominans. This particular genus of apes is characterized by a relatively large brain, limb structure adapted to a habitually erect posture with bipedal gait, well developed and fully opposable thumb, hands capable of powerful yet precision grips, and the ability to make standardized tools using one tool to make another. Many hominans emerged during the Pleistocene, some of them living cheek by jowl during this very eventful period of their evolutionary history. Among the hominans that lived on Earth in the Pleistocene, based on reconstruction by contemporary humans and listed according to their chronology were *Homo habilis*, *H. rudolfensis*, *H. erectus* also called *H. ergaster*, *H. antecessor*, *H. heidelbergensis*, *H. floresiensis, H. neanderthalensis,* and *H. sapiens.* There were other hominans as well, not mentioned in this list. Thus the Pleistocene Epoch may be quite accurately described as The Great Hominan Age. It was the time when these extraordinary great apes of Africa would establish their masthead on that continent and then proceed to spread around their planet. It was a period of unprecedented ferment and challenge for them.

The first clearly recognizable hominan to make an appearance during the Pleistocene was *Homo habilis*. Descending from *Australopithecus*, this first hominan showed up around 2.4 million BP during the early Pleistocene and hung on till about 1.4 million BP, surviving as a species for approximately one million years. *H. habilis* was the ancestor of *Homo ergaster* that lived in Africa from about 1.8 million BP to about 1.3 million BP. *H. ergaster* was the stay-at-home African cohort of a similar species, *Homo erectus*. While *H. ergaster* remained in Africa, *H. erectus* become the first hominan to emigrate out of Africa into Europe and Asia. Back in the African Rift Valley, *H. ergaster* would evolve into *Homo heidelbergensis*, presumably by way of an African branch of *Homo antecessor*[25]. A cohort of *H. heidelbergensis* would be another hominan to emigrate out of Africa into Asia and Europe, later evolving into *Homo neanderthalensis* there. The cohort of *H. heidelbergensis* that stayed on in Africa evolved into *Homo sapiens*, becoming anatomically modern humans around 200,000 BP while still on the African continent. *H. sapiens* would later emigrate out of Africa to dominate Earth right into the present time.

Based on what most human paleontologists now speculate from the available fossil record, a possible direct lineage for *Homo sapiens* from ancestral hominans could be conjectured up as follows. Before climbing onto that uncertain limb however, it should be strongly emphasized here that what follows is only a simplistic view of the likely evolutionary sequence. Human evolution is far more complex and enmeshed than would appear from this seemingly linear progression. Hominans may have hybridized with other parallel species resulting in an admixture of genomes and traits. With that precautionary observation, the following genesis for humans is possible: After separating from the genus *Australopithecus*, the first direct human ancestor to appear was *Homo habilis* (2.4 million BP to 1.4 million BP). *H. habilis* then begat *Homo ergaster* (1.8 million BP to 1.3 million BP), who begat *Homo antecessor* (1.2 million BP to 800,000 BP), who begat *Homo heidelbergensis* (800,000 BP to 200,000 BP), who then begat *Homo sapiens* (200,000 BP to now). All these dates are only conjectural and approximate. They represent one possible genealogy for *Homo*

---

25 At the time of this narrative, fossils of *Homo antecessor* had only been discovered in Europe. None had yet been located in Africa. Since *H. antecessor* would bridge the unaccounted time interval between *H. ergaster* and *H. heidelbergensis*, the presumption is made here that *H. antecessor* also originated in Africa and then emigrated to Europe, much like the other hominans did.

sapiens that these clever humans had formulated around the time Mac was on their planet. Like everything else, as knowledge too evolves, this genealogical sequence may be modified or changed.

The provenance of these various hominan actors has been questioned on occasion. Some paleontologists have proposed that the numerous pre-human hominans are merely phenotypes of a single species, *Homo erectus*, which left East Africa just short of two million years ago in the Early Pleistocene to disperse around the Old World. Five fossil skulls found at an archeological site called Dmanisi in the Republic of Georgia in the Caucasus, may offer some support to this view. All these Dmanisi fossils, believed to be about 1.8 million years old, have been classified as *Homo erectus* by their discoverers. They were found stashed individually in local caves after their owners were killed by predatory carnivores. Significantly, these skulls, particularly the last one discovered in 55 AP, though clearly suggesting a *H. erectus* origin to the examiners, also displayed a mosaic of features that are usually assigned to other specifically designated hominan species such as *H. habilis*, *H. rudolfensis*, *H. ergaster*, and *H. heidelbergensis*. However, since all these Dmanisi hominans had lived during a narrow time window of only about 1,000 years in the same Dmanisi district, it was broadly assumed that they all belonged to the same hominan species, *Homo erectus*. Comparative analysis revealed that variation among the different Dmanisi skulls was no greater than the variation commonly found among contemporary human or chimpanzee skulls. Their finders argued that if these Dmanisi fossils had been found at separate locations in Africa instead, they would likely have been classified as belonging to separate hominan species.

The obvious implications for human evolution from these Dmanisi fossils are indeed quite remarkable. If these assumptions prove to be accurate, they would certainly upend the existing taxonomy for the genus *Homo*. Many of the previously discovered and variously designated hominan species, except for *Homo sapiens*, would then have to be rolled into a single predecessor species, presumably *Homo erectus*. Thus, based on this speculative Dmanisi version, there would be only one hominan emigration out of Africa, that by *Homo erectus* circa 1.8 million BP. This single ancestor species would then presumably have developed locally into the racial and regional variants of *Homo sapiens* encountered today. This is in line with the old multiregional hypothesis of human evolution, in contrast to the currently endorsed out-of-Africa, or replacement theory of human origins.

Human culture, as people now living on their planet would recognize it, arose among *Homo sapiens* late in the Pleistocene Epoch. Art and music entered the human imagination, along with singing, dancing, cave painting, engraving, etching, and stone carving being among their recently acquired abilities. Highly motivated individuals, along with their kith and kin, would emigrate from their point of origin in Africa and eventually trek to every corner of their planet seeking opportunity and adventure. They sought a better and more secure future for themselves and their children provisioned with improved resources and greater possibilities. Humans continue emigrating to the present day in ever increasing numbers, as more effective ways of travel became available to them. Compulsive emigration is a unique and genetically driven behavioral feature of this cosmopolitan genus *Homo*, acquired along an evolutionary path from its territorially bound *Australopithecus* ancestor.

This deeply rooted emigration trait keeps *Homo sapiens* bound together as one contiguous species and is a major factor in their current planetary dominance. Galymonians recognize this feature from our own history.

The current epoch on Earth is called the Holocene. It began circa 11,700 BP, ending the Pleistocene, and continues to the present day. Human civilization grew exponentially in the later Holocene, and my intrepid friends even traveled to their Moon some 40 years ago. Humans physically landed on their Moon on July 20, 19 AP, and the American astronaut Neil Armstrong first set foot on the lunar surface the next day at 2:56 Universal Time.

The rate of biologic evolution on my host planet is exponential. Exponential change, also called geometric progression, occurs when the growth rate of a value is proportional to that value's current magnitude. The growth rate therefore compounds over time and grows at an ever accelerating pace, rather than growing at a steady and constant rate as in the case of what is called arithmetic progression. Exponential growth thus inflates rapidly, approaching an infinite rate of change if the passage of time itself remains constant. On the other hand, if time is accelerating exponentially, then more events will occur in each succeeding interval of time, even if the change itself proceeds at a steady pace. Of course, it is moot to the outcome if evolution is accelerating exponentially, or if time is accelerating exponentially instead. It is difficult for humans, enmeshed and bound within that time dimension, to tell the difference. A clue to this conundrum is that spacetime itself has been dilating ever since our Universe came into being, so events may indeed be transpiring faster and faster.

Visible life in the form of prokaryotes appeared shortly after the planet formed. They evolved, first slowly, through eukaryotes and multicellularity, and with gathering speed and momentum, into fish, amphibians, reptiles, birds, mammals, primates, hominids, and humans. After prokaryotes appeared on the early Earth, it took another 1,600 million years for eukaryotes to emerge from those prokaryotes, and another 1,000 million years for those eukaryotes to turn into multicellular organisms. Then 500 million years after that, fish emerged, 300 million years more and there were mammals, 140 million years later there were primates, and it took just 60 million years beyond that time for humans to make their appearance on my host planet. This exponential evolution of life continues onward ever faster, and will produce even more extraordinary creatures to come. That observation is another corollary to one of Mensa's Laws.

Modern chimpanzees are intimate kin to humans. More than 98% of their genome is identical. The progenitors of humans and those of chimpanzees split from a common simian ancestor about six million years ago in Africa, before the dawn of the Pliocene. Following this split, those fated to be the ancestors of humans entered the Pliocene as bipedal (upright and two-footed), sexually dimorphic (males larger than females), relatively bigger-brained (at least one-third the size of a contemporary human brain), and tribally cooperative apes called australopithecines. Their name is derived from the Latin *australis* for "southern" and the Greek *pithekos* for "ape," or "southern ape," so named because their fossils were first discovered by humans in southern Africa. The genus evolved in eastern Africa some 4 million years ago, before they spread throughout that continent. The australopithecines branched into two genera, *Australopithecus* and *Paranthropus*. The ancestral *Australopithecus* that led to *Homo* was sleeker and more gracile than its cousin, the bulkier *Paranthropus* that had diverged from *Australopithecus* by the beginning of the Pleistocene. *Paranthropus*, the robust australopithecine, followed a dead-end evolutionary path and was extinct before that epoch was over.

Around the same time that these australopithecines were actively evolving, their habitat in Africa was experiencing rapid transformation. The lush forests that once thrived extensively in that area, began receding apace as the climate changed and became drier. These accelerated climate changes are common in Earth's history and often result in major habitat modification for existing lifeforms. The forests were replaced by grasslands and savanna, thereby encouraging herbivores to proliferate. These herbivores in turn provided food for the large carnivorous canids and felids that preyed on them. The australopithecines then living in the forest, feeding primarily on fruit, were cramped for space as their forests shrank. One branch of these australopithecines, represented by *Paranthropus*, followed an evolutionary path that adapted them to eating more variegated vegetable material such as the grasses and shrubs now replacing their forests. To chew this new diet, they developed huge, broad, cheek-teeth covered with thick enamel, powered by large chewing muscles attached to their jaws, endowing them with wide faces. These adaptations gave the robust *Paranthropus* the ability to grind down tough fibrous foods, the "robust" in this case referring to tooth and face size, not to body size. These robust australopithecines became extinct during the Pleistocene, many of them prey to the large carnivores who hunted them down while they were grazing on grass and eating leaves. A second branch of australopithecines, the gracile *Australopithecus*, became hunters themselves and started adding meat to their diet. That was when these ancestors of humans switched from a vegetarian menu, to a meat containing one. These meat eating hominids survived, unlike their robust vegetarian cousins who perished. For the gracile australopithecines, the abundant energy from this new meat and fat diet fuelled rapid enlargement of their brains.

The species within the gracile branch of *Australopithecus* that would eventually lead to humans was a gregarious, taupe-colored animal with a bluish sheen, still sporting obvious fur on its sleek body. Males were a little under five feet tall and weighed about a hundred pounds. Females stood a foot shorter and tipped the scales at less than seventy pounds. Being bipedal allowed these creatures to free their hands so they could grasp objects securely, and carry food and their young around with them. By standing on their feet they could conveniently peek over tall grasses to scan for refreshments, or scrutinize their surroundings for lurking predators. They hunted only small animals at first—like Pleistocene hares, rabbits, and turtles—and scavenged for meat from remnants on kills made by the large carnivores; they loved eggs poached from birds' nests. In the beginning they subsisted largely on fruit and tubers, but became more voracious meat eaters with time. My contemporary human companions later gave this hominin, their likely direct ancestor, the binomial name *Australopithecus afarensis*. A fossilized partial skeleton of this ancestral being, nicknamed Lucy, was first discovered in 24 AP by the American paleoanthropologist Donald Johanson in Hadar, Ethiopia. This remarkable creature possessed both ape and human characteristics. They had small canine teeth like humans do, and stood on two legs and regularly walked upright. But they had apelike faces and crania, and long arms with curved fingers adapted to climbing trees. It is quite self-evident that the universal aptitude of modern human children to spontaneously climb trees is reflective of this ancestral heritage.

Australopithecus afarensis lived in Africa where they originated. These creatures are now extinct. During their heyday in the Pliocene, the genus *Australopithecus* included several contemporary and related species that ranged their native continent. For their time, they were brilliant creatures, endowed with healthy curiosity and a cooperative spirit. The gracile *Australopithecus* that led to the genus *Homo* first appeared to the south of the Nile River's headwaters in the Great Lakes region of east-central Africa. That spot was the cradle of humanity.

From there these human ancestors dispersed over a territory now occupied by the modern states of Tanzania, Kenya, and Ethiopia. Their adaptations for living both in trees and on the ground helped members of *A. afarensis* survive for almost a million years, even as the climate and environment changed around them. They are the best known of early human ancestors, and paleoanthropologists have uncovered the fossil remains of more than 300 *A. afarensis* individuals in the region.

Approximately 3.6 million years ago in what is now Laetoli in the East African country of Tanzania, two of these enigmatic creatures walked through fresh wet volcanic ash. When the nearby volcano erupted again not long after these animals

crossed, new layers of ash quickly covered the trail and preserved the oldest known footprints of early human ancestors
ever discovered by their modern descendants. Found in 28 AP,
the entire footprint trail is 88 feet long and includes fossilized
impressions of 70 individual prints[26]. Judging from the footprints, these human ancestors were bipedal, and their big toe
was in line with the rest of the foot. This meant that their gait
was more humanlike than apelike, as apes have highly divergent big toes—similar to opposable thumbs—that help them
climb trees and grasp branches with their feet. The Laetoli
footprints also showed that the gait of these animals was heel-
first, followed by the toes, reminiscent of the way humans
walk. The shape of the foot and the length and pattern of the
toes, strongly suggested these footprints were made by early
hominid ancestors of humans. The only candidate in this category living in the region at that time was *A. afarensis*, fossils
of which were found nearby in the same sediment layer as the
Laetoli footprints.

Later, in 57 AP, the first of many fossilized footprints
were discovered at a site called Koobi Fora near the modern
town of Ileret in Kenya. These Kenyan footprints were about
1.52 million years old and belonged to *Homo erectus*, or its
stay-at-home African avatar, *Homo ergaster*. The Koobi Fora
footprints clearly showed its owners striding along on two feet,
just like modern humans do.

A species is defined formally in Earth based biology as a
unique population of individuals with a segregated gene pool,

---

26 This extraordinary discovery at Laetoli was made by the famous British ar-
chaeologist and paleoanthropologist, Mary Leakey. Mary and her celebrated
husband, Louis Leakey, were renowned explorers in archaeology and human
evolutionary history.

restricted to interbreeding only with each other to produce fully fertile offspring who, likewise, can reproduce only with their own kind. Correspondingly, their genetic constitution is unique and does not extend beyond their genotype, a phenomenon called Reproductive Isolation. Species generally have a single point of origin on their planet's surface, from where they tend to radiate outward and occupy ever wider ranges. They would surely not be expected to appear independently as the same species, over and over again, at different geographic locations across their range. Certainly, organisms may undergo further speciation in their former common range, but modern humans everywhere on their planet today clearly remain one single species, since they can freely mate and reproduce with each other and have fully fertile offspring. As noted previously, some anthropologists have proposed a multiregional origin for *Homo sapiens*. This contrasts with the out-of-Africa model of human origin which remains the consensus view among modern scientists today. The out-of-Africa, or replacement model, asserts that humans evolved as a single, distinctive species only once in East Africa 200,000 years ago, and then dispersed from that location all across their planet, replacing other hominan species they encountered along the way. On the contrary, the now largely rejected multiregional model postulates that humans speciated separately, and also repeatedly, into *Homo sapiens* in Africa, Asia, and Europe respectively, from local populations of *Homo erectus* that colonized the Old World around 1.8 million years ago.

An instructive analogy here would be the evolution of elephants presently found in both Asia and Africa. Elephants are distant relatives of sea cows (manatees) and dugongs. They evolved from an aquatic mammal that used its extended nose or proboscis as a snorkel when spending long periods of time underwater. The common ancestor of elephants and mammoths, *Primelephas gomphotheroides*, thrived in the dense forests of east Africa during the late Miocene, approximately 6 million years ago. This ancestral creature migrated across the world and speciated in different geographic locations (multiregional) into the African elephant, the Asian elephant, the mastodon, and the mammoth. Mammoths and mastodons are now extinct.

Although the two existing types of modern elephants convey a close morphological resemblance to each other, they unambiguously belong to completely different species, and to different genera as well—*Loxodonta africana* (African elephant) and *Elephas maximus* (Asian elephant). These two separate elephant species are now genetically marooned, having attained reproductive isolation with distinct and unique genomes incapable of mixing together any longer. All modern humans however, have a congruous genome, indicating a common point of origin and clearly favoring the out-of-Africa model for their evolution. Of course, humans have acquired geographic or racial variations, but they continue as one authentic species for now. Admittedly, this situation need not be permanent. Populations do indeed speciate by natural selection as *Primelephas gomphotheroides* did when environmental conditions changed in its various habitats. In humans for instance, accelerated ozone depletion leading to increased ultraviolet radiation exposure may provide a selective advantage to alleles that confer protection from ultraviolet rays. Likewise, rapid climate change could apply selective pressure as the weather may permit. The level of access to material and intellectual resources could weed out a penurious population while boosting a well-endowed one.

The legendary story of Darwin's finches offers an instructive lesson here. During his iconic voyage of exploration around South America more than 175 years ago, the young scientist Charles Darwin picked up specimens of about a dozen finch-like birds inhabiting different islands of the Galapagos chain. Upon returning to England, Darwin presented the birds to an ornithologist who identified the specimens as belonging to different species. For instance, the birds possessed variously shaped beaks according to the type of food they ate: evolution, it seemed, had selected for beaks best suited to ingest the particular brand of food or seed available to finches on a given island. Darwin soon realized that if the finches had been confined to individual islands as they presumably were, then that isolation would account for the number of species among his sample of finches. These conclusions supported his evolving ideas on biologic evolution and transmutation of species.

It is therefore quite possible that humans too may speciate in the future, just like Darwin's finches did in the Galapagos Islands. For this to occur though, physical isolation of population cohorts is necessary to attain reproductive isolation. Certainly, most creatures distributed across their entire planet as these humans are, would surely have become reproductively isolated by now. And that is where humans defy the odds. Because of their irrepressible urge to emigrate and their unbounded sexuality, it is a formidable if not impossible task to maintain reproductive quarantine in this species. Every prior attempt by humans themselves to forbid miscegenation by legislating or socially imposing prohibitions on interracial mixing and mating in this species has uniformly failed.

Modern humans have now come to possess the tools and skills required to quite accurately rewind their evolutionary geography back to their ancestral homesite. Using recently acquired molecular technology, they are able to scrutinize their own contemporary genetic material collected from individuals around their planet, and analyze that material for mutations in nucleobases that have accumulated over time. Based on the predicted mutation rate, their scientists can extrapolate from the actual mutation count measured in each sample, back in time and space to the approximate period and physical location of their most recent common ancestor. Those lines for humans all converge on East Africa about 200,000 years ago. That was the approximate location and time when *Homo sapiens* first became a separate species.

Mac had the great honor and extreme good fortune to visit there on a recent weekend and meet with a tribe of anatomically modern humans fishing on the banks of Lake Kivu.

CHAPTER VI:

TRIBE

ovely Lake Kivu sparkles like a polished gem in the vast southern range of East Africa's Great Rift Valley. The lake itself is embedded in the Albertine Rift, the western branch of the East African Rift. The word *Kivu* means "lake" in the local language.

This lake noiselessly straddles the border between the modern countries of Rwanda and the Democratic Republic of the Congo, and covers an area of exactly 1,042 square miles. It is 55 miles long and 30 miles wide, holding approximately 120 cubic miles of freshwater. It discharges today into the Ruzizi River which flows southward from Lake Kivu into Lake Tanganyika. The Ruzizi is a young river, hardly 10,000 years old, and was not around when Mac was in the adjoining area. The Ruzizi formed when severe volcanism related to continental rifting created the Virunga Mountains, blocking Lake Kivu's former outlet to the Nile.

Lake Kivu is surrounded by spectacular mountains and eye-popping scenery. The gaping rift where the lake is located continues to be pulled apart by tectonic forces severing East Africa from the rest of the continent, disgorging volcanic activity around the area. Tectonic fissuring makes the lake especially deep—at its deepest it plumbs 1,575 feet. Lake Kivu now hosts an island called Idjwi within its ambit, the tenth largest inland island on Earth today. Idjwi had yet to appear when Mac visited the region approximately 150,000 years ago. That was almost 50,000 years after humans had first speciated in these very parts.

Lake Kivu is a most unusual species of lake. At the time Mac was on Earth it was regarded as one of my host planet's only three known "exploding" lakes. All three are located on the African continent. The other two lakes in this curious category, Lake Nyos and Lake Monoun, are tiny in comparison to Lake Kivu. The science of lakes, called limnology, explains the physical mechanisms involved in the cyclical explosion of such lakes.

In these exploding lakes, a gargantuan volume of gases from adjacent volcanic sources, mostly carbon dioxide and methane, continuously enters the lake from its surrounding basin. These gases dissolve in the lake and saturate the water at deeper levels, forced into solution there by the exceptionally high pressures found in the lower regions of these very deep lakes. The physics here is exactly similar to dissolving carbon dioxide under high pressure in a can of soda. Just as opening the can and decreasing the pressure, abruptly releases the dissolved gas in the soda, likewise, when the lake is agitated by floods or earthquakes, the gas-saturated lower waters are displaced from the bottom of the lake toward the surface, and the dissolved gas, now under reduced pressure, is catastrophically released from solution in the lake's water to the surrounding atmosphere, asphyxiating people and animals in the vicinity. This phenomenon is called a Limnic Eruption.

Just such a limnic eruption took place about 25 years ago at one of the three exploding lakes on the African continent. The event in question happened in 36 AP at tiny Lake Nyos in west-central Africa. This diminutive lake occupies a now dormant volcanic crater in an area less than two-thirds of a square mile, only a miniscule 0.06% of Lake Kivu's area. Yet, when the inevitably recurring limnic eruption occurred at Lake Nyos that day over 25 years ago, 1,700 people suffocated to death and 3,500 livestock were killed in nearby villages. If instead, it had been Lake Kivu where that eruption occurred, the consequences would surely have been magnified by thousands of times. Limnic eruptions occur at Kivu about once in every one thousand years. No record was kept by humans of the last one.

❧❧❧

The surface of Lake Kivu was literally alive and teeming with countless Nile tilapia[27] on that splendid day in May, circa 150,000 BP, when Mac visited a tribe of anatomically modern *Homo sapiens* living by its shores. These ancient people called themselves Itu-Kan, which means "Sky-People" in their native language. These noble Itu-Kan were busy hauling in the leaping tilapia by the truckload when Mac arrived.

It was a lovely morning that day in the divine land of the illustrious Itu-Kan. Their radiant yellow-white star had just arisen in the eastern horizon barely an hour ago. The pellucid dewdrops from last night, still dotting the leaves and the creeping grasses, captured and refracted countless photons streaming down from their glorious Sun, before evaporating

---

27 Nile tilapia (*Oreochromis niloticus*) is a tasty little freshwater fish indigenous to the region.

into the morning air, sparkling like diamonds as they vanished. A soft gentle breeze, more seductive than a lover's smile, wafted in from the warmer north, and mixing with the abundant sunshine, banished the last traces of lingering cold left over from the overnight chill. Songbirds sang lustily in the trees, joyously heralding the lovely day on tap. A lone eagle silently rode the sky. The Itu-Kan were blissfully at peace, and all the world was happy.

An older individual who Mac later discovered was called Master T'yu, emitted a threatening low-pitched growl when he first espied me in the distance. T'yu was bestowed the honored title of "Master" almost two years ago by his tribe, in recognition of his shamanic[28] skills and faithful service to his people. The title conferred upon him the position of both revered healer and respected soothsayer for the band. The nine other individuals corralling the leaping tilapia with Master T'yu using reed baskets, scattered at my approach before regrouping into a snarling and defensive knot around him. There were four females and five males in that tight phalanx, ranging in age from adolescents to much older adults, now fiercely poised with stone weapons and wooden sticks pointed in Mac's direction. These early ancestral humans were always fully armed wherever they went. Because of their nomadic ethos and absence of fixed storage quarters, they habitually carried their weapons on person and slept with them. Further away, five young and actively reproductive females—three heavily pregnant with child and two clutching tiny sucklings—huddled nervously by a clump of wild banana trees where they had just been rooting for edible tubers alongside two young men, when Mac first

---

28 A shaman is a person believed to use magic to cure people who are sick, divine the occult or hidden, and control future events.

appeared on the tribe's sacred territory. These seven were now anxiously shielding a gaggle of four squealing children in addition to the sucklings, all crowded in their midst.

The fabrication and use of dedicated tools by hominans began in earnest around 2.4 million years ago with *Homo habilis* in East Africa. Though its predecessor genus *Australopithecus* also used tools to perform tasks on occasion, those tools were not dedicated ones and were rather more ambiguous and provisional in nature, much like the tools used by modern chimpanzees today. The first specialized stone tool manufacturing process, known as the Oldowan industry by humans today and introduced by *Homo habilis* that many years ago, continued essentially unchanged for more than 700,000 years. Oldowan tools consisted mostly of choppers formed by striking one stone appropriately against another to produce a sharpened edge that could be used for cutting or sawing—the remaining unworked and rounded edge was useful for pounding and crushing. This Oldowan tool manufacturing industry of *Homo habilis* was successfully picked up by its descendant species *Homo erectus*—confusingly called *Homo ergaster* within Africa—which elaborated the technology into the more advanced Acheulean stone tool industry beginning around 1.7 million BP. The Acheulean industry remained the dominant tool making technology for another 1.5 million years until 200,000 BP when humans came along. The technique for making tools in the Acheulean industry was a refinement of the earlier Oldowan technique—namely, striking one stone against another—but the choice of stone was more selective now. A two-faced cutting implement emerged in the Acheulean called a hand-axe that was sharper, straighter, and had longer cutting edges than its ancestral Oldowan chopper. These tool techniques were absorbed and shared by later appearing hominans and passed on to their descendants. With time, other stone tool industries such as Mousterian, Perigordian, and Solutrean among them, were developed locally as these hominans migrated from Africa into Asia, Europe and outward.

Master T'yu's people clutched wooden spears about four feet long, nasty flint points inserted and fastened securely to the business end of the device, making for some very fearsome looking weapons. The weight and sharpness of the stone-bearing end gave these spears heft and lethality when hurled at an intended target. My new friends pointed those threatening spears directly at Mac. The males in that surly formation were shrilly hooting in unison, stretching their lips and conspicuously exposing their teeth, while also prominently displaying genitalia to me. The females appeared no less fierce. They jiggled their torsos, breasts flapping, a venomous gargling sound issuing from their throats.

These early humans were noticeably shorter in height and smaller in build than modern Bantu people who live in the same neighborhood now. However, the Itu-Kan were substantially taller and bulkier than the pygmy M'buti inhabitants who also live in that region today—but are being cruelly driven to extinction by their neighbors through war and genocide. Adult males among my new Itu-Kan hosts were a bit over five and a half feet tall and weighed around 140 pounds; adult females were just over five feet in height and weighed closer to 120 pounds. Sexual dimorphism was far less evident in these First People than in their erstwhile *Australopithecus* or earlier *Homo* ancestors.

By the time of Mac's visit, these early humans had lost much of their body hair. The only clothing any of them wore were knitted oblong pieces of coarse fiber hanging from a waistband of corded vines that adult males had draped over their external genitalia. Juvenile males, women and children remained completely naked. Physical clothing, a most curious feature among my human companions on Earth today—and surely unknown in any other species on their planet—was just beginning to enter the human behavioral repertoire.

The use of clothing to cover parts of their body is now very common among modern humans regardless of gender or age. The primary reason for this adaptation, certainly, was to buffer themselves from inclement weather. As these hominans eventually spread around the planet from their original toasty home in East Africa's Rift Valley, they were exposed to much colder climates than they were accustomed to in that warm tropical crucible where they first arose. Having lost the insulating fur of their mammalian ancestors, it became necessary for these naked apes to cover themselves with clothing—first in roughly processed animal hides, and later in sophisticated and fashionable textiles worn by contemporary humans today.

Yet the utilitarian value of clothing as protection against the elements is substantially different from that sense of propriety and decorum driving humans, especially adult males, to cover their external genitalia from the view of others. Notably, there are hunter-gatherer groups of *Homo sapiens* still living in isolated tropical regions like the Andaman Islands and the Amazon rainforest, who refrain from wearing traditional clothing. Yet in many of these settings, though females and juvenile males do not generally cover their genitalia, adult males do. The reason for this unusual cultural practice is not bashfulness of course, but a desire to telegraph nonaggression to other adults in sight. For often in higher primates, explicit display of adult male genitalia is a clear signal of aggression, indicating specific intent to challenge the other party. In this context, it is quite instructive to note that men from a stone-age tribe inhabiting North Sentinel Island on the remote Andaman archipelago in the Indian Ocean, brazenly display their genitals—even prominently bouncing them up and down with their palms—to communicate aggression and hostility toward intruders and unwelcome visitors. These North Sentinelese people continue to live their lives as ancient Paleolithic hunter-gathers once did, surviving by hunting, fishing, and collecting wild plants from the forest. *Paleolithic* is Greek for "Old Stone Age" coterminous with the Pleistocene Epoch, whereas *Neolithic* is Greek for "New Stone Age" commencing with the Holocene. The North Sentinelese perform no agricultural practices and therefore have yet to enter the Neolithic Age. These people number about 250 individuals who are extremely hostile and unfriendly to visitors from the outside. Adult males display their genitals to intruders as a warning before shooting arrows at them. Their culture and language are practically unknown to outside humans.

Master T'yu pacified his agitated people with a volley of clicking sounds and a sweeping display of hand gestures. He had correctly sensed that Mac was not an enemy to his clan and posed no threat to himself or his precious tribe, having quickly surmised that this stranger had entered their territory with peaceful intentions. In a curious display of hominid behavior, Master T'yu squatted at his knees and then quickly arose, three times in rapid succession, all the while emitting high pitched vocalizations and clicking sounds. That bristling phalanx of threatening females and males, who had earlier assumed a defensive perimeter alongside Master T'yu when they first noticed my appearance, now began to relax their aggressive body postures and tentatively lowered their spears. Even so, they continued to remain alert and observant, ready to respond instantly with lethal force if they sensed the slightest danger emanating from Mac. The five women clutching babies and children, who had just earlier been digging for tubers with the two men by the banana grove, were now huddled at the base of a large baobab tree (*Adansonia digitata*). These women were all cooing in a peculiar otherworldly tone that seemed to hypnotize and calm their little ones.

I approached Master T'yu very gingerly. We exchanged greetings using a stylized bowing gesture, much like people do even today in some human cultures when meeting each other. For example, bowing is considered very important in modern Japan, and children in that country learn how to bow properly at a very young age. Generally speaking, an individual of lower status bows longer and deeper at the waist that a relatively high-status individual. A sufficiently high-status person addressing a low-status one may only nod the head slightly, or not bow at all, while the lower-ranked individual bends deeply from the waist down. This reciprocal act of submission, symbolizing surrender or retreat in the primate context, is a common behavioral signal of nonaggression among Hominidae in general, occurring within all its current radiations including orangutans, gorillas, chimpanzees, and humans.

I smiled profusely, even obsequiously, at Master T'yu, but the shaman did not recognize my gesture nor smile back at me. Those delicate facial muscles for displaying emotions such as delight, fear, or astonishment, were not yet fully wired by his neurons into

the brain's limbic system where feelings and emotions originate—
that would come later in human evolution. Instead, he arched his
brows sharply and his nostrils flared; his eyes glowered, his pupils
dilated. It was not easy to quite figure him out. Apart from the
obvious display of free-floating anxiety in the behavior described
here, there was no clear element of fear, surprise, or curiosity in
his expressions or mannerisms.

Master T'yu spoke in a local dialect of click-language these
hominans were using in this district of Kivu to communicate
among themselves. This early click-language, supplemented in these people with voice production by the larynx, was
extremely limited in vocabulary, grammar and syntax, quite
unlike modern click-language which is a fluent tonal language
that uses supplementary clicking noises produced by a sucking
action of the tongue against different parts of the mouth. These
clicks are employed to distinguish between various shades of
meaning affixed to certain words, and to show degree, number
and gender for nouns.

Click-language appeared even before full evolution of the
larynx was completed to make laryngeal-language possible.
Unlike lung-driven voice production by the larynx which can
be as loud and sonorous as desired, the low volume of lingual
clicks made pure click-language audible only as a twittered
whisper, thus confining the sound to a restricted range. In some
animals, evolution had magnified a recipient's hearing ability
to compensate for a weaker sound source, as in elephants or
owls which can hear extremely low sounds at great distances.
Humans were not thus endowed.

This earliest form of language is still used to modify laryngeal sounds by certain groups of modern people living in
southern and eastern Africa today. The exclamation point (!)

is one of several symbols used for transcribing clicks—click-language itself does not have its own script. Modern variants of click-language belong to the extremely endangered Khoisan group of tonal languages. The language now used by the !Kung of the Kalahari Desert in southern Africa is an example of a click-language from this unusual language group.

Humans are currently the only existing species on their planet that can fluently employ speech to exchange information with each other. Spoken language is a relatively recent development in human evolution. Pre-human australopithecines used communication systems not very different from those of other great apes living today. Primitive language-like systems first appeared in *Homo habilis* around 2 million BP. It consisted mostly of modulated grunts and gestures. The evolution of spoken human language required the development of the voice box or larynx to articulate speech, the specialization of cortical centers in the brain to initiate and understand speech, the appropriate neural connections to hook the central/cortical and peripheral/laryngeal mechanisms of speech together, and the memory capacity and means to store and access the information content necessary for speech production. Spoken speech with standardized syntax and grammar did not substantially appear in humans until about 100,000 BP, and even then it remained rough and disjoined until the emergence of full behavioral modernity some 50,000 years after that.

"Say! Why? Here?" demanded Master T'yu in a dry, iterative tone.

He stared directly at me, all the time scanning intently for any unusual movement on my part. These early humans spoke in mostly short, declarative bursts of words, not in structured and complex sentences. The content of their speech was concrete,

and their ability to abstract or use figures of speech was fundamentally limited, or mostly absent. That advance had to await
further development of the brain's frontal lobe.

"I come from outside your garden, most worthy Master
T'yu," I replied, using concepts appropriate to his time and
culture, though the word "worthy" in my declarative sentence,
and the syntax and grammar of my speech, was much more
complicated that the old Master was used to. He appeared
unmoved.

"Here...why?" he repeated, pointedly.

"I be a friend. I pass through. I come in peace. I do not fight
with you," I continued, infusing much passion and emphasis
into my words, though my emotions were pretty much lost on
him.

Then pointing directly to myself I told him my name,
"Mac!"

Master T'yu scratched his head as if uncertain about what I
had just uttered. After a brief moment he replied, "!Mac?" The
clicking sound before the name indicated my gender. He then
added, "From where?"

"From the tribe of Galymon, sire," I intoned. Master T'yu
had not heard of them.

"!Mac," he beckoned, now pointing to himself, indicating I
should approach him. "Come."

I approached the shaman cautiously, my open palms and
fingers pressed together in front of me and pointing upwards in
a friendly *namaste* sign as used today by people in the Indian
subcontinent. I slowly inched forward in a crouched and conspicuously passive posture, until I was before him with my
head and naked torso lowered in a display of submission and
nonaggression, clearly demonstrating my peaceful intentions

and hoping everyone in the tribe would note and behave accordingly. We were all out in the open by the lakeshore where
the tribe had been fishing just before Mac had arrived on the
scene. The five women along with the little children, who had
earlier sought refuge by the baobab tree, now approached us
quite nonchalantly, the women chattering to each other and
making chirping noises among themselves. They seemed quite
relaxed and pacified by my previous interactions as they came
toward us. A young female in that group coquettishly bounced
her lactating breasts at Mac.

I was now standing hardly a foot away from Master T'yu.
He cautiously leaned toward me with his face and upper body
nervously poised over my crouched frame, and began by making a surprisingly deep and sonorous sound through pursed
lips. He then performed several grooming motions to my head
and face, running his fingers multiple times from front to back
through my shoulder length hair, and tugging frequently at
my short beard. Upon completing these grooming motions, he
sniffed deeply around my armpits and pubic area. Master T'yu
seemed reassured following this careful olfactory assessment.

Sniffing body areas in other animals of the same species
primes and alerts the sniffer to the aggressive or sexual posture of the sniffee. This information is communicated through
the agency of special molecules called pheromones which are
discharged by one individual and inhaled by other members
of the group, releasing specific behaviors in them. Numerous
creatures on my host planet, from bacteria to plants, and from
insects to mammals, emit these chemical signals to entice mates
and influence a multitude of other behaviors. Pheromones
were first identified and named by humans in 9 AP following
the discovery of bombykol, a powerful aphrodisiac secreted by

female silk moths effective over distances of miles—just a few molecules of bombykol are enough to induce male moths to fly to the pheromone-emitting female from miles away. In ovulating human females, pheromones tend to synchronize their menstrual cycles when they live together in common housing. Newborn human babies are guided to a mother's breasts by pheromones. People can detect alarm scents present in the sweat of fearful or anxious individuals. These chemical signals appear to affect the mood and cognition of humans and other creatures.

Pheromones are produced in microscopic quantities by modified sweat glands called apocrine glands concentrated in hirsute body areas in humans, such as the armpit and pubic regions. They are detected by the recipient's vomeronasal organ, an organ of chemoreception that is part of the olfactory system in amphibians, reptiles, and mammals. It is a second, completely separate sense of smell known as the accessory sense of smell. The vomeronasal organ is a patch of sensory cells within the main nasal chamber and detects moisture-borne odor particles such as pheromones—airborne odors are separately detected by regular olfactory cells located in the nose. After particles reach the vomeronasal organ, some of the chemical compounds they contain bind to receptor molecules in that organ, which then send sensory messages to the brain, profoundly influencing the social and sexual behavior of exposed individuals. Pheromones thus act like social hormones within a species. In contemporary modern humans, the vomeronasal organ is a vestigial structure, though it reportedly is physically present in over half of people studied. During the time of the Itu-Kan especially, this organ was fully functional and frequently deployed, as was just done by Master T'yu to me. Interestingly enough, a "pheromone nerve" or cranial nerve 0, also called the Terminal Nerve, is a clearly present cranial nerve. First discovered in sharks in 72 BP and later in humans in 37 BP, this pair of nerves runs from the nose directly to the brain in front of cranial nerve 1 which is the Olfactory Nerve traditionally regarded as the first of a dozen recognized cranial nerves. Certainly, during evolution, olfaction as a sensory mechanism arrived way before vision and hearing, and played a central role in the organization of behavior among lifeforms on my host planet.

When I entered the Itu-Kan's time and space, I had fully transfigured myself into a male human from that era, appearing on the scene as an older gentleman close to Master T'yu's deportment and vintage. The shaman himself was more than thirty years old, quite advanced in age for his time and place. He was surprisingly well preserved and nourished, and seemed quite healthy and vigorous for his age.

Early humans lived short and brutish lives. Life expectancy at birth for people in those days averaged hardly 20 years, if even that—many died during childhood, precious few saw three score and ten. Modern humans today in advanced societies live 80 years. Among contemporary great apes, chimpanzees live 40 years, gorillas 35, and orangutans 30. Maternal and infant mortality rates were sky high for these people. One in five females died during pregnancy or childbirth (20 percent then; 0.2 percent now), and greater than one in three live-births perished before the age of one (35 percent then; 5 percent now). Deadly insect-borne protozoan diseases like malaria and sleeping-sickness were endemic, while severe childhood malnutrition was widespread and resulted in retarded body and brain development in affected individuals. Parasitic infestations were routine, and chronic bacterial diseases like tuberculosis and leprosy were common[29]. Many died from injuries while hunting for food. All active and able bodied men and women participated in hunting and gathering protocols which were fraught with many risks and dangers. Since humans at this time were relatively few and their tribes widely dispersed and rarely in contact with each other, genocidal warfare had not yet become an issue then. That monumental catastrophe would arrive later to haunt and torment this species.

Surely among the more compelling features of *Homo sapiens* are their peculiar behavioral traits. These are specific goal oriented behaviors that were not commonly present in the other hominan species that once shared the planet with them. For example, Paleolithic humans pursued an eclectic range of prey animals for food, developing strategies to hunt animals of different sizes—large, medium, or small. They constructed snares and traps appropriate for the differently proportioned animals, and improvised special methods to harvest fish and shellfish. The tools they made reflected this broader selection of animals, manufacturing these tools in various sizes, including very small ones for hunting small game. These tools were also more sophisticated and versatile than those made by other hominans living concurrently. Humans were the first to frequently

---

29 Some of these abject conditions are still endemic on Earth today, especially in certain areas of South Asia and Sub-Saharan Africa. The percentages given in the text for morbidity/mortality among modern humans for these conditions is a global average. Individual countries can deviate widely on both sides of this average.

produce implements made of bone and ivory, and they developed new methods for making composite tools that contained different parts combined to form the final product. These humans also tended to forage over much longer distances than the other hominans did, thus giving them access to more and varied resources. In such cognitive, technical, and cultural ways, *Homo sapiens* was different from the rest of the hominans in their genus. A notable feature in the cognitive style of humans when compared to presently living non-human animals, is their approach to problem solving. Non-human animals tend to employ a "focused-beam" approach, where a specific solution is used to solve a specific problem, and none else. Humans, instead, prefer to employ a "flood-light" approach to problem solving, thus allowing them to adapt solutions designed for one problem to solve a related, though different problem.

The term Anatomically Modern Humans refers to *Homo sapiens* whose appearance and deportment are consistent with the range of phenotypes encountered among modern people living on Earth today. These anatomically modern humans evolved from more archaic phenotypes in the Middle Paleolithic, approximately 200,000 years ago. The emergence of these humans marked the dawn of a unique species, *Homo sapiens*, which includes all contemporary people now inhabiting my host planet. The oldest anatomically modern human fossils yet discovered by the descendants of these First Humans are the Omo remains from southwestern Ethiopia, dated back to approximately 200,000 BP. Other fossils of anatomically modern humans were found at Herto in Ethiopia dated to 160,000 BP, and at Skhul Cave on the slopes of Mount Carmel in Israel, dated back to about 90,000 years ago. These first humans, like the honorable Master T'yu and his cohorts, though technologically much more advanced than other hominans, had yet to experience the cognitive efflorescence that was later to become the defining characteristic of *Homo sapiens*.

That extraordinary mental flowering appeared quite abruptly in a group of anatomically modern humans in Africa sometime after 100,000 BP, and reached fruition approximately 50,000 years ago. It heralded the onset of a new breed of clever people called Behaviorally Modern Humans. The key to behavioral modernity—its defining characteristic—was symbolic thought. Evidence for this change can be found along the southern coast of modern South Africa. Important Paleolithic sites discovered there at Blombos Cave, Still Bay, and Howiesons Poort, dated between 100,000 BP and 59,000 BP, point to the first appearance of behavioral modernity in *Homo sapiens* during that important period of their evolutionary history. Significant findings at these South African sites pointing to the emergence of symbolic thought in these newly endowed hominans include engraved bone and ochre artifacts, marine shell-beads for ornamentation, decorated ostrich eggshells, and the methodical use of social space, indicating a novel breed of people with the ability for symbolic thinking, sharply enhanced cognition, and more effective ways of accomplishing their social tasks. As these cultural fossils in South Africa indicate, and 40,000 year old cave paintings in Europe demonstrate, the emergence of symbolic thought in these newly modern humans was the liftoff point for the never before seen cognitive efflorescence in this species. Symbolic thinking, which required abstraction, was that unusual ability to construct a representational model of the real world within their own minds and solve problems by manipulating those symbols safely in the mind itself, before trying it out on the real world.

Behavioral modernity generally refers to a set of traits that distinguishes contemporary humans and their recent ancestors, from all other hominans that ever existed on my host planet. It recognizes that inflexion point when humans began to demonstrate the ability to apply complex symbolic thought and express cultural creativity in their interactions with the environment and each other. These attributes are closely associated with the development of fluent spoken language, the embodiment of symbolism.

The abrupt onset and rapid spread of behavioral modernity at this particular time in human history suggests that a unique genetic mutation, directly affecting the organization of the brain itself, may have been responsible for this extraordinary event. Those newly acquired genes, bestowing great fitness on their owners, would be especially favored by natural selection to spread rapidly across the species, propelled by the emigratory and sexual dynamism of these creatures.

The brain is a central collection of nerve cells housed in the cranium. This organ ultimately hooks up with every possible nexus in the body, intimately coordinating all the organism's responses. The brain endlessly receives a constant barrage of sensory information from general and special receptors positioned throughout the body. After analyzing and considering this sensory inflow, the brain chooses an appropriate response for the body to execute and sends the message out. This motor outflow pathway from the brain to the head area in humans is by way of the cranial nerves. The cranial nerves, therefore, are the physical conductors of speech and emotions so characteristic of these behaviorally modern humans. These cranial nerves were evidently some of the major anatomic structures affected by that watershed mutation which quickly led to behavioral modernity in these hominans.

The brain's output to the rest of the body except the head, is by way of the spinal cord and its embedded corticospinal tracts. Much of this spinal output from the brain is directed to the extremities, especially the hands and fingers in humans. Symbolic art and creative expression such as painting and sculpture, and most importantly writing or written speech—the analog of spoken speech—are physically transmitted from the brain to the hand through the spinal cord by way of the corticospinal tracts. These systems would also have been impacted by that crucial behaviorally modernizing mutation. Even though these neural mechanisms had long existed in mammals and were therefore pre-positioned in humans way before anatomical modernity arrived 200,000 years ago, behavioral modernity had to wait yet another 100,000 years for the appropriate genetic mutation to bring it on.

Along with the rapid changes in human central nervous system organization during the Middle and Late Pleistocene, a brand new set of far reaching mental constructs became established in these hominans. Foremost among these constructs was the emergence of a new psychological paradigm called Theory-Of-Mind. This term describes the unique and exceptional ability of behaviorally modern humans to project and attribute mental states just like their own onto other humans, thus allowing them to comprehend and anticipate the intentions and actions of those other humans—virtually a form of mindreading. The uncanny ability to perform this remarkable cognitive feat appears in all healthy modern people in early childhood, certainly by age four. Theory-of-mind is innate in behaviorally modern humans, not acquired or learned post-partum, and like the ability for speech in these humans, the trait is directly encoded in their genes. This exceptionally powerful mental device creates a cornerstone for mutually cooperative alliances between these creatures, the magic to their social and cultural preeminence on their planet today. This new theory-of-mind led them directly to the Golden Rule underlying all successful human behavior, which advises people to deal with others as they would deal with themselves. It also taught them the Principle of Reciprocity as a useful guide to making inter-personal choices, intuiting that for every interpersonal action they initiate, there will be a predictable and corresponding reaction from the other party. An important understanding humans acquired with their new theory-of-mind is a model of the Continuous Mind. This ability allowed them to view events as transitioning from one frame to the next, not stuck in spacetime forever in its original incarnation. This was a quantum break from the Discontinuous Mind which had hitherto viewed the Universe as static and unchanging, stuck firmly into place in its current manifestation from the start by an unaccounted and unaccountable "manifester." Now the new continuous mind let them view their own mind—and by extension that of others—as fluid and prone to change by circumstances.

This natural aptitude for theory-of-mind is believed to be deficient in Autism. Autism is a spectrum of neuropsychiatric developmental disorders in humans present from infancy, certainly before the age of four. Autism is characterized by deficits in communication, forming relationships with others, and a failure to properly use language and abstract concepts to master the existing human and cultural environment. Autism arises from the failure of those affected with the condition to view others as one would usually view themselves. It is related to a brain dysfunction in establishing an adequate theory-of-mind and thereby anticipating the actions and expectations of others.

Comparatively speaking, the Itu-Kan were a robust and successful band of anatomically modern humans. They were well established in the territory they currently occupied. Counting every single individual in the clan hosting me that day, including all the sucklings and infants present, there were precisely twenty three of them. That made these people one of the larger and more dynamic tribes inhabiting the shores of Lake Kivu at the time of my visit there.

The size of early human groups usually depended on the availability of food, rarely exceeding two dozen individuals living together in any single tribe. On that scale, the Itu-Kan were on top of their game, a prosperous and successful tribe indeed. Groups of these early humans would split into smaller cohorts and move on if food resources became scarce in the area. Most group members were endogamous and had close kinship bonds with each other. Young reproductive females may migrate between allopatric groups—meaning clans that are separated physically and not usually interbreeding with each other. This exogamous behavior among actively reproductive females is also observed in modern chimpanzees and bonobos. Small, nonviable tribes may integrate with larger and more vigorous ones. These latter two actions favored exogamy and genomic mixing so that natural selection could operate more effectively.

Periodically, using seasonal or astronomical markers, regional bands of these early humans may temporarily join together into much larger mega-bands of up to 300 individuals in an area where resources are plentiful, to celebrate and assert their *joie de vivre*, and also to acquire and exchange goods and mates. This jubilant behavior involving the gathering of large numbers of people is deeply ingrained in human nature and continues to be practiced today by contemporary humans, though mostly now for religious reasons. The Maha Kumbh Mela, the biggest gathering of them all, a grand pilgrimage of religious devotees held every 144 years at the confluence of their sacred Ganges and Yamuna Rivers near Allahabad in India, attracted an estimated 100 million people over 55 days the last time it came around in 63 AP. A massive pilgrimage called the Hajj, conducted every single year by religious devotees who flock to Mecca in Saudi Arabia from across my host planet, drew approximately 3 million people in 62 AP.

Early Paleolithic hominans such as *Homo habilis* or *Homo erectus/ergaster* already had fairly complex social structures in place. *H. erectus/ergaster* was the first hominan species to develop central campsites or home bases, and then incorporate these sites into their hunting and gathering strategies. Their hearths and shelters go back at least 500,000 years. Once anatomically modern *Homo sapiens* arrived on the scene, this pace of societal change quickened and then simply took off like a rocket. Humans began to engage in inter-tribal trade for raw materials and resources as early as 120,000 BP. This trade between bands enhanced the overall security of the species by allowing commodities to flow, especially during times of scarcity caused by famines or droughts.

Paleolithic humans were fundamentally egalitarian in their customs. They rarely engaged in inter-tribal violence or war. War was unnecessary during the Paleolithic Age because of the extremely low human population density in those times. These people also had no formal leadership structure that recognized rulers or political authority figures, but rather made decisions affecting the tribe entirely by communal consensus. They had no formal division of labor, each member of the tribe being skilled in all tasks essential for survival. Every member contributed to the commonwealth according to ability, and received in full measure according to need. This early form of tribal communism was practiced to ensure equal distribution of food and other resources to all tribal members and thus avoid famine and deprivation for individuals which would be disastrous for group survival. It also served to maintain a stable food supply for the clan.

There was no overt sexism or gender discrimination among these early humans. Sexual division of labor was indeed quite flexible. Men actively participated in gathering plants, digging for tubers and collecting firewood, while women expertly hunted small game and assisted their male colleagues in driving herds of large animals over steep cliffs to plunge to death in the ravines below. There was an essential parity between men and women during the Middle and Upper Paleolithic, and this period was the most gender-equal age ever seen in human history so far. The institution of marriage which was later adopted to ensure maximum reproduction and swiftly swell population numbers, and the severe patriarchy associated with marriage that undermined gender parity, was still ominously tucked away in the future.

After the tense introductions and ritual displays of our initial meeting were over, we returned eagerly to continue fishing for tilapia. Everyone in the tribe who was physically able, including myself, enthusiastically joined in the operation—it was the perfect day for fishing! We were done by noon. The catch was enormous, possibly close to a thousand pounds of fresh fish to be decapitated, gutted, and cleaned. Once dried and smoked over a controlled fire, this cache of high protein food would last the Itu-Kan for weeks when supplemented by tubers and other vegetable material, including succulent berries and fruit foraged by their men and womenfolk.

The use and control of fire was an extraordinary cultural accomplishment for hominans. It is one of humankind's most essential and indispensable tools and helped set their path to civilization. Although *Homo habilis* was the first hominan to tinker with fire somewhere around 1.4 million BP—in fact, the first animal on their planet to ever do so—the controlled use of fire did not properly begin until the arrival of *Homo erectus*. Wonderwerk Cave in modern South Africa's Northern Cape Province contains evidence for fire use by *H. erectus* starting about a million years ago. The original source of fire was from lightning strikes that ignited blazes in the forest. Hominans would collect embers from these forest fires and keep those embers alive by adding fuel to it from time to time. Humans only learned how to generate fire on their own, using sparking devices, less than 10,000 years ago. Up until then they had to preserve embers from an existing fire for as long as they could, for if the fire died out they must wait for lightening to strike again. This ancient species-memory of preserving fire permeates human history right up to the present time. The "sacred fire" is even today kept perpetually alive in some contemporary homes in India, just as the Romans nourished a perpetual fire cared for by the Vestal Virgins in 2,500 BP, or the Greeks nursed and transported the sacred fire of Hestia during migrations in 3,500 BP. Until as recently as 200 years ago, the native people of the Andaman

Islands did not know how to generate fire from scratch, and therefore carefully preserved live embers in hollowed-out trees from fires produced by lightning strikes.

The first hominans to control fire gradually learned its numerous uses. They used fire to keep warm and cook their food. They lit it in their campsites for light, to repel insects, and to frighten away predators. They learned to employ it in fire drives for hunting, to singe leaves from trees to better expose hidden berries, and to clear forests of underbrush so that game could be better visualized and hunted. Without access to fire for warmth and protection from severe cold, these hominans— who lacked the protection of fur like other mammals adapted to cold climates—would have remained in the tropics of their origin and ventured no further.

Cooking food over fire before eating it was a cardinal development in the evolutionary history of these creatures. It was the physical key to proper nutrition. The technique of cooking is unique to their culture and has never been replicated by any other group of organisms on my host planet. The invention of cooking had a profound impact on these creatures. Cooking their food before eating the meal, selectively modified the anatomy and physiology of their digestive tract, making it considerably shorter and far more efficient in absorbing nutrients. Cooking allowed for easier chewing and digestion of the food, thus making extra calories available to fuel their energy hungry brains. In adult humans for example, the brain, though comprising hardly 2 percent of total body weight commandeers a full 20 percent of the body's total energy consumption. *H. habilis*, the first hominan to emerge from *Australopithecus* and did not cook its food before eating, had a brain only a little larger than its ancestor and had many apelike features in common with it. Yet *H. erectus*, when it emerged from *H. habilis*, was a radically more advanced hominan with a brain twice as large as its predecessor, smaller teeth, a more compact and efficient digestive system, and a body far more humanlike than apelike. Cooking made a substantial contribution to this development, and it is indeed doubtful if their brains would have blossomed without it.

Cooking their food over a hot fire is preferred by humans during food preparation because of the Maillard Reaction, an appetite-enhancing chemical process during cooking that both browns meats and also creates many of the flavorful compounds that humans find so delicious. The reaction is named after the French chemist Louis Maillard, who in 38 BP described how sugars and amino acids combine during cooking to create aromatic compounds that also happen to pack a lot of flavor. The Maillard reaction creates thousands of different flavor compounds depending on cooking time and temperature, as well as the type of sugars and amino acids present in the raw food.

The Itu-Kan kept their sacred fire lit and perpetually burning in a mysterious cavern by a hillside near Lake Kivu. Later in the day, after we had done fishing and joyfully romping in the heavenly waters of the lake, I would be awarded the rare honor of accompanying Master T'yu and a woman called !Ra into the bowels of that enigmatic cave to bring back live embers to cook dinner and light the campfires for the upcoming evening. The hearth were the perpetual fire was housed consisted of a raised platform of rocks topped by a thick layer of loose grey pebbles. Live embers nestled in a shallow depression in the pebble layer, glowing silently with a delicate—almost smokeless—steely blue flame. Right beside this small active fire, and stacked neatly alongside the platform of rocks, was a large pile of high quality anthracite coal that these Sky People had collected from a nearby coal-seam that had become exposed in the valley below. They called this material *!tch'ut*, meaning "burning rock" in their native tongue. This serendipitous discovery and use of coal for fuel was a major technological coup for scattered bands of humans living around this area of Lake Kivu. The clever Itu-Kan had established a protocol whereby someone was always scheduled to tend the sacred fire with nuggets of this clean-burning coal at all times of the day and night. Those who were assigned this most important fire-tending task were usually the elderly or disabled members of the tribe. Hominans had long since now become capable of tolerating, and even actively nursing and supporting, injured and disabled individuals among their kin. This empathy and altruism was later extended to those enfeebled by advanced age as well. Fossilized skeletal remains of hominans from long before the Itu-Kan show evidence of healed fractures that would not have been possible without communal care. As long back as 530,000 BP, ancestors of modern humans had already began helping injured, sick and elderly individuals, including some with severe congenital and degenerative disorders, to survive and even recover from otherwise life-threatening conditions.

It was evident to Mac while scrutinizing the limited world of the Itu-Kan, that these simple people had a long way to go before reaching full behavioral modernity. An early clue to the symbolic thinking that was yet to come was their belief in magic. Regardless, their speech was literal and rudimentary in content, with little evidence for symbolic thought or allegorical meaning. Looking carefully around me, I noted that the walls of the fire-cave were unadorned. They were completely devoid of the enigmatic art sometimes found on cave walls of human habitations from the Upper Paleolithic or the Late Old

Stone Age. The Upper Paleolithic was the period that began about 50,000 years ago, the era now associated with full behavioral modernity in this species. There was never such art or symbolism anywhere in that fire-cave by Lake Kivu. My beloved friends, the Itu-Kan, had not reached that stage yet. Their thought processes remained concrete and they were not quite able to imagine their world in representational terms. Allegorical thinking was barely detectable in these good people. Representational art only appeared robustly after the emergence of full behavioral modernity in the Upper Paleolithic as stated, and then proceeded to blossom with gusto in the form of cave paintings, decorative artifacts and personal jewelry. Engraving, carving, and sculpture—in clay, stone, bone, antler, and ivory—proliferated in the Late Old Stone Age. Commonly depicted themes included trees, animals and the human form, especially female shapes, particularly pregnant ones.

Creative expression flourished with behavioral modernity once that stage was reached. Substituting a symbol to represent something in real life is the beginning of abstraction and is unique to later appearing humans. It allowed them to conduct thought experiments in their minds by manipulating those symbols mentally without actually having to first physically try out the idea in the natural world to see if it would work. Thinking abstractly was the gateway to language, art, poetry, literature, science, and politics in which humans would excel one day. This process had just begun for Master T'yu and his people. Clearly, one of the strikingly evolved capabilities underlying modern human behavior is the ability to communicate habitually and effortlessly in symbols. The pervasiveness of symbolism in contemporary human culture is plainly evident in every single sphere of their lives. Common behaviors such as problem solving and long range planning are impossible without symbolic operations.

After our enthusiastic crew had finished landing the bountiful haul of tilapia that morning, the catch was quickly scaled, gutted, washed, and salted[30] by their lovely womenfolk, and then spread out to dry. The resulting product would be smoked over a fire and stored securely within a few days.

Evening approached and shadows lengthened as Earth's mighty star majestically descended into the serene western sky, framing the gorgeous landscape in a surreal glow. An enormous flock of rose-tinged pelicans squabbled as they foraged nearby, ignoring Mac and the Itu-Kan romping and playing in the celestial waters of Lake Kivu. Luckily for us, the ancestors of hippos and crocodiles had not colonized the lake. This curious anomaly continues to the present day. There is a distinct lack of wildlife around Lake Kivu in comparison to neighboring areas, because of the periodic local mass extinctions caused by limnic eruptions about once in every one thousand years.

The Itu-Kan had developed a two acre temporary homesite along a rocky promontory about a mile from the eastern shore of the lake. To reach the site from the lake you had to carefully walk north along a narrow boulder-strewn path that the tribe could defend from an elevated position on the promontory if the homesite itself was attacked by marauders. A few small caves were available for shelter along the rocky outcropping.

---

30 Sodium chloride, in the form of rock salt, was an essential and invaluable mineral collected and stored by hominans, beginning way back with *Homo habilis*.

The "maidan," a cleared swath of level land, opened out in front of the campsite.

We emerged from the lake, refreshed and squeaky clean, glistening with beads of crystalline water rolling off our backs. It was getting chilly as the temperature dropped. After drying ourselves under the afternoon Sun, we gathered in concert for dinner and dancing on the open maidan. Fresh fish from today, and scavenged carrion from yesterday, were grilling on a bed of coals. A comely young maiden sporting a flirtatious look, offered Mac a steaming hot tuber. Clusters of a delicately sweet-smelling fruit called odin, an aphrodisiac, were heaped to one corner. Potent buds of ganja or marihuana were passed around in lit pipes. Piling ourselves around heaps of sumptuous food, we stuffed our bellies until our stomachs virtually dropped to our feet, all the while quietly snorting fermented berry juice, nibbling aphrodisiacal fruit, and puffing on shared pipes of ganja. It was a great tamasha.

The Itu-Kan engorged themselves with calories whenever they accessed food, eating ravenously until they were literally stuffed to the gills. Their neural mechanisms induced this gluttonous behavior in anticipation of prolonged periods of starvation when food was scarce or unavailable in their precarious and dangerous world. They were therefore inherently prompted by their nature to carry as many calories as possible in reserve for a rainy day which was always guaranteed to come. Unlike other hominins, humans have a strong genetic predisposition to accumulate fat as adipose tissue, an evolutionary adaptation that served them admirably in the past when food supplies were uncertain and competition for limited resources was always intense—fat gave them a clear survival advantage over competitors. This curious behavioral relic still haunts modern humans and accounts for the epidemic of obesity presently sweeping affluent societies on their planet. Even though food supplies are now virtually unlimited and always available to most humans living in rich countries on Earth today, these people still respond to the sight or smell of food like their Paleolithic ancestors once did, thus consuming as much nourishment as they could at one sitting.

It was dusk now, and the late evening shadows were quickly lengthening into darkness. A waxing gibbous Moon was rising in the east, suffusing our maidan with that enchanting silvery moonlight so adored by lovers the world over. Yet romance and love, as humans experience them today, requires a clear aptitude for symbolic thought and expression, something the Itu-Kan still lacked.

Campfires were lit and fistfuls of lemongrass (*Cymbopogon* species) were sprinkled liberally into the flames to repel mosquitoes and other insects. Lemongrass contains citronella oil which is also an insect repellent when vaporized. Ancestors of the Itu-Kan had serendipitously discovered this relationship several hundred years ago while using dried lemongrass to fuel fires. They had noticed the absence of insects around those fires. Their brains were sufficiently complex by then to recognize and acknowledge this causal relationship, as well as to retain and transmit that memory to others. That is how discoveries are made by humans and broadcast culturally to succeeding generations through the mechanism of memes.

A melodic howl pierced the air, followed by another, then another, and soon a troop of aroused humans, both male and female, began stomping and chanting with rising vigor to the masterful measure of a handsome young lad beating rhythmically on a drum made from a hollowed-out log capped taut at both ends with animal hide. Now the passionate males of the tribe, inflamed and gyrating erotically, were all sporting stiff penile erections. Their testicles were conspicuously larger and hung heavier than those of their modern male descendants today. Since females routinely mated with multiple males then, individual male humans had to produce as much spermatozoa as possible to compete successfully within the common sperm-pool in the female's vagina, thus explaining the presence of larger testicles in these males to produce more sperm.

Before the dancing began, females of reproductive age had gathered in a tight knot at the center of the maidan. Now, as the beat picked up, they left that central location, their sexual arousal clearly on display, and joined the lustily dancing males further out on the maidan. As the beat continued in a hypnotizing cadence, skillfully syncopated by that handsome drummer-boy, the energized females and males of the clan, whipped up by berry wine and ganja topped with odin, were rocking and rolling furiously to the exotic pulse now pounding the air. Mac was stuffed with food, deliciously huddled on the ground alongside Master T'yu. We both watched the erotic dancing with mounting excitement.

Mating, like hunting and gathering, was a core responsibility of the tribe. Brutal living conditions in those times resulted in frequent deaths from disease and trauma, leading to a short life-expectancy for these humans. Therefore, early and frequent reproduction was given the highest priority by the tribe. This was imperative to underwrite group survival. Females became pregnant soon after their first ovulation, or shortly following menarche, and were well into child-bearing by their early second decade. By their early twenties they were mostly done. During their active reproductive life lasting about ten years, females were frequently pregnant or nursing. Miscarriages and maternal deaths were common. Each female may carry up to five live births to term in the course of her reproductive life. Of those live births, not more than two or three reached adulthood due to the high infant and child mortality rates prevailing at that time. A mother may succeed in raising just two offspring over her entire lifetime, barely enough to maintain the tribe's population numbers. Males had sexual access to all reproductive females in the group, and vice versa. The children of these unions were nurtured by the biologic mother, assisted by the entire tribe. Their fathers were anonymous.

Sexuality in modern Hominidae—the great apes—sheds valuable light on the sexual behavior of early *Homo sapiens*, here documented for the Itu-Kan. Two domains of sexual behavior are seen in great apes—monogamy and polygamy. In monogamy, one male and one female copulate and reproduce only between themselves. In polygamy, individuals copulate and reproduce with several different partners. Both males and females may adopt and practice polygamy. Hence within polygamy itself there are three sorts of possible liaisons: polygyny (one male/multiple females); polyandry (one female/multiple males); and polyandrogyny (multiple females/multiple males). Polyandry is uncommon among Hominidae. As a rough guide, sexual dimorphism, or the difference in male versus female body size, tends to correlate with these behaviors. When male dimorphism is prominent (gorilla, orangutan), polygyny appears to be the rule. When dimorphism is minimal (chimpanzee, human) polyandrogyny seems to be the preferred option. For most of their history, *Homo sapiens*, like the Itu-Kan, practiced a chimpanzee-like polyandrogynous sexuality. Only about 10,000 years ago in the early Neolithic, along with

marriage, did humans adopt polygyny or monogamy as reproductive strategies—they did so to achieve prolifically high
birthrates and rapid population growth. Of course, after marriage was invented, individual human males no longer had to
compete with other males as bulk sperm producers to successfully fertilize the now monogamous females; so their testicles
decreased in size to what is seen in male *Homo sapiens* today.

Homo sapiens are among the most sexually active of mammals that ever lived on my host planet. They are highly eroticized
primates, ready to copulate at a moment's notice. This insatiable
sexuality played a fundamental role in their astonishing biologic
success as a species. It was a major factor contributing to the
population explosion enjoyed by humans since the beginning
of the Holocene, and was indispensable for the overwhelming
planetary dominance they then established on Earth. Human
males, throughout their reproductive years, are ready to mate at
any time of day or night if given the opportunity to do so. Even
more remarkably in fact, human females are similarly endowed
and will copulate with an appropriate male companion even if
she is not ovulating at the time of sexual intercourse, or is pregnant or lactating while performing coitus. This is remarkable,
quite unlike the majority of mammalian females that will mate
only during estrus when they are ovulating and fertile.

As the drum pounded away in that fragrant maidan, dancing
couples stepped eagerly aside to mate. Copulation was notably
unselfconscious in these ancestral people, much like it is in all
other mammals. With hardly any inclination for symbolic or
representational thinking yet, and no theory-of-mind inherent
in their mental mechanisms so far, these anatomically modern
humans experienced sexual intercourse primarily as a physical
act without emotional attachments. It was done with gusto and

without embarrassment. Individuals mated with multiple partners. The incest taboo had still to appear in this species, and consanguineous couplings were common. Since tribes were small and isolated, they tended to be endogamous, and most members were related to each other. The tribal genome was therefore relatively homogenous. This, of course, would not be very conducive for genetic variation and natural selection to occur, so exogamy had to be encouraged. Exogamy took place primarily through voluntary female drifting between tribes as is often seen in chimpanzees and bonobos, as well as through mate-abduction. Tribes would raid each other if the opportunity presented itself, kidnapping females for incorporation and reproduction within the invaders' tribe, thus promoting needed exogamy. Bride abduction is still prevalent in several contemporary human cultures on Earth today.

The drumming was still pounding in my head as the frenzy on the maidan subsided. Music is clearly universal among humans and was established much before speech developed in this species. Music and rhythm is common to all peoples and cultures everywhere on my host planet, and must therefore have been written into their genes by natural selection to promote an important survival function. The indispensable role of music in humans, it seems, is to initially serve as the vehicle for special communication between a mother and her infant, creating that unique type of bonding necessary for the infant's care and nurturing. It explains the origin of the "sing-songy" baby-talk and lullabies that mothers routinely employ with their newborn babies. This style of musical communication, informally called "motherese," consisting of melodic sounds and body movements, triggers emotional bonding responses between the mother and her offspring which is so important to the infant's security and survival.

Sounds and rhythms are already imprinted into the newborn's brain. Unlike many other mammals which remain deaf throughout gestation and begin to hear only after birth, the human fetus can hear sounds after only 20 weeks of gestation, just halfway to full-term. The metronomic beating of the great maternal heart, the cadence of her breathing, the peristaltic movements of her intestines, the regular bounce of her walking, and other natural sounds and rhythms during pregnancy are all engraved in the newborn's brain. They had acted as a soothing pacifier and security blanket for the developing fetus. The effortless appreciation of sounds and rhythms by newborns is therefore already preprogrammed into the infant's behavioral repertoire.

Humans belt out songs by rhythmic contractions of their vocal cords, accompanied by reciprocal rhythmic movements of the rest of the body. Singing and music influence the brain's limbic system, releasing strong emotional responses in both the music producer and the listener of that music. Humans have adopted, and continue to employ, this motherese music tradition past infancy and into adulthood, now presented in the form of elaborate grown-up music and supplementing it further with musical instruments and active dancing displays. People use music for its powerful emotional effects in times of rejoicing as well as in times of sorrow, as martial music during wartime, and as a dependable messenger for love and romance. The form of music heard by listeners even influences the manner in which they think.

Besides music, competitive sports is another unusual phenomenon among humans. Sports developed as a mechanism to safely discharge and sublimate individual and group aggression without inflicting physical damage to opponents. That is why participatory sports is mostly engaged by post-pubertal and young adult males when testosterone driven aggression is at its highest—similarly aged girls do not seem to be as interested in competitive sports as males are. Sporting activity began as an extension of play activity which is often also observed in the young of several nonhuman mammals as well. In most of these other species however, play activity ceases after childhood, though it may persist into later life in a few nonhuman animals such as dolphins and porpoises. In humans characteristically, play activity, now as competitive sports, persists into adulthood. Sporting activity was especially congruous to their hunting ethos where team work and an *espirit de corps* were required for success. In sports, the goal of the enterprise is symbolic; therefore, some ability to abstract was first needed for a sports tradition to appear in this species. Sports displaces aggression into benign channels, thereby providing a way to produce a winner, while avoiding lethal conflict between adversaries. It effectively symbolizes the act of aggression, thereby making it innocuous and discharging the aggression as harmless play. Both individual and group sports are widespread in this species today, and international sporting events are regularly organized by *Homo sapiens*.

We were up shortly after their star arose the next morning. Master T'yu was silently gazing south as the new day dawned. Dawn and dusk are short and swift near the equator.

For many moons now, Master T'yu and others of his beloved tribe had considered moving the clan south toward the Cape of Good Hope, deep inside the southern African veldt and into the Kalahari Desert where the !Kung people live today.

The noble Itu-Kan were worried.

The honorable Master T'yu and his people all knew the terrible legend of the lake. That ancestral tribal memory recalled a fearsome monster that lurked at the bottom of Lake Kivu. This abominable creature was slated to emerge on an unknown day from the depths of the lake and devour every person and object along its deadly path. The noble Itu-Kan had to leave before that catastrophe struck. Here dwelt a historical memory, a collective consciousness of exploding lakes.

I gazed intently into Master T'yu's eyes. They were dull and hard to read. It would be another 100,000 years before the Itu-Kan reached full behavioral modernity and became fluent in facial and ocular expressions, and be able to transmit affect like humans do today. That could happen only as advanced neuronal circuits evolved and made complex connections—and that had to wait for now.

I looked into his eyes again. Mac knew that Lake Kivu was due for another limnic eruption in just eight short years from now. Could Master T'yu, their revered shaman and soothsayer, have known that too? I wished with all my heart that the noble Itu-Kan would soon emigrate south.

I then bid them adieu and left.

CHAPTER VII:
EMIGRATION

onsensus exists that the simian ancestors of humans—the upright walking apes—arose in Africa. Yet the progenitors of those very apes may have first trudged from Africa into Eurasia, and then back again to Africa during their evolutionary journey to becoming human.

Apes evolved in Africa at least 20 million years ago when that continent was an island separated by water from other land masses on Earth. The best known of these early African apes was *Proconsul* which lived in East Africa about 23 million years ago at the beginning of the Miocene Epoch. The Miocene extended from 23.03 million BP to 5.332 million BP, ending in the Pliocene. *Proconsul* was evidently an ape, but seems to have retained some monkey-like traits in its spine, pelvis, and forelimbs, suggesting the animal was a quadrupedal branch-walker threading atop tree limbs, rather than a brachiator swinging from branch to branch. Four fossil species of this ape have been identified. The primary feature linking *Proconsul* to apes is its lack of a tail. This animal, possessing a suite of Old

World monkey and ape characteristics, is tentatively placed by their modern human descendants in the ape superfamily, Hominoidea. Around 17 million years ago, lowered sea-levels provided a suitable land-bridge for these early Miocene apes to leave Africa and enter Eurasia, along with elephants, pigs, and rodents.

These apes had by then developed a thick coating of enamel on their teeth, enabling them to masticate harder foods such as nuts and seeds, an option not available to their *Proconsul* ancestor. This significant evolutionary adaptation allowed the Eurasian apes to diversify into at least eight different varieties within 1.5 million years of their emigration to Europe and Asia, from Africa. By 13 million BP, apes had spread throughout Eurasia, among which were *Dryopithecus* in Europe and *Sivapithecus* in Asia. They both had a remarkably similar anatomy to the modern great apes. These two lineages survived the major climatic changes that marked the end of the Miocene. While the other Eurasian apes became extinct by that time, these two remained alive by moving into southeast Asia (*Sivapithecus*) and back into Africa (*Dryopithecus*). The existing great apes seem to have descended from them. Phyletic analysis indicates that *Sivapithecus* is the likely ancestor of orangutans, while *Dryopithecus* is the probable ancestor of the African great apes, including humans. *Dryopithecus* fossils possessed a large frontal sinus—a cavity in the forehead lined with mucous membranes that produce mucous. This evolutionary feature links this animal to the African great apes and to humans, who all sport prominent frontal sinuses. Fossils of *Sivapithecus* lack this frontal sinus, exactly like contemporary orangutans do, thereby establishing a different evolutionary lineage for this southeast Asian great ape.

Dryopithecus likely left Europe behind and returned to Africa in the Late Miocene as climate change made Europe un-inhabitable for them. The rise of the great Himalaya along the northern edge of the Indian subcontinental plate, made Europe much cooler and dryer than before. Starting around 9.5 million BP, deciduous woodlands replaced subtropical forests in Europe, and many tropical animals perished on that continent as a result. Luckily for them, the ancestors of humans made it back to Africa.

This Miocene migration of apes from Africa to Eurasia, and then later some back to Africa, occurred long before the hominan emigrations out of Africa in the Pleistocene Epoch, described hereunder.

Among the hominans of East Africa during the Great Emigrations, the first to leave paradise was *Homo erectus*. This curious animal broke the mold and left its home in the Great Rift Valley, venturing further afield into the vast unknown spaces of its planet. Brave bands of these creatures emigrated from their birthplace, trekking into the broad and wider world beyond—that evanescent realm holding so many risks and rewards for them. Later, other species of hominans, including *Homo sapiens*, would follow this unusual example. The pristine course of the River Nile was the preferred route for these remarkable journeys. Like other creatures that migrate on land, these hominans also preferred to venture along well established waterways in order to ensure a source of that life sustaining liquid for themselves.

The Nile today is 4,258 miles long. It has remained just about the longest river on my host planet since the Late Pleistocene. The current Nile is one of several Niles that have flowed north in this region since ancient times. The Eonile, an ancestral Nile, once gushed in this area west of the present Nile, almost 10 million years ago in the Miocene. The Eonile's clearly fossilized watercourse can be visualized on satellite images of Earth today. The great river now has two major tributaries, the White Nile and the Blue Nile. The White Nile, identified as the primary river and the longer of the two branches, arises in the Great Lakes region of east-central Africa, with its most distant source located at latitude 2.32°S and longitude 29.33°E in the Nyungwe Forest near Lake Kivu. The Blue Nile emerges from the Ethiopian Highlands at Lake Tana, and travels westward toward the White Nile. The White Nile and Blue Nile merge and become confluent around Khartoum, the capital of modern Sudan. From there, the northern section of the single river flows almost entirely through desert, from Sudan to Egypt, bringing life along its shores—humans often refer to Egypt as the "Gift of the Nile." The mighty river languidly ends its course in the Nile Delta on the northern Egyptian coastline, emptying its drained and spent waters into the Mediterranean Sea.

Now carefully following the streaming river north from their home in East Africa's Rift Valley, intrepid bands of *Homo erectus* emigrated out of their natal continent about 1.8 million years ago. Some of them turned east at the confluence of the Blue Nile and followed that tributary upstream, heading south again and eastward toward the coast of Ethiopia, and across the now ice-breached Red Sea into Arabia and onward. Others continued along the main river downstream, heading north to the Mediterranean Sea. From there they crossed the Levantine corridor into Anatolia and then went on to Eurasia.

The Levantine corridor, for those dear readers not familiar with it, is the narrow coastal strip of land bordering the southeastern Mediterranean Sea and an important land bridge between Africa and Eurasia for migrating animals.

A striking feature of the genus *Homo* that immediately draws the attention of an extraterrestrial like Mac, is their inveterate penchant for emigration. Ever since the arrival of the pioneering *Homo erectus*, the act of emigrating away from their current local habitats and moving into foreign lands has been a deeply ingrained characteristic of these hominans. By and large, these animals have been among the most invasive species on my host planet, and humans, their only remaining representative on Earth today, are by far the single most invasive mammalian species the world has ever known. First appearing as a small group of hominans in East Africa hardly 200,000 years ago, *Homo sapiens* rapidly dispersed around the world, occupying and infiltrating every corner of their planet long before 15,000 BP. Their innovative ability to construct dwellings and don clothing to protect themselves from inclement climate and weather conditions, their cosmopolitan eating habits, their always prolific sexuality, and the reproductive spree they undertook beginning in the early Holocene, all contributed to this outcome. Nevertheless, though these other factors were helpful, their emigratory impulse alone was the key to their planet-wide dispersal. This irrepressible instinct to emigrate is a genetic fiat and lurks deep within their nucleobases. It is the quintessential emblem of their extraordinary success and prosperity.

Circa 700,000 BP, almost a million years after *H. erectus* left Africa, a cohort of another hominan species, *Homo heidelbergensis*, would also leave the mother continent and spread out into Europe and Asia. Before eventually disappearing from Eurasia, *H. heidelbergensis* would birth a successor species called *Homo neanderthalensis*[31] around 200,000 BP, which lived on in Eurasia till about 35,000 BP. Neanderthals went extinct after meeting humans. The cohort of *H. heidelbergensis* that remained in Africa would produce on that continent another brand new species called *Homo sapiens*—also around 200,000 BP and contemporary with neanderthals. This consummate new animal would in turn begin emigrating out of Africa for the first time around 130,000 BP. These emigrating Africans encountered the domiciled Eurasians—two sibling species from the same parent-stock but spawned on different continents—and a lethal existential struggle ensured between them. The Africans eventually won that round. Now in just a flash of geologic time after leaving home, that amazing creature *Homo sapiens* would spread out across the world to occupy and dominate its entire planet.

This compulsive emigratory behavior of these hominans is unique and unprecedented for any known vertebrate species on my host planet. No other large animal on Earth comes even close to this kind of rapid and systematic dispersal over ever increasing territory. Though many birds and certain ocean living creatures may seasonally migrate enormous distances between discrete locations, they do so specifically for breeding or feeding purposes only, and not to permanently occupy and inhabit a larger territorial space. These other movements are thus strictly migratory, not emigratory.

---

31 *Homo neanderthalensis* (neanderthals) began differentiating from their ancestor species, *H. heidelbergensis*, in Eurasia approximately 500,000 years ago. They completed full speciation around 200,000 BP. Neanderthals became extinct in Asia around 50,000 BP, and then disappeared from Europe around 35,000 BP.

The instinct to emigrate may well be imprinted in the hominan genome itself. For example, a particular gene in humans located on chromosome-11, designated the DRD4 gene, codes for a protein called DRD4 (Dopamine Receptor-D4 protein). DRD4 is a protein-receptor for the neurotransmitter dopamine, the chemical agent intimately associated with reward centers in the brains of animals. An unusual variant of this same dopamine receptor gene, a genetic mutation named DRD4-7R and often called by its informal moniker, the "novelty-seeking gene," is found in about 20 percent of humans worldwide. It appears that inheriting this mutant gene makes people more likely to take risks, explore new ideas and places, and seek multiple relationships and sexual partners. Along with other factors, it seems to induce these people to actively embrace movement and welcome change and adventure[32]. Presumably, this "emigration mutation" or something like it in the hominan genome, must have first appeared before *Homo erectus* began its perambulations, and was then inherited by successor species. These immense planetary emigrations, undertaken by a cabal of bipedal animals originating in East Africa, must evidently be fueled by a deeply embedded curiosity and an irresistible instinct for exploration imprinted into their hominan brains. Coincidentally, these movements were hugely assisted by the ongoing Pleistocene glaciation, when sea levels could fall almost 400 feet during glacial peaks, creating land bridges between continents for these creatures to cross.

---

32 This powerful emigratory impulse among humans can even be observed in their young. Not long after Mac departed their planet, hordes of underage children left their homes in Central and South America and traveled, unaccompanied by adults, to North America, crossing the Mexican border into the USA as emigrants. Some came from as far as 2,500 miles away. Many were fleeing extreme violence and oppression in their own societies. It was estimated that more than 50,000 minors fled to the United States in the brief span of just 9 months in 64 AP.

The Earth's ice ages are related to astronomical cycles caused by periodic drifts in the planet's rotational and revolutionary rhythms. For example, one such periodicity is Earth's axial precession, which refers to the cyclical wobble in the orientation of its axis of rotation—much like the wobbling of a spinning top—tracing out a pair of imaginary cones joined by their tips at the planet's center. The axial precession movement completes one full cycle every 25,772 years. This, and other astronomical periodicities, both longer and shorter in duration, combine to produce Earth's ice ages. There have been five major ice ages in my host planet's geologic history. The first one, the Huronian glaciation, occurred 2.4 billion years ago. The current ice age, called the Pleistocene glaciation, which began just 2.6 million years ago in the Pleistocene Epoch, continues to wax and wane regularly, right up to the present moment. Since the beginning of the Pleistocene glaciation, there have been more than ten successive glacial and interglacial cycles within that major glaciation so far, where cooling and advance of ice sheets across the planet would be followed some tens of thousands of years later by warming and their melting away, to be succeeded again by cooling and a new advance of the ice sheets. The Earth is currently in a balmy interglacial period that began with the Holocene Epoch around 11,700 BP and continuing to the present time.

It is indeed extraordinary to consider that in less than 12,000 years of the Holocene so far, Earth has witnessed the exponential trajectory of a single species, *Homo sapiens*, from preliterate hunter-gatherer to veritable atom-smasher, brain-surgeon, and space-traveler. Even more astonishing is that in just the last 100 years of a 200,000 year history as a species, humans went from riding horse-and-buggy to landing people on their Moon.

Homo erectus, like its fabulous future relative, *Homo sapiens*, was an inveterate traveler, dispersing its kind throughout the Old World. Besides migrating within Africa itself and populating that continent from their original home in the Rift Valley, the species emigrated out of Africa in the Early Pleistocene to as far away as Georgia in the Caucasus; Pakistan, India and Sri Lanka in South Asia; and to China, southeast Asia, Vietnam and Indonesia in the Far East. Some people have even suggested that these animals built rafts to cross bodies of water. Just a million years ago they were an immensely successful species on their planet, the dominant one around. Regrettably for them, their dominance and expansion did not last. Unfavorable climatic changes and conflict with other competing hominan species ensured their eventual downfall. *Homo erectus* went on to decline after peaking globally one million years ago, and the bulk of them were gone by 143,000 BP. A few rump populations lingered on terminally in the Indonesian archipelago until about 75,000 BP, when they too finally died out.

The extinction of all known hominans that ever inhabited Earth, with the sole exception of *Homo sapiens*, is a significant historical fact. As already noted, many individual species of *Homo* once walked my host planet. Those included *H. habilis*, *H. rudolfensis*, *H. erectus/ergaster*, *H. antecessor*, *H. heidelbergensis*, *H. neanderthalensis*, *H. sapiens*, and *H. floresiensis*, among other hominan species not mentioned here in this list. None live today to tell their tale except for *H. sapiens*. Where on earth did they all go? Some vanished because they could not adapt to changing environmental conditions. Others were systematically dispatched by fellow hominan species living alongside them—the winners more warlike and aggressive, more versatile and resourceful, than the losers. There was a time in history when the futures for these creatures seemed so promising, yet a goal they would never achieve, leaving only fossils behind as mute testimony to their advent on Earth. When *H. neanderthalensis* had the misfortune to encounter *H. sapiens* in Europe as the Pleistocene Epoch was drawing to a close, neanderthals rapidly disappeared from Earth in less than 10,000 years of that fateful meeting. Since neanderthals were a different species, their eradication was not technically genocide, though the process itself was similar to extensive genocides committed today by humans all across their planet.

Humans certainly had one insuperable advantage over all other competitors, and that was their ability to talk. Though some hominan species did indeed develop the aptitude for rudimentary speech limited to a few dozen words, humans alone had fully evolved the neural mechanisms and a specialized larynx for the fluent production of speech using a plethora of words. With the emergence of full behavioral modernity in *Homo sapiens* by the Late Old Stone Age and their simultaneous adoption of theory-of-mind, this successful appearance of a truly astonishing ability to speak allowed these humans to instantly broadcast and transfer their thoughts to each other effortlessly. By this very elegant mechanism, one individual could now transcendentally influence the behavior of another. It was indeed direct thought transference in the most literal sense, using language as the magic transmission vehicle. This extraordinary tool permitted individual humans to collaborate and function as a virtual super-organism and thus quite easily outcompete and dominate other hominan species that did not possess this unique ability like they did. Though these others were also conscious and self-aware, they could not transfer their awareness to each other as readily as humans could.

That made all the difference.

Mauer today is a village in southwestern Germany's Rhine-Neckar Valley, not far from the city of Heidelberg in the present German state of Baden-Wurttemberg. A solitary fossilized mandible, or lower jaw, of their ancestor *Homo heidelbergensis* was unearthed here by modern humans in 43 BP. It was discovered by a worker in a Mauer sand quarry. Among other fossils found with the Mauer jaw at the same location were fossilized remains of several extinct mammals that had lived there about 500,000 years ago, thus helping to fix a date for the hominan fossil itself.

The Mauer jaw is thick and broad; it lacks a chin. The teeth are unusually small for such a massive mandible. The jaw is elongated from front to back, indicating the individual who wore it in life had a projecting lower face. Since discovery of the Mauer jaw, fossils of *H. heidelbergensis* have turned up throughout the Old World, from tropical to temperate regions. Males of this species averaged 5 feet 8 inches in height, weighing about 150 pounds. Females were more like 5 feet 2 inches tall and weighed about 120 pounds. As these hominans migrated to colder climates, their bodies became more compact, thereby reducing overall skin surface area. This bent of body was more efficient at conserving heat than the tall thin body type associated with *Homo erectus*. The latter exposed more surface area proportional to body mass and was therefore more efficient for cooling off in a hot and dryer tropical environment.

As already noted in this narrative, the aboriginal East African stock of *H. heidelbergensis* separated into two cohorts, one group leaving Africa and the other remaining on that continent. The former evolved into neanderthals in Eurasia, the latter into humans in East Africa. Both sets of descendants from *H. heidelbergensis*—neanderthals and humans—appeared at the same time, around 200,000 BP, but on different continents.

The first cohort of *H. heidelbergensis* that left Africa dispersed widely across the Old World, colonizing Europe and parts of southern and western Asia, including China, India, and Indochina. These newer hominans from Africa encountered the far more ancient *H. erectus* populations already settled in Eurasia for more than a million years before them. These new Africans, upon meeting the old Eurasians, proceeded to unleash the most vicious attacks against the natives ever inflicted during the lethal hominan wars that engulfed their planet in the Pleistocene Epoch.

One phalanx of *H. heidelbergensis* migrating east into China settled around Dali some quarter million years ago. Dali, a site of paleoanthropological excavations by contemporary humans, is near the village of Jiefang in Shaanxi province of the modern People's Republic of China. Dali is best known for the discovery in 28 AP of a well-preserved 209,000 year old fossilized skull of *H. heidelbergensis*. The skull sports a mixture of both older and newer hominan features. It is low and long with a rounded occipital or back end, unlike the broad-based *H. erectus*, or the top-wide *H. sapiens* skull. The face of the Dali fossil is topped by massive brow ridges.

Mac traveled to the now famous Dali site back in 224,887

BP, for a peek at this illustrious hominan, the putative direct predecessor of both *H. sapiens* and *H. neanderthalensis*. This particular population of *H. heidelbergensis* that Mac visited in China, who had only recently colonized the area around Dali, were relentlessly waging an all-out war of extermination against the native *H. erectus* population peaceably living in the region for more than 500,000 years before the interlopers arrived.

H. erectus had once very successfully populated and flourished in the Old World for almost a million years before the new hominans out of Africa overran and destroyed their communities, driving them to the fringes of their range in Indonesia where they ignominiously died out in the Middle Pleistocene. *H. erectus* hunted smaller animals and was an active scavenger of carrion. Their diet included large portions of vegetable matter such as nuts, seeds, roots and tubers. In contrast, *H. heidelbergensis* was primarily carnivorous, actively stalking and hunting large mammals such as camels, horses, rhinos, and elephants in organized and efficient hunting groups. *H. erectus* was now also on their menu.

The word "cannibal" to designate humans who consume other humans for food, comes from the Spanish *Canibales*, a name given to the Carib people, a West Indian tribe once known to actively practice cannibalism—the Caribbean itself was in fact named after them. Cannibalism is common among hominans. Though one species of hominans eating the flesh of another hominan species is strictly speaking not cannibalism, it certainly does come awfully close. Modern humans today are known to eat other living hominids like chimpanzees and gorillas. In fact, this awful practice is now so common in Africa where these two nonhuman great apes naturally live, that it is very likely these apes may be exterminated rather soon. Classical cannibalism however, also known as Anthropophagy, refers exclusively to the consumption of human flesh by other humans.

Cannibalism in its pristine form has been practiced by *Homo sapiens* throughout their planet, and was once a widespread custom among them going way back into human prehistory. In Britain for instance, at the end of the last Ice Age, humans were using butchering techniques to strip flesh from the bones of men, women and children, processing the flesh of these slaughtered humans for food with the same expertise they used to process the flesh of other animals. Cannibalism prevailed well into modern times in parts of West and Central Africa, Fiji, New Guinea, Australia, New Zealand, Polynesia, Sumatra, and among certain tribes in North and South America. In some areas of the Pacific, human flesh was considered delectable eating, superior to other animal flesh, and called Long Pig. The Maoris of New Zealand often cut up dead bodies after a battle and feasted on the flesh. The Batak of Sumatra are reported to have sold human flesh in public markets before the arrival of the Dutch to Indonesia, who subsequently stopped the practice.

Now back to Dali during the Pleistocene. As Mac quietly surveyed the area, carefully examining the surroundings, a loud and clamorous commotion became unmistakably evident. A superbly coordinated hunting band of about a dozen young *H. heidelbergensis* males and females had just ensnared two fleeing tribes of *H. erectus* in a narrow ravine with no visible outlet. Trembling uncontrollably from fear and terror, and huddled at the end of this fatal cul-de-sac as their brutal killers approached them menacingly brandishing weapons, the terrified community of *H. erectus* suddenly collapsed to the ground atop their children in one enormous heap, trying desperately to protect their young from the anticipated assault by physically shielding their offspring with their own bare and exposed bodies. Whether they did this consciously or by instinct was difficult to tell, but the deeply rooted impulse of all Earth-based creatures to preserve and pass on their genes was clearly on display here.

Their attackers, now howling in unison, bounded up to their paralyzed prey, wielding clubs and spears. They bashed their victims' heads with the clubs—mercifully stunning them unconscious—while driving long spears through their hearts until their prey were all dead. Freshly coagulated blood soaked the killing field and made walking between dead bodies quite tricky because of the slipperiness. The gruesome carnage was meticulous and complete. The now slaughtered *H. erectus* had offered no resistance. It is not hard to speculate from this scene wherefrom humans get their deadliness.

The victorious *H. heidelbergensis* soon began butchering their dead victims, stripping the delicious flesh off the bones, and cutting out internal organs for consumption as well. A pack of clamoring *H. heidelbergensis* groupies had now entered the bloody scene and were busily assisting the elite hunters with the grisly exercise of carving the dead bodies now in progress. One indefatigable female in particular, a twenty-something with red hair and blind in her right eye now scarred where her eyeball had been, was especially skillful at cracking skulls with a heavy stone cudgel and expertly extracting the brain from the open cranial cavity. Brains were much prized as food because of their high nutrient and energy content, even more so than bone marrow which was always a delicacy for these hominans.

Like *Homo erectus* and most other species of hominans, *Homo sapiens* also speciated in East Africa. This was about 200,000 years ago. They too dispersed rapidly from their point of origin in the Great Rift Valley and colonized their natal continent first, before moving out into the larger world beyond. By 150,000 BP, humans had spread throughout Africa. Contemporary studies examining African genetic diversity among modern humans living on that continent today, point to the !Kung of the Kalahari in southern Africa as belonging to one of the oldest cadres of *H. sapiens* to have emigrated away from their cradle in East Africa. I do believe the honorable Master T'yu and the noble Itu-Kan made that crucial journey.

About 130,000 BP, a cohort of *Homo sapiens* then living in East Africa and kin to the Itu-Kan of Lake Kivu, elected to emigrate north along the Nile Valley watershed and follow the great river downstream like many of their ancestors had done before them. They were looking for new habitats and food sources, thereby seeking to avoid the adverse environmental conditions now mounting in the land they had always called home. Changing climate over the recent centuries with unreliable monsoon rains and aridity in the region, had degraded their ancestral homeland and reduced its yield to a bare minimum. The once predictable rains were shifting in a northerly direction, year after year, causing regional streams and rivers to dry out and vegetation to retreat northward. This pattern of desiccation had been going on for many generations now, until finally, concerned groups of these people made the difficult decision to leave their homeland and seek fresh pastures elsewhere.

These hardy bands of anatomically modern humans, tracing the Nile River downstream to the Mediterranean Sea, headed north across the Sahara over a swath of land known to them as Edon in those days. Edon, straddling the Nile, lush and green with vegetation then, was a ribbon of land snaking up across the lonely Sahara and heading toward the Levant, that narrow coastal strip marking the eastern Mediterranean littoral plain. But unlike the great success scored by *Homo erectus* 1.8 million years ago, this first emigration out of Africa by *Homo sapiens* failed disastrously. Those humans who made it to the Levant died out by 90,000 BP. Unluckily for them, their planet was passing through a harsh period of climate change, transforming the Levant and North Africa into extreme desert and killing this first exodus of humans to come out of the mother continent.

Then, beginning again around 80,000 BP, approximately fifty millennia after that earlier failed attempt at transcontinental emigration, new groups of *Homo sapiens* set out north once more, by first following the White Nile downstream as their unsuccessful predecessors had done before. These new emigrants, however, soon diverted to a different course. This second wave of humans left the waterway about where the modern city of Malakal is in contemporary South Sudan, and veered east across what is now Ethiopia, to Djibouti in the Horn of Africa. They then crossed the waters of the Red Sea at its confluence with the Gulf of Aden, thus entering Yemen in the Arabian Peninsula. This momentous crossing of the southern mouth of the Red Sea by humans occurred circa 75,000 BP. That pivotal crossing point, now called Bab-el-Mandeb or Gate of Scars, is about 12 miles wide today. At the time of the successful second exodus, that crossing was much narrower, as sea levels averaged 225 feet less than they do today because of the prevailing ice-age conditions on Earth at that time. Even though the strait was never completely free of water, scattered islands that could be reached by simple rafts became exposed by the sunken water level. Once they had crossed the Red Sea into Arabia, these intrepid humans began rapidly streaming across their planet.

These emigrating people split into two groups after that Red Sea crossing. One group kept due south and closely hewed to the northern coastline of the Indian Ocean, spreading along the southern border of the Arabian Peninsula through southwest Asia, Iran and Afghanistan, into the Indian subcontinent. The second group proceeded due north from Arabia, straight into Eurasia. Along the way, this second group split into three branches. One branch, the so-called Cro-Magnons, radiated west into Europe, eventually encountering and replacing the neanderthals who had been living there successfully for more than 150,000 years—neanderthals became extinct by 35,000 BP. The second branch made a complete U-turn after reaching Central Asia, moving south again into India. The third branch radiated eastward into China after hitting Central Asia, and then kept trekking south along the Pacific coastline of that enormous continent, into southeast Asia and Indonesia, eventually reaching Australia by crossing the Timor Sea circa 43,000 B.P. Humans had become successful seafarers by then. Way later, starting around 162 BP, a far larger cohort of *Homo sapiens* emigrated directly to Australia from Europe, after their ability to move around the planet was hugely enhanced by the extraordinary transportation technology available to humans by then. This later emigration simply swamped the earlier one, the new immigrants from Europe becoming the dominant human population in Australia today.

Occupation of the Americas occurred in two waves more

than 16,000 years apart. Around 17,000 BP, as the ice sheets advanced and sea levels fell, the first wave of emigrants, traveling eastward, arrived from northeast Asia to the Americas, entering the New World from Siberia and reaching Alaska by crossing what is today the Bering strait; at the time of that crossing, an exposed land bridge about a thousand miles wide connected Siberia to the western coast of Alaska. Having now successfully breached the New World, these emigrants then continued trekking southward and eventually reached Tierra del Fuego in the southern tip of South America by 11,000 BP, just as the Holocene Epoch was dawning.

The second, and much more massive wave of emigration to the Americas arrived directly across the Atlantic from Europe and Africa. It began as a trickle barely five hundred years ago in 497 BP, and then rapidly turned into a veritable torrent. Both the Africans and the Europeans sailed west across the Atlantic Ocean to reach the Americas. A remarkable maritime technology to move large groups of people across vast oceans allowed this huge emigration of humans from the Old World to the new one to proceed apace. The Europeans in this new wave came voluntarily, seeking greener pastures far away from a feudal and oppressive Europe. A spasm of genocide through war and pestilence followed their arrival in the two Americas. This tragedy almost wiped out the indigenous Native American population that had arrived there in the first emigration, and had already been living in the New World for many thousands of years. Overall estimates of the number of Native Americans who died in this encounter differ widely, ranging all the way from 3 million to 300 million fatalities. A reasonable figure may be 60 million or so dead natives, in the first 200 years of European emigration to the Americas.

The Africans in this massive emigration from the Old World were brought involuntarily as slaves to work for European settlers on their numerous American plantations, growing sugarcane and cotton for the lucrative European market. These Africans were systematically abducted from their homelands and then processed and shipped by the millions to the Americas not long after the Europeans arrived in the New World. Acquired in massive numbers by trade or capture, mainly along the Atlantic coast of West Africa, these imprisoned slaves were tightly packed into the poorly ventilated holds of large oceangoing vessels called "slavers," and transshipped across the Atlantic Ocean to the Americas. Almost a third of these captive African emigrants died during that deadly voyage, now memorably called the Middle Passage. Those dead and dying among this human cargo were tossed into the ocean to feed the fishes.

Slavery is the physical ownership and control of humans by other humans. It is a system under which people are treated as property, to be bought and sold for their uncompensated labor and other services. The word "slave" is derived from the Latin *Slavus*, later modified to Slav, the name given to an ethno-linguistic group of people inhabiting much of Eastern Europe and adjoining parts of Asia. Many Slavs were captured and then enslaved by invaders during the Early Middle Ages, hence "slave" to describe people forced into such servitude. The African slaves brought to the Americas by the Europeans were compelled to work endlessly long and brutal hours for their owners, in exchange for just basic food, clothing, and shelter. Their reproduction was carefully managed by their owners, and their offspring were considered slaves from birth. Slaves were shorn of all their natural freedoms and disallowed fundamental human rights.

Slavery itself has been a widespread custom among humans, practiced by diverse groups of people of all colors and sizes, ever since these hominans began settling down as agriculturalists during the early Holocene. Slavery as an organized practice did not exist when humans were exclusively hunters and gatherers. Ancient Persia, back in 2,500 BP, was the first human society on Earth to actually ban slavery by passing a law against it. In more modern times, slavery was first officially outlawed in England in 178 BP, and has since become illegal throughout my host planet, though it continues to thrive in modified and surreptitious forms in many poorer countries, especially in parts of Asia and Africa. Traditional slavery is still openly practiced in the modern African country of Mauritania, although it is not the only nation on Earth to do this. The number of salves in Mauritania was recently pegged around 600,000 men, women and children, or 20% from a nationwide population of 3,069,000.

Servants, a sanitized form of slaves, are widely used in South Asia. They may constitute almost 15% of the entire human population in this complex and densely populated region of my host planet. The South Asian countries of India, Pakistan, Bangladesh, Nepal, and Sri Lanka, with a combined population of 1.62 billion people packed into an area just half the size of the continental United States, probably has close to 250 million servants. Most servants are treated with barely more consideration than traditional slaves, though servants are not technically "owned" by their masters and have the option to leave. Many of them are mere children. Servants are forced to provide unending hours of personal and household services to their employers for hardly anything more than food, clothing, shelter, and possibly a tiny monetary allowance. These Asian countries export millions of these servants abroad, especially to the Arab Middle East, where many are egregiously exploited and abused by their alien masters, even tortured and killed in some cases, or publicly beheaded.

An unusual population of perpetually emigrating humans who have forever engaged and fascinated the imagination of people throughout their planet for many centuries, are those exotic and colorful folk called Gypsies. This group of humans, though unconfirmed, do indeed appear to be rather well-endowed with a high allele frequency of the mutant "emigratory" gene speculated on earlier. The nomadic or emigratory instinct in humans could be a holdover from their ancestral hunter-gatherer origins. Gypsies today are a widely dispersed group of people. They originated from an ancestral population of modern *Homo sapiens* in the Punjab region of northwestern India. Starting about 1,500 years ago, they emigrated out of India because of discrimination and oppression by their neighbors. Using the modern science of genomics, this emigration of gypsy people has been recently retraced back to their Indian homeland, circa 1,450 BP. One stream of these gypsy emigrants, calling themselves Dom, moved into Central Asia, Turkey, the Middle East, and North Africa; they number about 2 million people. A much larger second group, called Roma, dispersed widely into Eastern and Western Europe, and much later, to the Americas; they number close to 12 million individuals.

Huge planetary movements of humans in response to resource needs and security considerations continue to accelerate and spread around the globe. Millions of people emigrate every week across formal and informal borders into what is new territory for them. In contrast to today's copious global flow of emigrants, early human emigrations unfolded very gradually and deliberately, inching slowly over lengthy periods of time. In those earlier emigrations, movement across formidable land barriers and bodies of water was glacially slow and could take many generations to consummate. Those protracted journeys were fraught with immense danger and peril. The pilgrim's progress was tardy and sporadic, accomplished either on foot or on the back of pack animals. Unlike today's emigrations, those early ones demanded great sacrifice and forbearance to complete.

These circumstances would change dramatically with the introduction of mechanized travel following invention of the steam engine hardly 300 years ago. Fifty years after its creation, steam-powered vessels were navigating waterways, and fifty years after that, the steam locomotive made its appearance on land. Barely another fifty years passed before the internal combustion engine was invented in 90 BP, ushering in the automobile age. Not much later, humans were taking to the air with the first airplane flown in 47 BP by two brothers, Orville and Wilbur Wright of America. Remarkably, in the span of just 250 years, these humans zoomed from riding on camels to flying in airplanes.

These lightning fast developments in human transportation technology have enormously accelerated the mass movement of people around their planet. With chemical rocket propulsion now, these humans have launched themselves into extraterrestrial space, and some of them even hope to emigrate away from their home planet one day. To consummate this grand space odyssey, even more efficient ways of travel are being developed and tested by these hominans. Ion drives, magnetic sails, and stellar-wind powered sails, are even now being researched and deployed for eventual use by humans on those long interstellar journeys. Warp drives for faster-than-light travel by manipulating the very structure and fabric of spacetime itself have been speculated about by this adventuresome species. By contracting spacetime in front of them and expanding it behind, they expect to travel over vast distances pronto. If this species could only survive just long enough without imploding into extinction, either on their own or due to factors they cannot control, then they would surely be using wormholes to explore this Universe in good time, just as we are accustomed to doing today on Galymon.

Without a doubt, the irrepressible urge to emigrate is deeply embedded in the genetic code and behavioral repertoire of humans. It is the fountainhead of their being.

A calamitous geologic event that took place about 74,000 years ago brought humans to the brink of extinction. That monumental affair, called the Toba Supereruption, was the biggest volcanic eruption ever to occur on my host planet in the last two million years of its history. Right about the time the Toba supervolcano erupted, groups of humans were beginning to leave Africa across the Bab-el-Mandeb into Arabia, heading further and further away from the land of their origin.

The Toba Event took place in what is now Lake Toba, the largest active volcanic caldera to be found anywhere on Earth today. Lake Toba lies just 2° N of the equator, in the great big Indonesian island of Sumatra. When that supervolcanic eruption at Toba took place, an enormous mass of ash, magma and gas was very rapidly spewed into Earth's atmosphere from the planet's molten interior. The magnitude of this discharge was the equivalent of more than 650 cubic miles of dense rock being vaporized and vented as volatile volcanic products into the air.

The Earth's atmosphere is a layer of gases surrounding the planet and retained in place by gravity. The troposphere, the lowest portion of the atmosphere, begins at the planet's surface and extends straight upward to an altitude of about 10 miles at the equator and five miles at the poles. Most of the detritus from the deadly Toba explosion was deposited into the lower troposphere. The troposphere contains about 80% of the atmosphere's mass and 99% of its water vapor. The stratosphere comes next; it lies just above the planet's troposphere and continues upward for another 32 miles. That is succeeded by the mesosphere for an additional 52 miles. The thermosphere then follows to a depth of 300 to 600 miles. The exosphere finally tops out the atmosphere and merges imperceptibly into outer space.

So immense and powerful was the explosion at Toba that even though it took place in Indonesia, it deposited a layer of volcanic ash averaging six inches deep over the entire land area of South and South-East Asia, the Middle East, and East Africa. In some areas of South Asia, the volcanic ash from Toba lay three to fifteen feet thick. A blanket of ash descended on portions of the Indian and Pacific Oceans, eerily staining those waters a hideous gray.

This was by far the most perilous season *Homo sapiens* as a species had yet encountered since they first emerged in East Africa 200,000 years ago. Toba spewed forth its lethal emanations for weeks on end, poisoning all Earth and plunging the planet into disaster, pummeling its existing lifeforms with toxic fumes and acid rain.

The huge volume of debris dispersed into the lower atmosphere by that gargantuan volcanic eruption profoundly
impacted planet Earth's always impressionable climate.
Though the decrease in visibility directly related to suspended
volcanic ash and dust particles was relatively short-lived and
lasted less than six months, much longer-term planetary cooling
was initiated by volcanic sulfur[33] emissions. These emissions
produced a highly reflective sulfur-dioxide haze that remained
suspended in the Earth's upper atmosphere for many years,
reflecting solar radiation back into space. This cooling effect
plunged the planet into a decade-long volcanic winter. Summer
temperatures fell by greater than 50°F for more than six years
in a row. A thousand year mini ice-age descended upon the
bruised and besieged planet. Vegetation perished globally from
both the bitter cold and torrents of highly concentrated acid
rain. The Earth's human population was reduced from a peak
of about 150,000 individuals just before the eruption, to fewer
than 15,000 after the catastrophe. Nine out of every ten humans perished in the aftermath of Toba. During the height of
this decimation, fewer than 2,000 breeding human females remained on their entire planet.

The impact of Toba was simply breathtaking. Throughout an
arc then populated by these humans, extending up from Africa to
the northwestern shores of the Indian Ocean, more than ninety percent of all humans perished. Incredibly it seems, the species clung
on, though just barely, and survived this near fatal bottleneck in

---

33 Elemental sulfur is commonly associated with volcanoes. During an eruption, huge quantities of sulfur are expelled—along with other volcanic material—from the inferno's boiling cauldron. Elemental sulfur is also called
brimstone, an ancient name for this substance. Much of the sulfur becomes
oxidized to gaseous sulfur oxides that diffuse into the atmosphere, only to fall
back to Earth later as toxic acid rain.

its evolutionary history. That was the closest humans ever came to facing extinction until the present time. Humans were indeed lucky to survive that great catastrophe known today as Toba. During their second and successful emigration out of Africa when the explosion actually took place, they called it *Nakba,* meaning "Catastrophe" in the local dialect these humans were using at that time. This ancient word nakba survives in the Arabic language spoken today in that region of the world, and retains the same dreadful meaning—catastrophe.

These random catastrophic events are extremely difficult to predict and virtually impossible to anticipate. They occur with little or no prior warning and could inflict unimaginable violence on their hapless targets. They may happen at this very instant, or in time still later to come. It is not easy for modern humans, now almost 75,000 years in the future, to precisely reconstruct Toba's extensive impact on their species. Yet one conclusion is unmistakable—the close genetic similarity between people living anywhere on their planet today indicates a severe population implosion and an acute genetic bottleneck that this species encountered around the time of that supervolcanic eruption. All modern humans seem to have descended from a tiny ancestral population that survived the horrible Toba catastrophe, thus accounting for the close genetic similarity between all humans living on Earth today.

The monster volcano finally put paid to the remnants of *Homo erectus* still clinging to dear life on the few Indonesian islands they now occupied at the end of their remarkable odyssey on Earth. These creatures had once reigned as the dominant species on their planet, being the first in their genus to colonize much of the Old World. They were forced to participate in the Great Hominan Wars of the Pleistocene, and decisively lost that bloody struggle. The Toba explosion now permanently closed the book on their remarkable adventure. Doubtless, if Toba had not eliminated them, their slick human cousins would have performed that task with aplomb when they reached the redoubts of those remaining stragglers in Indonesia. Ironically, the first known fossils of the species *Homo erectus* ever discovered on Earth by modern humans was a cranial vault, a thighbone, and a few teeth belonging to an individual who once lived on these very same Indonesian islands, in Java to be exact. Dubbed Java Man, this fossil is now thought to be between 1,000,000 years to 700,000 years old. It was discovered in 59 BP on the banks of the Solo River in East Java by the Dutch geologist and paleoanthropologist, Eugène Dubois, about 120 years ago now. Dubois called the species he discovered in Java *Pithecanthropus erectus*, meaning "erect ape-man." His original name for this hominan was later reclassified to *Homo erectus*. Java Man had a cranial capacity of about 55 cubic inches or 900 cubic centimeters, a bit smaller than later appearing specimens of *Homo erectus*—and a habitually erect posture as indicated by the thighbone. The teeth were essentially humanlike. The particular creature represented by the fossils Dubois found stood about 5 feet 8 inches tall.

Enormous supervolcanic calderas are widely scattered on the surface of my host planet. These gigantic volcanoes erupt periodically, discharging hundreds of cubic miles of vaporized volcanic material into the air, causing catastrophic destruction to huge areas of the planet, and the extinction of large chunks of its biosphere. After the acute effects have subsided, major climatic disruption, planetary cooling, and acid rain, can prolong the misery for decades to come. On the land surface of their planet today, humans have identified six gargantuan calderas as possible sites for supervolcanic eruptions in the future. One, of course, is Toba in Indonesia; three are in the United States of America, one in Japan, and one in New Zealand. The supervolcano sitting in Yellowstone National Park in the state of Wyoming in America, is the one most immediately at risk for eruption among the six. The Yellowstone caldera measures about 45 miles in length and 34 miles wide. The bulk of Yellowstone Park, a popular tourist spot, is located inside this caldera. The caldera hosts many hot springs, the most famous being Old Faithful, a hot geyser that erupts almost like clockwork every 91 minutes. The floor of the caldera itself has risen about two feet in the last 90 years due to magma accumulation under it. This supervolcano erupts approximately every 600,000 years. The last eruption was 640,000 years ago, causing more than 240 cubic miles of volcanic material to be spewed as ash and larva into the atmosphere. No humans were present on Earth at that time to observe the fireworks.

Mac visited Indonesia at the time of the Toba Event. The few remaining bands of *Homo erectus* living in the area before the eruption were scattered in small isolated populations tucked around that immense archipelago. These semi-sapient beings who emerged around 2 million years ago, were the first hominans ever to leave Africa and colonize the Old World. They had even shared their planet with *Homo sapiens*. Now they were close to being gone forever. Though most of these creatures had disappeared from Earth by 143,000 BP, a smattering had stoutly persisted, hidden on verdant islands in Indonesia, much like orangutans are today. These doomed outliers were now finally earmarked for extinction. Nature can often be unfeeling and inscrutable in its ways. From supernovas to supervolcanoes, from black holes to the Black Death[34], nature is endlessly at work refining the cosmos.

Mac made landfall in northern Sumatra, only a few dozen miles from the venomous volcano. It was late evening in the middle of September 74,362 BP, just a few days short of the southward equinox. Something ominous hung in the air. A pod of local *Homo erectus* made up of two adult males, four adult females of which two were pregnant and one clutching an infant, and three juveniles, were gathered by the mouth of a shallow cave along a rocky hillside, readying themselves to retire for the night. Dusk was quickly lengthening into darkness around them. This weary band of ten individuals seemed anxious and disjointed as Mac looked on very concerned about their fast approaching doom.

Sexual dimorphism was rather pronounced in this species. Adult males were significantly larger than the females. Compared to their human cousins, these *H. erectus* females had narrower hips and flatter buttocks, looking almost boyish in profile. They appeared this way because their pelvic outlet was narrower and more apelike in structure than in humans, corresponding to the smaller head size[35] of *H. erectus* newborns. Still

---

34 The Black Death, by all accounts one of the most devastating disease pandemics in human history, was responsible for the deaths of up to 200 million people during its spread from Central Asia to Europe. It peaked in Europe for two horrible years from 602 BP to 600 BP. Plague, the disease responsible for the Black Death, is caused by the bacterium *Yersinia pestis*.

35 Adult *Homo erectus* had an average brain size of 60 cubic inches (about 1000 cubic centimeters) compared to 90 cubic inches (1,500 cubic centimeters) for modern *Homo sapiens*.

another apelike feature quite obvious in these creatures was the absence of prominent breast tissue in females, except for large nipples.

These ancient hominans were naked—they wore no clothing. They were covered with moderate amounts of reddish-brown body hair. The males were somewhat more hirsute than females and sported scraggly red facial hair, though the females themselves were quite hairy too. Their lips were prominent and everted in both genders, tinted a mottled bluish-black. Their skin was chocolate brown in color. *H. erectus* males generally ranged from over five and a half to nearly six feet tall, and weighed about 140 pounds. Females were closer to five feet in height and tipped the scales at around 100 pounds. Both males and females were skinnier and more athletically built than their corresponding human counterparts. Females among these hominans were accustomed to hunting alongside males.

Below the neck, except for the female breast and pelvic structures as noted, *H. erectus* was anatomically much like *H. sapiens*. Their arms and legs were shaped and proportioned like those of humans, giving them the ability to walk and run on two limbs as efficiently as their human relatives, making them excellent long-distance runners. Their heads, however, looked quite different. Their brains were about a third smaller than those of humans. The skull was flat in profile with little forehead visible. A ridge of bone ran front to back along the top of the skull for attachment of powerful jaw muscles. They had very thick skull bones with heavy brow ridges framing flat noses with flared nostrils. The braincase was narrow, receding backward to an elongated occipital pole. The palate was large, the jaw massive, with no chin. Their dentition was essentially human with some apelike features such as large, partially overlapping canines. The neck muscles were thick and well developed in both males and females.

The gaggle of *H. erectus*, gathered that evening by the mouth of their cave, were furiously gesturing and ululating to each other. Mac looked on in consternation, knowing what was soon about to happen. These doomed creatures had repeatedly felt strange sporadic tremors rattling the ground under their feet all afternoon, and were naturally very anxious and alarmed at this unusual development.

H. erectus had barely evolved the mechanisms for speech and therefore could only communicate vocally among themselves with an assortment of grunts and snorts, and a rare word or two thrown in. Consistent with the frontal compression and the narrowness of their upper skulls—even though set on a broad base—the underlying frontal and temporal lobes of their brain were relatively less developed. Since these regions of the cerebral cortex are fundamental to fluent speech functions, vocabulary and symbolic language had hardly yet appeared in *Homo erectus*. Their larynx had certainly been evolving toward more elaborate articulation of sounds, but the neuronal speech centers in their brain had barely begun to form—this adaptation would have to wait for their sister species, *H. sapiens*, to consummate. *H. erectus* used less than twenty separate words—in comparison, there are over 500,000 in the English language humans use today. Their words were almost all nouns such as *mada* (me), *yada* (you), *tada* (thing), *motu* (mother) and *otu* (child); they had no word for father. Just four verbs existed in their entire repertoire, one being *udo* (action). This verb meant voluntary action by the speaker to influence the outcome of an event.

Thus *"mada udo"* meant "me do (that)." *Udo* also had a noun form, *ud*, meaning "magic."

Two of the adult females were squatting and defecating to one side of a pathway. Suddenly, the darkening sky lit up with a surreal green glow and a series of ominous rumbles were heard coming from a westerly direction. The *H. erectus* group assembled in front of their homecave looked startled and obviously frightened. A piercing cry emanating from the throat of an adult male in the group, rent the air. Such warning signals, identifying danger, are common among cooperative primates. Within minutes, a hot sulfurous wind, gathering speed, whistled past our way. The now terrified hominans began to choke, descending into paroxysms of coughing. A gargantuan plume of volcanic gas trekked east into the troposphere, raining torrents of brimstone, pumice and ash onto the ground below. One by one, coughing and spluttering, the doomed hominans crawled and tumbled into their cave. They were all dead within the hour.

The Toba Event tragically ended the fabled planetary history of *Homo erectus*. But astonishingly, another species of hominan living in the same general area of this violent eruption survived the catastrophe and lived into relatively recent times—possibly even till the dawn of the Holocene. Remarkably, just as Java Man from the larger Indonesian island of Java was the first hominan fossil *(Homo erectus)* to be unearthed by modern humans back in 59 BP, this new creature nicknamed Hobbit was the last hominan to be uncovered by them before Mac left Earth—this one too in Indonesia. These Hobbit fossils were found in 53 AP on the smaller Indonesian island of Flores 112 years after the first hominan discovery in Java.

Just hardly a decade ago, in a limestone cave called Liang Bua (cool cave) in the lush Indonesian island of Flores approximately

1,750 miles due east of Toba, a joint Indonesian-Australian team of modern humans unearthed the fossilized remains of a diminutive hominan that had lived there at least until 17,000 years ago, if not into later times. They called this extraordinary creature *Homo floresiensis* with the moniker "Hobbit" after a tribe of dwarf humanoids in one of their popular children's fables. This hominan was only about three and a half feet tall when fully grown, roughly the same height as a four year old modern human child. Since the initial find on Flores, bits of scattered fossils representing at least 12 other individuals have been discovered at Liang Bua—the only site so far where *H. floresiensis* remains have been uncovered by modern humans. These fossils are dated between 95,000 years and 17,000 years old. Hobbits had small brains, relatively large teeth for their small size, no chins, receding foreheads, and forward-leaning shoulders. They had large feet and short legs. These creatures seemed to possess more "primitive" skeletal characteristics than did *H. erectus* or the other later appearing hominans.

Though diminutive in height, *H. floresiensis* was robustly built and capable of great physical endurance. These hominans were excellent hunters and feasted on a variety of animals. Adult males weighed nearly 70 pounds, all on a bristling frame of hard muscle and steely sinew. Females weighed about as much and were as tall as men, displaying little or no sexual dimorphism. Their favorite prey was the pygmy elephant *Stegodon florensis*—just three feet high at the shoulder and now extinct—which they enthusiastically hunted in well-organized teams. They also prized the flesh of Komodo dragons[36]

---

36 Komodo dragons often nip their victims with their teeth, introducing a toxic
     culture of deadly bacteria into the wound that would later kill the intended
     prey by sepsis or generalized blood-poisoning.

(*Varanus komodoensis*), a large and still surviving monitor lizard, some as long as 10 feet and weighing as much as 150 pounds. This unusual hominan had a small braincase about the size of a grapefruit that enclosed an elaborately convoluted brain averaging less than one-third of a modern human brain. The Hobbit brain was about the size and weight of an *Australopithecus* brain, far smaller in fact than any anticipated reduction of brain size for a corresponding reduction in body size that would be expected among hominans as a rule. Besides, the creature had a more primitive skeletal anatomy than any other latter-day hominan examined by modern humans so far. Yet, despite their small brains and presumably limited cognition, they made stone tools, hunted efficiently in cooperative groups, and may have used fire as well.

H. floresiensis could have reached the Indonesian islands from mainland southeast Asia during the last Pleistocene glaciation, the last ice age. That glaciation, which began about 110,000 BP, reduced sea levels and created land bridges from the Asian mainland to these islands. During the peak of that glaciation, a confluent landmass called Sundaland combined together Sumatra, Borneo, Java and some other islands of Indonesia, connecting them to the Malayan peninsula and mainland Asia. This gave the Hobbit a pathway to Indonesia. As the glaciers retreated, melting ice started flooding the ocean basin about 19,000 years ago, raising sea levels and breaking up Sundaland into the separate Indonesian islands humans recognize today, and confining those Hobbits to these islands. However, what remains puzzling and unexplained is how *H. floresiensis* reached Flores which was far east of Sundaland and always separated from that landmass by deep ocean. Were these Hobbits then seafarers as well? Still another mystery surrounding these creatures is how they got to southeast Asia from Africa. Stone tools dating back to 800,000 years have been found on the island of Flores. Did Hobbits make them? Did this hominan evolve locally from an earlier population of bigger-bodied *Homo erectus* through the classic process of island dwarfism—isolation on a small island with limited food resources and no predators—or did *H. floresiensis* represent a different and unique hominan lineage that emigrated independently from Africa to southeast Asia, just as its larger relative *H. erectus* did 1.8 million years ago?

When the Toba supervolcano erupted that fateful September evening more than 74,000 years ago, those Hobbits then dwelling in caves like Liang Bua in Flores and other distant places, amazingly survived the deadly fallout. Though the bulk of *H. floresiensis* living in southeast Asia perished alongside their larger *H. erectus* cousins in the Toba Event, a few plodded on for another 60,000 years on isolated island habitats in Indonesia. They then vanished from Earth at least 17,000 years ago if not later, after encountering *Homo sapiens* just as the Pleistocene Epoch was drawing to a close.

Besides cockroaches and microbes, humans may be the only other creature to have successfully invaded and occupied every imaginable habitat on their planet. Humans have convincingly established themselves as the dominant species throughout their world in just 200,000 years since their appearance in East Africa as the modern prototype. They are found all across the globe now. Their unique aptitude for speech and symbolic thought catalyzed an astonishing ability to manufacture and sustain environments physically and culturally conducive to them anywhere on Earth. In fact, humans were identified in every terrestrial habitat where Mac cared to look for them. They have even successfully carried their environment with them onto space stations in Earth orbit, away from their home planet itself.

This drive to metastasize and spread is deeply ingrained into the nature and character of *Homo sapiens*. It is the key to their success. The urge to occupy and populate territory far beyond their horizons, claiming those lands and resources permanently for themselves and their progeny, has always been irresistible to this species. The instinct to emigrate is indelibly branded into their DNA. This behavioral trait frequently causes conflict between various tribes of humans, as well as between humans and other species occupying the same real estate. The utter wantonness and brutality of these conflicts perpetrated by humans against other species, including their own, can be extremely distressing to any empathic extraterrestrial who may have witnessed them.

CHAPTER VIII:

SETTLEMENT

‍or most of their brief cosmic history, humans had been nomadic hunters and gatherers, clinging to the fragile and often unpredictable world they inhabited. This had always been the way of life for these creatures, a rigorous hunter-gatherer ethos bequeathed upon them by their ancestors. Hunting and gathering was the prevailing and customary lifestyle for these creatures, ever since *Homo habilis* emerged on my host planet almost two and a half million years ago in the Early Pleistocene Epoch. It was the rapid expansion and consolidation of this hunting instinct in *Homo* that marked this genus.

Individual humans sought to obtain food by stalking and hunting animals, fishing, scavenging, or foraging for edible plants, tubers, fruit, or insects. Upon securing provisions, these creatures often shared their bounty with other members of the group, developing reciprocal bonds and cooperative behavior among themselves. Their collegial hunting ethos greatly fostered these relationships—when hunting in groups they would rely on each other to ensure successful outcomes. It is important to note here that the whole line of hominans, beginning with *Homo habilis* and continuing right up to behaviorally modern *Homo sapiens*, had been hunters and gatherers for longer than 99 percent of their entire evolutionary history.

The appearance of cooperative behavior among primates probably dates back to an early common ancestor that lived more than 50 million years ago during the Eocene Epoch. It may seem at first blush that any development of cooperative behavior in animals must have been a slow and incremental process, only cautiously navigated by them step by step. Social or eusocial[37]evolution—and complex social structures in other species such as birds and bees—appear only gradually and by many small and tentative baby steps. Among mammals generally, solitary individuals first pair off as couples or live with a small group of their own offspring before including still other individuals into their orbit. It is from these initial units that eventually larger and much more complex societies emerge. Nevertheless, among primates in this case, the transition to cooperative behavior could have resulted much more rapidly. Approximately 52 million years ago in the Eocene, an early primate ancestor switched from being largely nocturnal to one that was active during the day. While an animal may prefer to be solitary and alone in the dark for reasons of anonymity and maximum stealth, a small primate, active during the daytime instead, would probably find safety in numbers by living in cooperative groups of its own kind. Cooperative behavior was likely born among these Eocene primates in this accelerated way.

---

37   Eusociality is the highest level of social organization in animals. It consists of overlapping generations within a society of adults where a single female, or a single caste of females produce the offspring—while castes of nonreproductive individuals cooperate in caring for the young.

The genus *Homo* as already noted, emerged from a group of gracile australopithecines about 2.4 million years ago in East Africa. Humans themselves separated out as a distinct species around 200,000 BP within that same region of Africa. As was characteristic for this group of animals, *Homo sapiens*, like their other hominan relatives, lived in small closely-knit bands or tribes of about a dozen to a score of related individuals sharing life together. These bands remained dynamically stable, with drifting of young reproductive females between groups. Human tribes functioned much like extended families—they looked out for each other and contributed to the common weal.

This keen reciprocal interest that humans showed in the welfare of each other, a bequeathal from their cooperative ancestors, would eventually lead to the vast and complex civilizations these hominans have successfully created for themselves today. The tribe itself was the first sovereign nation to appear in human history, even though its territory had no physical demarcation or boundary. It is relevant to mention here that even though the terms nation, country, and state are frequently used interchangeably by humans, there is an important difference. A state denotes a self-governing political entity and has the same meaning as a country; it is defined by physical territory within established borders. A nation on the other hand refers to a closely knit community of people who share a common culture. The label nation-state, therefore, refers to a nation that occupies a state or country. A nation of people can also inhabit several adjoining states or countries.

The term "hunter-gather" is used by modern humans to describe a specific kind of lifestyle that was followed by all peoples on their planet until agriculture was invented by them roughly 10,000 years ago in the early Holocene. In every hunter-gatherer syndicate, individual members were joined in close feeding and reproductive association with other members of the group. These groups were mobile in their predisposition and had no permanent home territory. They moved opportunistically from place to place, searching for food, water, shelter, and security. They were bound together by bonds of kinship forged by both family and familiarity, and reinforced by common aspirations and goals.

Though conventionally called hunter-gatherers, the earliest hominans lived mostly by scavenging carrion, and not primarily by hunting and killing large animals. For after all, they were only fragile primates not possessing any great strength or endurance. These early hominans quite advisedly avoided killing dangerously large animals themselves, and instead snacked on carcasses killed by other predators, or by consuming animals already dead from natural causes. No potential food source was allowed to go waste, including dead members of their own species. Living in diversified habitats permitted these animals to exploit and collect other kinds of food, such as marine and freshwater creatures, insects, birds' eggs, tubers, edible leaves, fruit, berries, and nuts. This allowed them access to a variety of foods, rather than merely scavenging for dead animals.

The australopithecine ancestors of hominans had only recently adopted bipedalism as their primary mode of locomotion, and were therefore still rather limited in their ability to use this form of mobility to actively pursue and hunt prey. Being only neophyte bipeds, they were naturally rather clumsy and heavy-footed in this operation. This limitation was carried over to *Homo habilis*, the first hominan to appear on the scene 2.4 million years ago. They too were unsteady on their feet. Not until the later emergence of *Homo erectus/ergaster*

approximately 1.8 million years ago, did mature and stable
bipedal locomotion finally appear in these hominans. That
milestone achievement was reached by the evolution and
shaping of appropriate musculature and ligaments for active
bipedalism, and the establishment of proper skeletal alignment
for endurance running over prolonged distances. These adaptations would allow humans, when they finally arrived on the
scene, to engage in a hunting style called persistence hunting.

   The technique of persistence hunting by endurance running
required these hominans to operate in the middle of the day
when it was hottest. Thanks to their bare skin and evolutionari-
ly modified sweat glands capable of superior thermoregulation,
humans could tolerate the heat far better than their putative
prey. Hunters would target a single animal such as a giraffe or
a gemsbok as the designated quarry, and persistently chase it at
fluctuating speeds ranging between the animal's trot and its gal-
lop. This alternating fast and slow mode of flight is extremely
energy inefficient and exhausting for the targeted animal. The
pursuit could continue for hours. The hunter may lose sight of
the quarry at times and then have to carefully track it by deductive means—such as understanding its behavior, following its
spoor, or observing other telltale signs like snapped twigs or
displaced vegetation—in order to ascertain the animal's flight
path. These skills required significant cognitive ability in the
hunter. The prey eventually overheats from the effort and is
now unable to continue fleeing. It suddenly collapses, crashing
to the ground incapacitated and helpless, the victorious hunter
now claiming the spoils.

Cooperating with each other in small isolated tribes, humans steadfastly remained hunters and gatherers for most of their evolutionary history. Their hunting and gathering methods steadily improved with time, becoming more sophisticated and complex as their cognitive functioning rapidly expanded. They developed new bone and wood implements, as well as more advanced stone tools to assist them in their hunting and foraging activities. Included now were improved models of spears and javelins in their hunting armamentarium. Sharpened bone or ivory points for spears resulted in greater penetrating power than the earlier flint tipped ones could ever provide. The spears themselves were refined and remodeled, becoming more aerodynamically efficient and providing the proper heft and balance for more accurate hurling. These improved spears, as well as the bow and arrow introduced 64,000 years ago in the Late Paleolithic, allowed for prey to be killed from a safe distance. The bow and arrow became a major hunting tool and was quickly adopted by people all over my host planet. It is still routinely used today by preliterate tribes for hunting and warfare, and by settled humans for recreation and sport—the latter thus recalling their Paleolithic ethos.

The boomerang, a flat missile made from a piece of wood often bent around the middle and operating like an aerofoil when hurled at a target, joined the hunting arsenal more than 30,000 years ago. It was good for hunting birds and small animals. Later, special boomerangs were designed to execute a parabolic flight path and return to the sender if the target was missed. A boomerang found along the Carpathian Mountains in Poland was made by behaviorally modern humans from mammoth tusk, and was approximately 30,000 years old. Australian

Aboriginal tribes took up boomerangs about 10,000 years ago and some of them still use this weapon.

Humans, along with some other later appearing hominans, developed a highly effective technique that employed bands of cooperating hunters to stampede herds of large prey animals—camels, horses, mastodons—into narrow passes that led to the edges of steep cliffs and precipices. The panicked animals, unable to turn back because of the goading hunters to their rear, would leap to their death into the ravines below. This technique required careful planning and more advanced cognitive skills on the part of these hunters than earlier hominans possessed. They accomplished this gory feat by encircling and driving the hapless animals relentlessly forward with stones, spears, arrows, and threatening sounds. This procedure was much enhanced by lighting brush fires behind the terrified animals to stampede them en masse to their death.

Paleolithic hunter-gathers tended to have relatively non-hierarchical and egalitarian social structures. Bands were usually made up of ten to twenty related individuals whose bonds of kinship cemented and reinforced group cohesion. The size of any particular band was regulated by the carrying capacity of the environment they occupied, determined by available food resources in the area. If provisions were generous and plentiful, the groups would maintain more robust populations. Conversely, if resources dwindled, usually the result of prolonged drought, larger groups of humans would split into smaller bands and migrate further afield to exploit a wider area. Warfare and violence over territory and natural resources were infrequent among these Paleolithic humans since tribes could easily move away to unoccupied territory and avoid direct conflict with other tribes.

These humans practiced a pure form of communism. All material assets were held in common by the entire group. Land was seen as belonging to everyone and owned by none. Social and economic equality, as well as gender parity, were generally observed among these Paleolithic hunter-gatherers. Every individual was valued for their contribution to the group, and every decision made by the tribe was done collectively by consensus and mutual agreement. There were neither rulers nor subjects among these Paleolithic people.

The invention and subsequent adoption of agriculture by *Homo sapiens* in the early Holocene introduced a monumental shift in this hunter-gatherer ethos and fundamentally altered the trajectory of this unusual species forever. Starting approximately 10,000 years ago, the development of agriculture and the domestication of animals for consumption changed the nature of human civilization. People no longer needed to roam endlessly as hunters and gatherers collecting food. They could now produce the food themselves in abundance, instead of just painstakingly gathering it in small quantities. The availability of surplus food then allowed these humans to mass into larger and even larger communities, thus forging a crucible that was conducive to thought and creativity. In less than 10,000 years of settlement, these newly sedentary humans with their swiftly expanding technology and burgeoning entrepreneurial spirit, were building empires, writing poetry, manipulating nuclear energy, splicing genes, and traveling to their Moon. It is indeed astonishing to contemplate the magnitude of this "Great Leap Forward" for *Homo sapiens*. It was as if a colossal sleeping giant had suddenly awakened. The rate of change in that brief span of time has been breathtaking and exponential. It continues to vigorously spike, thrusting humans into a brand new level of existence.

It should be noted here that so far in the history of *Homo sapiens* on their small planet, just a few game changing innovations have produced truly monumental effects that radically transformed life for them in completely unexpected ways. The adoption of tool use, control of fire, invention of agriculture, the Industrial Revolution, discovery of vaccines and antibiotics, mass communication, electronic computing, and just a few other watershed innovations have abruptly and magically transformed the future for this astonishing species. It may indeed be appropriate to compare this Anthropic Explosion of the End Pleistocene and early Holocene Epochs to the Cambrian Explosion of multicellular life that appeared on the same planet half a billion years before then. An important principle of nature is that fundamental change in a system does not always proceed in a gradualistic or incremental way. As a general rule, systems steadfastly cling to their old habits and customs and stubbornly resist paradigmatic changes to their structure. Only an entirely revolutionary development can produce something new. On Galymon we recognize this transmutational process inherent throughout the Universe. We call it Motaru, a term that finds resonance in the word catastrophism coined by Earth-based geologists. Geologic catastrophism proposes that the Earth has been affected in the past by sudden and unexpected events that had major consequences upon its form and function. Extraterrestrial bolide impacts or acute volcanism like Toba would be examples. Catastrophism contrasts with the geologic theory of uniformitarianism in which slow and incremental changes, such as erosion or weathering, shape the Earth's physical appearance.

Starting with the debut of *Homo habilis* the first committed and systematic tool user, the cultural history of these hominans is broadly divided into three contiguous periods by their latter day descendants. This classification was developed by humans so that hominan artifacts could be ordered and categorized sequentially, with the expectation that some system of chronology would emerge through this process. This concept came to be known as the Three-Age System and incorporated the view that different materials could represent different periods of time. These periods, named after their representative materials technology, came to be known as the Stone Age (2.6 million BP to 5,500 BP), the Bronze Age (5,500 BP to 3,000 BP), and the Iron Age (3,000 BP to 1,500 BP). The Iron Age ended the three-age formulation of human prehistory and was followed by the so-called Middle Ages (1,500 BP to 500 BP), and finally by the Modern Era (500 BP to the Present). The time intervals attached to these periods in this narrative are just composite figures, since the onset and termination of each age was not uniform and synchronous across the species, but varied from place to place around their planet.

The Stone Age itself is divided into two periods: the Paleolithic (Old Stone Age) with its chipped stone tools; and the Neolithic (New Stone Age) with its polished stone tools. Some archeologists on my host planet may insert a Mesolithic (Middle Stone Age) period between the two, but that distinction is rather tedious and is described for only a few groups of humans on Earth. The Paleolithic Age is contemporaneous with the Pleistocene Epoch which lasted from about 2.6 million BP to 11,700 BP. All the other subdivisions of human history are cramped into the short time period after the Paleolithic ended.

The Paleolithic Age began when *Homo's* ancestral genus

Australopithecus first picked up a crude stone tool at the dawn of the new Pleistocene Epoch. It continued from there past *Australopithecus'* immediate descendant, the erstwhile *Homo habilis*—that fine ancestral stone tool-making hominan from 2.4 million BP—for the rest of the Pleistocene Epoch. It ended at the start of the Holocene when glaciation and ice-sheets began retreating across my host planet due to a new warming trend.

The Neolithic Age succeeded the Paleolithic. It commenced on Earth approximately around 12,000 BP and continued into about 5,500 BP, eventually ending in the Bronze Age. Mac should emphasize here that the separation between Paleolithic and Neolithic is fundamentally a cultural one, not just a matter of materials and tool use. The transition was gradual. It is hard to delineate when one age ended and the other began.

The Neolithic Age lasted just a fraction of the Paleolithic. Humans were nomadic hunters and gatherers during the Paleolithic, whereas Neolithic humans were increasingly settled farmers and herders producing their own food rather than just collecting it from their habitat like their Paleolithic ancestors had done. Paleolithic humans used tools made of stone, bone, and wood for hunting and gathering, while Neolithic humans developed pottery and used more complex and versatile tools, some elaborated from metal, for farming and herding purposes. Neolithic humans developed barter and primitive forms of government, whereas Paleolithic humans did not have any of those institutions around.

The Paleolithic Age lasted almost 2.6 million years. It was a momentous season for the new genus *Homo* that had recently debuted in the Great Rift Valley of East Africa just as the Pleistocene Epoch began. This epoch may indeed be dubbed the grand and glorious Age of Hominans. Never before had Earth witnessed such action. Several species of the genus *Homo* lived alongside each other during this tumultuous period of their evolution. All of them made and used stone tools. Some migrated out of their natal continent and spread around their planet. They competed vigorously with each other for habitat and resources. The outcome of this deadly competition was the eventual disappearance of every other hominan species on Earth except for humans in what could be called the Great Pleistocene Purges. Yet even this carnage, extraordinary as it was, did not assume the magnitude of genocidal warfare that later engulfed humans in the Neolithic Age, only to continue magnified into the present time.

When the Paleolithic Age began, the genus *Homo* was confined to the Rift Valley inside East Africa. Then, starting 1.8 million years ago or shortly thereafter, that great pioneer *Homo erectus* emigrated out of Africa and colonized large parts of the Old World. *Homo antecessor* and *Homo heidelbergensis* would follow. Much later in the Paleolithic, *Homo sapiens* would initiate its own emigration out of East Africa to eventually disperse and populate their entire planet. When the Neolithic Age finally arrived about 12,000 years ago, they were the only ones left standing. The others had all vanished.

Homo floresiensis, that diminutive hominan living on Flores and nearby islands of Indonesia, was the very last hominan species to coexist with *Homo sapiens* on my host planet. That ended somewhere between 13,000 and 12,000 years ago, just as the Pleistocene Epoch was rapidly drawing to a close. Some contemporary human folklorists have suggested that the Ebu Gogo, a cadre of small human-like creatures that appear in the local human mythology of Flores, represented *H. floresiensis*. The Ebu

Gogo, described in these legends as incredibly fast runners, are said to have been hunted to extinction by the human inhabitants of Flores because the Ebu Gogo stole food from those humans. The Nage, an indigenous tribal people now living on the island of Flores, describe these extinct Ebu Gogo as pygmies with broad faces, wide mouths, and flat noses; their bodies were hairy, and their females had pendulous breasts. Some anthropologists suspect the Ebu Gogo actually referred to a species of monkeys.

*　　　*　　　*

Paleolithic people—hunters and gatherers by culture—led hardscrabble, nomadic lives. They lived in small isolated populations bound by kinship and genes, cooperating with each other to secure sustenance, shelter, sex, and safety. By the time the Neolithic Age rolled around, these same people had settled into a much safer and more sedentary way of life that also enormously magnified their food resources.

The discovery of cereal grains such as wheat and barley by humans, and the adoption of agricultural practices and effective crop management techniques thereafter, were the factors that brought about this monumental change in the lifestyle and culture of these hominans. Abandoning their long and familiar history as a food collecting species, they rapidly transformed themselves into a food producing one. This new way of living consisted of cultivating edible food crops, raising farm animals, and storing the food for future use. The manufacture of clay pottery by Neolithic people right about the same time made it more convenient for them now to cook their food, store provisions, and transport goods from place to place.

Late Paleolithic humans were familiar with wild wheat and

barley which they had collected for food as early as 23,000 BP. So, when Neolithic agriculture became possible with the retreat of glaciation and the melting of ice-sheets, humans were already accustomed and familiar with these cereal plants. These innovative hominans it must be mentioned, had already been planting fruit trees for centuries before embarking on a program of systematic cereal cultivation. Appropriately enough, human scientists in 56 AP discovered a cache of ancient figs in a dwelling they had excavated near the old city of Jericho in the lower Jordan Valley. These ancient figs were radiometrically dated to 11,400 BP and proved to be a rather unusual form of the fruit. They were a mutant, seedless variety of fig that could only be propagated by cuttings from their parent trees since they possessed no seeds. As seedless figs are more succulent and thus preferred for consumption, these pre-Neolithic humans had acquired the knowledge and the necessary skills to grow the popular seedless variety of figs from vegetative cuttings they obtained from parent stock.

Compared to their roaming Paleolithic ancestors, settled Neolithic people made more sophisticated and effective stone tools by grinding and polishing harder rocks than simply chipping softer material down to the desired shape as their Paleolithic predecessors had done. The cultivation of cereal grains encouraged these Neolithic people to invent more refined tools and farming implements, and join together into larger human settlements than just their own small tribe. Settlements required permanent dwellings and therefore the building of houses was a major cultural accomplishment for these people. Early Neolithic houses were either circular or rectangular in shape, depending on local cultural preferences. The structures enclosed a single room not more than 800 square feet in area.

Postholes were first made and timber then inserted into the ground to form a frame for the house and also to mark the door opening. Wattle, often plastered with mud, was used for the walls. Thatch—made from reed, straw, or palm leaves—covered the roof. More advanced versions of Neolithic houses had upper levels or attic spaces installed for storage, which could be accessed by ladders. These houses were built by pioneer farmers who had moved into the area, bringing with them the knowledge and skills needed to construct such buildings. Comparable houses are built and inhabited by people on Earth even today.

The building of complex and permanent dwellings by *Homo sapiens* is a relatively recent innovation in their social and cultural history. Humans are the only hominids that ever erected permanent houses to live in. No hominid ever did that before. The nonhuman great apes living on Earth today may build temporary "nests" for sleeping at night, but never permanent houses. That behavior began with the transformation of humans in the Neolithic to a sedentary and settled lifestyle. As nomadic hunter-gatherers, they had neither required nor occupied permanent dwellings. They had instead sought shelter in caves or built temporary structures—or nests—like all hominans did then and the non-human great apes still do today.

❧❦❧

Mac visited the tiny hamlet of Sofar to get a firsthand look at a Neolithic settlement circa 8,000 BP. Now in the territory of modern Sudan, Sofar nestled peacefully by the Nile, just as the Neolithic agricultural revolution was gathering steam in that region. It was a tightly knit community of eight Neolithic dwellings built at the Fifth Cataract of the Nile. The Cataracts of the Nile, six of them in all, are shallow white-water rapids along the course of the great river, extending upstream between Aswan in Egypt and Khartoum in Sudan. They all occur along a limited stretch of the river called the Great Bend where the Nile veers sharply off course before heading north again. Along this section, the river plunges about 1,000 feet in a series of six cataracts or waterfalls. The surface of the water in these cataracts is broken by numerous scraggy rocks and boulders sticking out of the river bed, including many rocky islets along the river channel there. The Fifth Cataract is near the confluence of the Nile and the Atbarah, the last tributary along the Nile's course before that fabulous waterway crosses the vast Sahara to reach the Mediterranean Sea.

I trudged along a well-worn footpath for about a quarter mile, away from the cataract, to enter the Neolithic hamlet of Sofar. Entrance to the bramble protected enclosure where the houses were built was through a narrow opening in this well-preserved bramble fence meant to keep lions and hyenas away from dwellings after dark. That is where I ran into Kla!

Kla! was a gorgeous 28 year old man, trim and supremely handsome. His piercing dark eyes, surmounted by a shock of grizzled weather-beaten hair and framed by his flowing beard, revealed a kind but determined face. Kla! wore his hair in dreadlocks as did most humans on my host planet prior to the introduction of reliable hair-grooming tools in the Bronze Age. Kla!'s dreadlocks were formed by leaving his hair alone and not brushing or cutting it, thus encouraging the hair to tangle together as it grew, producing the twisted and matted ropes of hair known as dreadlocks. Dreadlocks can also be created artificially by manually braiding the hair. Modern Maasai men from northern Kenya claim they have been wearing dreadlocks for as long as they can remember.

Kla! was the headman of this settlement of Neolithic humans by the Fifth Cataract of the Nile. Clan bosses by now had already appeared within human cultures. Kla! was actively helping a newbie to his settlement put up a dwelling on a piece of land in the village. With his extravagant hair cascading down broad and ample shoulders, Kla! hypnotically commanded his space.

It was 9 AM that morning at Sofar. Around the settlement were several neatly cultivated plots of chickpeas (*Cicer arietinum*) and barley (*Hordeum vulgare*) growing vigorously in the prolific sunshine suffusing that verdant landscape. Several obese feral cats, ancestors to future domestic cats (*Felis catus*) were lazily sunning themselves by a grain-storage bin near the settlers' houses. These feral felines were just beginning their relationship with humans almost 4,000 years before Egyptians depicted domestic cats in their art. The animal's appetite was what led to its domestication. The sequence began when farmers started storing grain that attracted rodents. This brought wild cats to the village, hunting these rodents. Over several generations, these cats adapted to village life but remained semi-feral, providing free pest control services, until people developed a fancy to cats and took them indoors.

With agriculture came marriage and patriarchy, two relationship styles wedded to each other and proceeding from the same principle. The human institution of marriage is certainly a curious arrangement unknown to any other hominan that ever lived before on Earth. It is thus not inherent to human nature, but extraneously imposed on them by custom starting in the early Neolithic. Marriage itself was uniquely developed by *Homo sapiens* to achieve rapid population growth and thus saturate their planet's habitable space with still more humans. This cultural strategy proved extraordinarily successful for the species. From just about 1 million individuals inhabiting Earth only 12,000 years ago, humans crossed the landmark figure of 7,000 million people or 7 billion living simultaneously on Earth when Mac was visiting their planet. That prodigal figure was hugely facilitated by inventing and implementing the radical institution of marriage.

Before marriage was adopted by them, humans averaged about two or three offspring per female, raised primarily by the mother nurturing just one child at a time. This pattern of reproductive behavior is universal for primates across their evolutionary spectrum. The core hominid family, like for most mammals, consisted of a mother and her kids, the biologic father serving no parenting role except to fertilize the female. Now however, the newly formed institution of marriage would provide humans with a robust two-parent family system to nurture a multitude of offspring simultaneously, thus allowing each human female to have twice or three times as many children as she would if she had to raise them all by herself. Customs quickly emerged to make marriage a strictly protected cartel with severe strictures and penalties—including death—for any individual rash enough to transgress its ordinances. These prohibitions were necessary because marriage itself was not native to this species and had to be severely enforced by harsh consequences for adulterous behavior.

Along with the institution of marriage came the odious system of patriarchy. In patriarchy, males are the dominant and central figures in every area of human organization, including decision making, leadership positions, moral authority, control of property, and dominion over women and children. Women were now essentially delegated to the role of baby-makers to rapidly increase Earth's human population. That objective, after all, is the definition of biological success for any species. Patriarchy was the penalty human females were made to pay as currency to compensate for the assistance they received from males in raising their many offspring. The commensurate social status given to women and men was no longer operative. Gender parity became a thing of the past. Men and women were no longer equal.

Kla! quickly finished helping the novice settler sink timbers for the new dwelling into the pre-positioned postholes they had dug. He used a rather unusual tool for his place and time—a digging device crafted from a sizable nickel-iron meteorite his father had found years ago when migrating to this location in the Sudan. Now an army of women, four of them Kla!'s wives, one a lovely nine year old, and numerous other adults and children from the settlement, gathered at the new homesite to attach and secure the wattle walls to the timbers and set the thatch roof in place. These early Neolithic humans were behaviorally modern by now, possessing a fully developed theory-of-mind and articulating fluent speech. The ones from Sofar used a clicking, tonal language to communicate. Their core cognitive functions were robust and well developed, though not yet quite as advanced as humans alive today—they would not have understood Einstein's Relativity. But they did know how to build durable houses.

The work on the house at Sofar was virtually completed before dark and the new neighbors moved in the next day.

Living first in scattered hamlets like Sofar, these early Neolithic humans would later go on to build immense towns and cities bursting with people. Abandoning their nomadic lifestyle tied to a hunting and gathering ethos gave these humans invaluable time and leisure to peruse specialized crafts such as pottery, woodworking, sewing, and weaving. The new technology of agriculture was the emblematic revolution of the Neolithic Age. This crucial transition for the human species from a food-collecting to a food-producing culture began in the Fertile Crescent.

The Fertile Crescent is a crescent-shaped strip of comparatively moist and fertile land located in southwestern Asia and northeastern Africa. It extends in a broad arc or semicircle from the Tigris and Euphrates Rivers on the east, to the Nile River in the west. It subsumes areas of fertile and arable land on hillsides and alluvial valleys. This crescent runs northwestward along the Zagros Mountains of Iran, loops around the northern rim of the Syrian Desert, continues southwestward on the eastern shore of the Mediterranean, and extends into the Nile River delta. The Upper Nile River Valley, the Tigris–Euphrates River Valley, and the Jordan River Valley are traditionally considered part of the Fertile Crescent. The earliest ever farming settlements on my host planet were located in this region. Preliminary cultivation of grains and domestication of animals first appeared in the Fertile Crescent by about 11,000 BP, and a lifestyle based on farming and raising animals from settled villages became established by 9,000 BP in the Tigris-Euphrates River Valley in present day Iraq. This arc of agriculture and animal husbandry continued into what are now parts of Syria, Israel, Lebanon, Jordan, Palestine, and the upper Nile Delta in Egypt. The Fertile Crescent was the incubator of human civilization. The first farmers of the Fertile Crescent raised barley, wheat and chickpeas, and kept sheep and goats, later supplemented by cattle and pigs.

Like an unstoppable contagion, this innovative new agricultural technology, first crafted and tested by *Homo sapiens* in that historic Fertile Crescent, disseminated swiftly eastward into Asia, northward into Europe, and west into Africa. Scattered farming communities appeared in Greece as early as 9,000 BP, plowing further north into Europe over the next 4,000 years. Complex agricultural settlements along the upper Nile River Valley of Egypt were forming around 6000 BP. This astonishing technology soon barreled eastward into the Indus River Valley now in Pakistan and India by 7,000 BP, and farming communities based on rice and millet cultivation reached the Yellow River Valley of China and proliferated into Southeast Asia by 5,500 BP. Neolithic culture also appeared in the Americas. Agriculture was independently discovered by humans in the New World where corn and beans were cultivated in Mexico and Central America from about 8,500 BP. However, fully settled village life was not established in the New World until around 4,000 BP.

This Neolithic Revolution quickly set the entire human world on fire—its momentum and spread were irresistible. It cannot be overemphasized here that this agricultural revolution was an exceptionally pivotal watershed event in the history of humankind. It was the engine that launched these hominans to the stars.

<hr />

Cultivation of food for later consumption is not just unique to humans. Other organisms do it as well. Many of them are insects. The aquatic larva of a species of caddisfly farms algae for meals. Some ants and termites cultivate and tend gardens of fungi as renewable food sources. The ambrosia beetle grows fungi in its tunnels, and the yeti crab nurtures bacteria on its claws for nutrition. The slime mold grows its own delicious microbes for dinner. Yet the human enterprise of agriculture is quite different from these other examples of food production. It belongs to an entirely new paradigm.

It began with the cognitively directed and purposeful collection of wild cereal grains representing ancestral strains of wheat, rice, barley, or corn. This was followed by planting that grain and then culling all the inferior growth, thus selecting the most robust ones for replanting. Through repeated cycles of planting, culling, and replanting, the process at last yielded domesticated cereal cultivars bearing bigger and more nutritious grain than their wild ancestors once did. In order to attain this desirable goal, humans had to first evolve a high degree of cognitive ability with well-honed observational, introspective, and abstraction skills—even before this sort of agricultural enterprise became climatically possible. That critical point in their cognitive development was only achieved by these hominans as the Holocene Epoch was approaching, thus explaining why the agricultural revolution occurred when it did. The retreating ice-sheets at the same time as agriculture was being developed by them was only coincidental, though it proved optimal for the enterprise.

The Bronze Age succeeded the Neolithic Age in the Old World when humans mastered the art of smelting metal ores and extracting the native metal from those ores. This important technology was serendipitously discovered when certain clays containing metallic ores—then used to make pots—were fired in kilns at high temperatures in a low oxygen atmosphere when the native metal magically appeared. The Bronze Age lasted from the end of the Neolithic in 5,500 BP to about 3,000 BP.

The 2,500 years of the Bronze Age saw the rise and consolidation of many great human civilizations on Earth. The very first one, on the banks of the Tigris and Euphrates, the Great Sumerian Civilization, reached its zenith in the Bronze Age.

Copper was likely the first metal mined and crafted into objects by humans. Native gold probably attracted their attention earlier than copper, but gold's softness and scarcity made it impractical for widespread use. Copper, too, was originally discovered in its elemental form and then later obtained by smelting copper ores. Modern estimates indicate that copper was known to humans in the Fertile Crescent almost 11,000 years ago, just as the Holocene Epoch dawned. Ornamental beads made from copper dating back to 8,000 BP were found at Catal Hoyuk in Anatolia, now in modern Turkey. Copper was one of the most important materials in the inventory of these hominans during the Bronze Age. Humans learned to combine copper and tin to make bronze which then replaced stone as a medium for making tools and weapons. The Bronze Age saw the early development and introduction of pictograms and related proto-writing formats that enabled people to start keeping records and document events as they happened. That allowed these humans to accurately communicate information to each other without just relying on their memories alone.

The Iron Age followed the Bronze Age. It is variously estimated by modern humans to have lasted for about fifteen centuries, roughly from 3,000 BP to about 1,500 BP. It witnessed important cultural transitions. The Iron Age was characterized by the smelting and widespread use of iron and steel in tools and in weapons manufacture; the metal still remains a stout pillar of modern life for these hominans. Another principle feature of the Iron Age was the introduction of alphabet characters to replace pictograms, leading to the development of a complex writing system. That laid the foundation for elaborate and highly accurate record keeping which in turn spurred industry and commerce, and facilitated an outpouring of literature that revolutionized human thought and behavior—after that, *Homo sapiens* would never be the same again. The Iron Age witnessed the rise of ancient Greece and Rome to the pinnacle of world civilization and power, and then saw them both fall to the ground and disappear.

The use of iron by humans actually predates the conventional Iron Age. People first became attracted to iron by its magnetic properties. As far back as 6,000 BP they were crafting iron artifacts from metallic iron meteorites. The word iron itself may have come from a root word meaning "holy metal" or "metal from the sky." The iron that was used by humans before the Iron Age had a higher nickel content than iron derived from native ores on their own planet; that nickel content is consistent with the composition of iron meteorites. Later on, during the Iron Age, humans discovered that when metallic iron was mixed with charcoal and heated to a high temperature, it seemed to become harder and stronger. The iron, in this situation, picked up carbon from the charcoal, turning itself into the harder material that came to be known as steel.

The Middle Ages followed the Iron Age. It technically began in 1,474 BP when Germanic tribes sacked the ancient city of Rome, ending more than 800 years of glory for that so-called "Eternal City." Humans mark that fall of ancient Rome as the end of their Ancient History. The next 1,000 years, from around 1,500 BP to 500 BP, are known to them as the Middle Ages. This was a period of enormous religious ferment and expansionism. Savage religious wars and brutal conflicts raced around my host planet. They have never ceased, and continue to rage on into modern times. The Arabs were the custodians of human civilization during the Middle Ages. They introduced novel concepts in optics, physics, and chemistry, and invented the crank-shaft, the windmill, and the fountain pen. Abu Ali al-Hasan ibn al-Haytham (985 BP–910 BP), also known as Alhazen, born in Basra, flourished in Cairo during Egypt's Fatimid Caliphate. He was a world famous scientist and philosopher who made extraordinary contributions to optics, astronomy, mathematics, meteorology, visual perception, and the scientific method. Quite possibly he was Earth's greatest known physicist for the 2,000 years between Archimedes and Isaac Newton. It was ibn al-Haytham who first figured out that vision was produced by light entering the eye—not by rays emanating from that organ and falling on external objects as the ancient Greeks had believed.

The Modern Era formally ended the historical Middle Ages. The Modern Era is considered to have started around 500 BP when humans, principally from Western Europe, commenced far-flung voyages of exploration by sea to locations around their planet. That launched the Age of Discovery. Others call it the Age of Colonialism when non-European cultures were subject to European domination. The Modern Era officially began in 462 BP when the great Portuguese navigator and explorer, Bartolomeu Dias, led the first European expedition around the Cape of Good Hope at the southern tip of Africa, thus opening a sea route to Asia by way of the Atlantic and Indian Oceans. The Modern Era saw the most incredibly explosive growth of pure science and ground-breaking technology that Earth has ever known, and witnessed the swift integration of this new science and technology into ordinary human affairs. That miracle continues unabated today, only much more accelerated now.

The Modern Era has been truly extraordinary with respect to human intellectual and material advancement. The accumulated progress in just those 500 years far exceeds everything achieved by *Homo sapiens* since they first made their debut on Earth 200,000 years ago. It began with the Copernican Revolution in 407 BP that gutted the privileged location of Earth and of humans in the Universe. Isaac Newton came along 144 years later and revolutionized mechanics and physics in his time. Then Charles Darwin, 172 years after that, rewrote the history of life on Earth. Albert Einstein in just another 57 years thereafter, discovered the principle of Relativity that forever changed the way humans view space and time in this Universe. In comparative terms, advances in the physical and biological sciences in just the last 100 years alone exceeds everything known to humans before that time. The Industrial Revolution, starting hardly 200 years ago, astronomically multiplied the material fortunes of this species. The Modern Era is indeed unprecedented in Earth history and its trajectory continues to soar exponentially.

Looking backward at this contagious fire of human civilization from today's vantage point, it seems apparent that its course was cradled along the way by a continuous line of exceptional civilizations in time and space. The Sumerians in the Bronze Age, the Greeks in the Iron Age, the Arabs in the Middle Age, the British in the Modern Age, and now the Americans in this Post-Modern or Electronic Age, have all been instrumental in this regard. There are more lining the future.

The Neolithic Revolution brought unimagined material prosperity to its acolytes—and yet it carried a sinister downside. Despite the cornucopia of gifts it lavished on its disciples, there was a Faustian[38] dimension to it. In exchange for the guarantee of food, shelter and safety, humans gave up their freedom of action. As hunters and gatherers for most of their evolutionary history, each individual had been his or her own master. No one else could order their lives, or dictate and control their actions. They were free spirits living in an egalitarian universe. Of course, they cooperated with each other in their hunting and gathering activities, and participated voluntarily in the tribe's culture and rituals, faithfully discharging any obligations to their clan. Yet, however short and brutish their lives may have been as Paleolithic people, they were always independent and self-reliant as individuals. These paleohumans served no master.

This intrepid hominan world succumbed to unimagined changes caused by the Neolithic agricultural revolution of the early Holocene. The first of these changes was social and cultural. The newly concocted institution of marriage—intended to supercharge reproduction and rocket their population numbers into the stratosphere—also destroyed prevailing gender parity in this species and introduced the stranglehold of patriarchy

---

38 "Faustian" comes by way of a German legend. Dr. Faust, it is said, was a highly successful and accomplished scholar who remained dissatisfied with his already high station in life. Faust therefore made an irrevocable deal with the devil's representative, Mephistopheles. Faust contracted to sell his "immortal soul" to the devil in exchange for unlimited knowledge and worldly power. According to the bargain, Mephistopheles with his magic powers would secure Faust all his desires for a term of 24 years, but at the end of that time his master, the devil, will claim Faust's soul, to be eternally damned.

into their societies. With respect to human population numbers certainly, this reproductive strategy was successful beyond their wildest imagination: in just the last 100 years alone, humans have geometrically inflated their population numbers from 1.7 billion in 40 BP to over 7 billion of them today—a surge of more than 400 percent during that brief 100 year window. Humans were a mere one million strong in 10,000 BP, a figure that had previously taken them 190,000 years to reach. It was the Neolithic invention of marriage that chartered this lightning course of population growth. Yet the downward spiral in the status of human females that came with this reproductive strategy quickly plummeted to a deep misogynistic bottom and remained stuck there permanently for more than 10,000 years. Only in the late Modern Era did this begin to change as human population numbers peaked and marriage got deemphasized as a consequence. It has been hardly 100 years now since this new gender dynamic appeared, though billions of girls and women around the world remain oppressed and exploited, even as recently when Mac was on their planet.

The other great change was in their economic life. The new paradigm of private property and the creation of large quantities of surplus wealth from mass agricultural production, allowed huge tranches of capital to become concentrated in the hands of a few artful individuals. Almost everyone else became subject to enslavement in some form or another, in exchange for survival necessities they were no longer able to produce for themselves like they routinely did during Paleolithic times. Thus the dehumanizing concept of slavery began to emerge 12,000 years ago for the first time in human history. It became appropriate now for one human to own another human, just like they would any other material possession, something unimaginable before the Neolithic Age. It would be inconvenient, nor was it customary, for nomadic Paleolithic hunter-gatherers to keep slaves. Even though slavery as a social institution has now been formally abolished on their planet, the tradition of labor by the many controlled by the capital of a few—an economic system called Capitalism which arose early in the Neolithic Age—continues untrammeled to the present time.

Ancient Persia under Cyrus the Great was the first jurisdiction on Earth to officially abolish slavery circa 2,500 BP. The last one was Mauritania which abolished it only in 31 AP. Regardless of these developments, many covert forms of slavery and indentured labor among humans persist to this day. The present phenomenon of Globalization[39] has vastly magnified this unhappy situation. Cheap human labor can now be bought and sold dispassionately on a planetary scale in anonymous capital markets controlled and operated by a propertied and affluent few, thus compounding this scourge of dehumanizing servitude. The vast majority of humans living on their planet today remain serfs, servants, or wage-earners entrapped by capital. Professor Albert Einstein, that admired scientist and savant, noted in an article published in 1 BP in the socialist magazine *Monthly Review* that, "Private capital tends to become concentrated in few hands, partly because of competition among the capitalists, and partly because technological development and the increasing division of labor encourage the formation of larger units of production at the expense of smaller ones. The result of these developments is an oligarchy of private capital the enormous power of which cannot be effectively checked even by a democratically organized political society."

---

39 Globalization is the tendency of businesses, technologies, and economic philosophies to infiltrate throughout the world. Alternately, globalization could also be considered as that inevitable process which will eventually produce a unified global culture and citizenship for all humans.

Yet still another unusual and coercive practice that arose in the Neolithic Age was the forcible incarceration, or imprisonment, of individuals deemed dangerous to society. These offenders were locked up in special institutions called Prisons, stripped of their freedoms, and involuntarily restricted to tiny prison cells for predetermined periods of time. Prisons are unique to *Homo sapiens* and are unknown in any other species on Earth. Humans themselves had no use for prisons during their long hunter-gatherer phase; incarceration of other humans was unimaginable to them then, and also impractical at the time. Yet, these dismal prisons quickly became common and widespread throughout the world, ever since these humans settled into large communities in the Neolithic Age. Unlike fraternal Paleolithic tribes, Neolithic settlements brought together a medley of strangers who had little in common and were therefore more likely to defraud or harm each other. Prisons were used to lock up such offenders. The primary purpose of prison is retribution for offenses against individuals and society, thereby setting an example for others to avoid such behavior. Rehabilitation is only a distant secondary consideration, if at all, due to fiscal constraints and disinterest by the authorities. Most culpable misdeeds are criminal ones, though in some cases they may be political or civil infractions. A few offenses such as murder—or adultery in some cultures— may incur the death penalty.

Every human society on Earth today possesses prisons, there are no exceptions. A prison cell—also called a holding cell or lock-up—is a miniscule steel or concrete room in a prison building where the condemned prisoner is held involuntarily. Modern prison cells usually measure just 6-feet by 8-feet in size. An open toilet and a sink are secured to the wall or to the floor. A single door with a small glass window for observing the prisoner, and a slot for passing food, opens into the prison cell. Only limited blocks of time are allowed for exercise and recreation. Guards are hired to manage prisoners and keep them in line. The prison milieu is harsh and punitive. In the United States, about 94% of prisoners are male, only 6% female. The vast majority of these prisoners range in age from early adolescence to young adulthood, a period when sex hormone levels peak and male humans can be especially aggressive and prone to physical and sexual violence. Racial and ethnic minorities, and other out of favor populations, are extraordinarily overrepresented in prisons. Prisons are avowedly one of the most unusual and dehumanizing institutions run by *Homo sapiens* anywhere on their planet today.

The metastasis of human settlements and the spread of agriculture was a seminal development in human history. In the face of these shattering events, a few human groups tried to buck the Neolithic settlement trend, clinging against all odds to their hunter-gatherer culture and way of life. Such people continue to survive marginally in the murky backwaters of humanity even today. They live in isolated clans and tribes, camouflaged in the forests and hillsides, the deltas and deserts, of their planet. The Mbuti of the Ituri, the !Kung of the Kalahari, the Veddahs of Ceylon, the Yanomami of the Amazon, and scores of others unnamed here, are examples of such people. Their numbers are rapidly shrinking, decimated by disease and genocide. Many are forced to surrender their sovereign cultures and reluctantly accede to a mode of life they had always dreaded, only to wither away and be killed or absorbed into encroaching populations, their stout hearts bursting with inconsolable grief. Their precious Paleolithic ethos, once shared by all the people of Earth, is now doomed to disappear into the mists of the hoary past.

The history of agriculture is closely linked to global climate change. The year 21,500 BP was roughly the peak of the Last Glacial Maximum (LGM) for the then ongoing Pleistocene glaciation. At the time of that LGM, mean global temperature plummeted to its lowest point for that glaciation cycle, and the spreading ice-sheets reached their maximum expansion. After that LGM passed, the planet again began a gradual warming trend. The northern and southern hemisphere glaciers retreated toward their respective poles, and forests began to appear where once stood only an expanse of ice-frozen tundra. Most humans moved northward—the southern hemisphere, with little land, was sparsely populated. These people now began living in larger and more sedentary collectives. The really big mammals, like woolly mammoths and mastodons that humans had hunted and consumed for thousands of years previously, vanished from my host planet, driven into extinction by rising temperatures and over-hunting by these hominans. People were now reduced to eating substantially smaller game like wild boar and deer. These people also collected scattered stands of wheat and barley in open meadows, and gathered mushrooms and acorns from the forest floor for food.

Then all hell broke loose again. Around 12,800 BP, toward the end of the Pleistocene, the brutal cold unceremoniously returned for another 1,300 years in what humans today call the Younger Dryas Period, named after a small arctic-alpine flowering shrub *Dryas octopetala*, that grows in cold climates and became common in Eurasia during this period. Glaciation resumed and forested areas shrunk once more or even disappeared from view completely. People dug in as best they could under these frozen and hostile circumstances. The Younger Dryas Period ended abruptly around 11,500 BP and Earth warmed once more, firing the opening salvo of the Holocene.

As the bitter cold lifted, the climate swiftly rebounded. In Greenland for instance, temperatures spiked 18°F within a decade after the Younger Dryas ended. Humans began to aggregate into large communities and developed increasingly complex social organizations and structures. In parts of the Fertile Crescent, these early settlers inhabited communities all year round. They traded actively in basalt which was used to manufacture ground stone tools, obsidian used for chipped stone tools, and seashells that were coveted for personal ornamentation. The first masonry structures were erected in the Zagros Mountains of Iran where people also collected seeds from wild cereals and domesticated sheep. Further along, the Neolithic period saw the intensification of wild cereal cultivation, and by 10,000 BP, fully tuned and domesticated versions of wheat, barley, and chickpeas became established in the area. Goats, sheep, cattle, and pigs were now being extensively raised in the hilly tracts of the Zagros region. This new technology of agriculture and animal husbandry radiated outward from this region and spread widely over the next one thousand years.

Unlike the surplus of meat in their earlier Paleolithic repasts, the new diet of these recently settled Neolithic farmers was predominantly vegetarian, made up mostly of grains, with meat now only an occasional luxury unless the meat-eaters were well-heeled as well. Common salt, or sodium chloride, a major dietary mineral and an essential supplement that animals need to maintain proper nutritional status, is severely deficient in a vegetarian diet which is poor in sodium content. Agriculture, therefore, became possible only as trading in salt was established by these hominans. Salt, as a consequence, features in many of the most important trading systems of the ancient world. Stately caravans, loaded with salt, plied the north African and west Asian deserts, faithfully transporting this precious commodity to its numerous consumers. The importance of this mineral is reflected in the word "salary" which means remuneration for work performed— *sal* is the Latin root word for "salt."

Approximately 9,000 years ago, early Neolithic farmers began joining together and formed small agricultural communes. Then 3,000 years later, more or less around 6,000 BP, these scattered agricultural communes had coalesced to form the first complex and centralized human civilizations on my host planet. These first civilizations blossomed astride four major river valleys of the Old World. These great river valleys, the cradles of human civilization, were located in western, southern, and eastern Asia, and in northeastern Africa. They each arose independently along river systems, marking the next big step in the consolidation and organization of human economic, political, religious, and social activities. They also spurred the emergence of government among these hominans now dominant on Earth. Such complex civilizations first formed along major waterways because rivers provided a predictable source of precious water for farming and other human activities, and also offered a reliable means for transportation within the area of civilization. These cardinal river valley civilizations were the prime incubators for global human civilization. The first one to appear was along the Tigris and Euphrates Rivers now in modern Iraq, followed by the Nile River in Egypt and Sudan, the Indus River in Pakistan and India, and the Yellow River in China.

The Tigris and Euphrates are the two rivers that fed the earliest human civilization on Earth, known now to modern humans as the Mesopotamian Civilization. This civilization first developed between the two rivers in the southern part of what is today modern Iraq. Scattered farming villages along the rivers banded together into urban centers with a common language, religion, culture, and political organization. The first inhabitants of this new civilization were called Sumerians. Starting around 5,200 BP, powerful Sumerian cities arose along the two great rivers and proceeded sequentially to dominate ancient Mesopotamia.

The Nile Valley was the axis of two prolific African civilizations, the Nubian Civilization in northern Sudan and southern Egypt, and the Egyptian Civilization in the Nile Delta of Lower Egypt. This great river along which humans had first emigrated out of their ancestral homeland, provided a reliable means of communication between the Nubian and Egyptian settlements and shaped the development of both civilizations, linking parts of sub-Saharan Africa to the Mediterranean Sea. Although both Nilotic civilizations arose on the banks of the Nile River, they developed along different cultural lines. Egypt united politically earlier than Nubia. The first ever pharaoh, Menes, ruled Egypt around 5,100 BP.

The Indus River begins its course in the western Tibetan Plateau of the Himalaya Mountains and drains a valley mostly in modern Pakistan today. This valley was home to yet another principal human civilization called the Harappan Civilization by modern humans. From about 5,000 BP onward, a complex urbanized society developed in the Indus River Valley on land now located in contemporary Pakistan and a strip of northwestern India. This ancient Indus Valley Civilization was dominated by several large cities. The most prominent of these cities, revealed by modern archaeology, were the urban centers of Harappa and Mohenjo-Daro.

The Yellow River or the Huang He, arises in the Bayan Har Mountains of central China and flows in a northeastern direction across China, carrying rich yellow silt all the way from Mongolia to the Pacific Ocean. The Yellow River Valley was the cradle of ancient Chinese Civilization. Humans in China were surrounded by mountains and desert and thus became quite isolated from other civilizations and cultures elsewhere on Earth. Early Chinese rulers built cities and fortifications in the Yellow River Valley starting around 5,000 BP. Though secluded by its geography, early Chinese Civilization developed in much the same fashion as did early Mesopotamian, Nilotic, and Harappan Civilizations.

These four classical river valley civilizations laid the groundwork for the political and social coherence on which all subsequent human civilizations are based. Its pioneering people built dwellings, erected monuments, made warfare, invented writing, established governments, devised money, wrote legal codes, and developed the social and political infrastructure necessary for civilization to function. Human settlements proliferated, and bustling towns and cities emerged. People became stratified into socioeconomic compartments, something they had never experienced before during their long Paleolithic prelude. Division of labor based on caste, class, and gender soon appeared in communities. These and other elaborate social constructs were imposed on them in order to manage the increasing complexity of life that had rapidly descended on these once free and simple people.

CHAPTER IX:

FAMILY

$\mathfrak{F}$ amily has many meanings. Here it refers to a structural and functional alignment among certain affiliated individuals within the larger social organization of *Homo sapiens*. Similar systems exist in other animals, including the living great apes to which humans themselves belong. These other systems will be examined to provide valuable insights on how human families operate.

The primary task of the family as a biologic device is to produce new individuals to augment and expand the umbrella group, and to replenish those members who have expired. To perform this indispensable function, the family has to create and maintain an appropriate milieu to efficiently raise, nurture, and socialize the offspring it produces.

Humans are mortal like most organisms on my host planet. Mortality is the state of being subject to Death. Death is the termination of individual existence and can occur in one of two distinct ways—the individual could be killed by an anomalous event or accident, or the individual may be programmed to die after a predetermined interval of time. Both mechanisms afflict humans. Since the act of dying permanently removes individuals from the ancestral group, the dead ones must be predictably replaced by fresh members if the species is to survive—for the species to pro-liferate, even more individuals must be reproduced than those that die. This generative function is assigned to the family.

Natural reproduction in humans, as in many multicellular organisms, is by sexual union. Male and female partners who are reproductively active copulate with each other and com-bine their respective gametes—the male Sperm and the female Ovum—to form a single fused cell called the Zygote from the Greek *zygotos* meaning "yoked". A zygote is the single-celled embryo that goes on to develop into a fully-fledged organ-ism. Before forming the zygote, the gamete from each parent, having previously undergone a special "reduction division" known as Meiosis, now possesses exactly half the total number of chromosomes (Haploid) than is found in all the other cells of that parent (Diploid.) The zygote therefore inherits exactly half its chromosomes from the haploid gamete of one parent, and the other half from the haploid gamete of the other parent, joined together to form the diploid zygote.

In the zygote, the two parental halves combine within a single nucleus, thereby reconstituting the full diploid number of chromosomes typical for that particular species. In the ma-jority of mammals[40], the zygote thus produced by the union of gametes, implants itself in the female uterus and develops into a viable organism. It is subsequently expelled from the

---

40 Monotremes are mammals that are exceptions to this rule. Unlike other mam-mals, they lay eggs instead of giving birth to live young. Monotremes are indigenous only to Australia and the adjoining island of New Guinea. They include the platypus, and four species of echidnas (spiny anteaters).

mother's uterus after a gestation period unique to each species. The human gestation period is approximately nine months or about 40 weeks. At birth the offspring is not yet fully developed. Especially in humans, the offspring emerges very fragile and extremely immature; it cannot survive outside the womb without extraordinary parental care and solicitude.

It should be noted here that new knowledge and technical ability now make it possible for humans to fabricate a complete and viable organism by Cloning a diploid somatic cell from a single individual. In biology, cloning is the process of producing genetically identical individuals from a single parent. Cloning occurs naturally when organisms reproduce asexually, such as propagation of plants from vegetative cuttings; or artificially, when identical copies of an organism are created from a single diploid cell using biotechnology. Humans have successfully cloned several species of mammals so far, thus eliminating, in principle at least, the need for sexual union in those animals for reproduction. The technique of cloning can be adapted for humans as well, though the practice has been prohibited so far for human reproduction.

Among *Homo sapiens*, the dynamics of sexual cohabitation between male and female partners within a family unit may occur through different modes of association between the cohabiting individuals. As previously described in this narrative, and repeated here for emphasis, two types of reproductive liaisons are possible among the participants. One is monogamy, the other polygamy. In monogamy, a single male and a single female have an exclusive alliance with each other and copulate and reproduce only between themselves—all offspring in that family unit are progeny of these two individuals alone. In polygamy, individuals copulate and reproduce with several different partners. Both males and females may adopt and practice polygamy. Within polygamy itself there are three sorts of possible liaisons: polygyny, where a single male cohabits with multiple females; polyandry, where one female cohabits with multiple males; and polyandrogyny, where multiple females cohabit with multiple males.

As a general rule, monogamy is rare among animals on my host planet. Less than 3% of mammals are monogamous. Monogamy is more frequent in birds. Pairing makes more sense for birds because successful child rearing requires both parents to incubate the eggs and provide food for their offspring which hatch from these eggs outside the mother's body. In mammals on the other hand, the fetus grows inside the mother and she lactates to feed her baby after birth, activities in which males can play no part, thus discouraging monogamy. Even among birds, though many are socially monogamous, sexual monogamy is much less common, with more than 30% of chicks in any nest being sired by someone other than the resident male. In mammals, examples of monogamy among primates are found in gibbons, a few marmosets and tamarins, and in some human cultures. Polygamy, by all estimates, is a far more common practice among mammals, including primates, with polygyny being the predominant mode. Behaviorally, the great apes follow this pattern.

Among primates in particular, sexual dimorphism, or the difference in body size between males and females within a species, tends to correlate with sexual behavior. When males are significantly larger than females, polygyny predominates; when dimorphism is absent or minimal, either polyandrogyny or monogamy is the rule.

On Galymon we have no genders and no sexual reproduction. Since galymonians possess an undetermined lifespan, and death occurs only infrequently by accident or suicide, reproduction is rarely an important issue for us. Our population has been stable now for over a billion Earth years, remaining at about the carrying capacity of our home planet. If and when offspring are desired, replication of the parent by multidimensional printing is readily available. It should be noted that humans themselves have recently started replicating simple objects by employing three-dimensional printing. 3-D printing is a process for reproducing solid objects from a digital model, much like producing offspring on Galymon. In the case of Earth admittedly, it may appear rather puzzling why evolution produced two distinct genders in most animals on that planet, when just one gender would have been quite enough and caused much less fuss to boot. Reproduction, it would seem, could be far more efficiently organized with only one gender to deal with. If two genders were really needed, then why not three, or even more?

Because lifespan is limited for the majority of Earth based organisms, the most important task for creatures on my host planet is to produce as many descendants as they can. Among plants and many lower animals, this function can be achieved without sex—sans eggs and spermatozoa. Ferns release millions of microscopic nonsexual spores that can grow into new plants if they fall on suitable ground. Numerous other plants reproduce asexually. In sea anemones, jellyfish, marine worms and such other creatures, organisms may bud children directly off their bodies, to spawn new and genetically identical individuals. All unicellular microorganisms reproduce by growing and dividing asexually, raising huge populations of similar descendants. Such asexual reproduction rests on the ability of cells to vegetatively grow and divide, a property common to all forms of life on Earth. Yet for the majority of animals on my host planet, especially the higher and more complex ones, sexual reproduction generally is the rule. Why is that so?

Though asexual reproduction can quickly create large populations of virtually identical individuals, it is of limited value in producing the genetic diversity required for natural selection to operate and bring about adaptive evolutionary change in Earth-based lifeforms. Quite evidently, in vegetative or asexual reproduction, all offspring are genetically the same as the parent. Therefore, susceptibility to an adverse or lethal condition affecting one progeny would quite likely affect all, and possibly none of them might survive the challenge. Sexual reproduction on the other hand, not only serves to replace expired individuals—as does asexual reproduction—but it also produces the genetic variation among offspring needed to survive under adverse environmental conditions. It thus offers a double guarantee. The fundamental distinction between the two types of reproduction is that offspring from nonsexual propagation have only a single parent and are thus all practically alike, whereas those from sexual reproduction have two parents and are never exact replicas of either parent, or their siblings. Sexual reproduction therefore diffuses genetic variation into otherwise congruent populations. For this very reason, sex became established on my host planet quite early in the history of life, thereby facilitating natural selection and environmental adaptation.

Genetic variation within species is essential for natural selection to occur. Even nonsexually reproducing unicellular organisms exchange genetic material directly between individual cells to augment genetic diversity by a process called Conjugation. In conjugation, two cells may line up with each other and hook their insides together using microtubules to exchange genetic material, after which the cells disconnect and go their separate ways. This early appearance of "pseudosexuality" or coupling behavior in prokaryotes eventually led to the clear morphological separation of the sexes in many multicellular organisms. This divergence between female and male sexes within a single species can sometimes be quite extreme, even to the extent that the genders may seem to appear and behave like completely different species.

The familiar egg-and-sperm scenario arose once binary mating systems became established. Some individuals (males) within a species began to specialize in producing immense numbers of small motile sperm, while other individuals (females) invested in a much smaller number of large nutrient-filled eggs. This new division of reproductive roles between female and the male genders was clearly a bonanza for evolution. Mathematical models seem to suggest that anything different from this binary prototype would be at a selective disadvantage due to the Principle of Parsimony. Nature can be fabulously extravagant if necessary, but when the same outcome can be obtained with fewer variables, then that would become the preferred pathway—two genders work just as well as multiple ones for genetic diversity in the offspring. This explains the absence of more than two types of sex cells in animals, and clarifies the reason why there are no more than two genders present. Two-gender sex differentiation thus evolved as the most efficient means to produce genetic variation in offspring, and may have arisen independently among different groups of animals.

In certain species, both sexes may be present in the same individual. Such animals are called Hermaphrodites. They do not comprise a third sex however, but rather possess both sexes jointly. Hermaphrodites tend to be found in animals that move sluggishly or may be stationary, and therefore less likely to mate actively. Having both sexes in the same animal is thus an advantage to them. Barnacles, sea squirts, slugs, snails, earthworms, flatworms, tapeworms and others are all hermaphrodites. Ovaries and testes, producing eggs and sperm respectively, are present in the same individual. Though self-fertilization does occur in these animals, cross-fertilization to ensure genetic variation is encouraged by certain reproductive strategies. Maturation of eggs and sperm in the same individual may happen at different times, or mutual copulation—where each member of a mating pair introduces sperm into the other during sex—may be adopted. Oysters and certain shrimp display sequential hermaphroditism, where the animal completely reverses its gender seasonally. In one breeding season it may be a fully-fledged biologic male, in another a complete female. This form of facultative biologic genderism is the norm among strong-force lifeforms inhabiting the neutron star Utu near the supermassive black hole at the center of the Sombrero galaxy (NGC 4594) in Virgo. That galaxy is 28 million light years from Earth. The Sombrero sports a central supermassive black hole of more than 1 billion solar masses, easily one of the largest such objects detected by humans from my host planet. Some of the lifeforms from Utu have recently colonized bits of the central black hole itself.

Mac began studying human family structure and dynamics by comparing related behaviors among the kindred great apes. Humans are animals differing from other animals on their planet not in kind, but only in the degree of development. Therefore, any study of family behavior in this species must be preceded by a sufficient knowledge of other mammals, especially primates, particularly the great apes. Great apes are primates belonging to the family Hominidae, presently consisting of four living representatives—humans, chimpanzees, gorillas, and orangutans. One common feature clearly present in all great apes and noticed immediately by any extraterrestrial visitor to their planet, is that they are all very social animals and gregarious by nature. They prefer not to function as lone operatives, but would rather band together in groups of varying numbers to accomplish their designated mission. Sophisticated team work and organizational skills within a hierarchical structure, and the common sharing of rewards and risks among the participants, are notable features of group behavior in great apes. These same animals display similar attitudes when operating as families.

❧⸙❦⸙❧

Orangutans are the only great apes living today that did not originate in Africa. Unlike their other three hominid brethren, orangutans evolved in Asia. Apart from humans, they are the only other great ape still naturally living outside Africa. Orangutans—*orang hutan* means "person of the forest" in the local Malay language—live in trees in the dense forest canopy and are primarily arboreal. They once ranged widely in Asia, from across the Indonesian archipelago, through southeast Asia, into mainland China. These gentle creatures had even discovered a form of herbal medicine, using the masticated leaves of the *Commelina* plant as an anti-inflammatory salve or ointment. Yet today, this winsome creature with the ruddy hair and pensive face has been lamentably reduced to just two tiny populations clinging desperately to shrinking enclaves in the Indonesian islands of Borneo and Sumatra. These close relatives of humans have been hurtling toward extinction ever since their unhappy encounter with the genus *Homo* emigrating eastward from Africa into Asia. Since then, orangutans have been reduced to less than 30,000 individuals today, divided between two species, *Pongo pygmaeus* the Bornean orangutan (about 20,000 left), and *Pongo abelii* the Sumatran variety (about 10,000 left). If this gruesome holocaust continues unabated, orangutans will all be extinct in barely a dozen years from now.

Orangutans are by far the most arboreal of the great apes and spend the majority of their life on trees in the confines of their tropical forest habitat. Fruit is the predominant component of their diet; they will also eat leaves, bark, insects, honey, and eggs removed from birds' nests. Orangutans spend most of their daylight hours alone, feeding, resting and traveling from place to place in their forested homeland. When evening arrives, they make nests in trees for the nightfall to come. After selecting a suitable tree, they climb to the proposed nest site and draw branches in, wedging the branches together at a central point to form a firm foundation. They then weave leafy branches onto this foundation, braiding the tips into a mattress. Some may add vegetation-derived pillows, blankets, and even rooftops to their nests. Orangutans can also improvise and use simple tools for capturing insects from tree-hollows, and extracting nutritious seed from hard-husked fruit.

Orangutans are considered the least social of the great apes. Their interpersonal behavior is sometimes described as "solitary, but social." They display marked sexual dimorphism: mature, sexually active males are more than twice as large as females. Dominant adult males have distinctive cheek pads and emit long calls that attract females while intimidating rival males. These long calls can penetrate over half a mile into the dense thick forest, and carry information about who is calling, and why. Younger males do not display these characteristics; they more closely resemble adult females in their mannerisms. Orangutan society is made up of "resident" as well as "transient" individuals of both sexes. Transient males and females meander broadly in the forest until they acquire a home range and settle down. These transient individuals travel alone, although as juveniles they may travel in small groups.

Adult males, as well as independent adolescents of both sexes, tend to be solitary and live by themselves. Resident adult females may reside with a child in a defined home range that overlaps those of other resident adult females who may be kin to them, such as mothers, sisters, or aunts. Upwards of one to several female home ranges are incorporated within the home range of a single adult resident male who is their primary breeding partner and sire for their offspring. Orangutans, therefore, have a polygynous mating system where one male breeds with several females; in this case the females happen to live in separate "households" or ranges. Since the ranges of resident males and resident females overlap, orangutans encounter each other and engage in brief social interactions.

The most significant social bonding among orangutans is between adult females and their dependent or recently weaned offspring. Since these animals are mostly solitary by nature, almost everything a young orangutan learns is from the mother. Females devote a great deal of time and effort to raising their children, one offspring at a time; the male provides no parental contribution. Females give birth only once in every seven or eight years. In the first year of an orangutan's life, the baby is almost permanently glued to its mother's body. For the following six or seven years, the offspring will never stray far from her side until the next sibling is born. After that, young females may linger a while and learn how their mothers care for newborn infants. Young males are evicted soon after the new sibling is born. Apart from humans, orangutans have the longest childhood dependency among animals.

Gorillas are in steep decline. They inhabit the vanishing tropical forests of western and east-central Africa. Presently two gorilla species survive, though just barely. They are the Western gorilla (*Gorilla gorilla*) and the Eastern gorilla (*Gorilla beringei*). Different races of these two gorilla species have been proposed by humans and given subspecies names: they are the two Western gorilla races (Western Lowland gorilla, and Cross River gorilla), and the two Eastern gorilla races (Eastern Lowland gorilla, and Mountain gorilla). Gorillas are critically endangered on their planet today, barely holding on to their disappearing habitat in Africa and being pummeled to death by the egregious poaching for their meat by murderous human cousins. Counted altogether, there are just about 100,000 gorillas of both species left on Earth, and among the races, only a few hundred Mountain and Cross River gorillas remain. In the not too distant future these precious gorillas will be gone from their old neighborhood, a few specimens prominently displayed in zoos around the world for humans responsible for their disappearance to observe and sadly reminisce.

Gorillas provide useful insights into human sexuality, family structure, and interpersonal functioning. Gorillas live together in small communities called troops that average about ten individuals each. Though the composition of troop membership may vary in particular cases, most gorilla troops tend to be composed of one mature adult male called a silverback, and multiple adult females with children that were likely fathered by the silverback himself. Silverbacks are typically over twelve years old and are so called because of the presence of silvery gray hair on their back, a sign of wisdom and maturity in the gorilla world. Silverbacks also possess prominent canine teeth that develop with maturity in these extraordinary creatures.

As the youngsters in a silverback's troop reach adulthood, they tend to leave their birth group and join other troops. Adult male gorillas may exit the natal group to establish their own troops by attracting emigrating females. In some ethnic gorilla populations, males may choose to remain with their natal troops and become subordinate to the reigning silverback. These subordinate males may occasionally sneak around the patriarch and copulate with a new or immigrant female when the old man is not looking. They may also get to replace him if the silverback dies or is deposed.

Gorillas demonstrate marked sexual dimorphism. Adult females are only about half the size of a silverback or even smaller. The silverback himself is the main focus of the troop's attention. He makes all the important decisions for his gorilla family. He mediates conflicts between individual gorillas, determines the group's movements, leads them to good feeding sites, and takes full responsibility for the safety and well-being of his troop. Backup protection for the troop may be provided by younger males subordinate to the silverback. These juveniles are known as brownbacks since they do not possess the sovereign's majestic silver hair on their backs.

Relationships between adult female gorillas vary within the troop, depending on the degree of consanguinity or biological relatedness among the players. Maternally related females in a troop tend to affiliate closely with each other and have friendly mutual interactions between them. On the other hand, unrelated females often act aggressively among themselves, and they could be quite mean and nasty to one another. These hostile interactions between females are often focused around social access to the silverback or another male member of the troop, with males intervening in fights between females. Adult females compete to groom and stay close to the silverback.

A female gorilla is ready to have babies when she is about eight years old. At birth the little infant weighs less than 4 pounds, while the mother can weigh over 200 pounds. Gorilla births are therefore quick and easy to deliver. The solicitous mother carries the tiny baby against her ample chest for the first several months until the infant can cling onto her back, which then frees the mother's hands for knuckle-walking and carrying food around. The newborn baby grows quickly. At 5 months it learns to walk, and by 18 months it can follow the mother on foot for short distances, though the safest place for the youngster is still momma's back as she navigates the dense vegetation of their forest home. Young gorillas learn by imitation. Even the dominant silverback is patient and gentle with them as they practice their newfound skills on him.

Gorilla family structure is exclusively polygynous. Multiple females share a common homebase with a dominant silverback with whom they all breed, raising their offspring within this highly patriarchal culture. The bond that a silverback has with his females forms the cornerstone of gorilla social life. These bonds between the silverback and his harem are maintained and reinforced by close physical proximity and grooming behavior. Having robust and enduring relationships with the dominant male is fundamental for gorilla females, as the male provides them with mating opportunities in addition to protection from predators and infanticidal gorilla males who would otherwise swiftly kill the babies. Infanticide is the killing of young offspring by an adult of the same species. One practical reason for infanticide by reproductively active males is to eliminate a rival's genes and substitute their own instead[41]. The death of her offspring allows the nursing mother to quickly become fertile once again and be sexually receptive to the infanticidal male, allowing him to propagate his own genes.

During her lifetime a female gorilla produces less than four offspring. She bears them one at a time and spaces them about four years apart. In this way she can devote all the energies of motherhood exclusively to raising a single youngster each time. Notwithstanding her sacrifice, the chances of surviving the first few years of childhood for a gorilla infant is less than fifty percent.

Gorillas communicate using about twenty-five different

---

41 Postpartum female infanticide was practiced by humans until relatively recent times. It is still occasionally seen in some cultures. In humans, most infanticides are committed by the biologic parent for social and economic reasons, not the step-parent for genetic ones. After humans recently acquired the ability to determine gender *in utero* using ultrasound, female feticide has become widespread in certain societies, especially in Asia. Millions of female human fetuses are killed before birth in China and India.

vocalizations. They are affectionate and patient with their children and often take time to play with younger members of the troop. Youngsters are disciplined whenever necessary with disapproving looks and disavowing body postures; they may also be scolded with reproachful vocalizations. No corporeal punishment is used.

※

Chimpanzees comprise two species, the common chimpanzee (*Pan troglodytes*) and the pygmy chimpanzee or bonobo (*Pan paniscus*). Certain subspecies of the common chimpanzee have also been named. Chimpanzees evolved in Africa and never left that continent. At the time of this writing they occupied a discontinuous and dwindling forest range in tropical Africa straddling their planet's equatorial line, from Guinea in the west through the Congo River basin in central Africa, to Uganda in the east. Bonobos are found only in the Congo region. The primary habitat of chimpanzees is the equatorial rainforest once prolific and abundant in Africa. Regrettably, deforestation in modern times has left only fragmentary patches of this once huge forest, displacing chimpanzees into drier and less hospitable areas such as exposed woodlands or even open savannah. Today, with the ecological collapse of their habitat and humans mercilessly hunting them for bush meat, there are less than 150,000 chimpanzees of all stripes left on their planet. The future of this most humanlike species is now considered extremely endangered or even doomed.

Chimpanzees are the closest living relatives to humans on their planet today. The two species split apart from a common simian ancestor approximately six million years ago. As already noted in this narrative, chimpanzees share upward of 98 percent of the genetic information in their DNA with people. Unsurprisingly then, chimpanzees are highly status conscious and acquire influence and rank by sharing food and other resources with their group. They employ hunting strategies that require communication and cooperation between hunters. Like humans, they can be manipulative and capable of deception. Chimpanzees can be taught to use symbols and recognize aspects of human language such as syntax, numbers, and numerical sequences. They show altruism, and engage in anticipatory planning.

Both surviving species of chimpanzees share comparable family structure and dynamics, though bonobos are far less domineering and aggressive than common chimpanzees, even as bonobos are more libidinous and sexually active among themselves. Bonobo social structure is considerably more egalitarian than the social structure of common chimpanzees. Bonobos also exhibit much stronger and longer lasting female-female bonding. Sexual dimorphism is minimal in chimpanzees and bonobos. Dimorphism in them is about the same as in humans. Adult females are about 80 percent the size of adult males.

Chimpanzees live in small communities or "villages" containing anywhere between 25 to 150 residents. These communities divide into smaller groups during the day to forage for food, or perform other duties such as policing or perimeter defense. Before their star sets for the evening, these denizens return to the village to retire for the night, each in their own individual bed made of leaves and twigs nestled in trees. These beds are made fresh each evening. Beds are only shared by a mother and her nursing baby. Sleeping in a fresh bed each day effectively discourages infestation by bed-bugs, lice, and other parasitic insects that may carry communicable diseases. Chimpanzees are also known to self-medicate with herbs. Along with humans living in the area, they ingest the pith of a small shrub that grows in tropical Africa called *Vernonia amygdalina*; commonly known as bitter leaf, they use it to control intestinal nematode infestations.

These great apes have complex social and family relationships within their community, spending a great deal of time together in intimate subgroups where they frequently touch, feel, and groom each other. At the core of chimpanzee social structure are the males who patrol the village and its environs. These males protect the community from predators, as well as other hostile chimpanzee tribes, and search for food and water resources for their own membership. Chimpanzees, like humans, are highly territorial and wage wars and kill other chimpanzees over land borders and access to resources.

Males usually remain in their native villages where they were born and raised. Females, instead, tend to leave their tribe during adolescence and migrate away from their village to join other chimpanzee communities, thus reinforcing exogamy and genetic diversity. Because of this pattern of female exodus, males within a community are much more likely to be related to each other than females are. Chimpanzees residing in a village tend to associate and socialize in smaller subgroups of various sizes. Individual chimpanzees have a high degree of autonomy within these social subgroups and come and go as they please. Hence these subgroups are protean in nature, and their composition is constantly changing. Chimpanzees are remarkably similar to humans in this respect.

Also much like humans, chimpanzees mate year round and

may give birth at any time during the year. Their mating behavior tends to be promiscuous, the female copulating with multiple males in her community. Sometimes a female may leave her own community to mate with males from another tribe and then return pregnant to her own village where she already has a support system in place to help carry her pregnancy to term. Especially among bonobos, eroticism and frequent sexual intercourse play a major role in the group's social cohesion. Individuals engage in mutual sexual activity and coitus when greeting each other and during play. They also customarily use sex for conflict resolution, as well as post-conflict reconciliation. Bonobos particularly, and common chimpanzees less frequently, engage in autoerotic, multi-partner, male-male, and female-female sexual activity, behaviors also found among humans on my host planet. Among bonobos especially, sexual interactions occur across and within all age groups.

In polyandrogyny, copulating females receive spermatozoa from multiple males. Therefore, the greater the mass of semen ejaculated by any one male, the greater his chances to fertilize the ovum, thus affecting individual fitness for that male—the number of genes he passes on to the next generation. Consequently, male chimpanzees and bonobos have large and heavy-set testicles to produce copious amounts of semen. Male humans, too, sported large testicles in their polyandrogynous incarnation, as noted for the noble Itu-Kan of Lake Kivu. Those testicles in humans shrank after polyandry was prohibited by the new institution of marriage introduced in the Holocene. The new polygynous regime did not require copious sperming of females since now there was no competition from other males in this regard. So just like orangutans and gorillas which are polygynous and have relatively small testicles, male humans too became selected for smaller gonads in the Holocene.

Care for the young in chimpanzees and bonobos is provided exclusively by their mothers; fathers do not participate. The physical and emotional well-being of their babies depend largely on the mothers' undivided attention to them. For instance, adult male chimpanzees may engage in infanticide on the little ones if maternal protection is lacking or inadequate. Mothers provide their children with food, nurturing and protection, and teach them the knowledge and skills they will need to live successfully and prosper in chimpanzee communities. Infant chimpanzees cling to their mothers' bellies during the first several weeks of their life. Like human newborns, but for less time, these baby chimpanzees are unable to sit up as their neuronal pathways are still immature and underdeveloped. This phenomenon of extended brain growth and maturation even after completing full gestation is called Neoteny.

Neoteny is an elegant mechanism devised by evolution to allow for more complex and sophisticated organisms to emerge. It is a unique process that prolongs the time available for organisms to mature, thus permitting them to acquire a higher level of organization and development. Neoteny prolongs immaturity in the offspring, thereby giving the beneficiary additional time and opportunity to develop more elaborate structures and functions. To put it another way, neoteny permits the developing individual to remain plastic and malleable for a longer time, before having to mature and settle into its final form. Though neoteny itself is a clever mechanism allowing for more developmental time to acquire advanced organization and behavior, it certainly places a severe burden on the parent because the underdeveloped offspring is much more fragile and vulnerable at birth and therefore more dependent, and for a longer time, on the caregiver for nurturing and protection. Neoteny is found in its most extreme form in *Homo sapiens*.

At six months of age, chimpanzee infants ride on mama's back, maintaining continuous physical contact with her throughout their first year of life. By age two they begin to individuate, moving and sitting independently from their mothers, yet remaining within her range of vision. By age three they may move beyond her visual range. At five they are weaned and childhood ends. A juvenile period follows and lasts another four years. These juveniles remain bonded with their mothers, but also begin to interact with others of their community. Emergent adolescent females now move between communities, and adolescent males engage with adult males in communal activities like hunting parties and boundary patrols.

⁕

The core family unit for mammals on my host planet is the female parent and her offspring. This basic mammalian model is faithfully followed in most primates as well. The role for the male animal in reproduction is to simply impregnate the female by fertilizing her ovum; males have no other role to play in propagating their kind. The only reason the male is even required is to provide the genetic variation needed for natural selection to operate; otherwise, males would have long since been discarded by evolution. Carrying the embryo to term and conscientiously raising the offspring until it can survive on its own has fundamentally been a maternal function in mammals. Certainly, this natural state of affairs would indeed be expected, since babies physically belong to their mothers for everyone to see. Fathers remain anonymous and have no role in that program. As noted in this narrative earlier, mammals, except for monotremes, are viviparous, meaning the female alone gives birth to live young which are evidently her own physical creation, after a period of gestation she completes entirely by herself. When live offspring appear, in every mammalian species including monotremes[42], the female parent singlehandedly provides food for her newborn in the form of milk expressed from her mammary glands. Males are not needed for any of this. Male mammals, therefore, lack the required anatomy, physiology, and psychology to provide services in this parenting context, and simply lack the necessary instinctual drive to contribute to individual parenting. Some may help in nonspecific ways, like the silverback does for his gorilla troop.

The invention and institutionalization of marriage among *Homo sapiens* drastically changed both human sexual behavior and their existing family structure. Marriage itself began hardly 10,000 years ago as the Holocene Epoch was gathering steam and humans abandoned their Paleolithic ethos to establish settlements as Neolithic farmers. Marriage was unnatural to them as hominins and was not a part of their biopsychology. The purpose of marriage for this most invasive of species was entirely utilitarian—to provide a framework on which to produce and raise a multitude of neotenous offspring and thus relentlessly proliferate their kind. Marriage proved to be enormously successful in this mission, increasing the human population by over 7,000-fold in that brief period of 10,000 years. Male humans were drafted into marriage by social customs to donate necessary parenting services to the mother to

---

42 Monotremes have no nipples and so the young, after hatching from eggs, simply lick the milk that oozes out from the skin of the mother's abdomen.

help her raise her numerous offspring required for this population surge. Because marriage is artificial and its purpose is fundamentally to grow a multitude of children, marriages tend to fail mostly after the children are raised.

The bonding and intimate relatedness between mother and child are both qualitatively and quantitatively very different from anything seen between father and child. Human fathers contribute 23 nuclear chromosomes to their offspring, and not much else. Mothers, apart from also contributing a corresponding complement of 23 nuclear chromosomes, are in addition the sole providers of all other cell components to their children, including mitochondria which have their own unique DNA. These mitochondria are the energy producing constituents of cells. The mitochondria in every cell of the offspring are direct descendants of the mitochondria present in the cytoplasm of the egg cell from the mother. The father makes no functional contribution of cytoplasm to the zygote, his entire donation being limited to one half of the nuclear chromosomes found in that cell. Structurally, the zygote is identical to the mother's ovum, except it has a diploid complement of chromosomes now.

Even more astonishingly, through an unusual biological phenomenon called Chimerism[43], this mother-offspring relatedness goes far deeper than just providing mitochondria and other cellular components to the fetus. During pregnancy, there is an actual physical exchange of complete cells between mother and fetus. Though this is a selective and not a wholesale exchange

---

43   Chimerism is a term in biology derived from the name for a fabulous beast in Greek mythology called the Chimera. The Chimera is a fire-breathing female monster composed of the parts of three animals: a lion, a snake, and a goat. In biology, an organism made up of cells from two or more individuals is called a chimera.

of cells—known as microchimerism—intact cells from mother and fetus do indeed colonize each other's physical bodies and remain in the recipient's system for life. Functioning adult neurons from previous offspring are found in maternal brains, and immunologic cells from their mothers continue to function in the offspring's immune system. All placental animals, including *Homo sapiens*, exchange cells in this way between mother and child, thereby cementing, along with other contributing genetic and environmental factors, the uniquely indispensable bond necessary for primary mother-offspring parenting to occur. In this very real sense, all humans are chimeras with their mothers. Whether male or female, every individual carries complete and functioning cells from their mothers throughout their lives, and all mothers harbor cells from their children for a lifetime. Fathers never get to participate in the formulation of their children in this extraordinarily intimate way. The primary biologic role for fathers is simply to introduce a single solitary sperm to double the number of nuclear chromosomes in the ovum to allow for variation to occur so that evolution through natural selection can work.

Clearly too, like no father can ever experience or even imagine, mothers are organically bound to their offspring by the process of pregnancy itself. Males do not become pregnant. Having a complete individual develop within one's own physical body during gestation, and then have that offspring emerge alive and fully formed through the birth canal, is a transcendental experience quite unknowable to males. This maternal perspective of actually creating her child forges an enduring physical and psychological bond unreachable to fathers.

Among orangutans, gorillas, and chimpanzees, as mentioned earlier, the female produces just one infant at a time which she then proceeds to raise over several years all by herself, until the offspring is grown and self-sufficient. Only then does the mother split form her child to once again become pregnant and raise yet another youngster. Orangutan mothers may birth two or three children in a lifetime and spend about eight years caring for each one of them. Gorillas have approximately four children per female and spend about four years with each offspring. Chimpanzee mothers also have around four kids, with the parent devoting about five years of her lifetime to each surviving child. Since nearly half or more of the progeny of these nonhuman great apes perish in infancy or early childhood, only just about enough adults survive to maintain stable population numbers. Clearly, this procreative obligation is an enormous imposition on the mother, demanding huge quantities of her resources and time for reproduction and child-rearing activities. Additionally, she risks considerable hazard to her own life and health from the pregnancy itself. The mother receives no direct material benefit from this effort. Raising children also extracts a societal cost on the group hosting the child. Obviously then, the only clear beneficiary is the species itself, which is thereby sustained and possibly even increased in numbers by the new members produced and added by females. For the individual female parent however, reproduction remains an enormously expensive liability. It is a huge sacrifice they perform for their species because the instinct to reproduce is powerfully vested in their female natures.

Evolution's introduction of neoteny in the higher primates, especially to the extent and degree seen in *Homo sapiens*, placed a steep and unsustainable burden on human females. The extremely fragile and delicate condition of human babies at birth, their demanding natures, their prolonged infancy and childhood, the delayed maturation of their brains and nervous system, and their insatiable curiosity and exponential learning curves, all made it very inconvenient for mothers to single-handedly raise their own offspring as the other great apes did. They desperately needed a helpmate.

This parenthood role quickly became overwhelming for human mothers as the Holocene Epoch was dawning. During their reproductive years, human females remain fertile and sexually active, and continue to become pregnant and produce offspring even as they are intensely engaged in raising a child already. This is a clear departure from the other great apes, solely for the benefit of population growth. It was certainly not uncommon among humans to encounter a mother with six or more vigorously consuming and growing children in her care, all together at the same time. A single human female is capable of having a dozen or more offspring during her reproductive lifetime. This task began at puberty with the onset of menarche[44] around age thirteen and could continue for twenty-five years or longer. The economic cost alone of raising a single human offspring from conception to late adolescence may require

---

44 Menarche heralds the onset of sexual maturity and cyclical ovulation in human females. Ovulation ends in menstruation if pregnancy does not occur in that cycle. These cycles are roughly in rhythm with their Moon's periodicity around Earth. The age of onset for menarche has been steadily falling for modern humans. In 90 BP it was 16.6 years for girls in the United States of America. In 53 AP it averaged just 12.5 years for U.S. girls, a drop of more than 4 years in less than 150 years.

as much resource as generated by the mother working full-time for five years of her life.

Among the core behaviors that led to the overarching dominance of humans on their planet, probably the most important one was the reproductive strategy they adopted at the beginning of the Holocene. By actively electing to raise multiple offspring in parallel, a genuinely novel model among hominids, these humans exponentially increased their numbers to rapidly populate the Earth. The population explosion achieved in this way by humans in so short a time is unparalleled by any other large mammal in the entire history of my host planet. This remarkable strategy sharply contrasts with the reproductive style of the other living great apes which as noted raise their young serially, one after the other, devoting large chunks of time to each offspring in sequence.

Because of the extreme neoteny of human development, and the long dependency period demanded by their young, the traditional mother-based family model for hominids would have been extraordinarily onerous and virtually unmanageable for single human females under this new reproductive regime. The plethora of offspring required to supercharge their population numbers would have been impossible for human females to accomplish on their own. That intolerable situation prompted these females to co-opt an appropriate male to assist them with rearing their children, a feat accomplished by overtly restricting their sexual activity to just that designated male. Thus did the institution of marriage first begin in the Neolithic Age.

In summary then, neoteny was the developmental key to the vastly superior cognitive prowess of *Homo sapiens* compared to all other hominids that ever inhabited their planet. Neoteny, however, then added prohibitively to parental hardship, prompting human females to either limit the number of offspring like the other hominids did, or else secure an alliance with a suitable male partner to help raise her numerous progeny. Humans chose the latter path, thereby inventing marriage and simultaneously kindling the extraordinary human population explosion that defined the Holocene Epoch right up to modern times.

Now, humans and chimpanzees, two closely related species, share in excess of 98% of genes in common. This metric measures all the genomic molecular differences between human and chimpanzee DNA. Most of these differences actually reside in the noncoding regions of DNA, or only affect coding regions in a manner that does not significantly alter properties of the gene products. If these factors are discounted, then the genomes of these two species are up to 99.9% similar in their makeup. Humans are therefore virtually identical to chimpanzees in their genetic blueprint. Yet they appear phenotypically very different from each other, principally in their respective cognitive abilities. What minor change in genotype could translate into such a profound difference in phenotype? The answer probably is a mutation that prolonged developmental maturation and thus introduced unprecedented neoteny.

A conspicuous difference between humans and all other primates is the timing of developmental events evidently produced by this genomic mutation. Because of this change, every single stage in life between conception and death is arrived at later in *Homo sapiens* that in other primates. Only the length of gestation[45] may be comparable between humans and the other living great apes, and that too was only because any further extension of

---

45   The gestational period is 40 weeks in humans, 34 in chimpanzees, 37 in gorillas, and 39 in orangutans.

gestation in humans would have made vaginal delivery virtually impossible for human females due to the anatomical limitations imposed by the mother's fixed pelvic outlet size and the baby's expanding brain and head size. Prolongation of gestation itself would have required major modifications in human female pelvic anatomy, something quite impossible to achieve in the time frame available for evolution to act in this instance.

The full-term human newborn, even after forty weeks of gestation in the maternal womb, is in fact a premature baby. The numerous hazards of prematurity have been deemed by natural selection to be a risk worth taking for a larger brain. No other newborn nonmarsupial mammal is more helpless than a human newborn. It takes *Homo sapiens* almost nine months to begin crawling on all fours, and about twice as long to walk unaided. This delayed maturation, or neoteny, though essential for human cognition to reach the towering heights it would scale later, nonetheless imposed an enormous burden on mothers. Coupled with the Neolithic population explosion being ignited now by surplus agricultural food production, human females found themselves no longer able to support and raise their multiple neotenous offspring on their own dime as hominid females had customarily done in the past. They were therefore compelled to resort to monogamous pair-bonding with a male for assistance in raising their numerous young. The new practice of marriage was the institutional means to that end.

This eventful period in human evolutionary history is swiftly drawing to a close. The enormously successful Neolithic reproductive strategy through marriage saw Earth's human population swell from under 1 million at the start of the Holocene to about 7 billion now, an astonishing increase by a factor of 7000, severely stressing the finite carrying capacity of their planet. Now that human populations are stabilizing after the exponential growth of the previous 10,000 years, this Neolithic reproductive strategy is no longer desirable, or even prudent. Earth's finite resources are stretched to capacity and any further significant increase in the human population would collapse the fragile ecology for *Homo sapiens*. That is exactly what the Malthusian Principle predicts.

Astonishingly though, contrary to the predictions of the Malthusian Principle—and possibly as negative feedback from this lethal population bomb—marriage rates are now declining, as birth rates fall and less babies are produced. Nearly 40% of births in the United States of America in 57 AP were to unmarried or single women. Among other highly developed countries surveyed at that time, the largest unwed birthrates in humans were in Scandinavia, with Iceland reporting 66%, Sweden 55%, Norway 54%, and Denmark 46%. Hardly a century ago, it would have been unthinkable for most humans in any country on Earth to imagine children born out of wedlock—such offspring were offensively called "bastards" then. Now it is becoming the rule, not the exception. That supercharged reproductive dynamism from the early Neolithic has changed radically for this species in barely five short generations to date. Major paradigm shifts frequently happen in this accelerated way.

The structure of the human family is indeed changing swiftly toward the traditional and more sustainable hominid pattern where the mother singly provides most parenting functions for a limited number of offspring. Maintaining population numbers, rather than growing it, is now the new reproductive paradigm. A tad over two offspring per human female would accomplish that goal admirably.

Annotating these observations for my esteemed readers now, humans were hunters and gatherers for most of their evolutionary history. They followed a reproductive strategy identical to their hominid predecessors, and similar to that practiced today by the other living nonhuman great apes: the mother singly parented and raised her offspring by herself, without post-fertilization assistance by the biologic father. As hunters and gatherers, female humans had only a few offspring that were raised serially and spaced widely apart, a pattern typical for hominids. These Paleolithic humans employed a mother-based family structure that is customarily found among primates and most other mammals. Bonding behavior for co-operative parenting by both female and male parent was absent during pre-Neolithic times. Paleolithic human sexuality was reminiscent of sexuality in modern chimpanzees and bonobos, the closest living relatives to humans on Earth today.

With the invention of agriculture by *Homo sapiens* in the early Holocene, and the resulting food-producing revolution of 10,000 years ago, human reproductive strategy changed dramatically. Now having access to reliable and plentiful food supplies, humans were able to devote enormous tranches of effort and resources to producing and raising babies. Mothers quit the old Paleolithic hunting groups to invest undivided time and energy to their numerous offspring, thus creating a clear gender division of labor in this species. The resulting tsunami of neotenous progeny clearly exceeded a mother's capacity to cope entirely on her own, thus requiring the active contribution of energy and resources by both biologic parents toward child rearing, a feature unusual for this clade of animals. Before that could happen though, the parents needed assurance that the offspring they were raising were indeed their own children, since the engine of natural selection clearly demanded the nurturing of one's own genes over that of a competitor's.

Confirming motherhood is straightforward and transparent, but fatherhood was always a matter of faith before the advent of modern genetic testing. It therefore became imperative among these hominans for the female to be monogamous to her mate so that the male can be assured that the offspring he is supporting is indeed his own and carried his genes and not that of another male competitor. Contrariwise, monogamy would not be required of males to establish parenthood. Instead, mating with multiple females would be far more effective in disseminating their genes. So the polyandrogynous sexuality as seen today in the less dimorphic chimpanzees and bonobos which was the norm for *Homo sapiens* before the Neolithic Revolution, now became gender restricted—polygyny was permissible, but polyandry was not. Appropriate marriage customs were soon developed along these lines. Although male monogamy among humans is the advertised mode in contemporary Europe and America, polygyny is common in Asia and Africa. Many males in monogamous cultures maintain mistresses, and numerous monogamists practice serial polygamy through divorce and remarriage. Polygamy is thus deeply entrenched in humans, as in other members of their hominid lineage, influencing the institution of marriage introduced by *Homo sapiens* in the Neolithic.

The institutionalization of marriage along these lines was established only after the Neolithic Revolution began to generate huge surpluses of food to support reproduction. Marriage itself did not exist before then. Therefore, draconian laws had to be promulgated and savage punishments enforced by human cultures to protect and safeguard this unnatural institution from breaking down because of its artificial and synthetic nature. One such brutal custom was the public stoning to death of adulterers who engaged in sexual activity outside of marriage. This practice was only too common in the past. Though adultery is now no longer a criminal offence in modern enlightened societies, it remains prohibited in some antiquated ones, and stoning to death in public of convicted adulterers is still reported from certain locations on Earth. In fact, stoning of adulterous couples to death occurred during Mac's visit to their planet. One such gruesome episode was videotaped by the enforcers and made available to curious viewers around the world. The unfortunate young couple were buried in a sandpit up to their necks with only their heads sticking aboveground; a cabal of angry villagers quickly dispatched the condemned duo with a volley of stones and brickbats.

Even if stoning adulterers to death is now rare compared to the past, the hideously macabre custom of "honor killing" remains quite active in some cultures today, though often unspoken and little advertised. The code operating here is dreadfully stark and chilling. Any contact, even just simple communication, between a man and a woman outside of customary marriage is considered so dishonorable to the girl's family that her relatives are entitled to seek murderous revenge for the infraction. Tradition requires the woman's family to first kill their offending member, before murdering the man who contacted her. Many cases of parents executing daughters, or brothers killing sisters, have been reported in public newspapers. Many more go unheralded.

The unpleasant aftermath of this Neolithic shift in human reproductive strategy and sexual behavior was the introduction of that odious social system known as Patriarchy, an oppressive form of societal organization in which males are the supreme authorities in society. Hence changing rapidly in the Neolithic from an egalitarian culture with no institutionalized gender discrimination, women became both politically and economically disenfranchised and subject to unreasonable male oppression. Females were now principally commissioned to child-bearing, a function indispensable to filling their planet with people. This female dispossession that began more than 10,000 years ago in the Neolithic went unchallenged until hardly 150 years before now. The country of New Zealand, then still a British colony, was the first ever human society on Earth to give women the right to vote in national elections in 67 BP, barely 130 years ago. Even today, in some countries on my host planet, women are not allowed to exercise their franchise due to legal or cultural prohibitions.

The Great Industrial Revolution[46] beginning around 190 BP, introduced a fresh dynamic to human reproduction and family structure. The astonishing material productivity of this new era, leading to the exponential growth of capitalism, materialism, and affluence, demanded the mass recruitment of people to staff and service the assembly lines and factories of this prolific new juggernaut. A readily available source of humans for factory work was the many home-based females still busily raising children the old-fashioned Neolithic way. So once again, following a 10,000 year hiatus between the Agricultural and Industrial Revolutions, human females rejoined a modified

---

46 The Great Industrial Revolution started about 250 years before Mac visited Earth. It began in England in 190 BP and spread globally, characterized chiefly by the replacement of hand-operated tools with power-driven machines. This power was initially derived from the combustion of coal.

"hunting group" now called the workforce, in steadily increasing numbers. Redirection of their attention and energies away from child production at home to the mass production of goods in factories, once again reformulated the female role in society and the associated family structure that went along with it.

The Industrial Revolution began to deconstruct the prevailing Neolithic mechanisms of family and child rearing on my host planet. It reoriented the human family back toward the more normative architecture that existed for these hominans during pre-Neolithic times. Yet those patriarchal Neolithic ways still stubbornly cling to certain human societies even today. There is one in West Asia where females are restricted from driving automobiles and kept segregated from unrelated males, confined to quarantined quarters at home in strict conformity with misogynous traditions and customs. Among other restrictions applied, females are prohibited from traveling anywhere without a male escort, and they may not open a bank account or start a business without the formal consent of their male guardian, generally a husband, father, or brother. In another egregious example from tribes living today in south-central Asia, young girls and women may be traded like chattel or personal property to pay debt obligations, or settle family or clan feuds, a custom called *baad*. The female gender role in these noxious patriarchal societies is restricted to bearing children and keeping house, often in a polygynous relationship, just like in the old Neolithic days.

The many discoveries and inventions of modern science and technology since the Industrial Revolution, incrementally controlled disease, poverty, famine, and pestilence among these humans. Improved nutrition, education, sanitation, and health-care allowed more people to live longer lives, and growing numbers of them to enjoy a full human life expectancy. Vast and devastating pandemics of smallpox, plague, and cholera came under control. Infant and child mortality, which had once been in the stratosphere, dropped back to earth with the introduction of modern vaccines and antibiotics. Maternal mortality rates plummeted with improved antenatal and obstetrical care. Human populations began to consolidate and stabilize in numbers, and the need to commit vast material resources and biologic energy exclusively to reproduction became much less important for species dominance now.

As a consequence of all this, birth rates dropped drastically in many advanced human societies, with fertility rates of just two children or even less per female being quite common in several countries today. It was no longer necessary for human females to produce numerous children as was previously the case, as most offspring now routinely make it to adulthood. Women were therefore once again able to support themselves, as well as raise their fewer offspring on their own. The state offered resources if needed. Women no longer required a permanent male resource provider, or husband, to accomplish that objective. This trend was fully evident by 62 AP when two-fifths of all children in the United States were being raised in single parent households, of which 85% were headed by single mothers.

In 7 AP, safe and effective hormonal contraception for women became commercially available. This seminal development permitted sex and reproduction to be predictably decoupled, allowing women to now decide if, or when, to have children. The synthetic steroid Mifepristone, commonly known as RU-486 or the morning-after-pill, was developed in France a generation ago. It is now widely accessible to human females of all ages to end unwanted pregnancies in the early stages. RU-486 acts by blocking the action of a naturally occurring substance called progesterone that sustains pregnancy, thereby terminating the condition. The drug first became commercially available as an abortifacient in 38 AP. These pharmacologic tools greatly eased the burden of child-bearing for women, thereby liberating them from the twin domains of marriage and patriarchy. Marriage as a cultural institution will disappear in due course, having very successfully served its purpose of expanding the human population on Earth from about 1 million in 10,000 BP to a planetary population of 7 billion humans on 31 October 61 AP, an eye blink in geologic time. The population of *Homo sapiens* is now fast reaching the carrying capacity of their planet, so that the institution of marriage with its passionate devotion to reproduction has become clearly counterproductive for the future of this species.

This trend by contemporary humans to transform the old Neolithic institution of marriage had already advanced a great deal by the time Mac visited their planet. The previously inviolable definition of marriage as an irrevocable, permanent, and lifelong union between a female and a male as endorsed by the Neolithic code, was drastically modified by latter-day humans. Divorce had already become commonplace and acceptable for this species over the last 50 years, and the trend toward increasing divorce rates has continued unabated. In many modern and successful human societies more than half of legal marriages end in divorce. For the year 61 AP in America for instance, 50% of first marriages, 67% of second marriages, and 74% of third marriages ended in divorce. A further categorical downgrading of the formerly impregnable institution of marriage began in 51 AP when the modern country of Netherlands in Western

Europe became the first ever jurisdiction on Earth to recognize same sex marriage, thereby upending the very meaning of that institution itself. Since then, several other important countries on my host planet have followed that example.

The Great Industrial Revolution transformed human sexual behavior and family organization. It set in motion an operant process to revolutionize the Neolithic family structure. The old patriarchal model had been specially formulated to inundate Earth's biosphere with humans. This vigorous reproductive strategy clearly demanded an enormous investment of biologic energy to the enterprise, shortchanging other investments for their future. Now that their planet has been saturated and overrun by these humans to the point of unsustainably for their kind, family structure is swiftly adapting to this new reality. The trend for *Homo sapiens* is now shifting back toward a traditional primate architecture, one where the core family unit is a mother and her offspring, the way it always was for hominids.

Human families are profoundly changing. The concept of family itself is in a state of rapid metamorphosis, evolving from mere biological kinship to one of shared values. It seems quite obvious now that just the accident of birth does not make family.

CHAPTER X:
SOCIETY

Society is always more than the sum of its parts. It is the matrix wherein those separate parts operate. Broadly speaking, society is a composite institution formed by its individual members, permitting those members to cohere harmoniously and integrate their actions within the ambit of an established and predictable order. That order, governed by the general principle of evolution, is forever changing and transforming over time. As a collaborative process, society endows its members with benefits that might otherwise not be available to them as individual players. This effect will operate both ways of course—society regulates the behavior of its parts which in turn influences the nature of society.

Two fundamental features mark all human societies on my host planet today—Caste/Class systems, and Division of Labor.

All human societies possess caste or class systems. These terms refer to patterns of social stratification by which certain categories of people within a given society are considered unequal and ranked according to a distinctive hierarchy. Such social disparity is characterized by dissimilar distribution of status, power, and resources. Caste is different from class by the degree of social mobility allowed in each system.

Caste, more prevalent in the past, is now mostly confined to the Indian subcontinent and its affiliated societies. It is a rigid and immutable social classificatory system based entirely on the circumstances of an individual's birth—the parents' caste is the offspring's caste as well. Caste is defined by skin color, race, lifestyle, occupation, and permissible social interactions. Beginning in ancient times, the subcontinent's culture systematically classified people within society into thousands of endogamous hereditary groups called Jatis. These jatis, according to certain Indian scriptures, are gathered into four Varnas or castes. The four primary castes are Brahmin (priests and religious functionaries), Kshatriya (rulers and soldiers), Vaishya (farmers, herders, craftsmen, and merchants), and Sudra (laborers and providers of menial services). Other people, primarily the many aboriginal inhabitants of India, were deemed so inferior in their social status that they were not included in any caste at all and remained outside the caste system. They were openly ostracized by the traditional castes and designated Pariah or "untouchables." Merely touching one of them physically was believed to cause ritual pollution in the toucher, requiring purification rites. Even today for example, in some Indian villages, pariahs are not permitted to draw portable water from the common village water supply for fear of polluting caste individuals who may use that same water source. Occasional reports of untouchables being brutally murdered for defying such odious and discriminatory customs are encountered in newspapers. Though such discrimination is officially banned by the authorities, the practice still continues among some caste Indians.

Class, however, is quite distinct from caste and exists in all contemporary human societies on Earth. It is a form of social stratification based primarily on education and wealth, not on heredity or birth. Class therefore allows social mobility for individuals who can, through their own efforts, rise to a higher class or fall to a lower one. It thus allows for continuous reshuffling of the pack, encouraging both merit and dynamism in society. Caste, instead, is fixed and permanent, enshrining privilege and dissing merit and equality.

Societies also practice division of labor, whereby categories of tasks and economic activity are assigned to particular groups of people based on age, gender, caste, class, or specialized training. Therefore, when different groups of people in a society engage in different economic activity, a division of labor is said to exist. For example, within a given society, one group may be responsible for planting and harvesting crops, another group tasked with hunting and trapping game—a division of labor would then exist between the two groups. By and large, the most prevalent division of labor is based on gender and occurs between males and females. As economic systems within societies become more advanced, division of labor takes more elaborate forms.

These two hallmarks of human society—caste/class systems and division of labor—are also found in certain other creatures on Earth as well. This latter type of sociality is called eusociality, a term noted before in this narrative. Eusociality, though displaying the two fundamental features of society, is different in its biology from human societies. Many eusocial insects, such as ants, bees, wasps, and termites, have castes with division of labor. In eusociality however, members of at least one social caste lose their ability to perform at least one function that is present in members of another social caste—such as reproduction, or food gathering. In this important way, sociality is different form eusociality. Honeybees for example, a subset of social insects belonging to the genus *Apis*, form complex societies with distinct caste systems and division of labor. Honeybees are the only insects domesticated by humans. They inherit their social roles entirely by birth. They have three castes: queen, drone, and worker. The queen and the worker have the same diploid genome but are phenotypically so very different from each other only because of the food they are fed as larvae. The drone has a haploid genome. The queen's function is to lay eggs, the drone's role is to fertilize the queen, and the worker's job is to gather provisions to feed the colony and raise the brood. Here then is a caste-based, nonhuman society with division of labor. Of course, unlike humans, the caste system and division of labor here are biologically predetermined. Among mammals, besides humans, only two other animals, both burrowing rodents or mole rats[47], have caste-based social systems. Again in this case, their castes are different from human castes because they comprise re-productive and non-reproductive populations, and are therefore eusocial castes.

Humans themselves surgically produce a eusocial caste within their own societies. These individuals, called Eunuchs, are castrated males with both their testicles removed. Testiculectomy (orchiectomy) could be pre-pubertal or post-pubertal. Pre-pubertal eunuchs are behaviorally non-libidinous and generally refrain from copulating as adults; this is not so for post-pubertal ones since they have already been exposed to testosterone. Male castration is very ancient among humans

---

47 The naked mole rat (*Heterocephalus glaber*) is a truly extraordinary animal in two other regards as well—it has an exceptionally lengthy lifespan of 30 years or more which is ten times longer than any other comparable rodent. And it is immune from cancer.

and long predates their written history. It was once extensively employed for social or religious purposes in certain cultures.

A useful way to imagine society is to think of it as a super-organism formed by a multitude of members. This is similar conceptually to individual biologic cells cohering to form a composite organism, which then has its own unique existence. Every object in our Universe, from quarks to galaxies, are organized into "societies" that are in turn members of still larger societies. Our Universe as a whole is the penultimate society, weaving all its constituent parts into one supreme company. For now though, as briefed for this mission before departing my home planet, Mac will examine human society according to the rules and regulations laid out by our Supreme Tribunal on Galymon.

Human society may be viewed as the embedding social matrix for *Homo sapiens*. Humans have a distinctive social, cultural, political, and economic structure. Considered as a species, these attributes have a common biological basis in human nature, and therefore all human societies tend to have similar fundamental characteristics. However, there may be clear and important differences in local values and expectations. To properly appreciate the social architecture of this species at the time of Mac's visit to their planet, it is necessary to examine their previous societal history, as human society has continuously evolved since *Homo sapiens* first speciated some 200,000 years ago.

Today, humans control all the available space on Earth and live on most of its land area. Currently there are more than seven billion individual humans residing in 242 separate political units[48], some large and some small, each with its own government. There are certain differences in how individual human societies are specifically organized at the local level—these differences will be considered when appropriate. However, *Homo sapiens* is a single species with a global distribution and has common behavioral and organizational patterns that have produced a universal human culture beyond these local variations. That makes it possible for individual humans to move alongside and integrate with other human groups elsewhere on their planet without too many difficulties. Like other animals on Earth, humans associate in predictable ways. They form very similar collaborations regardless of their geographic location. Nevertheless, distribution of knowledge and material resources, as well as access to advanced technologies and devices, are not uniformly dispersed around all human societies. Some are grossly lacking in these attributes, others are richly endowed. Autocratic cultural systems, suppression of free speech and expression, and opposition to education, particularly female education, are largely responsible for this disparity among human populations. These differences account for the variation in the local structure of human societies, even though the transactional forces operating within them are very similar.

It is necessary here for the benefit of those esteemed readers who may not be familiar with human manners and customs, to

---

48 In 62 AP there were 242 political units on my host planet (206 sovereign states—some disputed or claimed by others; and 36 dependent territories). Russia had the most land area (6.59 million square miles), Vatican City the least (0.44 square miles); China had the largest population (1.34 billion), Pitcairn Islands the smallest (66).

provide a general account of how these people exchange goods and services among themselves. This knowledge is essential for understanding the structure and functioning of human society. The societal process facilitating this crucial activity is called the Economy. Humans are material beings and need material objects to exist and function on their planet. Beside the basic requirement for food, clothing, and shelter, they also need numerous other goods and services to fulfill their many wants and desires. All this is accomplished through the economy.

The word "economy" derives from the Greek word *oikonomia*, meaning "household management." For post-Neolithic humans, this refers to the efficient exchange of goods and services between people in a "household" or social group. To accomplish this objective, value must be ascribed to each good or service exchanged. This value is determined as the product of two separate functions—Necessity and Scarcity. The first of these attributes, necessity, is a primary component of value; goods or services will have no conventional economic worth if they did not satisfy a perceived necessity[49]. The second variable, scarcity, then adds to the value of the product to be exchanged.

Necessity creates demand for products and thus attaches value to them. For example, hungry humans looking for wheat to eat create a demand for wheat. Wheat therefore assumes value as it is necessary to assuage hunger. Because of its value now, other humans will work to produce wheat for those seeking to acquire it. This creates the classic cycle of Demand and

---

49 There remain some exceptions. Occasionally these hominans ascribe meaningless and exorbitant value to products that, though relatively scarce, have no utilitarian function to speak of. The metallic element gold and other "precious" metals are examples of this anomaly.

Supply. As demand rises, supply follows along with it, until such time that supply can no longer keep up with demand and the product therefore becomes scarcer. On the supply side, even if demand remains constant, drought or disease affecting the wheat crop would likewise make wheat scarcer. As scarcity mounts, the product becomes dearer and therefore more valuable. Consequently, as the price of wheat progressively rises, people will curtail their demand for the product and switch to other possibly less expensive sources of food such as rice or corn. This new slack in demand for wheat decreases its scarcity, increasing its supply, which in turn makes wheat less expensive. The cheaper wheat once again stimulates demand for the product, the demand eventually catching up with the available supply and producing a feedback loop between the two functions. In this manner, necessity and scarcity influence and modulate supply and demand. This simple principle is the ballast of all economic activity among these hominans and is appropriately called the Law of Demand and Supply.

An effective transfer mechanism is evidently needed for economic activity to proceed apace and for goods and services to be equitably exchanged. This was initially accomplished by Barter. Barter involves the exchange of a desired good or service for a similarly valued good or service—such as a bushel of wheat in exchange for a leg of lamb if each of these items were judged to have the same value at the time of the transaction.

The earliest commodity ever used for barter among humans was not a good or product, but a service. Prostitution is a form of sexual barter found in every human society on Earth and is an ancient practice among these hominans. This form of barter is also found in other animal species besides *Homo sapiens*. Adelie penguins (*Pygoscelis adeliae*) are birds that nest along the Antarctic coast in the southern hemisphere of my host planet. Female penguins engage in sexual intercourse with strange males in exchange for nest-building pebbles. These birds are monogamous by nature and remain coupled in exclusive pairs. They build their nests on the ground using pebbles which they collect from the surrounding area. During the nest building season, females will go out alone to collect pebbles; their mates do not suspect their spouse's methods. The female targets a single male working on his nest hoping to attract a permanent female partner. The pebble-seeking female penguin performs a courtship dance before the single male, offering herself as his nesting partner, leading to sexual intercourse with the new male. But she has no intention of settling down with him. After copulation, the sex-bartering female penguin appropriates some of her john's nest building pebbles and then quickly waddles off to her own mate, adding the pebbles to the nest they are building together. Prostitution in penguins is an example of barter. Likewise, female chimpanzees barter sex for food. Humans have an adage identifying prostitution as the oldest profession in their species. It was indeed the earliest form of barter.

Yet barter in most cases is cumbersome and difficult to consummate. If, for instance, someone wanted a chicken and possessed a surplus of apricots for bartering—then the transaction could only be concluded if the owner of the chicken reciprocally needed apricots. If the chicken owner wanted honey instead of the proffered apricots, there could be no deal and barter would fail. In order to complete the transaction therefore, a third person must be found who wanted apricots and had honey to barter for it. The apricots are first exchanged for honey with this third party, and the honey then exchanged for the chicken between the two original parties. Multiple intermediaries may be required for successful bartering, depending on the goods or services desired. This sequence of needs, known as Coincidence of Wants, is incommodious and burdensome to navigate. Humans therefore invented a tool called Money to circumvent this impediment. It functioned as a mechanism to override improbable coincidences of wants.

Money has three functions: it is a store of value, an accounting unit, and a medium of exchange. Firstly, money is a symbolic store of value, meaning that it retains a designated value and thus permits postponement of consumption until some desired future date. Secondly, money is an accounting unit, meaning it allows assignment of value to different goods and services without having to compare the items directly; thus, instead of saying a goat is worth seven bushels of wheat, it can be noted that a goat, or seven bushels of wheat, are both worth a similar unit of money. Thirdly, money is a medium of exchange; it represents a convenient and efficient way for individuals to trade goods and services among themselves.

It is most important here to emphasize that money is entirely a symbolic creation of these hominans and has no intrinsic value of any sort by itself. Money merely serves as a token of exchange, unsupported by anything of material worth. Its import is acknowledged only because of prevailing custom, and resides solely in common convention, and the acknowledgement of those who use it. Backing the "value" of money with a material doodad is meaningless. For example, a fixed quantity of gold or some other material has at times been guaranteed in exchange for a unit of money. This protocol is patently absurd and imparts no difference to the currency in question; it merely substitutes one token (gold) for another (money). Money can have no "gold standard" except for the voluntary acquiescence of those who receive it. Money is an instrument, not a commodity.

Money physically takes the form of an object that is compact and portable, and instantly recognized as such by individuals in the society where it is acknowledged as currency. Mollusk shells were once commonly used as money by *Homo sapiens* in many parts of the world. Some variety of shell money as a medium of exchange was used by humans at one time or another on every continent of my host planet. Shell money consisted either of whole sea shells or pieces of them carved into beads. The variety most frequently used as currency around the world was the shell of a species of small sea snail, *Monetaria moneta*, the money cowry. This species of marine snail was most abundant in the Indian Ocean and acquired by these hominans in Madagascar, the Maldives, the Island of Ceylon, the Malabar Coast of India, and the island of Borneo in the East Indies. The official currency of the Kingdom of Kongo, a sovereign nation in west-central Africa till about 100 years ago, was shell money known regionally as the Nzimbu. One hundred nzimbus would pay for a hen, 2,000 a goat, 10,000 a wife. The shells were obtained from a secret island and their "minting" was an exclusive royal monopoly. Back 3,000 years ago, cowries were used in China as currency; they were so important that the Chinese character for money was the pictograph of a cowry shell. Shell money, once used widely around their planet, remained the primary legal tender among humans in some areas of the world until at least the beginning of the last century.

Clearly, the downside to shell money is that a society using it as the national currency may lose control over its money supply, since anyone living in an appropriate coastal region could simply go looking for the right seashells by the seashore and automatically mint as much money as they pleased. This would of course expand the money supply, or the money in circulation, and thus lead to inflation in the market prices for goods and services—there would be more money now chasing after the same pool of goods, so the goods get inflated in price. Shell money therefore could only be monetized in inland regions that lacked open access to the ocean and its money cowry. By controlling the quantity of cowries in circulation, the incumbent monetary authority of that jurisdiction would then effectively control the money supply and thereby regulate the cost of goods and services in that society. This is exactly what modern monetary authorities such as the People's Bank of China or the United States Federal Reserve System, and other national banks do to their own currencies every day. Similarly, by actively expanding or shrinking the number of cowries in circulation, the putative Cowry Monetary Authority could buffer the economic cycle and maintain steady economic growth in its own jurisdiction.

Physical money today is usually configured as an elaborately printed rectangle of paper or an intricately embossed metallic coin, no different in function from cowry shells. It is manufactured by the issuing authority in a form that is difficult to reproduce, and is declared illegal to duplicate by that society's governing authority—exemplary punishment is meted out to those that counterfeit the currency. Increasingly now among these hominans, money itself in its physical form is rapidly disappearing. Instead, it is stored and exchanged as electronic notations, credited or debited to the transactor's account. Especially for large transactions, physical money is no longer used.

The concept of money is found in no other species on Earth

except for humans. Starting in a rudimentary way, money is now standard issue in every human society. As Paleolithic hunter-gatherers, humans were mostly self-sufficient animals. Living in small tribes, they could generate their own requirements and did not need to formally exchange goods and services with each other. If they did, simple barter was good enough for them. All that changed after people settled into pan-tribal societies. Individual humans then began to specialize in producing only particular goods and services which had to be exchanged with other humans, frequently strangers, in order to satisfy their different needs and wants. So these clever hominans invented a token of exchange, a symbol of value that they call money, in order to consummate those transactions.

Money is created by fiat and conjured out of whole cloth—just like cowry shells. It is minted by the monetary authority of the society using that particular currency. Money is not a commodity; it serves merely as an instrument of exchange, an accounting device to keep track of actual commodities bought and sold by the participants to the transaction. Money that is accumulated and stored as purchasing power for future use is known as wealth.

⁂

Anthropologists on my host planet classify human societies into three successive types. These are, sequentially designated as Pre-Industrial, Industrial, and Post-Industrial societies. They span an interval of approximately 200,000 years, extending from speciation of *Homo sapiens* to contemporary modern times.

Pre-industrial society refers to human societies operating

at a level that existed before the Great Industrial Revolution. These pre-industrial societies occupied 99.9% of the entire time period that human societies have existed on Earth. In these pre-industrial societies, food collection and food production are the main economic activities, and are accomplished predominantly using human and animal labor. Pre-industrial societies are subdivided into five classical types based on the level of technology used by its members, and the primary method they employed to acquire food. These five classical ones are: Hunter-Gatherer, Pastoral, Horticultural, Agrarian, and Feudal societies. Functioning models of all these five pre-industrial societies still exist on Earth today.

All people were hunter-gatherers until about 12,000 BP. In these first human societies, the main form of food acquisition was by collecting plants and hunting animals in the wild. Because of the onerous task of finding food this way, individual hunter-gatherer societies rarely exceeded 25 members at any one time, and were constantly moving in search of food and sustenance. Being nomadic, these early humans did not make permanent dwellings or live in established villages. They sometimes improvised temporary shelters or used grottoes or caves when available. Social status was usually equal among individuals in these societies and there were no castes or political office holders among them. They did not practice any overt form of gender discrimination. There was little or no division of labor in these societies except for maternal child rearing, and everyone participated in all necessary activities as needed by the group. Though eventually during the Holocene, these hunter-gatherer societies morphed into modern human societies, a few still cling precariously to their past in isolated habitats on their planet, facing almost certain disappearance in the foreseeable future.

The first pastoral societies arose from hunter-gatherer
bands in the Fertile Crescent about 11,000 years ago. Pastoral
societies had a more efficient form of subsistence than did
hunter-gatherers. Pastoralists developed skills for domesticat-
ing herd animals like cattle, goats, and ducks, and therefore
did not need to search for food on a daily basis. They were
nomadic in their existence, moving their flocks and herds from
one pasture to another, based on the seasons and the availability of forage for their animals. As their food supply was more
reliable, these pastoral societies were able to support larger
numbers of people than hunter-gatherer societies could. Their
populations ranged from hundreds to thousands of people.
Because surplus food was available, fewer hands were needed
to produce it. This freed people in pastoral societies to engage
in specialized economic activity such as making tools, fashion-
ing weapons, manufacturing clothing, and designing attractive
ornaments, thereby leading to a division of labor. Production
of surplus goods and services led to trade, which in turn led
to inequality, as some individuals and kinships acquired more
goods than others. These successful individuals and their relatives accreted power and influence onto themselves on account
of their increased wealth. Later, by generational transfer of this
wealth and power, those attributes became more patrimonial.
Over time, hereditary chieftainships emerged which is the usual form of government in pastoral societies. Today, pastoralism
as a way of life is in rapid transition as more people choose a
settled lifestyle to replace their nomadic ways.

Horticultural societies produced food by growing fruit,
grain, and vegetables. Their level of technology was comparable to pastoral ones. To grow their crops, horticulturists cleared
plots in forests and jungles, often employing slash-and-burn

methods to accomplish this objective. When Mac was on their planet, millions of humans on the large Indian Ocean island of Madagascar were slashing and burning immense tracts of priceless tropical rain forest to temporarily grow crops, especially their staple food, rice. Forests were also rapidly cut and harvested for wood, which after conversion to charcoal, is the primary fuel Madagascans use for cooking. Numerous rare and exotic creatures found nowhere else in this Universe, having lived for millions of years in Madagascar's tropical rain forests, are vanishing right along with their precious habitat. As these pristine forests speedily disappear under this savage human onslaught, the red gravelly soil they once held in place for millions of years, quickly erodes away under the heavy monsoonal rains, leaving behind gaping pink wounds lacerating the hillsides. From up in the air this grim pattern looks alarmingly like their planet was bleeding to death.

After cutting and later burning the vegetation in the cleared tracts, horticulturalists let the resulting ashes fertilize the soil. Then, with simple tools and human labor, they cultivate this land for one or more seasons. When the land later goes barren, they clear a new plot and let the old one revert to its natural state, sometimes returning to the original plot to grow crops there again. By rotating their garden plots in this way, they could remain in a given area for fairly prolonged periods of time, prompting them to build semi-permanent or even permanent villages. These villages may contain anywhere from 20 to 2,000 individuals or more, depending on the quality and extent of land available for cultivation.

A surplus of food from this method of production led to a more complex division of labor, comparable to that found in pastoral societies. Specialized roles among horticulturists included craftspeople, traders, priests, and medicine-men. This specialization inevitably resulted in an unequal distribution of wealth and prestige in these societies. As in the case for pastoralists, chieftains arose among these people, and together with their kith and kin, wielded much political power and influence. Caste systems were established. When Mac visited Earth, pure horticultural societies were fast disappearing, most of them absorbed by their settled neighbors. Those that are still alive and active today usually operate in closeted forests in the deep interior of countries, or on isolated islands far out at sea. Such horticultural societies have virtually no access to modern information technology available to other contemporary people living elsewhere on my host planet.

Agrarian societies used more advanced agricultural technology than was ever employed by horticulturalists. They produced large surpluses of food by cultivating grain and other crops on huge tracts of land. Agriculturalists plowed and tilled the ground, raised farm animals for both labor and food, rotated crops, and fertilized their fields with manure and compost. People settled permanently in one central location and no longer moved from place to place in search of sustenance. Vastly increased food supplies in agrarian societies led to huge increases in population like never before seen on their planet. Villages proliferated and the number of people living in them exploded. The villages coalesced into towns and cities, becoming centers for extensive trade and commerce. These new urban agglomerations supported rulers and legions of administrators, soldiers, politicians, tax-collectors, educators, craftspeople, merchants, traders, priests, and doctors. Division of labor and social stratification became ingrained in their organizational structure. Caste and class systems were set solidly in place.

The status of women now declined precipitously. In earlier human societies, women shared labor equally with men and gathered as much food as the men did. Their status was therefore equal to men in those societies as status and prestige in the group depended on how much of the proverbial bacon an individual brought home to the tribe. Now, as food supplies zoomed in agrarian societies as a consequence of the Neolithic Revolution, women assumed a lesser role in securing sustenance for the settled group and were therefore marginalized and subordinated to men. Patriarchy became enshrined. The new custom of marriage ushering a zealous commitment to reproduction, along with patriarchy, was particularly devastating to the status of women. This gender discrimination in humans only began to be reversed after the Industrial Revolution in 190 BP. Astonishingly, political equality between men and women which was lost around 10,000 BP in the early Neolithic was restored just hardly 100 years ago when the right to vote in public elections became generally available to women around the world. Though hard to believe, women's suffrage and political rights came very late in the day. In fact, in a few jurisdictions on my host planet it was still being denied to females at the time Mac visited Earth.

As towns and cities expanded, agrarian societies came into conflict with neighboring ones for control of land and resources. Accordingly, systematic and premeditated warfare on an extensive scale became an integral part of these societies. Standing armies were formed. Captives were taken and slavery was institutionalized. Farmers and other producers of goods and services supplied the soldiers with food, armaments and other necessities in exchange for protection from attack and pillage by their enemies. Rulers and an aristocracy with high social status emerged. These nabobs and baboos headed increasingly complex, opaque, and often corrupt forms of government and other institutions. They often implemented policies for the benefit of their own class or caste, rather than for society as a whole. Taxation as a means to accomplish these objectives was enforced by these rulers on ordinary members of society. Agrarian societies still remain quite widespread on Earth today, especially in Asia, Africa, and South America. They function at a more archaic level than do industrial societies.

Feudal societies are structured on ownership and control of land by a few individuals, and was a regressive byproduct of agrarian society. Unlike traditional agrarian society where there is a relative degree of freedom and choice for the individual farmer who could freehold land, in feudal society the land is owned and controlled by relatively few individuals called Landlords. The bulk of the population in these societies worked as peasants or serfs for the landlord, toiling and farming the land for the benefit of its owner. These peasants remained vassals under feudalism, each generation passing on their bondage to the next. A caste system was therefore deeply embedded in these societies. Peasants cultivated the master's lands and paid homage to their lord in exchange for protection and rations. Feudal societies have mostly disappeared among these hominans today, though these systems still thrive in certain regions of my host planet. In parts of South Asia where such systems remain active and influential, the enterprise is called the Zamindari system. The feudal lord is the Zamindar.

All five societies chronicled so far belong to the

pre-industrial period of human history. This period began with the speciation of *Homo sapiens* in East Africa around 200,000 BP and concluded in 190 BP with the start of the Industrial Revolution. Although these pre-industrial societies still exist on my host planet, they are only vestiges now of their former robust selves, mired in the backwaters of global industrial and post-industrial civilization. They will eventually wither away.

The Great Industrial Revolution that began in England 252 years before Mac's mission to Earth from Galymon happened, was a watershed event in human history, a truly monumental game changer for this species. It belongs in the same league as the control of fire or the invention of agriculture was to the future of *Homo sapiens*. It enabled these hominans to create a brand new type of society called industrial society, a novel and exceptional form of social organization that endowed humans with enormous power and influence, investing them with enduring control over their environment. Industrial society is quintessentially characterized by the use of external energy to vastly amplify the output of a society. This output was further leveraged and multiplied by an elaborate division of labor. The primary source of energy for this enterprise was combustion of fossil fuels such as coal and petroleum products. Innovative technologies, developed in Britain and Western Europe at the start of the industrial era, allowed industrial societies to capture and harness this energy, channeling it to the mass production of material goods. This enabled such societies to support huge populations with relative ease. The first device for powering machines in the industrial age was the steam engine where steam to drive mechanical pistons was produced by heating water over coals. This was followed later by the internal combustion engine and the electric motor.

The key manufacturing technology emblematic of the Industrial Revolution was the mass cloning of individual parts which were then assembled to create the final product. Ever since the first stone artifact was fabricated by hominans more than 2 million years ago, and until the dawn of the industrial age, every single finished product had to be painstakingly created, one item at a time, by a skilled craftsman working exclusively on its production. No two products were ever identical and their components could not be interchanged. The genius of the Industrial Revolution was the mass duplication of parts by creating lathes and other machine tools that reproduced individual parts in massive quantities and with high precision. These duplicate and interchangeable parts could then be rapidly assembled into large numbers of the finished product. Mass production was the magic formula of the Industrial Revolution, the mantra that worked magnificently.

In order to achieve massive food production in industrial society, the task of farming was transferred from individual farmers to large commercial farming operations. Machines for farming crops, along with advanced agricultural practices such as pump irrigation and chemical fertilizers, and the mass propagation of animals for human consumption, maximized the production of food while simultaneously minimizing the need for human labor. This surplus labor, now no longer required for food production, was moved to factories and put to work at mass producing manufactured goods, a process further enhanced by mechanization. Mechanization led to automation, a technique where machines performed on their own, bypassing the need for continuous input from human operators. These redundant humans could now be shifted to work in service industries such as sales, transportation, education, and healthcare. In this remarkable way, by leveraging the energy initially released through the combustion of fossil fuels, and then applying that energy to perform work by interposing mechanical devices along the energy gradient, these hominans were able to multiply their work output by several orders of magnitude.

Industrial society enforced urbanization, as countless workers migrated to centers of production where they could engage in the manufacture of goods and provide services to each another. As more and more people moved to these urban centers and settled thereabouts, enormous cities surrounded by teeming suburbs appeared. These highly urbanized areas were powerhouses for massive economic activity on a scale never before seen or even imagined by *Homo sapiens*. Surely, these hominans had now embarked on a highway with no exit ramps. They were headed at ever accelerating speed toward an exponentially more complex and demanding future, a way of life that held many hazards, but also the promise of uncommon rewards. There was no going back to Eden[50] now.

The fabulous riches disgorged by industrialization would have put even Croesus[51] to shame. This wealth, however, was not fairly distributed across the population, but was concentrated instead in the hands of a small coterie of individuals along

---

50 Eden is a mythical location in the folklore of people who once lived in the Levant, which they believed was their original home. It is portrayed as a benign and bucolic place where plentitude, peace, and immortality reigned forever, and where every human need was magically fulfilled without the requirement for any thought or effort.

51 Croesus, who died in 2,497 BP, was the fabled king of Lydia, an ancient country that would have been located where Turkey is today. Legend has it that Croesus possessed wealth beyond human imagination, and the metaphor "as rich as Croesus" is still used by humans to describe a spectacularly wealthy person.

with their relatives and friends. They were the people who controlled the means of production in industrial society and for whom the teeming masses toiled endlessly. Labor was indeed cheap and pay was minimum. Child labor was widespread and common. Workers were brutally exploited by the propertied classes and had to drudge under dreadful and dangerous conditions. They were exposed to every hazard imaginable but received none of the profit from their hard work. The rapacious capitalists who now possessed and controlled all this enormous wealth were the reborn slave masters of this new age, the abused workers the reclaimed slaves. Capital trumped labor in every imaginable way for the first one hundred years of the Industrial Revolution. The odious social model of feudalism or zamindarism returned with a vengeance, only this time the zamindar was the factory owner and the formerly abused peasant was now the industrial worker. This comparison may in fact be too generous to those industrialists: no feudal society had ever achieved the degree of polarization between the few haves and the legions of have-nots than did early industrial society.

The extraordinary magnitude of resource and wealth concentration in the hands of a few syndicates thriving within huge population centers—even entire nations—proved highly toxic to the wellbeing of these early industrial societies. This dynamic was brilliantly portrayed by Charles Dickens (138 BP–80 BP) in his many memorable novels. Dickens, a celebrated English author and social critic, is considered by many humans as one of the greatest novelists that ever inhabited their planet. He wrote several serialized novels during his time that are treasured and read by people to this very day. Dickens lived in England as the Industrial Revolution was taking off. After his father was imprisoned for unpaid debt, Dickens was sent as a young boy aged twelve to work in a shoe-polish factory. Later as an adult, Dickens wrote evocatively about the culture of poverty and injustice in the England of his time.

The insatiable need for raw materials to stoke the fires of industrial production in these societies gave rise to the era of ferocious mercantile colonialism when much of the non-European world was subdued and occupied by industrialized Western European countries. These colonies served primarily as a source of raw materials for European factories, but also as captive consumer markets for their manufactured goods.

Such festering imbalances caused severe social tensions within industrial societies during the first century of industrialization. Worker revolts were put down brutally by the propertied class using physical force or economic deprivation, often with the help and active participation of incumbent governments and the ruling class. North American and European workers began organizing unions to collectively oppose this brutality and to demand their rights to a living wage and decent working conditions. The Union Movement gathered popular support and gained increasing strength after 100 BP, and effectively started challenging flagrant capitalism in the years that followed. The heroic martyr James Connolly, a revolutionary workers' leader during those barbarous times, challenged the English capitalists with his Irish labor movement. In the year 34 BP, Connolly led the Easter Rising in Dublin proclaiming the Irish Republic. That rebellion was mercilessly attacked and crushed by capitalist forces, the wounded Connolly later propped up in a chair and shot by an English firing squad.

The Union Movement of the last century engaged and tamed the ruthless capitalism of the Industrial Revolution. It was one of the most effective ways that humans had ever devised for promoting justice and equity for the masses. The notion of a living wage, safe working conditions, gender parity, arbitration of grievances, prohibition of child labor, the five-day work week and eight-hour work day, overtime pay, health and retirement benefits, vacation time and holidays, are all precious gifts from this Union Movement to ordinary working men and women in many countries around the world.

Yet ever since these workers' unions arose as an antidote to laissez-faire capitalism, attempts by the owning classes to undermine and destroy unions have continued unabated, scoring significant successes of late. Overall union membership has declined over the past decades, and the bargaining power of unions has been severely curtailed as a result of cynical anti-union efforts by local and national governments controlled by the capitalists. Moreover, unions are mostly present and active in rich Western countries. In much of the poor and underdeveloped world where the vast majority of workers live and toil, unions are often rudimentary or frequently absent.

In reaction to the unfettered capitalism of the early Industrial Revolution, Communism emerged as a sociopolitical counterpoint. The term communism comes from the Latin word *communis* meaning "common." Communism is a political and economic doctrine that aims to replace private property and the profit motive of capitalism, with public or communal ownership of property and natural resources. This includes sole control of the means of production for all essential goods and services in a society. Communism is thus an extreme form of Socialism, the distinction being communism's adherence to the revolutionary socialism of Karl Marx (132 BP–67 BP). Socialism itself is an ancient practice among humans, harking back to the time when *Homo sapiens* emerged as a distinct species in the Pleistocene when all resources were considered common property of the tribe. Marx, a renowned German philosopher and economic idealist, who later settled in England, expanded this aboriginal foundation of socialism into the sociopolitical doctrine of communism.

Marx argued that the motivating force of capitalism is the exploitation of working labor, whose uncompensated work is the ultimate source of profit for the capitalists. Marx made the revolutionary observation that value was created by labor alone, and that capital had nothing to do with creating value. By pushing down wages and squeezing the worker even further, the capitalists who owned the factories and therefore the means of production, would extract even more profit for themselves and become even wealthier. As a result, capital, or money, continually concentrated in the pockets of the few capitalists in society at the expense of the multitude of workers who toiled to produce it.

Marx described this dialectic—the tension between conflicting ideas or forces—as the defining feature of all human history. He identified two main social groups or actors in this ongoing dialectical struggle: one was Labor which he called the proletariat or workers, a group that included anyone who earned their livelihood by selling their labor and being paid a wage for their time. The other was Capital which he called the bourgeoisie or capitalists, who obtained their income from the surplus value they confiscated from workers who created that wealth in the first place. Marx urged the proletariat to unite as one body and rise en masse in a revolutionary class struggle against the bourgeoisie—a stance enshrined in the famous communist motto, "Workers of the World, Unite!" Marx envisaged these united workers would nationalize all private property as well as the means of production. This struggle or dialectic would eventually create a classless, moneyless society where the utopian doctrine, "From each according to his abilities, to each according to his needs" would finally prevail. That was communism's ultimate goal.

Industrial society catalyzed astonishing changes in the social structure and behavioral organization of humans. In two exceptionally important areas it was enormously influential—the division of labor, and the role of gender. As already noted in this narrative, the qualitative division of labor among individuals within human societies is quite a recent development in the history of this species. Throughout its hunter-gather stage that lasted for almost 190,000 years of its 200,000 year history, *Homo sapiens* showed no predilection for any significant and sustained division of labor in its group organization. Most members of the tribe did whatever task was at hand and necessary to do, based on their knowledge and skill. Age and health conditions certainly played a role, particularly for the very young, the very old, and the infirm. However, all able-bodied individuals, whether female or male, undertook and shared multiple tasks and activities required for individual and group survival. There was no formal division of labor among hunters and gatherers. All humans of either gender were considered equal as regards to occupation and status.

Once these redoubtable humans abandoned their hunter-gather ethos and settled down cooperatively into larger communities producing food rather than simply collecting it, they began to allocate particular tasks among themselves. The earliest division was based on gender. Men were given tasks that demanded greater physical prowess, while women were assigned duties that did not require as much physical strength and could be performed closer to home while raising children within the new institution of marriage. Warfare, construction of dwellings, hunting, bartering and trading, were predominantly male activities. Cooking, cleaning, making clothing and pottery, schooling the young, and nursing the sick were usually female functions. Agriculture, which required soil preparation, planting seed, weeding, and cultivating the crop, was shared by both men and women, though males governed and dominated the operation. Men's work now got generally judged by society as more valuable and essential than women's work, thus leading to a demotion in the status of women from the old hunting and gathering days. An obdurate patriarchy emerged. This gender based discrimination became culturally imprinted into their societies through memes, and remained unchanged for almost 10,000 years thereafter. Barely a century ago did this imbalance between men and women begin to get reset, though sex discrimination still persists in some form or another in all human cultures on my host planet even today.

As humans continued to grow and develop their societies, acquiring sophisticated technologies and more complex ways of manufacturing goods and providing services, the existing division of labor expanded from just between the genders, to within the genders themselves. This became quite important in industrial societies. The principle underlying this division of labor is quite straightforward—it is linked to specialization in the production process. Complex jobs are more cost effective to accomplish if done by many people, each performing a single task, rather than one person doing the entire job by mastering and executing multiple tasks on their own. Thus this new division of labor assigned different tasks in the assembly line regardless of gender to different individuals possessing different skill-sets. This division of labor is the basic principle underlying the assembly line, the heart of the mass production process.

Just as gender based division of labor produced a difference in status between men and women, non-gender based division of labor, likewise, resulted in unequal distribution of status among different workers of the same gender. Some jobs were held in high esteem and provided greater social status and income than did others. This phenomenon enhanced caste and class distinctions in society. Groups of workers called guilds emerged in the industrial age to perform special services, such as printers, tailors, and apothecaries. Guilds were professional castes, different from social castes, and were formed on the basis of occupation usually passed on from father to son. Still other humans were grouped into classes of unskilled workers such as meatpackers, farmhands, longshoremen, and laborers. This work-related stratification of people rapidly morphed into social discrimination, and then—joining hands with gender, caste, and class discrimination—became a fixture of human societies everywhere. Notably though, in advanced secular countries, this unsavory feature has been steadily declining over the past decades.

❧❧❧❧❧

The clear biological and behavioral distinctions between males and females in this simian species is the overarching factor influencing the nature and configuration of human society. Since society is an epiphenomenon of the humans in it, this striking gender difference is a primary factor in shaping it. As Mac observed upon first arriving on my host planet, humans—quite unlike galymonians—come in two distinct genders or sexes—male and female. An exasperated male human once remarked to me, "Men are from Earth, Mac, those women are from another whole different galaxy!" as he struggled with the demands of a messy divorce. The converse, of course, is equally true. To a novice unfamiliar with such gender differences, the two sexes may indeed appear much like separate species.

As noted before, sexual differentiation into female and male genders is widespread among multicellular organisms on Earth, and evolved to ensure genetic variation in the offspring so that natural selection could operate effectively. Yet creatures bearing no gender are far more common. Galymonians are not the only beings in our Universe to come in just one prototype. Non-gendered creatures are everywhere. One need not go to distant locations in the cosmos to observe unigenderism. It exist abundantly right here on my host planet. The word unigender is used here only for convenience since the term is meaningless when gender itself does not exist in an organism.

Unicellular archaea, bacteria, and protists, and many multicellular organisms like most plants, several invertebrates, and over two dozen vertebrate species have only one gender. The Mexican whiptail lizard, *Cnemidophorus neomexicanus*, is an example of vertebrate unigenderism. This reptile flourishes today across the western range of the Mexico-United States border in North America. The whiptail lizard species first originated in this range by hybridization, or cross-mating, of two related bi-gender lizard species living in that area. Hybridization produced only one gender of offspring. Virgin birth, or parthenogenesis, allowed the resulting unigender population to reproduce and evolve into a distinct species consisting of a single gender able to propagate its own kind.

Since the very structure and configuration of human society is clearly determined by the nature and characteristics of the main performers, both female and male, an overview of gender differences is therefore essential to understanding human societies and how they organize and operate. As Mac remarked earlier, the differences between these males and females are startling. It begins right in their chromosomes.

The human genome, as noted before, has 46 chromosomes made up of two sets of 23 chromosomes each. One set of 23 chromosomes comes from the female parent, the other set from the male parent. Of these 23 pairs of chromosomes, 22 are called Autosomes—each chromosome in any one pair of autosomes matches its twin. The single remaining pair in that full set of 23 chromosomes—called Sex Chromosomes—come in two distinct configurations dubbed X and Y. These two do not match each other. Females carry two X chromosomes designated XX, and males carry one X and one Y chromosome, designated XY. A human egg or ovum, after meiosis or reduction division, contains just one set of 23 chromosomes and is said to be haploid. The sperm, after its own meiosis, is also haploid, having only one set of 23 chromosomes. Fertilization between the ovum and the sperm brings the two haploid sets of chromosomes together in the zygote to form a new diploid individual who now once again carries the full complement of 46 chromosomes. The egg's sex chromosome is always X, since the pre-meiosis female germinal cell is XX. In sperm on the other hand, half will contain the X chromosome and half the Y chromosome, since the pre-meiosis male germinal cell is XY. If an egg fuses with a sperm carrying the X chromosome, the resulting individual is a female (XX). If it fuses instead with a sperm carrying the Y chromosome, the resulting individual is a male (XY). The differences between males and females start right there. It is encrypted in their very genes.

To begin with, women and men are physically different from each other. On average, males are half a foot taller than females and weigh about 15% more. They have significantly larger muscle mass and are almost 45% stronger in upper body strength and 25% in lower body strength than females. Externally, their most sexually dimorphic parts are the chest, the lower half of the face, and the area between the waist and the knees. Women have breasts for lactation; men do not lactate. Men have larger waists compared to their hips; women have larger hips surrounding an enlarged pelvic outlet, an adaptation for birthing offspring with large skulls. Their reproductive systems are entirely different. Gonads are located within the abdominal cavity in women; they hang outside in men. Men possess a tubular, erectable organ called the penis to deposit sperm during the act of intercourse; women have a corresponding cavity known as the vagina to receive the sperm. The vagina leads to a saclike organ called the uterus where gestation takes place; men have no uterus. Men have more facial and body hair than women. On average, men carry more melanin pigment on them, making their skin, eye, and hair appear darker in color that the typical female of their cohort.

Adult male *Homo sapiens* have a larger trachea and more bronchi in their respiratory system; their average lung capacity is about 50% greater than the females. They have larger hearts, higher red blood cell counts, higher hemoglobin levels, and higher levels of circulating blood-clotting factors. Females have increased white blood cell counts and more dermal pain receptors than do the males.

Men and women literally sound very different. The male voice is about an octave lower than the female voice. The female is higher pitched. This startling difference between adult male and female voices is instantly recognized by humans of both genders without any need for visual cues. The male voice itself evolved through sexual selection by their females. Hominan women preferred a lower pitch and octave in their men's voices when selecting for sexual partners. Such a voice predicted greater sexual and reproductive fitness in the male due to the higher testosterone levels it reflected. Testosterone, the male sex hormone, modulates voice and makes it sound deeper by affecting the structure of the larynx and vocal cords. This voice change starts right around puberty with enlargement of the larynx, otherwise known as Adam's apple, in young adolescent males.

Testosterone is synthesized by the male gonads or testicles. It is the preeminent male sex hormone, producing all the effects of masculinity in males. Its production peaks during male puberty, then slowly declines for the rest of the individual's lifetime. Testosterone promotes physical and psychological aggressiveness in males, and encourages resource acquisition, homesteading, mate capture and the territorial guarding of females from other males—all important markers for sexual selection by females. Testosterone also figures in alopecia or baldness in men. Loss of head hair with age is common in male *Homo sapiens* but rare in females. Though "baldness" genes are equally inherited by both men and women, its phenotype is seen predominantly in men because the baldness gene requires testosterone to be expressed—so women, though they possess the gene, do not go bald since they lack testosterone. However, they remain carriers for baldness in their male offspring.

Corresponding to testosterone in males, estrogen is synthesized by female gonads or ovaries. It is the premier female sex hormone. It engenders all the effects of femininity. It too peaks during puberty in females, though unlike the male sex hormone, it drops off sharply at menopause after the female has completed her reproductive life. Estrogen triggers ovulatory cycles, dampens aggression, promotes gentleness and nurturing, encourages mate selection, and drives the female psychologically and physically to reproduce offspring. These two sex hormones thus play a major role in ensuring the continuity and survival of this bi-gendered species, setting and shaping the ethos and architecture of human societies.

Today on average, women live about five years longer than men—this gap in life expectancy between men and women has been narrowing over the past several decades. There are many other anatomical, biochemical, and physiological differences between the two genders than those briefly listed here. Further details are found in data uploaded to Alka on Galymon.

Besides clear physical differences, there are also significant psychological and cognitive differences between male and female humans. Male brains are about 10% to 15% larger than female ones, though this ratio decreases or vanishes when total body mass is taken into consideration as well. There are also meaningful gender differences in brain structure itself. Men have larger parietal lobes and therefore better spatial and navigational abilities as these functions are handled in that part of the brain. For the same reason, men possess better numerical and mathematical skills as a group—though some individual women may have exceptional ability in this area—and men on average have superior three-dimensional viewing skills for mental imagery. Women generally have larger expressive and receptive speech centers in their frontal and temporal lobes respectively, and are therefore on average superior in language processing; they communicate more fluently and have greater sensitivity to emotional signals than men do. Again, some individual men may possess extraordinary language and emphatic skills. Male brains are superior at handling visual and visuo-spatial information. Females are more sensitive to smells and olfactory inputs. The deep limbic system where emotions reside is larger in females than in males. This allows women in general to better communicate feelings and empathize with the feelings of others. However, this also makes women more susceptible to chronic stress, and to anxiety and depressive disorders.

Male and female humans generally display very different gender dispositions and existential agendas. Those dissimilarities are clearly evident in their biologic natures and begin to be established from the moment of fertilization onward. All embryos start out phenotypically female. Left to their own devices, they would all be girls. Anywhere between 4 to 8 weeks after fertilization of the ovum, the putative male embryo carrying the Y-chromosome begins to secrete testosterone from rudimentary gonadal cells, channeling the embryo in the male gender direction. Putative female embryos carrying the X-chromosome do not secrete an equivalent hormone for feminization; they simply continue to develop along their initial pathway. If not for that gender-switching androgenic stimulus at that key early developmental stage, all embryos would naturally grow to be females.

Approximately 120 male embryos are conceived for every

100 female ones[52], but male embryos are more delicate and vulnerable to external conditions and thus have a higher mortality rate throughout gestation. Proportionally more male fetuses miscarry or abort spontaneously. Because of their higher prenatal mortality, only 105 male babies are born for every 100 female babies delivered. Male mortality continues a tad higher throughout childhood, so that by puberty and the start of reproduction, the sexes are about equally balanced. Male mortality remains slightly higher throughout life, so that at the end of the human life cycle there are more women than men alive. Male fetuses, on average, are more physically active *in utero* than females. They are also a bit heavier and longer at birth. Female fetuses progress a little faster in skeletal growth—girls are 4 to 6 weeks ahead in bone development than boys at birth. Overall, neoteny lasts a bit longer in boys than in girls.

Play activities and related behaviors are quite distinctive between boys and girls, long before sex hormones accentuate those gender based differences. Girls are more sociable than boys, but prefer to play with just one other person; boys prefer a larger group to play with. Boys are more likely to indulge in rambunctious play; girls play more gently. Girls generally prefer passive toys like dolls and toy houseware; boys favor action oriented ones like toy guns and cars. Girls, quite unlike boys, like to adorn themselves and wear shiny body jewelry and facial makeup, continuing this behavior throughout their lives. The universal predilection of female *Homo sapiens* for body ornamentation is indeed extraordinary. Color preferences between the two genders are quite distinctive. Boys seem to

---

52　The higher conception rate for male over female embryos may be due to the greater motility of the male-determining sperm which carries the shorter and lighter Y-chromosome, and not the fuller and heavier X-chromosome.

be more partial to the blue end of the visual spectrum and girls to the red end. "Blue for baby boys, pink for baby girls!" say humans. As adults, men appear to favor sky colors, women earth tones.

Females are inherently more compliant than males with existing laws, social customs, and rules and regulations. Physical and sexual violence—either within societies, or between societies as in war—is almost exclusively a male province noted most prominently in post-pubertal and young adult males, corresponding to higher testosterone levels in that age cohort. Mass killings that happen sporadically in human societies are almost exclusively done by males. In this regard, all manner of criminal behavior is generally far more common in males than in females. Incarcerated males in prison populations outnumber females by over nine to one.

Men tend to prioritize their own status in society as important markers for their self-esteem, and place great value on how highly others in their social group view them along a social dominance hierarchy. Women are significantly less into social status and more into family, because they alone are the propagators and proliferators of the species. Indeed, women had even forgone gender parity in the early Neolithic and submitted themselves to patriarchy in order to power the new supersonic population express. Finally, in this whole domain of gender differences it should be noted that men, compared to women, have greater variability across traits in general, and therefore tend to be overrepresented at both the high and low ends of the distribution curve for human gender traits.

There are other important differences between the sexes. Though both men and women possess quantitatively comparable cognitive abilities, there are obvious qualitative differences in how they perceive and interpret the world around them. This is a delicate issue for discussion among modern humans. The president of a leading American university was cashiered out of his job not very long ago for calling attention to these gender differences. Because creative energy in males is not especially directed into physical reproduction, they tend to channel those energies into other areas of life and creativity. It is therefore hardly surprising to an extraterrestrial like Mac that most notable explorers, inventors, religious and political leaders, scientists, and philosophers, have all mostly tended to be males—at least so far—in the recorded history of *Homo sapiens*. More research publications in scientific journals are authored by men. Women are clearly underrepresented in the fields of science, technology, engineering, and mathematics. This gender disparity may arise because corresponding female creative energies are more fundamentally focused on biological reproduction and the indispensable function of creating new individuals to populate and sustain their species. Women are existentially focused on reproduction, and unlike men, it is a profound instinctual drive in them. They alone have the unique ability to birth babies and experience the psychological meaning of having another complete human being emerge from within their bodies, a process unknown and unknowable to men. For men, reproduction is merely an unplanned epiphenomenon of their sexuality and not the primary driver for their lives. The American physician and poet Oliver Wendell Holmes, father to the famous jurist of the eponymous name, when lecturing students in anatomy at his medical school in Boston, held up a female pelvis and announced to the all-male class of that era, "Gentlemen, this is the triumphal arch under which every candidate for immortality has to pass!"

These gender predispositions may be changing apace in this late Modern Era. As women begin to disengage further from physical reproduction and making babies, then just as in men, their creative juices will be channeled into non-reproductive goals. In the past few decades alone, woman have been successfully competing with men in those very bailiwicks men hitherto monopolized, and giving them a major run for their money. It may not be too long before both female and male *Homo sapiens* show equal prowess and similar accomplishments in all fields of human endeavor.

The prominent gender differences between men and women have exerted a profound influence on the structure and functioning of human societies. They powerfully molded the way these hominans choose to organize themselves and discharge their numerous obligations and commitments.

CHAPTER XI:

RELIGION

A facet of *Homo sapiens* not ever seen today in any other species on Earth is a curious phenomenon called Religion. Commissar Ra-him who once headed the Folkways[53] Commissariat in the Collegium of Pansophy on Galymon, published extensively on this arcane subject. Mac applauds the learned Commissar's excellent monograph on this matter called, *Religion: A Peculiar Institution.* The renowned Commissar describes in this book the unusual role religion and like-minded constructs played during the first emergence of sapience among particular lifeforms in our Universe. Commissar Ra-him's analysis of the subject also applies in a most meaningful way to humans. Mac will borrow freely from my esteemed colleague's learned views on this question of religion. Though the worthy Commissar is now fully retired and no longer active in our Collegium—having moved to a different galaxy upon his recent retirement—Mac was fortunate enough to prevail

---

53   Folkways are practices, customs, and beliefs shared by members of a group as part of their common culture.

upon the enigmatic Ra-him for important advice and feedback on this portion of my manuscript.

Religion, as it applies to humans on Earth, is a numinous belief system peculiar to this hominan. It presupposes the existence of an anomalous supernatural agency—with its own plans and purpose—controlling the origin and eventual fate of the entire Universe. This power is endowed with every imaginable and unimaginable ability, including the astonishing talent to abolish universal laws. That preternatural entity is called God. This evoked god unilaterally conjures up every conceivable object there is, including that god's proponent *Homo sapiens*. Of course, not every human believes in such a supernatural creator or creators, but many still do at this juncture in their evolutionary history. Yet core believers in this unusual formulation of reality have steadily declined in numbers, commensurate with increasing understanding of the natural world available to them over time.

The natural purpose of religion when it first appeared in hominan culture was to make sense of the physical world and provide an explanation for prevailing events impacting their temporal existence. Of course, humans could only offer explanations based on their current knowledge and understanding. Anything inexplicable was attributed to a supernatural agency. For example, earlier humans had no clue what caused lightning and thunder. They ascribed these events to celestial forces and imagined gods as their causes, propitiating those gods with offerings and prayer. Later however, as sapience advanced and they understood the science behind lightning and thunder, those same gods were banished and forgotten. It was hardly 2,500 years ago that the noted Greek geometrician and philosopher, Pythagoras, of the eponymous theorem fame, suggested

Earth too was a sphere based on the observed geometry of the Moon and the Sun. Humans had assumed previously that Earth was a flat disc because it seemed counterintuitive to believe otherwise—as far as they could tell, Earth's surface seemed quite flat to them in all directions.

Before Nicolaus Copernicus, hardly 500 years ago, humans believed their Earth was intentionally placed by their creator at the center of the Universe. That was then the prevailing geo-centric view of the cosmos. That assumption, of course, proved most embarrassing to both themselves and their gods after Copernicus demonstrated that the prevailing geocentric view was incorrect. The great mathematician showed through dili-gent astronomical observations that Earth, and the other planets known at that time, all orbited the Sun instead. This clearly contradicted the orthodoxy endorsed in their scriptures which they believed came from their god. It then took centuries of violent debate and summary judgments against the Copernican view before the actual cosmic reality of Earth's position in its stellar system became generally accepted by these hominans.

Thus the miraculous creator proposed by humans to explain the workings of their Universe could only be endowed with knowledge and understanding that they themselves possessed at any given time. The virtuous Copernicus had just extended that limit, and god had yet to catch up with him.

Humans are the only species on their planet to display this behavior called religion. The appearance of religion in these hominans was closely linked to the emergence of self-consciousness or sapience. It is necessary to pause here for a moment wise reader, and reflect again on two quite different attributes of living creatures noted before in this narrative—consciousness (sentience) and self-consciousness (sapience).

Consciousness, or sentience, is mandatory to lifeforms everywhere, as they all have to be aware of their environment in order to seek food, avoid enemies, reproduce their kind, and thrive in whatever way they can. Sentience, then, is simply the possession of sensory mechanisms to feel out one's surroundings and determine its nature, a prerequisite for any creature to live anywhere in the cosmos.

Self-consciousness, or sapience, instead, is a much rarer phenomenon among organisms in our Universe. It is the uncommon ability to be aware of being aware. Sapience, then, is the capacity to possess self-awareness and thus understand how actions can influence outcomes in the future. It is the ability to apply knowledge and experience to manage that future. For example, humans know that if they planted lemon seeds in the ground, lemon trees would emerge from those seeds and the trees, in turn, would bring them more lemons in the future. That is sapience. Though rudimentary sapience may be present in a few other living species on Earth besides humans—such as the other great apes—yet nowhere on their planet does this quality manifest to the extent and abundance found in *Homo sapiens*. This sapience is the product of innumerable interactions among countless individual neurons[54] joined together in a synaptic network in the cerebral cortex of their brains. That higher neuronal interactivity can be computed for the brains of different animals. Humans score highest in this metric by a mile. This quality of

---

54 The average adult human brain has approximately 86 billion neurons. This compares to 14 billion neurons in a baboon brain, and about 30 billion neurons in a gorilla brain.

sapience uniquely endows them with the capacity for abstraction and to think in representational terms and thus conduct thought experiments that imagine the future before it arrives. Sapience is thus qualitatively different from sentience, which is a concrete process and addresses only current reality. Sapience anticipates future reality.

Once sapience was established among these hominans, it began to have a curious effect on their behavior. Observing events around them, they discovered that others with whom they coexisted and established close relationships, their kinfolk and fellow tribes people, quit living and died after a certain interval of time. Using their newly acquired sapience and projecting those observations into the future, they realized that they too would inevitably perish and disappear from the physical world. For the first time now in the history of life on my host planet, a creature had become self-consciously aware of its own impermanence. A clear acknowledgement of mortality and the inevitability of death and oblivion began to take shape in the hominan mind. That is when god, religion, and the afterlife emerged.

Now, if individual existence inevitably led to death and oblivion after a brief lifespan, what then is the purpose of struggling to live and succeed in a world saturated with fearsome odds guaranteed to slay them sooner or later? Mastering and dominating their environment, the hallmark of hominan behavior, would have no meaning and appear futile to these newly sapient creatures who now understood that in a relatively few years they too would be dead and gone, their lives snuffed out like the animals they hunted and killed. What on earth would motivate them to engage vigorously with their world and persist in the voyage of discovery and invention that would eventually lead them to split the atom and transport humans to their Moon?

Unlike other creatures who had no intimations of mortality and therefore lived their lives with gusto until the moment of their death, these latter-day hominans knew only too well that they were earmarked to perish. With this new knowledge of death, they might quite logically have given up their appetite for advancement and lived their lives without strife like the proverbial Lotophagi or lotus-eaters. These lotus-eaters were a fanciful tribe of people described by the blind poet Homer in *The Odyssey*, written circa 2,750 BP. The mythical Greek hero Odysseus encountered them in *Odyssey IX*. They were believed to occupy an island off the coast of Tunisia in North Africa. This island, probably modern Djerba—dubbed "the land of the lotus-eaters" by Homer—was the site of an exotic "lotus" plant. The fruit of this plant, the primary food of the people on that island, was a powerful narcotic causing the natives to sleep their whole lives away in blissful apathy.

The improbable answer to the conundrum of death for these inventive hominans was to invoke a creator-god who would ensure continuation of their lives after they died, in a special world located outside their terrestrial plane. Conspicuously to the mind of an extraterrestrial, this formulation did not usually include other living creatures that coexisted with humans on Earth, the covenant of immortality being guaranteed only to members of their own species. Thus was formal religion born among these humans circa 50,000 BP. It developed rather late in hominan evolution, in tandem with full behavioral modernity, right about the time that sapience was robustly emerging in these creatures. This new construct of religion served as an important ligament during the cognitive transition of *Homo sapiens*, arising from the way their brains operated. Upon establishment, religion then provided a *raison d'etre* for living, a justification for being, a purpose for existence. It assured these hominans, now that they could anticipate their own impending demise, that their individual existence would not abruptly perish with death but would last forever in another world. Later, the concept of an immortal "soul" emerged in the lexicon of these people. This new soul was often described as an ethereal substance, temporarily inhabiting the mortal body, and representing the eternal and imperishable "self" that had an existence separate and distinct from that body. A creator god (or gods) was an essential part of the package.

It is indeed remarkable to note that the institution of religion is universally present among *Homo sapiens* wherever that species may reside on their planet. It transcends age, gender, geography, race, ethnicity, and culture, and therefore must have played a critically important role for this species during its evolution. That crucial period may now be coming to an end. Though the practice of religion itself was still widespread among my esteemed human friends during Mac's mission to their planet, it is quite evident now that religion has been declining in scope and meaning for these people throughout the late Modern Era. When formal religion was first established in the Late Pleistocene, its hegemony was unquestioningly accepted by all people on Earth. However, in recent Holocene times, beginning just a few hundred years ago, as humans became more informed and knowledgeable in their outlook, they began to require less religion to give meaning and purpose to their existence, and sought more authentic ways to resolve the issue of their own mortality.

Though the aptitude for religion or "religiosity" is embedded within their genetic constitution and still remains deeply ingrained and influential in human nature—thus explaining the prevalence of religion among these hominans worldwide—the practice of religion itself is declining sharply among their kind. Hardly a century ago, practically everyone was religious and few, if any, questioned its authenticity. Yet a global survey done in 62 AP revealed that only 59% of people worldwide now considered themselves religious, 23% were nonreligious, 13% were atheists, and 5% were of unknown persuasion. This falling trend in religious faith is attributable to religion's essentially transient role during the emergence of sapience for certain lifeforms—as described in Commissar Ra-him's celebrated book. Apart from communist countries where it is officially discouraged, religion is more prevalent today in poorer and less developed societies than in wealthier and more developed ones. For instance, in that same 62 AP survey cited here, 93% of people in Nigeria said they were religious and only 1% claimed to be atheists, while in Japan, just 16% said they were religious and 31% were atheists.

⁂

Unlike all other creatures that ever lived on Earth before them, latter-day hominans, now just beginning to acquire sapience, were the only animals on my host planet to bury their dead. This internment ritual began in the Late Pleistocene about 100,000 years ago, almost 50,000 years before religion itself was formally established. That period in their evolutionary history when these hominans first became cognizant of their own mortality and began to bury their dead, ushered in the belief of an afterlife. It heralded the forthcoming era of religion as a major cultural phenomenon in human affairs. Religion, for these newly cognitive animals, was to become an essential survival tool if they were not to turn into the legendary lotus-eaters of Homer's ancient epic. Both neanderthals and humans have left fossil evidence of intentional burials from those times.

Mac attended a neanderthal burial event 62,062 years ago in the Zagros Mountains of West Asia. It was about six o'clock in the morning on a calm June day. The body of a 22 year old male neanderthal killed the previous day while hunting wild horses with his comrades, lay naked on the floor of a cave within a mountainside. That cave, known today as Shanidar Cave by my modern human companions, is located on Bradost Mountain in the Zagros range. The site that Mac visited for the funeral is now part of Erbil Governorate in the Kurdistan region of modern Iraq.

Homo neanderthalensis completed speciation in Eurasia about 200,000 years ago, at exactly the same time that *Homo sapiens* appeared in Africa. They both had a common immediate ancestor, *Homo heidelbergensis*. Thus humans and neanderthals were sibling species from two cohorts of the same ancestor, the former speciating in Africa, the latter in Eurasia. Neanderthals went on to dominate Europe as well as southwestern and central Asia. These enigmatic creatures declined after encountering humans migrating out of Africa, and finally disappeared from Earth about 35,000 years ago.

Neanderthals were shorter and bulkier than their human cousins. Adult males were rarely more than five and a half feet tall. These males could weigh as much as 160 pounds or more, with no unsightly fat, just heavy bones and hard muscle. Adult females averaged about five feet in height, weighing in at about

130 pounds. Neanderthals were predominantly carnivorous. Their diet consisted mostly of butchered meat from big game animals they killed using elaborate group hunting techniques. At home they loved to engorge themselves on chunks of savory fire-roasted meat, done rare and liberally seasoned with salt and aromatic herbs. Active neanderthal hunters could devour as many as 4,000 or more calories per day to meet their high energy needs, reaching upwards of 5,000 calories daily in the frigid winter months. Neanderthals had to ensure a significant salt intake to compensate for salt depletion in sweat during strenuous hunting activity. They enjoyed fermented berry juice, but otherwise consumed little in the way of vegetable matter. Like other major carnivores, neanderthals had an acute sense of smell and could detect the scent of prey from long distances away. They had huge noses and enlarged paranasal sinuses to complement their highly developed sense of smell, including detection of pheromones using their well-endowed vomeronasal organ. These anatomical adaptations for olfaction caused the middle section of their face to protrude like a snout, a condition called maxillary prognathism. Their chins were small and quite inconspicuous.

Homo neanderthalensis lacked the necessary configuration to their larynx and vocal cords to comfortably articulate spoken speech. Their larynx—or Adam's apple—was much closer to the mouth and not near the middle of the neck like in their human cousins. It was the lower positioning of the larynx that gave humans the early ability to produce a much wider range of sounds than any other animal on their planet. In newborn human babies the larynx is much closer to the mouth as in adult neanderthals, but in human infants it begins its descent toward the middle of the neck as speech develops.

Neanderthals instead, had their larynx permanently glued close to their mouth and were therefore dumb, though only in the sense that they could not speak—cognitively they were much like humans. In fact, their brains were slightly larger than the ones their human cousins sported. Even among humans, though spoken language began to appear before the time of my dear friends the Itu-Kan, human speech mechanisms did not fully mature until after 50,000 BP.

The FOXP2 gene, found in other animals as well, may be related to language in humans. In songbirds, this gene appears to facilitate the development of singing. The gene is located on chromosome-7 in humans and codes for the synthesis of a protein called FOXP2 (Forkhead box protein P2).This protein affects neuronal plasticity in human brains and is probably related to language development in this species. It is noteworthy that an abnormal FOXP2 gene in humans leading to defective FOXP2 protein synthesis, results in severe language disorder. Neanderthals and humans inherited the same FOXP2 gene from their common ancestor, *H. heidelbergensis*, and therefore possessed the central or cortical capacity for language. However, they clearly lacked the peripheral or laryngeal mechanism for speaking. Spoken language was therefore very rudimentary among these stocky neanderthals and was restricted to only a few vocalizations like those found in modern gorillas. They were therefore unable to transmit their thoughts to other neanderthals using the efficient mechanism of spoken speech like their human cousins routinely did.

Communication among neanderthals was accomplished by complex hand signals and eye blinks, along with graceful body movements and gestures, resulting in an exceptionally fluent neanderthal sign language resembling a form of esoteric dance—they were called the "dancing ones." For this reason they hunted in compact groups since they could not effectively communicate over longer distances without direct eye contact—spoken language would have carried further afield and not required sight or visual cues. Also for the same reason, they did not operate after dark. In order to put their remarkable sign language skills to good use, neanderthals had to be constantly visible to each other, placing them at a significant competitive disadvantage to humans. Because they communicated by sight rather than sound, they possessed supreme vision—neanderthals had twelve times as many photoreceptors in their retina than did humans, thus virtually picking up every photon on tap.

Under the right conditions, much like their human cousins, neanderthals would stampede prey over steep cliffs and have them plunge to their death into the ravines below. At other times, upon cornering a prey animal, and unlike humans, individual members of the entwined neanderthal hunting group would charge the besieged and now extremely dangerous beast head on, driving flint-tipped wooded spears into the body of the countercharging animal at close range. This was lethal combat and frequently resulted in injuries and broken bones to the neanderthal hunters, even death in many instances. The dead hunter, now laid out in Shanidar Cave that June morning in the year 62,062 BP, had died in this exact way the previous afternoon.

Melancholic silence permeated the inside of the funerary cave that day. A tight knot of individuals, about a dozen of them, adults and children alike, both male and female, clustered around the body of the dead hunter. He was clearly one of their bravest and one of their wisest to boot. All of 22 years old, this handsome individual was at the summit of his life—neanderthals did not live much beyond their late twenties. Lethal hunting injuries, infections, and lately, predation by their human cousins, made life short and brutish for them. Neanderthals with their robust noses could smell these humans from great distances away and tried hard to avoid those murderous cousins. A pale teenaged female with freckles and red hair was tenderly stroking the dead hunter's frozen and lifeless face, now set in rigor mortis. A lover perhaps? A mother of his children?

Outside the cave, not quite eighty feet to the left of the opening, a shallow grave had been freshly excavated and was now ready to receive the body of the deceased hunter. In complete silence, a small group of assembled individuals picked up the dead body from inside the cave and carried it gently to the freshly dug grave outside. Reverentially, they placed the body in the grave, curling the corpse into a fetal position with the head facing east. The young female who had been lovingly stroking the dead hunter's lifeless face inside the cave, now quietly stepped up and gently dropped a handful of brightly colored flowers she had carefully gathered in the valley below. Her touching gesture of goodbye was sublimely soulful and poignant. Next, a strapping young lad barely eleven and on the cusp of puberty, hair just sprouting on his pubes, probably an apprentice hunter under the deceased neanderthal's tutelage, gingerly approached the open pit and placed a sparkling new flint ax in the grave. His beloved teacher will need that tool in the hereafter. The group by the graveside stood in immaculate silence for several minutes after that. Not a word was uttered, not a tear was shed. Those neuronal circuits for weeping or expressions of grief that humans would evolve, were not present in these neanderthals. Their profound loss and sorrow, though not vocally or emotively expressed, was indeed supremely palpable.

A large pile of stones lay heaped to one side of the grave. These stones had been carefully collected by these creatures the previous afternoon and early that morning, in preparation for the funeral. A wizened old female of advanced age, well into her mid-thirties and riddled with arthritis, now emerged from the mouth of Shanidar Cave. She carried the meaty thigh of a freshly butchered antelope slung across her right shoulder. Limping painfully to the open grave, she dropped the chunk of meat beside the dead hunter, amply provisioning him for his journey into the afterlife.

Immediately upon the old woman completing her task, the stones piled by the graveside were cast over the dead hunter's body by the folk who were gathered there for the burial that somber June morning. After the stones were all in, they scattered several inches of soil over the stones to level the grave. Right thereafter, as if carefully choreographed, every one of them assembled at the funeral that day joined in a complex flurry of hand signals, eye and body movements, comparable in content to the wailing and sobbing of their vocal human cousins in similar circumstances. Then they all left the scene noiselessly.

This simple neanderthal burial in 62,062 BP contrasts vividly with a splendiferous one in 3,229 BP, performed by humans living in southern Egypt. Those people belonged to the New Kingdom under the Nineteenth Dynasty of Pharaohs, or emperors.

The grand ceremonial burial of the dead Pharaoh Seti in the Valley of the Kings, across from the west bank of the Nile near Thebes, now modern Luxor, is an astonishing monument to human pageantry and credulity. Seti's tomb is a huge underground structure, a gargantuan warren of corridors and chambers excavated meticulously into the surrounding limestone, and occupying an area larger than a modern American football field. The tomb's construction was accomplished by the labor of tens of thousands of workers beginning many years before the pharaoh himself died. A fifth of the entire national treasury for ten years was lavished on the project. Extravagant paintings and inscriptions on the walls of his underground vault explained to the dead pharaoh in detail the exact roadmap to follow to the hereafter. Though vastly different in both scope and magnitude, the two burials—one neanderthal and the other human—were identical in design and purpose: to equip the dearly departed for the journey into the afterlife.

Other Egyptian pharaohs, instead of going underground, built enormous aboveground structures in pyramidal shape to serve as their burial site and portal to the afterlife. One such structure is the Great Pyramid of Giza built on the outskirts of modern Cairo where the Pharaoh Khufu from the Fourth Dynasty of the Old Kingdom was buried in 4,516 BP. His Great Pyramid, 455 feet tall, measures well over a football field in height. It is the largest of the surviving Egyptian pyramids and is now recognized as one of the Seven Wonders of the Ancient World by contemporary humans.

The son and successor of Seti, the Great Pharaoh Ramesses II who died in 3,163 BP, is acknowledged by humans today as the greatest and the most powerful pharaoh in all of Egyptian history. When young Ramesses was just fourteen, his father Seti appointed him Prince Regent over the entire empire. Ramesses lived to be ninety when the average life expectancy in Egypt at the time was not much more than thirty. He led successful military expeditions north into the Levant and south into Nubia, greatly expanding Egyptian territory and the hegemony of his empire. He had scores of wives and hundreds of children, and later Egyptians took to calling Ramesses II "The Great Ancestor" for this reason. His hideously shriveled and mummified body, removed from its elaborate tomb in the Valley of the Kings, is now on public display in Cairo's Egyptian Museum. Ramesses the Great was known to the ancient Greeks as Ozymandias, King of Kings. In 132 BP, the English Romantic poet Percy Bysshe Shelly published a haunting poem, *Ozymandias*, a memorable sonnet to all hubris and vanity, worth contemplating here:

I met a traveler from an antique land
Who said: Two vast and trunkless legs of stone
Stand in the desert. Near them, on the sand,
Half sunk, a shattered visage lies, whose frown,
And wrinkled lip, and sneer of cold command,
Tell that its sculptor well those passions read
Which yet survive, stamped on these lifeless things,
The hand that mocked them, and the heart that fed;
And on the pedestal these words appear:
"My name is Ozymandias, king of kings:
Look on my works, ye Mighty, and despair!"
Nothing beside remains. Round the decay
Of that colossal wreck, boundless and bare
The lone and level sands stretch far away.

Recorded human history, directly witnessed and documented by people living at the time of the event, is hardly 6,000 years old. Ironically enough, Archbishop James Ussher, religious Primate of All Ireland, declared in 300 BP that based on the chronology in his scriptures, Earth was created in 5,954 BP. That would make it about 6,000 years old now, only about as old as recorded human history. Considering the 200,000 year existence of humankind as a separate species on their planet, a timeline supported by biological and paleontological evidence, it does seem rather astonishing that every bit of directly recorded first-person information humans have about themselves comes from just that tiny slice of their recent antiquity. Of course, *Homo sapiens* could not start documenting their eyewitness history until after they had invented writing. That pivotal development, a cultural watershed for this species, happened around 5,500 BP when the ancient Sumerians, domiciled then in southern Mesopotamia now in modern Iraq, felicitously invented Cuneiform script for writing and record-keeping.

Cuneiform, derived from the Latin word *cuneus* meaning "wedge," was the first written script among these hominans. Cuneiform writing was executed by using a wedge-shaped stylus to make impressions on a soft surface such as clay which could later be hardened. Early cuneiform script consisted of representational images, or Pictographs, of the actual information recorded. This pictographic script then underwent many changes over more than 2,000 years, becoming progressively more symbolic or abstract in style. Cuneiform script was completely replaced by alphabetic writing in the Roman era starting around 2,700 BP. No cuneiform systems anywhere on my host planet are currently in use for writing by humans today.

Because of this novelty of recoded history, it is difficult for Earth-based historians of religion to precisely count the number of individual religions that have come and gone since that peculiar institution was first established on their planet. Estimates range from 3,000 to 30,000. For humans today, there are twelve so-called "classical" religions available to them. These religions offer quite divergent doctrines regarding the origin and sustenance of the natural world. They officially promulgate various formulations, not always compatible with each other, to explain the human condition, its provenance, and destiny. With respect to a particular religion's followers, it is astonishing to note, especially to an extraterrestrial like myself, that the likely reason a person professes one particular religion over another is simply because they were born into that religion. No rational choice is customarily involved in selecting one.

The dozen classical religions, by number of adherents in 62 AP, were as follows: Christianity (2,280,616,000), Islam (1,553,189,000), Hinduism (942,871,000), Buddhism (462,625,000), Sikhism (23,739,000), Judaism (14,824,000), Taoism (8,429,000), Baha'i (7,337,000), Confucianism (6,516,000), Jainism (5,277,000), Shinto (2,772,000), and Zoroastrianism (179,000). Of course, there are many other religions and cults as well.

The number of followers for the twelve classical religions add up to 5,308,374,000. An additional 802,971,000 belong to various folk/ethnic religions, or to other unspecified ones. That makes for a grand total of 6,111,345,000 humans who nominally claim adherence to one form of religion or another. There were 7,021,836,000 people living on Earth before Mac departed their planet. Therefore, 910,491,000, or 13% of humans, did not subscribe to any religion. These nonreligious people were either Agnostics or Atheists. An agnostic is an individual who concludes that the existence of a divinity or god is both unknown and unknowable. An atheist goes even further than that and rejects the notion of any god or divinity ordering the Universe. It should be noted here that both Buddhism and

Confucianism, though classified as religions, are non-theistic in structure and do not explicitly recognize the existence of a creator-god. They are therefore essentially agnostic in nature.

The earliest forms of religious belief among humans attributed a unique and immutable essence (or soul) to all objects around them. This view of the natural world, called Animism, is still found among some people on Earth today. It holds that there is no separation between the spirit world and the material world, and that souls or spirits exist, not only in humans but also in other animals, plants, rocks and geographical features, including all natural phenomena such as clouds, wind, lightning and earthquakes. But this ecumenical view of the cosmos became increasingly restricted as humans became more anthropomorphic in their outlook. In time, inanimate objects lost their souls, followed by the desouling of plants and nonhuman animals. Ultimately, only humans remained endowed with this special commodity.

The earliest religions bestowed a facade of immortality on individual humans by way of their "immortal" souls, and that central theme of assuring eternal life continues to remain the bedrock of religion today. This basic module was later embellished with specific codes of conduct in respect to work, family, sexuality, ethics, and morality. These later features of religion were used to facilitate a more harmonious social order for humans in their present life, a welcome dividend of the religious regime. Transgression of these divine edicts, as people were solemnly warned, would undoubtedly result in eternal punishment. That tended to keep them in line.

The persona of the supernatural creator and director of the Universe may take different forms in the many religions now operating on my host planet. To begin with, Theism is the belief in the existence of an external creator responsible for everything—its opposite is Atheism which rejects the notion of god. Theism among these hominans may be divided into four subtypes: Pantheism, Polytheism, Henotheism, and Monotheism. Pantheism is the belief that everything is divine and that the Universe is identical with god; this universal god is therefore not personified in any single entity. Polytheism is the belief in multiple personified deities, usually presented as a pantheon of gods and goddesses, each divinity having its own attributes and fixed characteristics. Henotheism is the belief in a chief god, yet accepting the possible existence of other lesser deities as well. Monotheism is the belief in a single god or creator, to the exclusion of all others.

Religion among humans began as animism. At this stage of their religious development, no creator-god was invoked by them. Pantheism is related to animism, though it is not the same. Animism acknowledges that everything in nature possesses a soul, but not that the souls of everything in nature are the same. Animism thus excludes Monism which pantheism embraces. Monism holds that all things in the Universe are reducible to one common substance, and thus concludes that the fundamental character of the Universe is unity. Animism, instead, emphasizes the uniqueness of each individual soul and rejects the monistic view. Therefore pantheism, unlike animism, is monistic, believing everything shares the same spiritual essence—rather than having distinctly separate spirits or souls as animism proposes.

The cultural institution of religion then continued to develop in tandem with the elaborate cognitive evolution of these hominans, particularly in *Homo sapiens* after the appearance of behavioral modernity in that species during the Late Pleistocene.

Then rather abruptly around 12,000 BP, just as the Pleistocene Epoch was hurtling to a close, the "god-factor" became separated from the natural world and instead endowed with its own supernatural character and independent existence outside of nature. This was a critical juncture in the evolution of religion among these hominans. Soon humans were supplicants to this disembodied divinity, faithfully building sanctuaries to worship and propitiate this newly created god, now taken out of the natural world and placed in a supernatural domain endowed with infinite power and authority.

The first temple ever built by humans to venerate this new divinity was just north of the Fertile Crescent in today's southeastern Turkey on a hill now called Gobekli Tepe, or Potbelly Hill. This god-sanctuary was built 11,600 years ago by stone age people who were all hunter-gatherers then, not too long before permanent settlements and agriculture began. Though organized religion was still to emerge and had to wait for the first stable civilization to appear in Sumer, tribes were already making pilgrimages to worship at Gobekli Tepe. This god-sanctuary preceded by several centuries the Neolithic Revolution when humans established permanent settlements in the Fertile Crescent. Upon establishment, these new settlements would then permit these hominans to conveniently organize rituals and offer routine worship and sacrifice to placate the recently reformulated gods. Some gods demanded human sacrifice[55] which was also on the menu.

Religion helped enforce order and fostered a common social currency on these newly settled hunters and gatherers.

---

55 Religious human sacrifice was frequently practiced by many human cultures throughout recorded history. Now banned and considered murder, it still occurs, though rarely.

Lacking familial kinship bonds to underwrite tribal loyalty, these unrelated settlers substituted the new religion for the old consanguinity as cement for social bonding. Ever since that time, religion has served as a formidable talisman for tribal identity, forging communal solidarity between clans of unrelated people. But by a perverse calculus, it equally promoted conflicts and wars between heterogeneous tribal groups who did not profess the same religion. These savage religious conflicts and brutal holy wars would torment *Homo sapiens* and lay waste to many hundreds of millions of human lives in the course of their sanguineous history. It continues today.

⁂

Polytheism, adorned with its many gods and goddesses, was the first organized religion on my host planet. Among Earth's present religions, Hinduism, a polytheistic creed, is the oldest one in existence today. A form of proto-Hinduism first flowered around 7,500 BP in the Sumerian cities of Mesopotamia. It had no single founder. It was a polytheistic doctrine exulting a pantheon of gods and goddesses, each divinity influencing some aspect or other of a person's life. These numen—the spirit presiding over an object, place, or situation—required to be bribed and propitiated with prayer, sacrifice, and offerings, in order to ward off trouble and ensure good fortune to the householder. A fat priestly caste soon emerged to perform these rites and rituals.

That first Neolithic religion spread westward from the Fertile Crescent into the Mediterranean littoral, and mixing with local traditions, invested ancient Egyptian, Greek, and Roman religions with their slew of divinities. Those Mediterranean incarnations of this Neolithic creed eventually declined and disappeared. Notwithstanding, another branch migrating southeastward into India thrives today as modern Hinduism, one of Earth's major contemporary religions.

The earliest preserved scripture[56] of Hinduism in India is the Rig Veda, a collection of hymns compiled around 3,500 BP. Hinduism later incorporated a tripartite divinity of three super-gods (Trimurti) surmounting a medley of lesser gods and goddesses. The three super-gods were a Producer or Creator (Brahma), a Preserver or Sustainer (Vishnu), and a Destroyer or Transformer (Shiva). These three divinities directly or indirectly influenced all human affairs. Transcendent even beyond the Trimurti is a genderless, formless and impersonal absolute called Brahman (no relation to Brahma), the categorical quintessence of everything there is in the cosmos. In this respect, Hinduism is a monism. It is also pantheistic and henotheistic, not simply polytheistic. The ultimate goal of existence according to Hinduism is to comprehend and unite with Brahman, thus reaching moksha or liberation from bondage to the unending cycle of existence. This is achieved by devoted study and ceaseless effort, striving always toward the objective of merging with Brahman the monistic absolute. If an individual is not successful in accomplishing this task during a given lifetime, the soul is reincarnated in flesh again and again, for as long as it takes, for liberation to be finally achieved.

Hinduism, unlike other classical religions practiced by present day humans, permanently assigns people at birth to one of four immutable social castes based on their parentage.

---

56 The scriptures of Hinduism are numerous. They include Vedas (revealed wisdom), Upanishads (listening to a teacher), Puranas (legends and speculative history), and the great Itihasas (epics) of Ramayana (journey of Rama) and Mahabharata (great story of the Bharat dynasty); the Bhagavad-Gita (song of god) is part of the Mahabharata.

This caste system is relentlessly hierarchical and has important social consequences for the assignees. No individual effort or scheme can ever alter one's designated caste.

Buddhism, a major world religion, was founded 2,540 years before Mac visited Earth, by a man named Siddhartha Gautama (2,513 BP–2,433 BP). Siddhartha was born in Kapilavastu by the foothills of the Himalayas, in what is today modern Nepal, near that country's southern border with India. Siddhartha later came to be known as Buddha, meaning "Awakened One." Siddhartha was the son of King Suddhodana and Queen Maya. Suddhodana was chief of the Sakyas, an Indic people inhabiting the region at that time.

Buddhism developed within a Hindu society which was the prevailing religious tradition in that area during those times. Moreover, during this period, Jainism, yet another classical religion from India, was also prevalent in the local region during Siddhartha's time. Jainism championed the principle of active nonviolence toward all living creatures and emphasized the spiritual equality of every single form of life that exists in the world, no matter how trivial or insignificant it may appear to be. Jainism does not believe in a creator-god, though it does allow that humans have the capacity to evolve spiritually into godlike creatures. According to Jainism, the Universe is eternal and was never created nor will it ever cease to exist—it does not posit a superior power to make the Universe or govern it. Mahavira (2,549 BP–2,477 BP), who gave Jainism its present form, was born in what is now the modern Indian state of Bihar. He was the last and most renowned member of a long pedigree of Jain savants or Tirthankaras. Mahavira was a contemporary of Siddhartha. Some speculate that Jainism had an influence on Siddhartha, though orthodox Buddhists today reject that proposition.

As a young man, Siddhartha devoutly sought to find an antidote for human misery and suffering. Hardly 29 years old, he relinquished his patrimony and all its opulent luxury, abandoning his home and family for the life of an itinerant mendicant. He subjected himself to the most extreme forms of self-abnegation and physical deprivation. Upon reaching the age of 35, and now close to death from the unremitting privation he had inflicted on himself, the desperate prince sat in deep meditation under a pipal tree (*Ficus religiosa*) in a place now called Bodh Gaya in India. At that moment and in that place, overcome by extreme hunger and fatigue, Siddhartha Gautama is said to have attained enlightenment and become Buddha. There, according to classical Buddhist teachings[57], he had discovered the Middle Way, a path of moderation, away from the extremes of self-indulgence and self-abnegation.

Siddhartha's way begins by first acknowledging the "Four Great Truths." The first truth is that all existence is sorrow; life survives only by exploiting and destroying other life around it. The second truth is the cause of this sorrow, this "deep disease of life" as Siddhartha called it. He claimed that this misery, this unquenchable sorrow, sprang exclusively from desire, meaning attachment to the transient and impermanent world and its contents. Since those inevitably perish, they are doomed to disappoint and thereby inflict sorrow. The third truth according to Siddhartha, is that this unremitting sorrow that all life is heir to can indeed be conquered by prying away and eventually detaching those lethal bonds of attachment. The fourth truth is

---

57 Buddhist scriptures are many. They are assembled in a tripartite collection called the Tripitaka (triple basket). The triple basket is composed of Sutra (discourses), Vinaya (rules for the clergy), and Abhidharma (philosophical and psychological analyses).

the path that must be followed in order to reach this desired objective.

That path he called the Eightfold Path to be traversed by cultivating the following eight qualities: right doctrine, right purpose, right discourse, right behavior, right purity, right thought, right loneliness, and right rapture. It is a progressive journey, trod with unswerving effort and commitment, which becomes easier to travel with experience gained over time. At the end of the road is nirvana, literally meaning "extinguished" as in a flame put out, and refers to the sublime peace and imperturbable calm after the raging fires of desire and delusion are finally laid to rest. Siddhartha makes no allusion anywhere to a creator-god in the quest for nirvana, and Buddhism is fundamentally nontheistic in its outlook, if not arguably atheistic. Despite this character of the religion, devotees of different Buddhist sects may often venerate images of Buddha or other deities in their worship and rituals.

Back in ancient Egypt, the Pharaoh Amenhotep IV (3,330 BP–3,284 BP), after ascending the throne in 3,301 BP, abruptly changed the longstanding polytheistic religion of the Egyptians in the fifth year of his reign. Amenhotep summarily rejected the existing polytheistic conclave of gods and goddesses, choosing instead to pay obeisance to only one supreme creator-god he called Aten, identifying that god with the solar disc. This new monotheistic religion of Atenism, freshly imposed on a prevailing culture of polytheism, provoked a great deal of controversy in the Egypt of that time.

Atenism was one of the earliest, if not the first, experiment in monotheism among humans. Its founder, Amenhotep IV, changed his imperial name to Akhenaten—meaning servant of Aten—and made Aten the only god of the Egyptian state. Other gods were ignominiously abolished, their names expunged, and their temples abandoned. Nonetheless, this first monotheism did not last long. Soon after Akhenaten's death, the old polytheism was enthusiastically restored by its former priests and practitioners. Akhenaten's son and successor, the famous boy Pharaoh Tutankhaten, was enjoined by the restored polytheistic priesthood to personally reject Atenism and change his name to Tutankhamen instead. Atenism, banished as the state religion within three years of Akhenaten's death, rapidly disappeared from the scene.

The second experiment in monotheism was a runaway success. It eventually affected approximately 55 percent of Earth's human population who are nominally monotheists today. It was first crafted by a man called Moses (3,341 BP– 3,221 BP), an aristocratic Egyptian of Israelite descent. The Israelites were a Hebrew-speaking Semitic people originating in the Fertile Crescent during the Neolithic period. Moses was a second-generation Egyptian born to Hebrew parents, Amram and Jochebed. He was adopted as a foundling by the reigning pharaoh's daughter and raised to adulthood among Egyptian nobility. Moses is said to have lived for 120 years, an improbably long time, especially for someone in the Bronze Age.

Moses advocated a monotheistic religion called Judaism derived from the ethnic traditions of the Hebrews, or Jews. Hebrew mythology traces these traditions down from Adam, the first ever human said to be created by their god Jehovah or Yahweh. A presumed forefather of the Jews, Abraham, a protagonist from Ur in ancient Mesopotamia—a reputed descendant of Adam that first human—is believed to have entered into a covenant or agreement with Jehovah. This covenant guaranteed Abraham and his descendants protection and victory over

all adversaries, if the devotees of Jehovah scrupulously followed that god's every edict and injunction.

Judaism, along with the other Semitic monotheisms that
followed it, regard Abraham as a Prophet. Prophethood has
its origins in Hebrew tradition. Prophets are individuals who
exhort their fellow humans to a cause, reputedly prompted
by divine inspiration, and are considered messengers through
whom the divine will is communicated to people. Abraham's
oracular patrimony was internalized by three other monotheistic religions—Christianity, Islam, and Baha'i—all borrowing
from this peculiar Jewish prophetic tradition. These monotheistic faiths are appropriately called Abrahamic monotheisms.
In contrast, Sikhism, a monotheistic religion promulgated in
India by Guru Nanak (481 BP–411 BP), is a non-Abrahamic
monotheism.

Moses was 57 years old when Akhenaten died in Egypt.
Being a scion of the Egyptian establishment, Moses was quite
familiar with the heady new monotheism of the deceased pharaoh and was disappointed to see Atenism eclipsed so soon
after Akhenaten's death. The eminent Dr. Sigmund Freud, a
renowned Austrian neurologist and father of modern psy-
choanalysis, noted and commented on these matters. Freud,
indeed, for a quite different reason, should be acknowledged
for illuminating some important aspects of theory-of-mind,
introducing the now familiar and far-reaching psychological
construct of Ego (conscious mind), Id (unconscious mind), and
Superego (sense of right and wrong).

In a remarkable monograph, *Moses and Monotheism*,
published in 13 BP, Freud applies psychoanalytic theory to religious history, postulating that Moses was an ethnic Egyptian
who allied with a cult of Egyptian Israelites and led them to

freedom after Akhenaten's death, grafting the deceased pharaoh's monotheism onto their religion. Freud speculated that these emancipated Israelites, in due course, rebelled against Moses and killed him. They later merged with another tribe that swore allegiance to a fierce volcano-god called Yahweh. Years after the murder of Moses, the rebels regretted their action and perforce invented the concept of a "messiah" to personify their hope for the return of Moses as their savior.

The traditional history of Moses, certainly, is quite different from Freud's psychoanalytic accounting of events. After the murder of an Egyptian slave-driver, Moses fled Egypt to Midian in the northwestern Hejaz region of Arabia where, according to Jewish scriptures[58], he encountered the god of the Hebrews masked in a fiery bush, who commanded him to return to Egypt and deliver his fellow Hebrews from bondage. Moses returned to Egypt as ordered. After challenging the reigning pharaoh and inflicting a gruesome series of ten disasters or "plagues" on the Egyptians with the collusion of his partisan god, Moses was allowed by the besieged pharaoh to lead his people out of Egyptian bondage. He led them toward Canaan, the land they believed was promised to them by Jehovah. Along the way, it is claimed, Jehovah gave Moses a set of Ten Commandments, the first of which enjoined the Jews to worship no other god except Jehovah himself.

Thus was the doctrine of monotheism reborn not long after Atenism died, appearing now as Judaism, the religion of the Hebrews. It was founded by their prophet Moses, although

---

58 The Tanakh and the Talmud are the primary scriptures of Judaism. Tanakh is an acronym for its three components: Torah (Five Books of Moses), Nevi'im (Prophets), and Ketuvim (Writings). The Talmud is a compendium of rabbinical or priestly commentaries on a variety of subjects affecting society.

Jews claim that their history goes back to Abraham and even before him to Adam. Judaism is an ethnic monotheism based on the tribal traditions of the Israelites. Its covenant was restricted to Jehovah and the Jewish people. In return for the many favors that Jehovah has done for them, Jews are sternly enjoined by their religion to follow a rigorous code of behavior and revere Jehovah the god of Israel, faithfully following all his laws and commandments.

The Jews, as heralded in their scriptures, had a historic tradition of yearning for a supreme leader from amongst their clan, a political and military hero who could vanquish their enemies and lift their nation to the pinnacle of greatness. They referred to this cultural icon as Mashiac, meaning messiah or savior. An itinerant Jewish preacher called Jesus (1,954 BP–1,920 BP), born in the town of Bethlehem now in modern Palestine, was hailed by his adoring followers as just such a mashiac predicted in the Jewish scriptures. Jesus was the son of Joseph and Mary. Subsequent tradition held that Mary conceived Jesus directly by an act of god, remaining a virgin herself, and therefore Joseph was not Jesus' biologic father.

During the time of Jesus, the Jews were under colonial occupation by the Romans. Following the Roman conquest of Judea in 2,013 BP by Gnaeus Pompeius Magnus or Pompey the Great, the subjugated region was divided into five district councils or Sanhedrin. Roman rule was fully consolidated under Herod, a client king appointed by the imperial power. Pining for a savior to deliver them from that occupation was both unsurprising and palpable among the local Jews. Nonetheless, Jesus informed his followers that he was not a worldly messiah, but rather a heavenly one sent by god his father to redeem them from eternal damnation. Jesus later came to be regarded by his partisans as the only "begotten" son of this father-god, the putative creator of the cosmos, who was now personally involved in the salvation of individual humans through his earthly son, Jesus. The religion of Jesus thus presumed the existence of a uniquely personal and anthropomorphic god. Jesus preached a doctrine of unconditional love, humility, and forgiveness, notably excoriating the hypocrisy and self-righteousness of his fellow Jews of that time. Needless to say, that position made Jesus very unpopular and threatening to the local Jewish authorities now under the jurisdiction of Pontius Pilate, the Roman prefect of Judea.

The religion of Jesus later came to be known as Christianity, derived from the word "Christ" meaning messiah. The scriptures[59] and doctrines of Christianity derive from Judaism and its traditions. Yet, the majority of Jews living at the time of Jesus rejected the claim to messiahship and implicated Jesus with sedition. He was tried for this offense, convicted, and then executed by crucifixion at the age of thirty three. Christians believe that Jesus literally died for their sins, thus paying the ultimate price required for their redemption and everlasting existence. They also believe that Jesus was restored to physical life and ascended to heaven three days after he died on the cross.

Following Jesus' death, his posthumous disciple Saul, known to Christians as Paul, a tent-maker born in the city of Tarsus in Turkey, converted to Christianity from Judaism after encountering a vision of Jesus. He became the main sponsor

---

59 The Christian scripture is called the Bible, claimed by them to be the inspired word of their unitary god who has three manifestations: the Father, the Son, and the Holy Ghost. The Bible is made up of two components: the Old Testament which is essentially the Jewish Tanakh; and the New Testament that describes the life and teachings of Jesus as compiled by his disciples and admirers after his death.

and proselytizer of the Christian religion. Paul had his conversion vision on the open road while on a journey from Jerusalem to Damascus in Syria, to arrest Christian converts in Damascene Jewish communities, on the authority issued to him by the Jewish high priest in Jerusalem. After his own conversion, Paul made the crucial decision to extend the religion of Christianity to both Jews and non-Jews alike. Paul thus expanded the hitherto ethnically restricted monotheistic covenant between Jehovah and his chosen Hebrew people, to all interested parties regardless of their tribe or ethnicity. This strategic move by Paul made Christianity available as a religion to Gentiles or non-Jews as well, thus opening up the new religion to many more people and ensuring its widespread distribution. Before Paul, Christianity was restricted to Jewish communities only.

Muhammad (1,380 BP–1,318 BP), the son of Abd'Allah and Aminah, was born in the city of Mecca, now located in modern Saudi Arabia. Orphaned at an early age, Muhammad was first raised under the guardianship of his paternal grandfather, then later, after his grandfather expired, by his paternal uncle. His father died before Muhammad was born. His mother passed on when he was just six years old. Muhammad was the founder of another major transnational monotheistic religion called Islam. The Arabic word Islam means "submission"—to the will of their god Allah—and a follower of that religion is therefore called a Muslim, meaning "one who submits."

According to Muslim tradition, Muhammad was 40 years old when he encountered an angel called Gabriel in a cave on Mount Hira near Mecca, where he had gone to meditate as he often did. The angel commanded him to, "Recite!" As Muhammad complied with the command, words his followers believe issued directly from their monotheistic god, burst from the new prophet's lips. Over the course of some 22 years, Muhammad received a series of such revelations that were compiled and canonized as the Quran, the basic scripture[60] of Islam.

Muslims trace their religious patrimony through Abraham's older son Ishmael, while Jews do so through his younger son Isaac. Much like Judaism and Christianity, Islam lays claim to a line of Hebrew prophets. In Islam, this constellation includes Jesus and Muhammad as well. Muslims assert that Muhammad is the last of this prophetic line and there would be no further prophets after him.

Muhammad proved a highly successful religious, political, and military leader, who skillfully compounded both the religious and the secular aspects of human life into the rubric of his new religion—there is no separation of these two spheres of human activity in Islam. Now aged 60, just two years before his death, Muhammad's forces conquered his hometown of Mecca where the Muslim prophet had fled persecution eight years earlier. Upon entering the now vanquished city, Muhammad banished the numerous polytheistic deities from Mecca's house of worship the Kaaba (Cube), and imposed a supreme god, Allah, as the only one worthy of submission and adoration. Islam is a strict monotheism exhorting complete obedience to its god, along with constant mindfulness of

---

60 The Quran (or Recitation) is the primary scripture of Islam. Adherents of that faith claim the Quran to be the direct word of their god Allah, revealed serially to their prophet Muhammad. A subsidiary doctrinal source in Islam is the Sunnah or Hadith, compilations by various authors portraying the biography, statements, and actions of Muhammad, considered by Muslims as important tools in understanding the Quran, and a source for Islamic jurisprudence or Sharia.

Allah's judgment. Just as the Hebrew god Jehovah once was for the Israelites, Allah was once a principal god for the Arabs in pre-Islamic Arabia. Arabian religion before Muhammad was a polytheism, where people worshiped an assemblage of gods and goddesses enshrined in the Kaaba. Some would choose a principal deity, like Allah, for special adoration, a form of henotheism. Muhammad's posthumous father Abd'Allah himself, whose name means "slave of Allah," was such an individual.

There are numerous religions humans profess and practice today, packaged in many different flavors and configurations. Confucianism, a religion originating in China, is entirely nontheistic in nature and invokes no god or divinity in its ethos. It was founded by the Chinese editorialist and politician, Confucius (2,501 BP–2,429 BP), who propounded an ethical system of behavior based on duty and filial piety. The core of Confucianism is humanism which extols the value and sanctity of humans. Confucianism focuses principally on family and kin, not on gods or an afterlife.

Taoism was another Chinese religion that emerged in the same period as Confucianism. Taoism offers as its central creed the imperative of living in harmony with the Tao or "The Way." Taoism had several contributors, foremost among them a quasi-historical figure called Lao Tzu who is alleged to have been a contemporary of Confucius, though humans today have no documentation of Lao Tzu's birth or death. Taoism is a preppy polytheism recognizing many divinities who engage in different celestial administrative functions. However, the Tao itself is not a deity. It is purely a metaphysical formulation.

The primary objective of Taoism is to unite with the Tao and harmonize one's will with nature, thereby achieving the capacity for effortless action in the natural world. There are some faint echoes here with our own secular outlook on Galymon. The Yin-Yang principle is fundamental to Taoism. It clearly postulates that all aspects of being are composed of complementary forces that depend on each other: they do not make sense if considered independently on their own merits or demerits alone. Thus there is feminine and masculine, darkness and light, hot and cold, wet and dry, action and inaction, positive and negative, death and life, and so on. This duality is not exclusionary, but complementary. The key to success is to perfectly balance the dualities and achieve eternal harmony. In this manner, the practitioner of Taoism is able to lead a frictionless existence and distill anything that is needed for life out of the cosmos itself, much like pulling rabbits out of a hat.

Homo sapiens first developed religion in the Late Pleistocene and thereafter natural selection fixed it in their genome, with the phenotype expressed in their cognitive and behavioral repertoire. This adaptation then quickly dispersed worldwide among their kind. Religion is now a universal phenomenon among these hominans. No human group anywhere on their planet, whether living in primitive tribes or in advanced civilizations, lacks this extraordinary institution. A propensity for religion, or religiosity, has been clearly favored by natural selection and is now an inherited trait in this species. Evidently, this "religiosity gene" must certainly have played an important survival function for these hominans and increased fitness during a period in their evolutionary history, given that religion is so ubiquitous among them. This critical period for religion started just as sapience was emerging 100,000 years ago. It was a construct necessary to transcend the alarming intimations of mortality that came with sapience. Now at last religion may have finally played out its role.

It is necessary here to separate process and content. Religiosity—the process—is inherited and universal to all humans. However, any one particular religion—the content—is clearly acquired and provincial. Stated another way, the biologic mechanism underlying acquisition of religion is similar in all humans, yet there are many religions with surprisingly dissimilar content, all claiming to be the correct and only indisputable one. As an analogy, language centers in the brain are similar in all humans, but each language is different and one language cannot be understood by another language-speaker. So too, much like the difference between computer hardware and software, religiosity may be imagined as hardware the same in all people; the individual religions themselves are software programs that download onto that hardware but are each unique and diverse.

Counting every shade of religion on my host planet today, from tiny tribal ones to global behemoths, and figuring in the copious denominations found within each religion itself, the total number of current religions on Earth may reach 200 or more. They propose contrasting visions of god, creation, the material world, human life, and destiny. Obviously they cannot all be right, and it is most unlikely that any have captured the truth. These old religions are all outmoded cosmogonies now, based on information and insights humans had many centuries or millennia ago. As a reminder of the paucity of knowledge and understanding in those times when humans conjured these religions, it should be recalled that people did not even have the faintest idea then about what made their Sun shine. Humans only unraveled that small mystery in modern times, hardly 90 years ago, when the British astrophysicist Arthur Eddington first suggested in 30 BP that the Sun produced its energy from nuclear fusion of hydrogen atoms. Humans had believed until then that the Sun was a huge ball of fire, exactly like the common carbon fires they knew on their own planet, just on a much grander scale.

The quintessential conundrum about the nature of existence, recognized by all sapient beings in our Universe, is the profound paradox between freewill and predestination. Each one logically precludes the other. If indeed there is an unbreakable chain of causality extending from the past through the present into the future, then destiny will always prevail and nothing can ever change or alter outcomes. This notion of determinism, also called fate, provides a framework for some religions. Other religions on my host planet contend freewill is paramount and that the future is plastic and yet unborn, to be determined by choices freely made in the present. These opposite existential viewpoints are clearly incompatible with each other. They have been debated throughout human history, at least since these hominans acquired the necessary sapience to ask this fundamental question. Religions earnestly offer explanations to resolve this implacable dichotomy, but none of those explanations are logically appealing or intellectually satisfying.

On Galymon we approach this conundrum rather differently. We recognize that freewill and predestination can coexist in a single domain together only if they both desire the same outcome. In other words, what freewill wants is what destiny ordains. These two agencies—freewill and destiny—are perfect mirror-images of each other in the realm we inhabit. In our world, the god inside is exactly the god outside. Whenever these two forces are at variance with each other, then, like matter and antimatter, they will surely annihilate each other every time.

The future of traditional religion on my host planet was once cogently addressed by the same eminent Dr. Sigmund Freud encountered earlier. Freud published another monograph in 23 BP called, *The Future of an Illusion*. Therein Freud defined religion as a false belief system, or illusion, merely representing wish fulfillment. Among the wishes seeking fulfillment are the psychological yearning to cling to the security of a parent figure, the hope for the continuation of earthly existence in a future life, and the desire for immortality of the human soul.

Commissar Ra-him would surely agree with Dr. Freud.

CHAPTER XII:

GOVERNMENT

"Humans are political animals," said the great Greek philosopher Aristotle more than 2,300 years ago. He was right.

"Politics" derives from the Greek word *polis* meaning "city." It described how humans debated their positions and exercised power among diverse populations such as those who live in a city. After their long libertarian Paleolithic existence, a deference to higher authority became necessary in the Neolithic to ensure order and predictability within the new cities they built, since humans had to now perform tasks and obligations not expected of them as hunter-gatherers. Therefore, by way of politics, a system of cooperation was established and people made to adhere to rules and regulations, a form of organization that came to be known as Government.

It was the Neolithic Age that first saw humans adopt this elaborate system of mass interpersonal organization called government. This development was the direct outcome of small nomadic tribes joining up into larger communities of settled farmers. As a result of settling permanently to engage in agriculture, these hominans were forced to abandon their simple and nonsectarian ethos as free-roaming hunters and gatherers, and adopt a more regimented lifestyle as settled farmers. Packing large numbers of them into compact areas created many problems for these people. Clearly, a major area of concern was the spread of communicable diseases that took a heavy toll on them until sufficient herd immunity had built up in the population. Such disease epidemics could easily wipe out large numbers of these people in a hurry.

Another concern to these early Neolithic people was that any inappropriate or unsavory behavior on the part of individuals could significantly impact others living around them. This required imposition of order, by force if necessary, to regulate improper activities and deviant behavior and avoid chaos inside crowded human settlements. Government became the instrument of that control. Therefore, the one single defining feature of any government—from the most benign to the most malignant—is its monopoly over Police Power, or the authorization to use physical force. In this way, formerly free choices and unrestrained actions of individual humans were subordinated to the interests of the larger community. That was how government first began, barely 7,000 years ago in human history.

Politics, the art of governing, emerged as the engine of power among these hominans during the Neolithic. It became the mechanism by which people engaged each other. Control of this mechanism naturally led to authority or power. Power itself, at least among humans currently inhabiting Earth, can best be understood as the ability to influence the behavior and actions of others. The wellspring of all power among *Homo sapiens* is the ownership and control of resources, both the tangible variety and the intangible kind.

The vastly amplified food production spurred by the Neolithic Revolution led to an explosion of humans occupying their planet. As already remarked, the earlier deadly Toba Event circa 74,000 BP had decimated nearly nine out of ten humans living on Earth at that time, reducing all of humanity to less than 15,000 people and bringing the species to the brink of extinction. Following recovery from that catastrophe, and until the development of agriculture in the early Holocene, Earth's human population had stabilized and settled around 1 million people who subsisted entirely by hunting and gathering food. This lifestyle required, and resulted, in a low population density imposed by the unpredictability and scarcity of food resources. The entire population of humans at the start of the Holocene roughly 11,700 years ago, was not substantially different from the planetary populations of other great apes living alongside humans at that time. Of course, among the Hominidae alive when the Holocene began, all hominans except for *Homo sapiens* had been eliminated.

Humans then invented agriculture. With this revolutionary new technique came the mass production of food without exposure to the extreme dangers experienced by their hunter-gatherer forebears. A torrential explosion in their population numbers followed, powered by the newly established institution of marriage. It had taken all of 190,000 years after speciation for *Homo sapiens* to achieve a worldwide population of just over 1 million individuals by 10,000 BP. Yet hardly 2,000 years later, by 8,000 BP when Mac visited Sofar, there were five times as many, the population of humans pushing the 5 million mark. This phenomenal growth continued to explode geometrically. There were almost 50 million people in 3,000 BP, 400 million in 500 BP, 1 billion in 100 BP, 3 billion in 10 AP, and 7 billion when Mac visited their planet in 61 AP. In just the final 10,000 years of a 200,000 year history, these formidable hominans had increased their numbers by 7,000 times. That growth was unprecedented for any large mammalian species ever in the history of their planet.

There was no pressing need for political government so long as humans were just few and scattered across their range. The largest social groups operating during their long Paleolithic diaspora as hunter-gathers were small tribes where each adult member essentially had an equal voice in tribal adjudications. Authorities, if they even existed, had strictly limited powers. Most tribes did without them. Marriage to goose population numbers, and patriarchy with its associated concentration of power and privilege for men, had still to emerge. This form of pre-political social organization can still be found among the few remaining hunter-gatherer societies scattered around my host planet today.

Starting in the Fertile Crescent, and then inexorably spreading elsewhere, the rise of settlements after 10,000 BP began to change this pristine state of affairs. Jarmo, an ancient Neolithic hamlet east of the modern city of Kirkuk in northern Iraq, was the first agrarian commune established by humans on their planet. Though other Neolithic settlements were also formed around the same period as Jarmo, at sites around Damascus in Syria, Jericho in Palestine, and Jubayl in Lebanon, these other locations were only intermittently occupied by humans and not used for persistent and organized agriculture until after 6,000 BP.

Jarmo was first settled in 9,040 BP during the early

Holocene, by hunter-gatherers who had emigrated out of Africa some 70,000 years earlier. At its peak, the village had roughly 150 people residing in 25 houses on about four acres of land. Jarmo was charmingly nestled in a belt of oak and pistachio woodlands at an elevation of 2,625 feet above sea level, on the northern foothills of the Zagros Mountains separating modern Iraq from Iran. The good people of Jarmo cultivated wheat, barley and beans, and raised sheep, goats and pigs. They bred domesticated dogs from wolves, and were among the first humans to manufacture pottery.

The electrifying transformation in the culture of this species that emerged with agriculture would forever change the trajectory of *Homo sapiens*. Not long after appearing in Jarmo and spreading along the adjoining foothills of the Zagros Mountains, this seismic revolution spilled south, caressed by the nurturing arms of the Tigris and the Euphrates Rivers. Then, this brand new agricultural enterprise followed the enchanted course of these two great rivers through the heart of Iraq to the Persian Gulf in the Indian Ocean 400 miles away. Agricultural settlements cascaded down the rich alluvial plain between the two mighty rivers, along an area the ancient Greeks would later call Mesopotamia, literally meaning "between the rivers." It was here that itinerant Paleolithic tribes first abandoned their old nomadic life of hunting and gathering, settling down instead to a new life of farming and herding.

And so was born the Neolithic Age with its transformative agricultural revolution that in less than 10,000 years would propel these humans into extraterrestrial space, away from the gravitational clutches of their own rocky planet.

This novel agrarian way of life beginning in Jarmo, moved south to first produce the Samarra culture of middle Mesopotamia. Settling on the plains just north of modern Baghdad, these Neolithic Samarra people began to irrigate their crops and manufacture a distinctive style of pottery they exported to surrounding areas. The Samarra people in turn became the Ubaidian culture further along to their south. The Ubaidians continued this southward thrust toward the Persian Gulf to emerge as those superlative Sumerians who built the first systemic and stable human civilization on their planet. It is known today as the Sumerian Civilization, the forerunner of all other civilizations on Earth. The ancient Sumerians drained the surrounding marshlands to grow crops, developed trade with neighboring settlements, and successfully established industries such as pottery, masonry, weaving, and the fabrication of metal and leather.

Sumer, from the Akkadian word *Sumeru* meaning "land of the civilized lords" was what their neighbors called the territory of these extraordinary southern Mesopotamians. In their own native language the Sumerians called themselves *ug sag gigga* or "the black-headed people" to distinguish their own kind from those others to the north. This was indeed the same Sumer where writing as cuneiform script was first invented by *Homo sapiens* around 5,500 years ago. The unique distinction of being the first durable metropolis on Earth belongs to the legendary Sumerian city-state of Eridu in southern Mesopotamia.

Sumer straddled the Tigris and Euphrates, the mother rivers of human civilization. Several city-states blossomed in Sumer, starting with Eridu in 7,520 BP. Eridu developed not too far from the west bank of the Euphrates at the very southern end of Mesopotamia, not long from the border with modern Iran and the Persian Gulf. After emerging as a loose confederation of hamlets occupied by Neolithic farmers, Eridu proceeded to consolidate successfully during the middle Holocene to become the first functioning city-state ever established by humans on my host planet.

Over a span of approximately 2,500 years following Eridu, Sumer hatched more than two dozen independent city-states in southern Mesopotamia. These self-contained bailiwicks were separated from each other by canals and stone boundary markings. City-states with names such as Ur, Uruk, Lagash, and Kish, among others, were clustered to the north and west of Eridu in the rich riparian plain between the two great rivers. Here indeed nested the primal engine for all subsequent global human civilizations.

As agriculture spread in Mesopotamia and crops were intensively cultivated, elaborate irrigation techniques were developed and employed by Sumerian farmers. Canals were trenched from the rivers to supply water to growing fields. Controlling the flow of water down these canals soon had to be coordinated by a central canal authority so that downstream fields were not deprived of water as upstream ones were being fed. Other issues needed addressing as well. A reliable calendar had to be devised so that farmers would know when the spring floods were expected to arrive. Property rights such as ownership of slaves[61], animals, houses, and fields had to be authenticated and acknowledged.

---

61 Institutionalized human slavery first appeared in the culture of *Homo sapiens* in Sumer during the Neolithic Age.

Unlike the case for hunters and gatherers who associated in small fraternal tribes during their earlier Paleolithic incarnation, these new Neolithic city-states of Sumer could house huge populations of 5,000 people or more at any one time. Individuals in these agglomerations lived in close proximity to each other and were quite likely to be strangers among themselves. Because of this unfamiliarity between people, there was the clear risk of personal and property crimes such as murder, rape, assault, and robbery. These criminal activities had to be proscribed and prevented by adequate policing under the control of a central authority. That authority could also adjudicate and mete out punishments for the offenses. The heads of the first Sumerian cities, which were little more than enlarged villages at that time, gradually began to assume these ruling responsibilities, eventually going on to acquire the regal trappings and functional attributes of monarchs or sovereigns. Monarchy, literally meaning "rule of one" was therefore the first form of political governance invented by humans. It was founded in Sumer more than 7,000 years ago.

Inevitably, the young cities of Sumer began bickering and fighting over the allotment of river waters, the upstream cities naturally wanting to dominate this valuable resource at the expense of downstream ones. Their new wealth also attracted the covetousness and greed of nomadic tribes milling outside the yet relatively small area of civilization. Large scale systematic warfare, probably the most potent force of historical change for these hominans since giving up their hunter-gatherer ethos, now loudly proclaimed its bloody and lethal arrival.

During their prolonged pre-settlement Paleolithic phase, these hominans had indeed engaged in sporadic inter-tribal conflict over access to resources and mates. That behavior was already instilled into their hominid heritage as seen today also in modern chimpanzees. However, these earlier Paleolithic skirmishes were rather infrequent and easily defused. In those ancient times, these hominans had lived in small isolated tribes that rarely encountered each other. The whole planet was wide open territory for them then. If they did happen to run into another group of humans and tensions became unbearable, they could always gracefully move on to other empty pastures. This peaceable strategy was no longer available once humans congregated into permanent settlements. Military leadership therefore became an important attribute of successful monarchies and remained so throughout the long history of that institution.

The wars of Sumer exposed for the first time another imperative of governments—the quest for empire. The need to defend and define frontiers drove rulers to enhance and expand those boundaries. Monarchs, of course, had to pay troops to fight their wars, and also pay for the weapons to prosecute them. They did this by plundering their enemies or invading and occupying new lands and usurping its resources. They also compelled their own subjects to surrender a portion of income to the royal treasury as a levy to support the monarch's domestic and foreign agendas. Thus it was in Sumer that the lucrative business of taxation first appeared in the crowded lives of these hominans.

Humans had lived on Earth without the benefit of government for most of their evolutionary history. This state of affairs is called Anarchy (rule of none). Monarchy (rule of one), the first of four forms of government invented by these hominans, appeared in Sumer around 7,000 BP. This was followed by a hiatus of several thousand years before the other three forms of government emerged, all in ancient Greece around 2,500 BP. These other three forms of government were Tyranny (also rule of one, á la monarchy), Oligarchy (rule of few), and Democracy (rule of all the people).

These four primary archetypes of political governance were formally identified and named by the ancient Greeks. Aristotle, around 2,300 BP, authored a scholarly work addressing the nature of politics and government among humans. Therein he posited that the ruling element in a society, "must be one man, or a few men, or the multitude," thus deftly defining monarchy, tyranny, oligarchy, and democracy. Aristotle's work on this subject titled *Politics* (literally meaning "things concerning the city") comprised eight separate monographs. His classical insights on this topic remain relevant to this very day. Aristotle is historically credited with being the first person to delineate the forms of government on his planet. People continue to use his classification of government even today, thereby showing that the types of government presently existing on Earth have changed little since Aristotle's times.

Monarchy was the principal form of political governance in settled human societies until as recently as 250 years ago. During the entire Neolithic Age, through the Bronze, Iron, and Middle Ages, and well into the Modern Era, most human civilizations were ruled by monarchs or sovereigns, except for notable interludes in ancient Greece and Rome.

Monarchs were solo agents, virtually all male, who asserted the privilege and authority to rule over others. Many claimed this authorization was bestowed on them and their descendants in perpetuity by a creator-god, and thereby affirmed a celestial right to rule over their subjects. Incredibly, this fatuous claim was recognized and endorsed by humans as the "divine right of kings" until quite recently. That right was first secured by demonstrating leadership, intelligence, good judgment, political sagacity, strong alliances, and the use of force when necessary. But once a monarch was established on the throne, it was conceded by his subjects that his oldest male offspring would succeed him after his death, by reason of divine dispensation and popular tradition. This resulted in subsequent monarchs ruling simply by inheriting the job, not because of any exceptional qualities they possessed, preventing other talented individuals in a society from becoming the sovereign instead. Certainly, fresh individuals would appear from time to time and depose the reigning monarch and his dynasty, but only to impose their own personal rule and dynastic successors in turn. Monarchies were never meritocracies.

The first king to rule on Earth was Alulim of Eridu from that astonishing civilization called Sumer. The Sumerians were indeed a rare and unusual breed of hominans credited with many firsts and numerous landmark achievements in the annals of their species. They broke the mold, marking a seminal inflection in the calculus of humankind. The Sumerians formed the first stable civilization, first systematic crop irrigation, first calendar, first organized religion, first practice of slavery, and the first codification of laws. They produced the first city, first king, first government, first warfare, and the first imposition of taxes. They invented writing, reading, arithmetic, astronomy, metallurgy, the sailboat, the wheel, and the plough. Many tools and products humans use today, such as serrated saws, chisels, hammers, nails, glue, hoes, axes, knives, flutes, and stringed musical instruments, were all first made by Sumerians. These amazing people reset the template for their species.

Mac visited the Sumerian city-state of Lagash in 4,361 BP to observe and research these extraordinary Sumerians and the institution of government they forged in Mesopotamia more than 7,000 years ago. My objective was to gather firsthand details of that important hominan achievement that I would include in my report to our High Tribunal back on my home planet. My visit to Lagash occurred in the seventh year of the reign of Ensi (king) Enmetena who ruled Lagash for 27 years in those ancient times. Lagash itself was founded more than 6,000 years ago, and at its peak about 300 years after Mac visited, the city-state covered an area of 620 square miles and contained 17 large settlements, eight district capitals, and more than 40 villages. Lagash was the largest city in the world from 4,025 BP to 3,980 BP.

This magnificent city-state of Lagash lay in southern Mesopotamia, northwest from the confluence of the two great rivers, not far from the west bank of the Tigris. It was located just 18 miles east of its major rival, the competing city-state of Umma. Lagash and Umma had long been at war over the location of their common border. More than 3,000 combatants from both sides had been killed in the years since the conflict began several generations ago. Exactly 139 years before Mac visited the region, a comprehensive peace treaty had been imposed upon the warring parties by the then Sumerian Lugal (emperor) Mesilim who ruled from his capital at Kish. By now, the hegemony of empire had already entered human affairs, once again starting in Sumer. This imperially sponsored treaty was ratified by the ensis of both Lagash and Umma who were in office at that time.

That official treaty of 4,500 BP between two established governments, called The Peace Treaty of Mesilim, was the first international treaty in the annals of humankind. By articles of that compact, the great Lugal Mesilim redrew the boundaries between Lagash and Umma, and specified the rights and responsibilities of the two sides regarding use of an irrigation canal along that border. Mesilim erected a stele, or stone pillar, at the designated border to advertise the treaty, and inscribed the agreement reached between the two opposing parties on that stele. Regrettably, Lugal Mesilim's peace treaty would not remain a permanent solution to the conflict. A later ensi of Umma named Ush, publicly repudiated the treaty and defiantly smashed the Stele of Mesilim, resuming the war with Lagash. That war continued even as Ensi Enmetena ascended the throne of Lagash in 4,368 BP. The ensi of rival Umma at that time was a warlord named Urlumma. Just a few years into Enmetena's reign, the young king marshaled his troops and engaged Urlumma and his army on the plains of Ugigga in a historic battle for ascendancy.

The Battle of Ugigga was decisive. Urlumma's army was utterly crushed and nearly 600 of his soldiers lay slain on the battlefield. Many more were bloodied and wounded. Urlumma himself fled to Umma, followed in hot pursuit by Enmetena who captured the defeated ensi in downtown Umma and slaughtered Urlumma on the spot. Enmetena returned triumphantly to Lagash, placed a new stele on the border, and enforced the boundary to his own specifications now. Umma became a vassal of Lagash and Enmetena expanded his hegemony over the area. This pattern of war and conquest would later became very common among humans all across their planet.

The suburb of Girsu was the main religious center for

Lagash when Mac visited the area. Girsu's huge temple complex was called Eninnu. Eninnu was crowned by a ziggurat as was customary for all Sumerian temple complexes. Along with the main structure, the complex also housed other supplemental buildings. The ziggurat itself was a massive pyramidal affair surmounting the main building, made of successively smaller decks built on top of each other and tapering to a narrow flat summit. Its core was made of sunbaked bricks, while kiln-fired bricks were used for the outside facing. The ziggurat was believed to be the dwelling place of the principal god for the temple. The massive Eninnu temple was dedicated to Ningirsu the great god of war and agriculture, who was also the patron deity of Lagash.

Sumerian religion, the first organized mass religion to appear anywhere among these hominans, arose in southern Mesopotamia approximately 7,500 years ago. It was a polytheism like modern Hinduism. Sumerian polytheism venerated a host of gods and goddesses. Enlil and Enki were the head gods on Earth. They are depicted as incoming cosmonauts who created humans, perhaps by directed panspermia. Ningirsu was already mentioned; others included An (god of Heaven), Ninhursag (goddess of Earth), Inanna (goddess of Fertility), Utu (Sun god), Nanna (Moon god), Irkali (goddess of Death), and numerous other deities representing forces and circumstances affecting the human condition. Sumerian polytheism and its analogs, such as Hindu, Egyptian, Greek, and Roman religions, were the predominant international faiths across all global civilizations until replaced by monotheism starting about 2,000 years ago.

As was customary in Sumer, the people Mac encountered in Lagash were divided into three social classes. Those of royal birth, the political and military elites, and the priests, belonged to the upper class or Amelu who were the most powerful and privileged of the lot; they were the nobles, religious functionaries, military officers, and government bureaucrats. Next came the lower class or Mushkinu, the bulk of the population, made up of farmers, traders, potters, brick makers, and other free citizens. Last came the slaves or Wardum.

Slavery was common in Lagash and throughout Sumer, but it was not a permanent condition. Slaves were permitted to earn and hold assets, own property, and improve their lot by learning and acquiring a skill. Many slaves in Lagash, by this way, were able to eventually buy their freedom. Slaves were usually captured in wars and traded at public auctions. It was also possible for free men and women to become slaves: debtors could voluntarily be slaves to pay off debts, or criminal offenders forced into slavery. A man may sell his child or even his entire family into slavery if that was his only way to obtain food or shelter, pay taxes, or repay obligations owed to others. By law, the period a family could be held as slaves was limited to a maximum of three years. Slaves were generally treated well, though they could be whipped for misbehavior or sloth. Attempts to run away ended in severe punishment.

Exchange of goods and services in Lagash was by barter. Credit or debit accruing from these barter exchanges were recorded in Shekels on clay tablets using cuneiform script and reconciled during subsequent transactions. The shekel was first introduced by religious authorities in Sumer. It was a metallic token crudely embossed with symbols of fecundity—since it was the Bronze Age now, metals were being fabricated. On the obverse of the coin was a figure of Inanna the goddess of

fertility, and on the reverse was depicted a sheaf of wheat. The
she in shekel meant "wheat" in their tongue, and *kel* stood for
a measure like "bushel." Worshippers at a temple would be
given the appropriate number of shekels in exchange for their
tithes such as wheat. These shekels entitled male supplicants
to have sexual intercourse with female acolytes residing on the
temple premises who were believed to physically represent the
goddess Inanna. Sexual intercourse with the fertility goddess
endowed the devout worshippers with potency and transcen-
dence in all departments of their life. A comparable tradition
within Hinduism in India was customarily practiced until fairly
recently. The temple sex workers in India were called devada-
sis, meaning female acolytes of a god.

Mac stopped over at Ensi Enmetena's royal compound.
His spectacular capitol complex was near Lagash's city center
on about two acres of prime real estate. A wide ditch, almost
eight feet deep, fed by a canal from the Tigris and loaded with
hungry crocodiles, ominously circled the premises. A magnificent boulevard, beautifully landscaped with tall palms and
leafy redbud trees, was smartly lined with soldiers bearing
ornamental spears when Mac visited the site. The boulevard
snaked across that crocodile infested moat into Lagash's fortified capitol district. Three prominent structures inside the royal
compound caught my eye. These buildings were all intricately
faced with kiln-fired mud bricks over sunbaked ones, the walls
then smoothly plastered with a cement like substance and elaborately decorated with pigments of various colors, blue and
gold predominating.

The first structure was an enormous building, the royal
household, where Enmetena with his forty royal consorts and
their numerous young children resided. The other two structures,

though still quite large, were appreciably smaller than the royal palace. The one close to the palace was essentially a huge chamber where Enmetena held regular audiences surrounded by his courtiers and other high government officials. During these grand assemblies, scheduled on eight auspicious mornings of each lunar cycle determined by the court astrologer, public issues were discussed, laws and regulations reviewed, and royal proclamations and edicts promulgated. The third building, located just inside the entrance to the capitol compound, was the government's executive office building. It was crammed to capacity with bureaucrats earnestly receiving and dispatching emissaries to and from the city, running the machinery of government, and stoutly enforcing the monarch's edicts and decrees.

Mac was lucky to be in the capitol complex on a day the ensi held court. Enmetena became king when he was barely fourteen years old. He had hardly turned seventeen when he vanquished Urlumma of the rival city of Umma. Now just twenty-one, the young ensi was considered a god by his subjects, the spiritual offspring of Lagash's own patron deity, the great god Ningirsu.

I watched keenly as the handsome ensi confidently strode into the great chamber. The young man was robustly built, a tad on the heavy side, his face and head shorn of all hair, torso completely bare, a sarong like garment draped around his hips and extending to just above his knees. His feet were clad in elegant leather sandals. Just as Ensi Enmetena entered, a courtier stationed at the ostium to the chamber called out in a deeply resonant voice, "Hear ye all who would live, behold the most beloved son of our great god Ningirsu!" Enmetena bound into the chamber, stepped onto a dais, and there seated himself on an exquisitely crafted cathedra embellished with gemstones and precious metals.

After a few housekeeping chores, the agenda for the day was introduced by the honorable Chief Minister. On the docket was an explosive dispute over allocation of water from the Tigris River. Endu, a prominent entrepreneur and proprietor of a brick manufacturing company employing hundreds of Lagashians, had been demanding a larger water quota for one of his brickworks from a common canal that also supplied the extensive wheat and barley fields of Amul, an aristocratic landowner and relative of the ensi. The public conflict between Endu and Amul, now going on for three years, had already claimed the lives of nineteen men. The dispute was the subject of avid gossip by the general public. The case could not be resolved in the lower tribunals because of powerful political interests on both sides. It was therefore referred to the ensi for disposition.

Enmetena had carefully reviewed the case with his senior advisers. His Law Minister had suggested making no change in the water distribution scheme, since Amul was traditionally entitled to his entire allocation even though he did not always use the full quota of water himself, selling the surplus to downstream peasant farmers in exchange for labor. Moreover, the minister had noted, Amul was an amelu of royal blood and the ensi's relative. Endu was a mere commoner, a mushkinu.

But when the verdict was delivered that morning, Enmetena ruled in favor of Endu, not only because Amul did not always use his full water allocation himself which was a major point of contention between the litigants, but also because the taxation rate for manufactured products such as bricks was significantly higher than the rate assessed for agricultural products such as wheat or barley. Since the amelu owned most of the cropland around Lagash and monopolized state power as well, they conveniently held taxes low for agriculture.

Monarchy, that earliest form of government invented by humans, remained the predominant model for governance amongst these hominans well into the Modern Era. With the singular exception of a few hundred years during the first half of the Iron Age, when Greece, and then Rome, experimented with other forms of political organization, monarchy remained the primary form of government for people across my host planet. It is puzzling why humans would have permitted the eminently crucial function of government to be monopolized by a single family lineage in succession forever. The answer probably lies with the emergence of patriarchy in this species at about the same time when monarchy appeared. Patriarchy concentrates power among humans into the hands of a ruling male who is then free to pass on the mantle to his son. The institution of monarchy is quite reminiscent of the model humans adopted in the early Holocene for the newly devised patriarchal family system they put in place to supercharge reproduction in their species. Now the nation itself was imagined as a patriarchal family, and the king represented the male parent or patriarch of that family. Just as the traditional family patriarch held suzerainty over his household, the king likewise held absolute power and authority over his nation's subjects and passed on that power to his eldest son after his incumbency. It is not at all a coincidence that monarchy and the patriarchal nuclear family both began collapsing around the same time in the late Modern Era.

This governing formula by sovereign monarchs went unchallenged by the governed for most of the 7,000 years since these ruling houses were first established. Then abruptly and very swiftly, starting hardly around 250 years ago, monarchies began to disappear like snowflakes in hell. Many were violently extirpated from the body politic, others defanged and transformed into symbolic institutions where the reigning monarch was stripped of executive power and authority. Today, only six absolute monarchies[62] anachronistically cling to power on my host planet. This transformation came about in the most unusual way.

The famed land of ancient Greece, tucked into the northern Mediterranean littoral, was the singular birthplace of the three other forms of government invented by *Homo sapiens*. As noted in this narrative before, these other three forms of government are tyranny or dictatorship, oligarchy, and democracy. To properly appreciate the emergence of these alternate forms of government requires a brief overview of ancient Greek history. Modern people separate this history into six overlapping eras, designated as Minoan Civilization, Mycenaean Civilization, the Greek Dark Ages, and the Greek Archaic, Classical, and Hellenistic Periods.

The human footprint in Greece goes back to Late Paleolithic times, not long after these emigrating hominans colonized the Levant following their successful exodus out of Africa. During the early Neolithic period, almost 9,000 years ago, people formed

---

62 Just six absolute monarchies were left on Earth by 62 BP. Four were in western Asia clustered around the Persian Gulf (Saudi Arabia, United Arab Emirates, Oman, and Qatar), one was in southern Africa (Swaziland), and one in southeast Asia (Brunei).

small settlements on the Greek mainland near the Gulf of Corinth. They dispersed around the Aegean Sea over succeeding millennia, populating the surrounding Greek islands including the island of Crete where they established their first major civilization known today as the Minoan Civilization (4,500 BP–3,350 BP). Like all civilizations of that time, it was ruled by monarchs.

Minoan Civilization was replaced by Mycenaean Civilization (3,350 BP–3,050 BP) arising on the Geek mainland in the area around southern Greece and the Peloponnese[63]. Mycenaeans, like Minoans, were divided into kingdoms ruled by monarchs. Mycenaean Civilization eventually collapsed, besieged by external tribes like the Dorians from the north and the so-called Sea Peoples from the south, who were encouraged to attack the Mycenaeans because of festering internal conflicts within Mycenaean society itself.

As Mycenaean Civilization crumbled, the entire region entered a period of steep decline known as the Greek Dark Ages (3,150 BP–2,700 BP). Several factors conspired to cause this rapid civilizational collapse, including foreign invasions, civil wars, clusters of volcanic eruptions, earthquakes, severe drought, and epidemic diseases. The population imploded sharply, writing and literacy virtually disappeared, no more monuments and palaces were built, vital trade links were lost, and towns and villages abandoned. Kings and armies, with their bureaucrats and administrative systems, simply vanished. Ancient Greece during this dark period was fragmented into

---

63 The Peloponnese is a large southern peninsula on mainland Greece, south of the Gulf of Corinth. The area has been inhabited by humans since Late Paleolithic times. The name derives from the mythical Greek hero Pelops who is said to have conquered the entire region. The iconic Olympic Games traces its origin to the cult of King Pelops. The famous Peloponnesian War (2,381 BP–2,354 BP) was fought by Athens and its League of city-states, against the Peloponnesian League led by Sparta. Sparta eventually won.

assorted local neighborhoods organized by households and kinship groups resembling communities that had once existed in earlier Neolithic times.

After 2,750 BP, a radical reconstruction of culture and civilization finally banished the Dark Ages tormenting ancient Greece. Dubbed the Archaic Period (2,750 BP–2,430 BP), it created the three new systems of government—oligarchy, tyranny, and democracy. The Archaic Period saw the Greek population rebound vigorously with the establishment of new townships and the expansion of old ones. A brand new alphabet was borrowed from the Phoenicians. Literacy and intellectual ferment resumed in that previously demolished civilization. This active period witnessed the formation of Greek city-states or poleis (plural of polis) and the steady rise of Greek colonies around the Mediterranean and Black Seas.

Mountainous terrain in Greece made it difficult for any community at that time to dominate more than a few square miles of land. The city-states were therefore modest in size. They were exposed to enemies and vulnerable to invasion. Territorial integrity required every adult male to be prepared and willing to fight, defending their polis at all times. In exchange for this great devotion and sacrifice, a measure of personal autonomy and freedom had to be offered to individuals by the authorities. In this way, here in the precincts of ancient Greece, for the first time ever in human history, the concept of Citizenship was born.

The city-states that emerged at the end of the Greek Dark Ages began their provenance ruled by a Basileus, meaning a hereditary king. Many of these monarchs were soon overthrown, governments being run by other political arrangements. The most common replacement for monarchy during this period was oligarchy, or rule by a few. The oligarchs came from a select group of the wealthiest citizens of the state. Such an oligarchic government, controlled by a syndicate of wealthy individuals, is also called a plutocracy. Many oligarchies tend to be plutocracies, but not all[64] by any means.

The oligarchs of Archaic Greece possessed powers usually held by a monarch. Although these powers were presumably spread among the ruling oligarchs, the collective scope of their power was notably totalitarian. As is customary in most oligarchies throughout human history, the laws that were promulgated by the Greek oligarchs or their representatives, and promptly endorsed by the judiciaries they installed, benefited the privileged few at the expense of the multitudinous poor and middle classes. This process resulted in an immense transfer of property and wealth in a few short generations to the already very rich upper crust of Athenians. Many in the middle and lower classes soon became bankrupt. The majority of the population, now impoverished, accumulated mountains of debt. People unable to discharge these debts lost standing as free citizens through laws enacted by the oligarchs, and were then designated as slaves in bondage to their wealthy creditors.

As a matter of interest here, at a doppelgänger conference in the Collegium of Pansophy on Galymon, Professor Tao wryly noted that a similar dynamic was in effect right now on my host planet. The good professor observed that the United States of America, the most powerful and influential country on Earth when Mac was visiting their planet, had embarked on a gargantuan transfer of wealth to the rich in the decades following

---

64 Governments in most communist countries are usually non-plutocratic oligarchies; communist oligarchies call themselves Politburos. Military governments not ruled by a single military dictator also tend to be non-plutocratic oligarchies; they frequently use unusual names to describe themselves, such as National Salvation Council.

30 AP. For example, by 57 AP, the top 5% of the population owned almost two-thirds of the entire country's wealth, the remaining 95% left to haggle over a skeletal one-third. This ratio comfortably exceeded the monopolization of wealth by even the oligarchs of Archaic Greece. This degree of maldistribution in wealth and power among the population of any country on Earth has never before been seen outside the early Industrial Revolution in England.

Whenever public resentment to these developments in Archaic Greece peaked from time to time and a popular uprising seemed imminent, the ruling oligarchs and their rich allies employed violent police action to suppress the disgruntled masses. Eventually however, a charismatic individual would appear on the scene to co-opt the anger and resentment of the people, and by securing the alliance of common soldiers they would overthrow the ruling oligarchs and seize political power. These individuals came to be known as *tyrants*, meaning "supreme rulers" in the original Greek, and the governments they ran were called tyrannies—in modern usage, a tyrant would be a dictator and his government a dictatorship. Tyrannies often began when the polis faced a crisis. Tyrants were very similar to monarchs in their role and functioning, except for the fact they had seized power illegally through force and therefore suspect, as their incumbency was not sanctioned by tradition or the so-called divine right of kings. Furthermore, tyrannies were not dynastic in structure, though many attempted to make their tyrannies hereditary just like monarchies; only a few succeeded.

Tyrannies were inherently unstable, though some did manage to complete successful terms. The tyrant's power depended on control of armies and backing from the people, obtained either by fear of punishment or by favors bestowed on the populace.

Tyrants could cancel debts, release citizens from slavery of debt-bondage, ease taxation on the masses, and confiscate wealth from the rich for distribution to the poor. However, due to the general instability of this system of government, mostly because of questions about the legitimacy of the ruler, tyrants held power for only modest lengths of time before being driven out of office. Despite all this, tyranny was a frequent political arrangement in Greece during the Archaic Period.

Monarchies, oligarchies, and tyrannies functioned in this way before a new form of government emerged some 2,500 years ago in the historic land of ancient Greece. For the first time in human history, a paradigm shift in the structure of government appeared in the city-state of Athens right by the Aegean Sea. What was most extraordinary about this new system of government was the translocation of power from the ruler to the ruled, a novel form of governing through self-government. It was called democracy, literally meaning "people power."

This astonishing development in human affairs, spliced briefly into the long thread of monarchy dominating government since that institution was first established, showcased an alternative, non-authoritarian form of governance for these settled hominans. Though this first experiment with democracy hardly lasted 200 years in its premiere Greek incarnation, and was then crushed by monarchy and the other forms of authoritarian government, Athenian society of that time is appropriately credited by people living on Earth today with bestowing the gift of democracy on them, a system that would eventually become the leading contemporary form of government on their planet.

The historic city of Athens, now capital of the modern European nation of Greece, hosts a population of 664,000 people today. In the year 2,500 BP, the city-state of Athens, made up of the central city of Athens itself and the surrounding territory of Attica, held a population of about 300,000 people. That number was truly enormous for those times, given that the entire planetary population of *Homo sapiens* then was only 70 million, compared to 7 billion now.

Of those 300,000 people living in ancient Athens, nearly 150,000 were slaves, and another 50,000 were metics—resident aliens and foreigners. Neither category were considered citizens and were thus proscribed from participation in Athenian democracy. Of the remaining 100,000 native Athenians, about 70,000 were women and children not franchised. That left about 30,000 adult male citizens, twenty years of age or older, entitled to fully engage in Athenian democracy. No further requirements such as rank, education, or financial standing applied to this latter group to qualify for participation in their democracy. It was a completely nondiscriminatory system, though limited to male Athenian citizens over the age of twenty.

This new form of government called democracy, first established within the historic precincts of ancient Athens, was a Participatory Democracy. In such a democracy, every eligible citizen was entitled to directly vote their preference on proposed legislation in an inclusive citizen's assembly. Yet, this form of participatory or pure democracy did not outlive ancient Greece and is not practiced anywhere on Earth today except in muted form in two small districts or cantons of modern Switzerland. Democracy in its modern avatar is known as Representative Democracy, first formulated in ancient Rome where constituencies of citizens elect one of their own to represent them jointly in an assembly. These representatives then vote on proposed legislation on behalf of their electors. Clearly and unsurprisingly of course, representative democracy is always susceptible to co-option by oligarchs and other interest groups. Those agents frequently attempt to influence the votes of elected representatives by either financing their electoral campaigns and bribing them with money and favors, or else cynically threatening to defeat them in the next election by demonizing recalcitrant representatives while funding their compliant opponents. For exactly this reason, these oligarchs and interest groups have always vigorously opposed any public funding of political campaigns, then as now.

Greek democracy emerged in stages as responses to political, social, and economic conditions during those times. The city-state of Athens had once been ruled by kings. As in many Greek poleis during the Archaic Period, monarchy in Athens had given way to an oligarchic form of government managed by a group of political overlords called Archons (rulers) who hailed from aristocratic families called Eupatrids (well-fathered). These privileged eupatrids extemporaneously made all administrative and legal decisions for the polis. There was no written law. Over time, the people were no longer willing to accept these arbitrary oral rules conjured up as needed by these aristocratic Thesmothetai—those who lay down the law.

Responding to this incendiary problem, the archons appointed a rather callow 29 year old legislative assistant called Draco in 2,571 BP to tabulate and produce a written civil and penal code for Athens based on existing practices. Draco's constitution replaced the prevailing system of arbitrary law by a written code to be enforced by a court. Known for its extreme harshness, the word "draconian" has come to refer to similarly unforgiving laws and regulations. For example, any debtor unable to pay, whose social standing was lower than the creditor, was forced into slavery to that creditor. Punishment was more lenient when the applicable social status was reversed. The death penalty was liberally prescribed. When asked about his use of the death penalty for even minor offenses, Draco replied that he considered those lesser crimes to indeed merit the death penalty and only regretted he had no greater punishment to impose for the more serious ones. Draco was crushed to death in a theater as he turned fifty. In just one area of law however, Draco showed some rare judgment: for the first time in judicial history, he formally classified homicides on the basis of intent into intentional and unintentional varieties, thus distinguishing murder from manslaughter.

Over the next three decades, matters tracked insuperably downhill. The mounting debt-bondage among the common people to wealthy creditors under Draco's draconian laws, led to deepening political unrest and disaffection among the toiling masses. Furthermore, rich people who were not aristocratic by birth, demanded a share of political power with the entrenched eupatrids.

Six years after Draco's death, in an effort to address the mounting popular discontent and brewing constitutional crisis, an impeccably credentialed man named Solon (2,588 BP–2,508 BP), an eupatrid himself who claimed descent from the legendary Greek hero Heracles (Hercules), was chosen as archon in 2,544 BP to reform Athenian law and avert a looming revolt by the dispossessed public. Posterity would remember him as Solon the Lawgiver for the far reaching reforms he instituted. Solon quickly repealed Draco's laws except for the one on homicide. He promulgated a new code called the Seisachtheia, or "relief from burdens" law. Solon's new charter immediately cancelled all outstanding debts, emancipated all enslaved debtors, reinstated all land confiscated by creditors back to their former owners, and strictly prohibited the use of personal freedom as collateral in all future debts. Solon also placed a ceiling on the amount of property any Athenian could own, in order to prevent the excessive accumulation of land by powerful families.

After addressing the immediate constitutional crisis in this way, Solon reformed government to establish proper foundations for the participatory democracy that was to come. Before Solon's reforms, the eupatrids claimed a monopoly on government solely by reason of their birth. Solon replaced the hereditary aristocracy with one based on wealth, thus opening up the institution to more people. He established four classes of humans depending on how much property they possessed. Citizens were permitted to run for designated offices based on their class, the richest given the most slots and the most influential positions. The Pentacosiomedimni were the wealthiest, followed by the Hippeis, then the Zeugitae. Solon sagely added a fourth class, the Thetes or peasants, who owned little or no property but were still citizens, admitting the thetes for the first time to the Ekklesia or assembly, the parliamentary forum for all Athenian citizens. Only slaves, foreigners, women and children were left out. Thus were the fragile seeds of democracy planted in Athens by Solon the Lawgiver.

Soon after Solon's archonship ended in 2,515 BP, political factions and conflicts re-emerged in Athens. People living on the coast (the Coast Party), made up mostly of the middle and lower classes or Demos, favored continuing Solon's reforms. People in the plains (the Plains Party), formed by eupatrid aristocrats or Aristoi, opposed the reforms and wanted the old feudal system restored. As the conflict escalated, an aristocratic warlord called Pisistratus, a nephew of Solon, seized the occasion to wrest control of Athens in a coup in 2,510 BP. Though twice driven out of Athens after his coup, Pisistratus returned each time and finally consolidated power as constitutional tyrant fourteen years later in 2,496 BP. He was backed in this effort by a foreign army as well as his newly forged Hill Party composed of people not in the other two traditional Coast and Plains parties.

Pisistratus, a populist, preserved and extended his Uncle Solon's laws. His tyranny was friendly to the lower classes. Pisistratus died a natural death in 2,477 BP, aged 78 years old. The tyrant was succeeded by his two sons, Hippias and Hipparchus, who ruled jointly after their father died. Hipparchus was killed thirteen years later in 2,464 BP. The murder, actually the result of a love feud, was quickly branded a political assassination. His brother Hippias kept the tyranny going for another four years until an exiled group of Athenian aristocrats known as the Alcmaeonids, led by a man called Cleisthenes, persuaded the Spartans to invade Athens and depose Hippias, who then fled to Persia in 2,460 BP.

Cleisthenes (2,520 BP–2,457 BP) is recognized by modern humans as the founder of democracy on their planet. In the three short years between expelling the tyrant Hippias and his own death at the age of 63, Cleisthenes brought democracy to Athens.

Athenians joyously celebrated their emancipation from tyranny after Hippias fled. Cleisthenes, now sixty years old, the one man more than any other responsible for this liberation, sensed power within his reach. But almost immediately another eupatrid leader called Isagoras emerged to oppose him. The upper-crust Plains and Hill Parties threw their support behind

Isagoras. Cleisthenes responded by allying with Athens' lower-crust Coast Party and proposed a series of sweeping reforms that would bestow a fully equal and peer citizenship status on all free male Athenians over the age of twenty, without regard to wealth or social status. Cleisthenes won the bid for power and introduced his reforms. Thus was democracy first born in Athens.

Isagoras would not quit. He induced the Spartans to invade Athens again, this time to expel Cleisthenes, portraying his rival's democratic reforms as an exemplary threat to Sparta's oligarchy itself. Sparta obliged, driving Cleisthenes into exile and leaving a garrison behind in Athens for good measure. Yet, when Isagoras tried to repeal the new Cleisthenian constitution, the people of Athens rose up in arms and threw out the unpopular Isagoras and the Spartan garrison to boot, inviting Cleisthenes back to complete his democratic reforms. Cleisthenes died not long after returning to Athens. He is remembered today as having introduced a radically new system of self-government to *Homo sapiens*.

Cleisthenes also introduced the practice of Ostracism to Athens. Under this unusual protocol intended to protect and preserve democracy in Athens, a vote by more than 6,000 Athenian citizens against any person would exile that individual from Athens for a period of 10 years. The intent of ostracism was to banish any overambitious citizen who accumulated too much power and thereby posed a threat to Athenian democracy, thus keeping them from sabotaging this new form of government and imposing tyranny again. Under the system of ostracism, the exiled man's property was preserved and unaffected, but he himself could not be physically present in the city of Athens. After the period of exile was over, he was allowed to return to the city and resume life there without restrictions.

There were many defenders of this first democracy after its extraordinary debut in Athens. Foremost among those defenders was the illustrious Pericles (2,445 BP–2,379 BP), a renowned statesman and brilliant military general, much admired for his peerless oratorical skills. Pericles was a great patron of the arts and literature. It was because of his unceasing efforts that Athens acquired its reputation as the cultural mecca of ancient Greece. Pericles embarked on a beautifying agenda for the city, starting an ambitious building program continued after his death which eventually generated most of the surviving structures still standing today as relics on the Acropolis of Athens. This site is a citadel built on a high rocky outcrop above the city. The Acropolis contained the Parthenon, that famous temple to the city's patron goddess, *Athena Parthenos*, Athena the Virgin.

The democratic system in Athens was not without its internal opponents. When Athens was weakened during the disastrous Peloponnesian War with Sparta, these opponents conspired to lead oligarchic counterrevolutions in 2,361 BP, and then again in 2,354 BP. Yet the Athenian oligarchs found it impossible to maintain themselves in power, and democracy was restored each time. But for rare misadventures[65], Athenian democracy operated with justice and equity for all its citizens, flourishing during the Classical Period (2,430 BP–2,273 BP) that followed the Archaic Period in ancient Greece.

Athenian democracy ended and was replaced by monarchy

---

65 The great philosopher Socrates (2,420 BP–2,349 BP), one of the wisest humans who ever lived on their planet, was tried and executed when he was 71 years old in democratic Athens on the charge of influencing and corrupting the minds of young people with radical ideas. He was convicted of this charge and sentenced to die by drinking an extract of hemlock (*Conium maculatum*) that poisoned him to death.

after Athens was defeated by the Greek kingdom of Macedon in 2,288 BP. Athens continued as a major Greek city under the hegemony of the Macedonian kingdom and prospered during the Hellenistic Period (2,273 BP–2,096 BP) that followed the Classical Period of Greek history. The Greek empire ended in 2,096 BP when the Greek Achaean League was defeated by Rome at the Battle of Corinth led by the Roman general Lucius Mummius Achaicus.

❦

A Republic is a country that is *res publica*, Latin for "public thing." It is not the private property of its rulers. Government positions are filled by election or appointment to office, not by inheritance. The republican concept was first developed in ancient Rome after the Roman monarchy was overthrown in 2,459 BP. The Roman Republic was disbanded in 1,977 BP when Caesar Augustus was installed as the first Imperator (emperor) of Rome. In modern usage, humans apply the term republic to any country where the head of state is not a monarch. Thus a republic could be a dictatorship, oligarchy, or democracy. The Roman Republic, in fact, experienced each of these three forms of government at one time or another during its existence.

Except for the remarkable Greek and Roman interludes, monarchy was the usual form of government in all human societies across their planet until quite late into the Modern Era. The global spread of European colonialism, beginning around 450 BP, had effectively brought most of Earth under the rule of European monarchies over the following 400 years.

Earlier challenges to monarchy, apart from the Greek and Roman precedents, were vanishingly rare. Monarchy, invented by the Sumerians 7,000 years ago in Mesopotamia, was still the only game in town. A notable attempt by English aristocrats to restrain the absolute authority exercised by their sovereign did not last long. They had corralled their incumbent King John in 735 BP into endorsing the Magna Carta or Great Charter, and thereby to agree that the king's will cannot be arbitrary and that no "free man" could be punished except by the "lawful judgment of his equals or by the law of the land." Yet the Magna Carta itself was later degraded and defanged. Then, more than four centuries later in 301 BP, as a consequence of economic and religious tensions besetting England, the reigning monarch at that time, King Charles, was overthrown and beheaded by the English Parliament representing the Commonwealth of England and led by Oliver Cromwell. The monarchy, however, was restored eleven years later in 290 BP. Over time, the British monarchy transitioned to the constitutional form of today. The British monarch now functions as the symbolic head of state with no executive power, while executive authority is vested in an elected Parliament and Prime Minister.

The first substantial strike in the Modern Era against monarchism was deftly delivered in 174 BP in North America. On July 4 of that memorable year, representatives from thirteen British colonies on that continent, jointly assembled in Congress as the United States of America, adopted their iconic Declaration of Independence in the city of Philadelphia. That document proclaimed their joint decision to end political control by England over their governmental affairs. Declaring independence from the British Crown under King George III, they sighted their "unalienable" rights and the insufferable tyranny of the king as reasons for their action. After a successful War of Independence led by the formidable George Washington against the British colonialists, the rebels went on to establish a representative democratic republic on their continent with the great George Washington himself as its first President. The American Republic continues to this day.

Hardly more than a dozen years after that watershed rebellion in North America, the fiery French Revolution in Europe sounded the death knell for executive monarchies on that continent and around the world. The European Enlightenment, also called The Age of Reason, launched in the third century BP by that continent's extraordinary scientists and philosophers[66], encouraged people to question the validity of dogma and absolutism in all areas of thought and faith. Sapience, it seems, was now swiftly proceeding in this species. Inspired by this movement, the French people in 161 BP stormed an old prison fortress in Paris called the Bastille, signaling the start of their grand revolution. That same year, their representatives meeting in a National Assembly, issued the famous Declaration of the Rights of Man and of the Citizen. Three years later they arrested their monarch, King Louis XVI, declaring the French Republic in 158 BP. The king was beheaded by guillotine the next year. Though monarchy made a comeback in France a dozen years later in the avatar of Napoleon Bonaparte, the first Napoleon, and was resurrected several more times until 80 BP, its fate and eventual demise were sealed. In less than two short centuries after the French Revolution, monarchies would practically disappear from Earth, replaced predominantly by republics, and a few constitutional monarchies. Just a smattering of absolute monarchies still persist in the vanishing world of monarchial government.

---

66 They include Francis Bacon, Johannes Kepler, Thomas Hobbs, René Descartes, Baruch Spinoza, Isaac Newton, Jonathan Swift, Voltaire, Jean-Jacques Rousseau, and many others.

The two great World Wars of the last century both originating in Europe—but reverberating around the planet due to
the extensive physical colonization of the world by European
powers—sealed the fate of executive monarchy as the principal form of government for these humans. The First World
War (36 BP–32 BP) severely weakened and disoriented these
European monarchies, roiling the vast international empires
they had created and controlled over the past centuries. The
Second World War (11 BP–5 BP) resulted in rapid planetary
decolonization and the emergence of numerous republics in
territories once ruled by colonial empires.

The past century may be called the Graveyard of Monarchies.
Many were violently overthrown by revolution or war, or summarily abolished as part of the decolonization process. This was
a brand new experience for this young species, ever since the
middle Neolithic when imperialism and empires first began to
be established. The Mexican Emperor Maximilian of the Second
Mexican Empire was executed in 83 BP. Brazilian Emperor
Pedro II was overthrown by a republican military coup in 61
BP. The end of the First World War saw the defeated German,
Austro-Hungarian, and Ottoman Empires dismantled. The ancient monarchy of China expired in 38 BP when Sun Yat-sen's
revolution overthrew Emperor Puyi. The Russian Revolution of
33 BP abolished the Tsarist monarchy of that country, culminating in the execution of Emperor Nicholas II and his family.
Rapid decolonization after the end of the Second World War in
5 BP saw much of south and southeast Asia, and most of Africa,
emerge as republics from the colonial yoke. What is most astonishing about these events is that this entire sea-change in
human political organization transpired in hardly more than
200 years after the tenacious 7,000 years of monarchy on Earth.

Such transformational paradigms have happened before and is a noteworthy feature of change—when change begins it can occur swiftly and lead to a new level of organization.

Monarchy as the default form of government for humans was done. Republics—ruled by democratic, oligarchic, or dictatorial governments—replaced them.

On Galymon we have no government. The Supreme Authority of our High Tribunal exercises no police power and is thus devoid of any governmental authority. Our tribunes are picked at random from among our population and serve out their terms with high honor and great dedication. Our tribunes assemble as a peer group with no leadership module endorsed or acknowledged. Since all galymonians function at the exact interface of free will and destiny, no government is ever required.

CHAPTER XIII:

WAR

{Q}uite unlike any other species on Earth today, organized killing of humans by other humans, a gruesome practice called War, is actively pursued by *Homo sapiens* wherever they may live on their planet. Although internecine killing is also found among chimpanzees who are humankind's closest living relatives today, this signature form of homicidal behavior—to the extent and scope observed in this case—is peculiar to humans and deeply embedded in their biology. It portends enormous consequences for their future. Especially noteworthy is the unprovoked and indiscriminate slaughter of unarmed noncombatants or civilians, an activity called Genocide. Though genocide should logically include any killing between species within an identified genus, in the case of humans however, since they are now the only existing species in their genus, the term genocide for them has traditionally come to refer exclusively to humans killing other humans alone.

There is little practical difference between war and genocide, yet humans use much wordsmithing to distinguish between the two. War is defined by them as a state of armed conflict between people representing adversarial nations or political states, as well as between opposing groups within a single state or territory, a form of war known as Civil War. Genocide, by their definition, distinguishes customary killing of armed combatants in wars, from the exceptional killing of unarmed civilians and noncombatants. Even this definition of genocide is sharply curtailed in the text endorsed by an international consortium of countries called the United Nations (U.N.) in its Resolution 260 IIIA ratified by the United Nations General Assembly in 2 BP. This U.N. Resolution defines genocide as "...acts committed with intent to destroy, in whole or in part, a national, ethnical, racial or religious group..."

The United Nations is an organization headquartered in the city of New York in the United States of America. It represents a desultory attempt to showcase a new international order that has never delivered on its grand promises. It was founded in 5 BP by the triumphant victors of the Second World War, right after that brutal war ended. It offers membership to every independent country on Earth. These countries, each possessing a single vote and assembling democratically as the U.N. General Assembly, issue resolutions that carry no statutory authority. Executive power, instead, is vested in the U.N. Security Council controlled by only five "permanent member" countries (Britain, China, France, Russia, and the United States) which together account for a mere 27 percent of the Earth's entire human population today—and that too, largely on account of the People's Republic of China. If China was discounted, that figure would shrink to just 8 percent of world population. The U.N. is a text-book example of an international oligarchy.

Any major war waged by humans with their lethal modern

war machines inevitably results in widespread civilian casualties and numerous noncombatant deaths, often in greater numbers than combatants killed. Precisely for that reason, the U.N. definition is careful not to define war itself as genocide, since that would make its most powerful member countries genocidal, even though *Homo sapiens* as a species most certainly is. Thus, the wholesale bombing of enemy cities and the indiscriminate massacre of civilians living in those cities would, surprisingly to many of my esteemed readers, not necessarily meet U.N. criteria for genocide. Instead, a specific intent to eliminate just a particular category of humans belonging to a circumscribed group of them has to be clearly demonstrated to qualify for the crime of genocide as defined by the U.N., which would then expose the perpetrators to possible indictment and prosecution for War Crimes and Crimes Against Humanity by an appropriate international tribunal. Without doubt, any such action by aggressor groups—called ethnic cleansing—would unambiguously qualify as genocide under whatever definition is employed. But the phenomenon of genocide itself has a much broader meaning in biology, and pertains to any internecine killing within the ambit of a single species. Under this biologic definition then, genocide would subsume all manner of organized killing within a given species and is better described as Endospeciocide. Socially sanctioned homicide carried out by one human population against another is genocide by definition, regardless of the intent or motivation of the murdering party. For this reason, the terms "war" and "genocide" are used interchangeably here. For purists however, there remains one essential distinction between the two: in war the enemy is not killed if the losing party surrenders; in genocide the victims are killed regardless.

Humans had developed and formulated a general code of behavior to be followed by combatants during wars. These conventions are commonly called Rules of War.

Though armed conflict among humans is as old as humanity itself, massive internecine warfare is a fairly recent development, found only since Neolithic times. Certainly, humans gruesomely dispatched multitudes of other hominans to death during the Great Hominan Purges of the Pleistocene, but those victims were from other species within the genus *Homo*, not humans themselves.

There have always been customary practices in warfare among humans, though only in the last 150 years have countries formulated international rules to limit the effects of armed conflict among themselves, motivated no doubt by the humanitarian considerations they aver, but certainly also to reduce violence directed at their own side. The Geneva Conventions and the Hague Conventions are the main vehicles humans have devised to regulate modern warfare. Often called International Humanitarian Law (IHL), it is also known as the Law of War, or the Law of Armed Conflict. Its principles derive from the laws of natural justice and moral commandments to respect one's enemy, as well as from various treaties that encourage a universal law of decency and dignity in the ugly business of warfare if possible. Though IHL does not determine war's pretentious claims to legality, it does attempt to minimize its destruction and brutality through rules that govern the means and motivation for battle. While it is clear that humans frequently violate these rules of war, the seven basic principles enshrined in IHL do remain admirable objectives to mitigate the bloody and tragic practice of warfare. These 7 rules of war may be summarized as follows:

1. Civilians who are not combatants must be spared from attack at all times.
2. All civilian non-combatants are entitled to their physical security and mental integrity, and should be protected without discrimination.
3. Killing or wounding an adversary who surrenders or can no longer fight is prohibited.
4. Weapons of war that are likely to cause excessive or unnecessary loss and suffering are forbidden.
5. All medical personnel and hospitals must be spared from attack, and the wounded and sick treated even if they are from the enemy side.
6. Everyone is entitled to judicial protections, including trial by court, and no one can be subjected to cruel or unusual punishment.
7. Captives of war are entitled to their own religious or political beliefs, can exchange news with their families, receive aid, enjoy basic legal safeguards, and must be protected from violence or reprisals at all times.

Still another very troubling aspect about waging war is when—if ever—war is justified. Because war is a common behavioral trait among them, these hominans have attempted ever since ancient times to seek justification to wage wars and vindicate the death and destruction caused by this lethal enterprise. As a result of those considerations, humans have developed the rather curious concept of Just-War to exculpate themselves and to rationalize this deadly undertaking. Just-war, by their own reckoning, is a war that a society is permitted to wage under certain compelling conditions and circumstances.

The Indian chronicle Mahabharata, written almost 2,500 years ago and attributed to the sage Vyasa, offers some of the first written discussions in human history about the parameters for a just-war. The narrative describes a legendary battle that was fought on the plains of Kurukshetra in northern India about 500 years before the epic itself was written. It recounts a dynastic succession struggle between two groups of cousins—the Pandavas and the Kauravas—for their ancestral kingdom of Kuru with its capital at Hastinapura. One of the five Pandava brothers, who are collectively the protagonists in the saga, asks if the suffering caused by war can ever be justified under any circumstances whatsoever. A lively discussion follows about rules of engagement, such as proportionality, just means, just cause, and fair treatment of captives and the wounded. Criteria are then established for the impending Kurukshetra War. Not long after the Mahabharata was written, the Greek philosopher Plato, and still later, the Roman philosopher Cicero, made similar contributions to the paradoxical notion of just-war.

The 7 cardinal principles of a presumably just-war can be summarized in the following way:

1. A just-war can only be waged as a last resort after all non-violent options have been exhausted before the use of force can be justified.
2. A war is just only if waged by the legitimate political authority of a society; even just causes cannot be served by actions taken by individuals or groups who do not constitute a legitimate authority sanctioned to act by the war-making society.

3. A just-war can only be fought to redress a wrong suffered, the only permissible objective of war being to indemnify that injury.

4. A just-war must be waged with a reasonable chance of success; deaths and injury incurred in a hopeless cause are not justifiable.

5. The ultimate goal of a just-war is to re-establish peace, and the peace so established should be preferable to the peace that would have prevailed if the war had not been fought at all.

6. The violence used in the war must be proportional to the injury suffered by the warring party in the first place; states are prohibited from using more force than is required to attain the limited objective of correcting that injury.

7. The weapons used in a just-war must clearly discriminate between combatants and non-combatants, as civilians are never permissible targets in war and every effort must be taken to avoid killing them; their deaths may be justified only if they become unavoidable victims of a requisite attack on a military target; even if attacking an authentic military target, all civilian deaths cannot simply be dismissed as collateral damage.

The 7 Rules of War, and the 7 Principles of Just-War, outlined above, apply primarily to conflicts between traditional nation-states. Non-state actors, asymmetric forces, or sectarian groups fighting each other or the state, may not follow these conventions. Often, established states themselves cynically ignore these rules when fighting among themselves.

The invention of gunpowder by the Chinese more than a

thousand years ago, and its later adoption and widespread use in warfare by numerous European armies, introduced a new and deadly calculus to the gruesome annals of war making by these hominans. It was now possible to inflict extensive damage to enemy formations from behind safe distances using projectiles powered by gunpowder. Human ingenuity tirelessly enhanced and proliferated these tools of destruction, fabricating ever more lethal weapons capable of producing even greater carnage during combat. Evolution of armaments and their delivery systems, especially in the past 100 years, brought biological, chemical, and nuclear weapons to the fray. These had the potential of indiscriminatingly destroying large populations regardless of their combatant status. Such diabolical devices were therefore known as Weapons of Mass Destruction (WMD).

Biological agents composed of deadly virions and bacteria that produce lethal diseases such as smallpox, anthrax, and plague, have only rarely been employed as WMD by humans because these biological agents do not kill immediately upon contact and require an incubation period of days before they cause morbidity and mortality in their intended victims. Furthermore, the invaders themselves are equally susceptible to these infective agents which cannot be effectively quarantined and isolated just behind enemy lines. It is alleged that European colonists distributed smallpox-tainted blankets to Native Americans in the New World, and that Japanese invaders polluted Chinese drinking-water wells with cholera bacteria during World War II.

Chemical weapons such as phosgene, VX, and sarin gas on the other hand begin to effect the physiology of the victim almost immediately upon contact. They have a circumscribed duration of action and can be introduced into enemy lines without exposing the attackers, who can wear gas masks to avoid toxic effects. Chemical WMD have been employed during war by many nation-states well into contemporary times. Particularly valuable to their users besides the death and suffering they cause is the terror they instill in the enemy.

The use of nuclear WMD has so far been limited to just two instances in human history, both times in 5 BP by the United States of America against the Empire of Japan. Nuclear weapons deliver their deadly punch by transforming ordinary matter into explosive energy. They come in two different types: fission devices (atom bombs), and fusion devices (hydrogen bombs). Fissile material such as isotopes of uranium or plutonium are split in atom bombs, whereas hydrogen isotopes are fused together in hydrogen bombs. Chemical explosives are employed to detonate a fission bomb, while a fission bomb itself is used to detonate a fusion bomb. Only about 0.1 percent (in fission) to 1 percent (in fusion) of designated matter is converted to energy in these bombs, but even just that little bit of matter produces an unmatched tsunami of energy.

Because of their deadly and grotesque nature, and potential for massive and indiscriminate killing of people, humans have attempted to ban the use of WMD over the last century. A protocol to prohibit the use of biological and chemical weapons, referred to as the Geneva Protocol, was devised in 25 BP and signed by the majority of countries on my host planet. Exactly 47 years later, the Biological Weapons Convention of 22 AP became the first multilateral disarmament treaty banning the production or stockpiling of an entire category of weapons—in this case biological weapons. The Chemical Weapons Convention of 43

AP did the same for chemical weapons, banning their production or stockpiling as well. Some countries have ignored these protocols and conventions, a few even recently using chemical weapons in warfare. Still others, having formally acceded to the conventions, have yet to eliminate their stockpiles of prohibited weapons. There is, of course, no moratorium on the production, stockpiling or use of nuclear weapons in war, the Big Kahuna in the mix, the most destructive of the lot. The persistent refusal of world powers to authorize international prohibitions on the production and stockpiling of nuclear weapons like the existing conventions on biological and chemical weapons—or to even expressly forbid the actual deployment and use of nuclear weapons in war—is entirely disreputable and the reason is completely transparent to any concerned extraterrestrial visitor to their planet.

The reason for this reluctance by the major powers to prohibit nuclear weapons is quite clear—it is the emblem of their formidability that the lesser powers do not possess. A nuclear weapon releases a gargantuan blast of energy in the form of heat and lethal radiation causing immeasurable damage to the intended target. Nuclear weapons are compact and efficient devices that can be accurately directed from anywhere on their planet to any intended target on Earth, and are extraordinarily powerful and destructive to boot. Long is the list of carbon based sapient lifeforms in this Universe that have incinerated themselves and their progeny in such thermonuclear fire. Compared to nuclear weapons, biological and chemical weapons are indeed just small potatoes with limited scope and effectiveness; they can be manufactured by almost any country on Earth today with only a modest investment in technology and resources. Nuclear weapons on the other hand require a great deal of highly sophisticated technological know-how and material resources to produce. Those are very prohibitive for most countries to acquire. Therefore these weapons are limited to the already powerful ones[67]. Hence, the campaign to ban biological and chemical weapons, conspicuously championed by those same powerful countries already possessing nuclear weapons, never challenges the right of those nuclear countries to stockpile nuclear weapons for themselves. The nuclear-weapon states, especially the five permanent member countries dominating the U.N. Security Council, are quite unwilling to give up their nuclear weapons monopoly, or allow other states to possess them. The egregious hypocrisy of this position should be clearly evident to everyone.

⁂

Mac traveled back to 21 AP and visited the now vanished city of Tentulia for a firsthand look at war and genocide among behaviorally modern *Homo sapiens*. Tentulia was then in the Ganges Delta of Bengal in South Asia. The Ganges Delta is formed by the distributaries of the Ganges and Brahmaputra Rivers. This delta incorporates the modern country of Bangladesh to the east, and the Indian state of West Bengal to the west. It is Earth's largest delta and its waters empty into the Bay of Bengal in the Indian Ocean. The Ganges Delta measures approximately 220 miles along its border to the sea. Tentulia was plunked in the middle of this delta, right along the Indian border of the then

---

67 Only nine countries on Earth had nuclear weapons when Mac visited the planet. They were the United States, Russia, Britain, France, China, India, Pakistan, Israel, and North Korea.

Pakistani province of East Pakistan. East Pakistan was soon
to secede from Pakistan and become the brand new country of
Bangladesh that year. Tentulia had once been a peaceful bucolic
setting with a different name and character. The location had
served as a regular meeting place for a band of local pastoralists who herded ducks in the surrounding waterways and paddy
fields interlacing the river system.

Starting that inauspicious spring of 21 AP, more than ten million terrified humans fled an escalating genocidal civil war in
the great Bengali heartland, desperately seeking refuge across
the border in India. In an instant, Tentulia, that formerly tiny
meeting place for duck pastoralists, perched high on a dry
promontory in the emerald countryside, suddenly swelled in
population to more than 64,000 profoundly stricken people trekking frantically to that place for respite, drawn from among the
many millions fleeing for their lives to India. The new city that
took shape sprung up virtually overnight and was called Tentulia
because of the endless sea of tents dotting the area as far as any
human eye could see. On that evanescent border between India
and the Pakistani province of East Pakistan, soon to become
Bangladesh, Tentulia hurriedly arose, straddling a pathway to
relative safety in India. The sprawling Indian city of Kolkata,
then known as Calcutta, lay just 60 miles to the west of Tentulia.
Columns of battered people shorn of every modicum of respect
and human dignity, desperately clutching terrified children, their
meager possessions wrapped in small bundles, arrived endlessly at this sad and forlorn place to rest awhile before continuing
their frenzied journey deeper into India.

The people died like flies in Tentulia. Acute gastroenteritis
with severe dehydration and malnutrition usually did them in.
Waterborne diseases like cholera and typhoid were rampant.

The entire landscape reeked of gangrene and human excrement. The distinct odor of death and depravity hung around every corner of that terrible domain. Children were especially affected, little girls and little boys writhing in agony, dying in the most miserable ways. The wretched elderly, even if they made it alive to this vicious Jahannam, had little hope of survival after entering this horrible hell. Scarce food and other valuable resources in Tentulia were specially earmarked by families for able-bodied individuals in their active reproductive prime, since they alone could pick up the pieces and propagate their genes once this brutal holocaust had run its terrible course. The especially unlucky ones at either end of their life cycles—the very young and the very old—were quietly ignored and left to die on their own time. Survival sex, where young women and girls bartered sexual services for bare survival necessities, was practiced here just as in other brutalized human societies. People became utterly expendable. Dead bodies were hastily dumped into the surrounding waterways without any obvious mourning or funerary rituals for the departed. Decaying corpses floated out to sea, or drifted ashore and were scavenged by wild animals like hyenas and jackals.

But even inside this ugly crucible of despair and degradation, the human enterprise occasionally triumphed. A magnanimous man would quietly donate an extra blanket to a shivering stranger sprawled naked on the ground in the chill of a cold Bengali night. A loving mother would starve herself in order to feed a dying child. It is noteworthy to observe that this astonishing spirit of altruism and sacrifice in the face of overwhelming adversity and danger has redeemed many imperiled groups of *Homo sapiens* from annihilation in the past. Even their continued existence today as a species has depended on those remarkable qualities, characteristics that once saved them from indubitable extinction after the monstrous Toba supervolcanic eruption.

The kindly citizens of the former Federal Republic of Germany (West Germany) had generously donated an enormous consignment of milk powder to feed the star-crossed children of Tentulia. Crates of this milk powder, in giant stacks, were piled high inside three gargantuan tents erected on a maidan in that stricken city. The milk-feeding scheme was administered by volunteers from neighboring India—a country with limited resources itself that was forced to levy a 25% postal surcharge on all letters mailed from its territory during that period to fund its refugee relief effort. Every afternoon, giant cauldrons of water would be boiled over a charcoal fire. Vats of milk would then be reconstituted from the German milk powder and ladled out to thousands of children patiently lined up in front of a large feeding trough. The children were required to drink the milk on site in the presence of the volunteers, because if allowed to take the milk home it could be appropriated by relatives and the children themselves may not get any to drink—so desperate had life become in Tentulia. After consuming the nutritious milk, the children would lose some of their torpor and become more active, raising their voices and playing games as children are wont to do when they gather.

The roots of the Bengali genocide date back to 3 BP. In August of that inauspicious year, Great Britain, the colonial ruler of British India at that time, partitioned the country into two separate polities. They did this just before granting independence to British India. That division was based entirely on sectarian religious considerations and served no other intent or purpose. It was proposed by some leaders of the Indian Muslim community at that time, who feared domination by the Hindu national majority after the British quit, and therefore demanded their own Muslim majority country carved out of pre-independent India. The British were only too eager to comply, and some whisper, weaken the country before they were evicted from India. That independence itself was the result of an arduous freedom struggle by the native population led by the indomitable Mahatma (Great Soul) Gandhi. Mohandas Karamchand Gandhi (81 BP–2 BP), patriot and faithful practitioner of the irrepressible principle of nonviolent civil disobedience that led to Indian independence, also inspired movements for civil rights and political freedoms elsewhere on my host planet. The mahatma called his method *Satyagraha*, Sanskrit for "truth force." His victory over colonialism in India soon led to the decline and fall of political colonialism around the world.

British India was divided that year into two independent successor states based on religion—one a majority Hindu nation that retained the old name of India, and another, a Muslim one called Pakistan. The bloody partition of British India in 3 BP forced a massive translocation of people, based on their religious preferences, between the two newly independent countries, resulting in more than a million humans slaughtered in cold blood during that partition. But that is a different story, one that led to the Bengali genocide 24 years later.

Pakistan, when it was created, consisted of two very culturally different territories, one to the east and the other to the west, separated by more than 1000 miles of their former Indian homeland. East Pakistan bordered the Bay of Bengal on one side of the subcontinent, West Pakistan the Arabian Sea on the other, with all of India between them. Ethnically, the inhabitants of East and West Pakistan were substantially different in physiognomy, culture, and language. Their common identity was essentially limited to the Muslim religion. Even though East

Pakistan with a population of 73 million people in 21 AP considerably exceeded West Pakistan's population of 64 million at that time, political power was mostly concentrated in West Pakistan which dominated and economically exploited its more populous Eastern cohort. It is revealing to consider that these respective population numbers before the Bengali genocide were later dramatically reversed. Just forty years on, in 61 AP, Pakistan (former West Pakistan) had about 187 million people, while Bangladesh (former East Pakistan) had only 142 million. Though this population turnabout is partly attributable to higher fertility rates in modern Pakistan compared to Bangladesh, some of this difference is clearly a result of the earlier Bengali genocide.

An all-Pakistan general election was held around the turn of the year that Mac visited the region. As expected, a majority of National Assembly seats in the country's parliament was won by the then more populous Eastern polity. The result of that general election, however, was summarily suspended by the West Pakistan based military regime. On 26 March 21 AP, just 24 years after the creation of Pakistan, the whole edifice came crashing down. Mounting political alienation and Bengali nationalism in East Pakistan that followed the prorogued National Assembly, was met on that ominous day with savage force and massive destruction by the ruling elites of West Pakistan in a brutal military crackdown called Operation Searchlight.

The murderous orgy began with the raping and killing of students and teachers at the main university in the Eastern capital city of Dhaka and quickly engulfed the entire province. It ended nine months later with an estimated 3 million people[68]

---

68   Three million is the number provided by the Government of Bangladesh for those killed in the war and genocide of 21 AP. Higher and lower figures have been offered by others.

liquidated in East Pakistan by their fellow compatriots from the West, aided by East Pakistani collaborators. After the genocidal forces were finally defeated by the extraordinary bravery and resistance of local Bengali freedom fighters called Mukti Bahini, helped by neighboring India, the newly independent nation of Bangladesh emerged from the ashes of East Pakistan on 16 December 21 AP.

Tentulia, in the fall of that miserable year, was surely one of the most pitiable places on Earth. Sporting the form and appearance of a local pastoralist herding a small flock of well-behaved ducks, I surveyed the sea of humanity that had descended on the once tranquil countryside surrounding our traditional meeting place. Slowly inching my way toward a knot of people clustered around a small pond polluted with human excreta, I noted scores of people with severed arms and legs milling around the area. They were stoically bearing the intense physical pain, faces ashen from blood loss and terror, their severed limb stumps crudely wrapped in filthy rags. This lamentable congregation, about five hundred in all, whimpering from hunger and exhaustion, was truly dreadful to behold, even for a widely traveled extraterrestrial such as myself.

Their misfortune was commonplace throughout this bleak landscape. A group of nearly 700 people had fled a besieged southern suburb of Khulna, 40 miles east of Tentulia as the crow flies. Khulna, in the central part of the Ganges Delta, was a city of almost 400,000 inhabitants at the time of this tragedy. That unlucky metropolis was suddenly savaged by military gangs and their collaborators in the middle of October of that horrible year. Tens of thousands of civilians were massacred. Whole families were sadistically tortured and killed, children beheaded in front of their helpless parents, women and girls mercilessly raped and dismembered by young male combatants barely past their teens. Pregnant females had abdomens slashed open, live fetuses literally torn from ripped wombs. The degree of cruelty and mindless violence was incomprehensible.

The rag-tag crew of people fleeing Khulna that mid-October night trekked frantically westward toward the relative safety of the Indian border, finally reaching Tentulia after trudging across fields densely mined with explosives by the invaders. Many died during that cruel exodus, often blown to bits by buried mines along the way. About 500 survived that apocalyptic journey and were now milling around that polluted pond on the outskirts of Tentulia. They had lost everything—their dignity, their physical and mental integrity, their material possessions, and their sense of permanence. Adults groaned gruesomely from pain and fatigue, children screamed from hunger, diarrhea, and abdominal cramps.

I approached a man about 40 years old, squatting dazed on the ground, his right leg and left arm shattered beyond repair. Crudely improvised rag tourniquets applied above the wounds staunched blood loss. Jagged bone ends protruded from his severed limbs. I offered him a jug of clean water which he gratefully accepted with his intact right hand and swallowed in one long gulp.

"What happened to you?" I inquired softly.

He stared back at me in stark bewilderment, all human emotion drained from his dumbfounded face. I reached into a cloth pouch I carried across my shoulder, searching for a laddu, a confectionery popular in that region of Asia. I placed the soft rounded object on his outstretched right palm. He devoured the yellow sweetmeat in an instant, restoring some color and animation to his numbed features.

"Habibul Rahman," he croaked, indicating his name, tears welling from his anguished eyes. He then proceeded to recount this ghastly tale of horror and debasement.

Dr. Habibul Rahman was—until he fled Khulna two nights ago—a senior lecturer in invertebrate zoology at a local college in his home city. As a young lad of seventeen, just out of high school in Khulna, he was awarded a full academic scholarship, with room and board included, to study at a prestigious college in West Pakistan where he finished his undergraduate education, majoring in zoology. After completing his postgraduate studies and successfully defending his doctoral dissertation on an arcane area of termite entomology at a major university in Karachi, Dr. Rahman returned to his hometown of Khulna in East Pakistan to join the faculty of the Zoology Department at the local college. Now more than a decade at that college, he was an outstanding teacher, adored by his students and admired by colleagues.

Dr. Rahman hailed from a polygynous tradition. He had four wives as permitted by his religion and culture. Together with the wives, he had six children. Dr. Rahman lived in a modest suburban home not far from the college campus where he taught. His four wives and five of his six children lived with him in that house. His oldest son, a strapping lad of sixteen and captain of his high school cricket team, had recently joined the Mukti Bahini guerillas defending their homeland, and had moved out into the countryside with them. Dr. Rahman's youngest child was an adorable little three month old baby girl born to his second wife earlier that year. The Rahmans were a closely knit and loving family who cared deeply for each other.

The family had just sat down to dinner on that savage night the genocidal forces invaded their house. Just as they were starting to eat, the terrified household heard heavy footsteps stomping up the pathway leading to their home. A loud explosion quickly demolished their front door and several armed boys and men burst into the house. "Where's Shajahan?" they yelled, referring to the Rahman son fighting with the Mukti Bahini. Then they lined the doomed family along a wall, including the infant child, and shot them all in the head, one by one. They left Dr. Rahman alive to tell the tale.

☙❧

Pakistanis are not any more or less cruel than other humans on their planet. Tentulia, even with all its unspeakable horrors and grotesque brutality, is not exceptional in this regard. Countless Tentulias have besmirched the barbarous post-Neolithic history of this species. During older Paleolithic times, these humans exterminated other hominan species. Now war and speciocide were endemic among *Homo sapiens* themselves. Unmistakably, imprinting for lethal conflict is deeply embedded in their biology.

Central Africa with its ethnic divisions and belligerent states has been a charnel house for war and genocide in recent times. The Democratic Republic of the Congo is a country located in central Africa around the mighty Congo River, home to chimpanzees and gorillas. It is the second largest country in Africa by area, and with a population of over 75 million people now, the fourth most populous country on that continent. Congo's Democratic Republic borders a slew of other central African nations. Endlessly savage conflicts between regional states, and civil and sectarian wars inside them, have resulted in indiscriminate massacres and escalating genocide since 46 AP. Considered the deadliest conflict in African history and involving nine states and over 20 armed groups, the wars in the Congo have already killed 5.4 million people in the dozen years since they began. Describing the carnage to a reporter, a victim once remarked, "The soldiers came and started to shoot our men and boys, and rape our girls and women. They stole all our food and said if anyone spoke out they would be killed."

Elsewhere in the Congo, a pre-literate population of indigenous pygmy people called Mbuti, spread over 25,000 square miles of the Ituri rainforest, are in mortal danger of extermination. The Mbuti are hunters and gatherers currently numbering about 35,000 individuals. They have lived in this area since humans first emerged as a distinct species right in their own backyard. Shortly they may all be gone. In adjoining Rwanda, a country bordering Lake Kivu where Mac met the noble Itu-Kan those many long years ago, nearly a million Tutsi people were systematically murdered during just 100 days of 44 AP by their Hutu neighbors and compatriots. Approximately 15% of Rwanda's entire human population at the time was massacred in cold blood, and its resident Tutsi population virtually extirpated. In the Darfur region of western Sudan, nearly 500,000 peasant farmers have been killed so far by marauding tribes of Janjaweed on horseback and camels, in an ongoing genocide that started in 53 AP and continues uninterrupted to the present day.

Over by southeast Asia, the deadly Cambodian genocide unleashed by the communist Khmer Rouge government led by their murderous leader Pol Pot, consumed the lives of at least 2 million people through political executions, starvation, disease, and forced labor. That unfortunate country, then called Democratic Kampuchea, saw unparalleled savagery for four brutal years from 25 AP to 29 AP. A full quarter of the country's human population died in those four miserable years. Huge mounds of bleached human skulls, piled high and exposed for all to see, bear mute testimony to this monstrous abomination. More recently in Sri Lanka, a 27 year old civil war between the majority Sinhalas and minority Tamils, that had already claimed upwards of 60,000 lives on both sides, ended in 59 AP with the relentless bombardment and killing of 40,000 trapped Tamil civilians by the soon to be victorious Sinhala army.

The grisly European holocaust that lasted for six hideous years from 11 BP to 5 BP, was a horrific enterprise of official state murder by a popularly mandated German government led by the diabolical Adolf Hitler and the German Nazi Party. Throughout Germany and across German-occupied Europe, 24 million people in all were ruthlessly exterminated by summary executions, forced labor in concentration camps, starvation, and disease. Multitudes were gassed to death in specially designed killing rooms called gas-chambers. Out of a population of 9 million Jews who resided across Europe before the holocaust, approximately 6 million of them were systematically murdered by the Nazis. The Jews of today have a word for this meticulous mass slaughter. They call it *Shoah*, meaning "catastrophe" in Hebrew. On top of this egregious brutality, 16 million Slavs consisting of numerous Russians and Poles, and more than a million Gypsies, not to mention several other groups such as Freemasons, homosexuals, and the disabled, were also systematically murdered and dispatched by the Germans.

From 26 BP to 3 AP more than 20 million people perished in the former Soviet Union from purges and forced deportations during a nationwide political reorganization by the avuncular though lethal communist dictator Joseph Stalin. After Chinese leader Mao Zedong's successful communist revolution creating the People's Republic of China, more than 40 million individuals lost their lives between 1 BP and 25 AP in the political and cultural upheavals that accompanied his revolution. Countless other mass killings and uncounted genocides have been perpetrated by these hominans in every single territory and civilization on Earth. These pogroms are unending, and it must be noted here that Mac has so far been accounting for less than 100 years of their sanguineous history. It barely scratches the surface of their bloody pedigree.

The drive to subdue and occupy new lands and territories, and to control and exploit their human and natural resources, would propel many Western European nations—especially Spain, Portugal, Britain, Netherlands, and France—to expand overseas and colonize most of their planet's land area. This colonial enterprise called Imperialism that began approximately 500 years ago was shut down only recently. It has been hardly 50 years since classical global colonialism largely ended. At its peak in 12 BP, the British Empire alone, the largest single empire one group of humans has ever assembled so far in the history of their planet, encompassed a land area of more than 13 million square miles accounting for almost one quarter of Earth's land area. More than 450 million people, about 20 percent of their planet's entire human population at that time, lived within its boundaries. It was said in those days by the people of Earth that "the Sun never set over the British Empire." Indeed, that was literally true.

Many millions of people, some figure as much as a quarter billion or more, were liquidated as a result of colonialism and its racialist policies and practices. Just the colonization of the Americas alone may have killed over 50 million Native Americans in a cultural genocide of war, pestilence and imported diseases. Losses in Asia and Africa amounted to many scores of millions more. The aboriginal population of Australia estimated at about 1 million people when European settlers first arrived there almost 225 years ago, was virtually wiped out on that continent before slowly recovering to about 500,000 today. In the beautiful island of Tasmania, then called Van Diemen's Land and now part of Australia, the entire aboriginal population was physically hunted down and killed in just four short years beginning in 122 BP during the so-called Black War. There were some 4,000 Native Tasmanians living in Tasmania before the Europeans arrived. These First Tasmanians were all dispassionately exterminated in their own homeland by invading tribes from Europe.

War and genocide, as old as humanity itself, has since become massively prevalent with passing time and the corresponding growth in human population density. There is ample documentary evidence attesting to this trend ever since these hominans started keeping written records of their activities circa 5,500 BP. The past millennium of human history is especially riddled with genocide, of which the last 100 years are particularly odious and may be accurately called the Age of Genocide. This relentless genocidal age is far from over. On the contrary, these pogroms and massacres are clearly gaining momentum and charging full speed ahead.

War is waged for two primary reasons by humans on my host planet. These reasons may be grouped as either material or ideological. War may be engaged for material reasons such as to seize or defend territory, or to control and expand resources. War is also championed for ideological reasons such as those ignited by religion, political views, or culture. Though all wars are miserable and messy, ideological wars are particularly distressing.

For as long as they were nomadic hunter-gatherers with a low population density, humans found it unnecessary to engage in large-scale wars among themselves, even though they possessed the behavioral propensity for doing so—that module is genetically programmed into them. The disappearance of every other hominan species by the beginning of the Holocene, except for *Homo sapiens*, bears ample testimony to their aggressive and lethal nature. Regardless, massive and systematic killing within the same species, properly called endospeciocide, is rare among creatures as a rule. This would naturally seem to make the most biologic sense, since species are expected to proliferate and increase their numbers, not kill each other off and decline in population. Though individual members within a given species may compete and even kill each other over access to food and mates, they would surely not engage in wholesale massacres and genocide of their own kind as practiced by humans every day. Endospeciocide, it should seem, would be a taboo in biology. Certainly not for *Homo sapiens* it appears.

This injunction against endospeciocide applied to humans as well during their long Paleolithic season. Though raids by Paleolithic tribes on each other did indeed occur as evidenced by the behavior of existing hunter-gatherers on Earth today, human groups only occasionally encountered each other then and so there was little pressure to display communal aggression within the species itself. In case conflict arose during their occasional encounters, adversarial tribes always had the option of retreating into plenty of available space and thus avoid lethal confrontation. Food and other resources to sustain a hunting and gathering ethos were widely distributed across the biosphere and always accessible to them—there was no imperative need to fight to the death with other tribes for these resources. And of course, in those less contentious times, there were no cultural or religious inducements to wage war. Such sectarian preoccupations had yet to emerge and consolidate themselves into the behavioral and social fabric of these hominans. Humans in those halcyon days were nomadic tribal people living in small isolated clans that did not routinely accumulate material possessions nor personally harbor any passionate ideological convictions. For them, just survival and reproduction was good enough. Except for the occasional opportunistic raid for female mate-abduction which still happens today[69], not too many factors operated as triggers for intraspecies conflict in those times.

All this underwent a monumental sea-change around 10,000 years ago. The ongoing wholesale transformation to Neolithic culture, and the blossoming agricultural revolution that heralded the dawn of the Holocene Epoch, witnessed increasing numbers of humans abandon the foraging lifestyle of their nomadic ancestors and establish themselves in permanent, year-round settlements. These settlements produced enormous food resources by way of the new agricultural technology being implemented, the surplus food now able to support ever more settlers. With the adoption of marriage as a new cultural institution and the associated reproductive strategy these hominans

---

69 Customary bride abductions are reported in many contemporary societies. In the Arsi region of central Ethiopia, a man, in collaboration with his friends, may kidnap a girl, hide his intended bride and rape her repeatedly until she becomes pregnant. As the father of her child, the man can then claim her as his wife. Comparable practices in some ethnic groups are reported from several countries, including Azerbaijan, China, Georgia, India, Kazakhstan, Kenya, Mexico, and Vietnam, among still others.

devised at the start of the Holocene, human population numbers swelled exponentially. These pivotal developments set the stage for the promiscuous rise of large scale warfare and the proliferation of genocide in this species.

Organized warfare involving a substantial commitment of men and arms to that violent enterprise first attained its present incarnation in iconic Sumer of southern Mesopotamia. Those first wars were waged between the dynamic city-states of Sumer for hegemony and control of territory in their vicinity. From Sumer, warfare accompanied human civilization wherever it spread on their planet. Settlements, with their accumulated wealth and tempting stockpiles of treasure, quickly became alluring targets for hordes of rapacious marauders lurking along their borders.

More than 4,300 years ago, Sargon, a water-carrier's adopted son abandoned as a newborn by his mother, became king of Akkad in central Mesopotamia now in Iraq. He had been a gardener before. Sargon created one of the very first empires on Earth by conquering the city-states of Sumer to his south, thus founding the Akkadian Empire. It is rumored that Sargon advanced all the way to the shores of the Persian Gulf and there giddily waded into the warm waters of the Indian Ocean, naked as a jaybird. The Akkadian Empire went on to control all of Mesopotamia, the Levant, and parts of Iran.

Though far less technologically advanced than the Sumerians, the new Emperor Sargon had more weapons and troops than they did and that made all the difference. After sacking Sumer, Sargon embarked on a violent, blood-soaked campaign to subjugate the entire Fertile Crescent. Records written after his death attest that Sargon once marched into a city called Kazallu, turning "[Kazallu] into a ruin heap, so that there was not even a perch for a bird left." More than 50,000 people were massacred during Sargon's depredations in the Fertile Crescent, a huge number dead for that time. From these inauspicious beginnings, human warfare grew unbridled in both scope and intensity over the next four millennia, becoming today's huge tactical operations capable of killing millions of people in a single campaign. Just in the last 100 years alone there have been over 50 or more wars of all sizes, staged in every corner of my host planet, killing more than 200 million people in that brief period—the mere lifetime of a single centenarian.

The young Alexander III of Macedon (2,306 BP–2,273 BP), also called Alexander the Great, cobbled together an extensive empire in just twelve short years, stretching all the way from Macedonia in northern Greece, south to Egypt, east across the Levant, the Fertile Crescent, Persia and Afghanistan, then across today's Pakistan and the mighty Indus River to northwestern India. Alexander was barely 20 when he succeeded his father and began his conquests; he died in Babylon just short of 33 years old. In the course of Alexander's rampage, more than 325,000 soldiers and civilians lost their lives—again, a huge number in those times. Opposing cities were pillaged and put to the torch. During Alexander's siege of the Phoenician city of Tyre, now in Lebanon, 8,000 inhabitants were massacred and hurled into the sea, and 30,000 enslaved. When Massaga, the capital of the Assacenes in the northern Indus Valley surrendered, it was recorded that, "Alexander not only massacred the entire population of Massaga, but also vented his rage upon the buildings." When Alexander's boyhood friend and gay lover, Hephaestion, unexpectedly died after a drinking bout with the king while visiting Ecbatana—now Hamadan in western Iran—Alexander is reported to have become so bereaved and disconsolate over his lover's demise that he had the local Kassite population massacred, believing they were somehow responsible for Hephaestion's death. That Kassite massacre was thorough and comprehensive.

The bloody Battle of Kalinga in 2,211 BP, a massive and unprovoked attack by ancient India's Mauryan Emperor Ashoka (2,254 BP–2,182 BP) on the bordering kingdom of Kalinga for territorial expansion and hegemony, was the single bloodiest battle ever fought in human history. Kalinga resisted valiantly, but was no match for Ashoka's brutal strength and savagery. Some modern human historians estimate that as many as 300,000 combatants from both sides were killed in that single sanguineous battle. It is reported that during the encounter, the River Daya by the battlefield turned red with blood, and mighty Yamaraja, the king of death himself, was seen triumphantly dancing between heaps of dead bodies piled high on the ground. More than 150,000 Kalinga worriers and about 100,000 of Ashoka's own soldiers were slain in that battle. Ashoka the Great became so mortified and remorseful over his barbarous act that the shaken emperor vowed never again to engage in warfare, a promise he kept faithfully. Ashoka dedicated his life after Kalinga to unfailing solicitude and devotion for all life on Earth, even building hospitals in his territory for non-human animals.

Genghis Khan (788 BP–723 BP), born Temujin in the Khentii Mountains of Mongolia, founded the blood-drenched Mongol Empire that grew after him to become the second largest empire ever seen on Earth, and the largest contiguous one in human history—only the enormous British Empire, discontinuous and coming much later, was a smidgen larger. At its zenith in 671 BP, the Mongol Empire encompassed more than 12 million square miles of contiguous territory in Eurasia, occupying 22 percent of the planet's total land area. It housed 110 million people, or 25 percent of the Earth's entire human population at that time.

Genghis Khan came to power by uniting the nomadic tribes of northeast Asia. These tribes, marauding the vast Asian steppes, were fierce warriors and expert horsemen looking to pillage the prosperous settled communities around them. After founding his empire, Genghis Khan unleashed his Mongol Hordes whose savage invasions eventually resulted in the conquest of most of Eurasia. These brutal campaigns were frequently accompanied by wholesale massacres of civilian populations. Estimates indicate that over 45 million people were slaughtered in these Mongol onslaughts, amounting to more than 10 percent of Earth's entire human population at that time. Traveling through Kiev, now the capital of modern Ukraine, an European envoy to the Mongol court in 704 BP succinctly observed, "When we were journeying through that land we came across countless skulls and bones of dead men lying about on the ground. Kiev had been a large and heavily populated town, but now it has been reduced almost to nothing."

The two great global wars of the last century, both originating in Europe, proved to be endless killing fields consigning countless humans to horrible deaths. The first of these terrible wars, called World War I, was waged to maintain the balance of power on the European continent. It raged mercilessly for four savage years from 36 BP to 32 BP, sucking all the major powers on Earth into deadly combat. Upwards of 30 million people were killed in that dreadful conflagration which was immediately followed by an influenza pandemic called the Spanish Flu that killed an additional 70 million humans battered and weakened by the war.

World War II, coming barely twenty years later, initiated by Germany under Chancellor Hitler and espousing the bogus ideology of racial supremacy, quickly polarized world powers into opposing camps. That grisly conflagration pulverized humans across their planet in a barbarous war lasting six gruesome years. Notorious for mass civilian deaths and the only use of nuclear weapons in warfare by these hominans so far, the Second World War resulted in an estimated 65 million fatalities, making it probably the deadliest single conflict in human history to date.

Ideological, religious, ethnic, and cultural conflicts have frequently been vehicles for war and genocide among humans throughout their history. Religion has been an especially virulent actor in this regard. Religious war, also called "holy war" or *bellum sacrum* in Latin, is war waged because of religious and doctrinal differences between the warring parties. The ferocious Muslim onslaught that catapulted out of Arabia some 1,400 years ago and surged into Asia, Africa, and Europe for over a thousand years thereafter, Islamized large swaths of the Old World. It also produced many massacres of "infidels" in its wake. These massacres continue sporadically to the present day.

The Christian counterattack included the European Crusades into the Muslim heartland of the Middle East starting in 854 BP and continuing intermittently over the succeeding centuries. The siege of Jerusalem by Christian forces in 851 BP resulted in much of the city's predominantly Muslim and Jewish population slaughtered in cold blood. A Christian Crusader, eyewitness to the massacre at that time, noted, "When the pagans had been overcome, our men seized great numbers, both men and women, either killing them or keeping them captive, as they wished." He went on to starkly describe that orders were issued for, "all the Saracen [Muslim] dead to be cast out-side because of the great stench, since the whole city was filled with their corpses; and so the living Saracens dragged the dead before the exits of the gates and arranged them in heaps, as if they were houses. No one saw or heard of such slaughter of pagan people." The Christian re-conquest of Spain from the Muslims that raged for many generations and the Ottoman wars in Europe were all very bloody affairs. A series of brutal religious wars followed the Protestant Reformation in Europe. Known today as the European Wars of Religion, they were fought between Christian factions and resulted in innumerable deaths—some say 50 million.

In the past century alone, many ethno-religious conflicts have flared and many continue combusting to this day. The genocide of Christian Armenians by Muslim Turks during and after World War I left more than a million Armenians dead in its grisly wake. The Israeli occupation of Palestine and their endless wars and humiliation of the Palestinians, the wars in Chechnya and Nagorno-Karabakh, the Yugoslav wars, the Indo-Pakistan wars, the American invasions of Afghanistan and Iraq, the sectarian Syrian civil war, the wars in Mali and South Sudan, and religious wars in Nigeria and the Philippines, are just a few random examples of this genocidal genre.

Ferocious massacres between the Sunni and Shia sects of Islam, initiated in 1,294 BP at the infamous Battle of the Camel near Basra in Iraq, rages on in many parts of the Muslim world today. This unrelenting conflict between the two Muslim sects has persisted on my host planet for more than a millennium now, and demonstrably illustrates the deeply rooted and relentless nature of internecine warfare and genocide in this species. The Sunni-Shia schism is based on a disagreement among Muslims regarding the protocol for succession and leadership of their community after their founder, Muhammad, died. The division, therefore, is essentially a political one, not a doctrinal issue. The soon to be Sunnis, who now make up nearly 86 percent of the 1.6 billion Muslims worldwide, averred at the time that the new leader should be chosen by consensus from among any of the faithful in their community. On the contrary, those who were to became the future Shia, now about 12 percent of Muslims worldwide, insisted that the succession should stay within their prophet's family and household. The principal antagonists in the fateful Battle of the Camel were Ayesha, Muhammad's young widow, and Ali, the newly appointed leader of the Muslim community who was also their prophet's cousin as well as his son-in-law married to Muhammad's only daughter Fatima. The battle was fought in the vicinity of Ayesha's camel—hence Battle of the Camel. The Battle of Siffin in Syria a year later in 1,293 BP, and then, in 1,270 BP, the iconic Battle of Karbala near Baghdad in Iraq, cemented the Sunni-Shia split. This toxic dispute has remained intractable right to the present time, flaring up perennially in the form of wars and massacres between the two sides. At the time Mac was done visiting Earth, this Sunni-Shia civil war and genocide was once again raging in Syria and Iraq with devastating effect across the volatile Middle East, and multitudes of individuals on both sides of the divide were being horribly mutilated and killed en masse.

The relentless conflict between America and the Sunni Islamist *Al-Qaeda*, Arabic for "The Base," ignited after an asymmetric attack by Al-Qaeda on the United States of America in 51 AP. It resulted in the wholesale invasion of Afghanistan and Iraq by America and its partners. A study published in 56

AP in the British medical journal Lancet, estimated 654,965
excess Iraqi civilian deaths attributable to the Iraq war during
the three years preceding the study.

In India, systematic genocide of Adivasis by the dominant population continues unremittingly, abetted by elected
local governments. Adivasis are the aboriginal human settlers of the Indian subcontinent and presently number about
104 million people in a total population of 1.2 billion. They
largely dwell in forested regions of that country and eke out a
precarious living by harvesting and utilizing forest products.
Regrettably for these First Indians however, their lands contain giant treasure troves of priceless mineral deposits that
are greedily coveted by Indian and other multinational cor-
porations. The adivasis, therefore, are egregiously driven out
from their lands and livelihoods, and forced into settlements
that are virtual concentration camps where they languish miserably and die, their stout hearts now broken and bursting
from the ignominy.

By and large, just religious and ethnic conflicts by themselves over the ages have probably consumed the lives of more
than 430 million humans across my host planet.

War and genocide among *Homo sapiens* is a never ending
affliction for these creatures. It marks an alarming course of
escalating violence and death for this species. Lamentably, that
has become the prevailing meme ever since these hominans
formed permanent settlements circa 10,000 BP. As described
here in this narrative, this killer behavior is deeply disturbing
and will doubtless torpedo these creatures into early extinction

unless they defuse that deadly momentum. All species on Earth are indeed transient and do not last forever. Mammalian species have an average lifespan of about 1 million years from speciation to extinction, though some may persist for as long as 10 million years. Humans have already been on their planet for approximately 200,000 years. The question is not if they will eventually become extinct, but rather if they will unduly hasten that departure.

Killing of other species or exospeciocide—unlike endospeciocide—is found throughout Earth's biosphere. Clearly, that too is far more prevalent among humans. The disappearance of all other hominans except for humans was a harbinger of this behavior. The hunting to extinction of mastodons, woolly mammoths, giant beavers, saber-toothed cats, and numerous other large mammals during the later Pleistocene and early Holocene is a somber commentary on this incorrigible human trait. That behavior continues unabated today, measurably accelerating with time. The wholesale elimination of the Tasmanian tiger *Thylacinus cynocephalus*, the largest known carnivorous marsupial of modern times by emigrant humans Down Under 75 years ago, the remorseless destruction by settlers of immense herds of bison that once roamed the North American plains just 100 years ago, and the extermination of the dodo bird by itinerant sailors on the Indian Ocean island of Mauritius 300 years ago, are only a few of the more famous examples of this exospeciocidal behavior by humans. There are countless others.

The entire population of West African lions is now down to under just 400 animals, with less than 250 of them in the active breeding group. In just the last 40 years, populations of other large mammals in West Africa have declined an average of 85 percent, mostly to supply the booming bushmeat trade.

Chimpanzees, gorillas, elephants, rhinos, and other large forest mammals may become extinct in Africa within 50 years,
if hunting them for meat to feed hungry human populations
continues as the current pace. Each year, rural people in central
Africa consume 2.2 billion pounds of bushmeat, the equivalent
of eating 4 million cattle every year. Ecologists have estimated that if the current human-induced planetary extinction rate
continues unchecked for another 300 years, then quite possibly, 75 percent of all existing mammalian species would have
disappeared from Earth by that time. Though natural extinction is quite common and mundane, humans have thoroughly
distorted that process. Only about 0.05% of the roughly 4 billion species that evolved on Earth remain today. In the past
however, this extinction rate was balanced by the evolution
of new species. That sensitive equilibrium has been savaged
by human-induced extinction which is 1,000 times the natural
rate, thus putting it on par with the five big planetary mass extinctions on record to date since the Cambrian.

In contrast to exospeciocide that is directed at other species and is quite common on Earth, endospeciocide, or killing
within a species, is rare in nature. If species are to proliferate and fill their environment with replicas of themselves, they
plainly cannot tolerate mutual destruction within their own
ranks. Exceptions to this rule, besides humans, include an
ant species, *Pheidologeton diversus*, which habitually invade
each other's nests, kill opponents, and force captors to work
as slaves for the winning side. Honeybees evict drones from
their hives when winter approaches to conserve resources, the
drones dying from cold and starvation outside the hive. Some
mammals, such as lions and Hanuman langurs, may practice
infanticide soon after a new male deposes the old patriarch and

takes over his harem. Chimpanzees may sporadically battle and kill each other in communal group conflicts over food and territory. These exceptional behaviors may narrowly represent a particular survival strategy for the species in question. But this is quite unlike the mindless killing of their own kind routinely practiced by humans. Nowhere on their planet, not even remotely, can any other creature compare with the breadth and extent of the crass endospeciocidal behavior so promiscuously displayed by *Homo sapiens*.

Even before the Holocene, these humans had displayed an astonishing technological ability propelled by a singular psychological trait unusual in any other Earth based species. That was the tendency to "maximally extract" resources from their environment. This kind of exploitive behavior has become deeply ingrained in their psyche and influences the fundamental conduct of these hominans. Generally speaking, organisms tend to consume only as much resources as they may require for the moment, confident that a further supply will always be available when needed in the future. A few of them, such as squirrels and honeybees, may hoard extra resources seasonally to tide them over a limited period of scarcity. But none do so as zealously as *Homo sapiens*. Only humans remain forever obsessed about extracting and hoarding resources endlessly, until they eventually exhaust the natural supply of those resources or reach the limits of their current technological capability to extract them any further. This psychological penchant for maximally extractive behavior is emblematic of these hominans. It is their sine qua non.

Humans now wantonly indulge in this kind of wholesale exploitation of resources with little concern for the future. For instance, their massive extraction of fossil fuels is bound to deplete that dwindling resource in all its forms in hardly more than a century. Humans themselves are well aware of this but do not seem to care beyond their own individual lifetimes. At their present rate of consumption, they burn through 32 billion barrels of oil a year. Estimates place their planet's proven oil reserves at 1.48 trillion barrels remaining. Therefore projecting their consumption rate, without even factoring in any future growth in usage, humans can expect their available oil reserves to last them less than 50 years. Tar sands may hold another 2 or 3 trillion barrels of oil. If it could all be economically extracted, that may last about 75 years. Planetary coal reserves, estimated at 950 billion tons in all, will hardly last much more than 100 years at current consumption of 8 billion tons a year. Estimated natural gas reserves of 6.6 quadrillion cubic feet will suffice for another 50 years at their present usage of 112 trillion cubic feet of natural gas every year. This unstoppable hydrocarbon energy extraction and consumption by humans is certainly a most lethal addiction for them.

Incalculably more sinister and foreboding by any estimation is the effect this prolific use of fossil fuels has on atmospheric carbon dioxide levels, that potent greenhouse gas produced by carbon combustion. Recounting that fossil fuels were formed at a glacial pace by plants slowly removing atmospheric carbon dioxide through photosynthesis over hundreds of millions of years, it would seem obvious to anyone that venting all this extracted carbon back again into the atmosphere in just a few short human generations is a certified course to disaster and global speciocide.

Humans often consider the year 190 BP as the start of their Great Industrial Age. As already noted here, this era began with the burgeoning use of fossil fuels to power steam engines that in turn ran machines capable of mass production, a completely new paradigm for these extraordinary hominans. Soon the aggregate output for humans increased by several orders of magnitude. The capacity to employ and manipulate vast quantities of external energy to elegantly accomplish a mountain of biologically useful work was the key to this novel and unprecedented development in the history of my host planet. No other species on Earth had ever been there before. The Industrial Revolution began to inexorably alter their planet's features in many unexpected and alarming ways. Mechanization—by leveraging and multiplying collective human activity—soon began to affect the Earth's atmosphere, its land and oceans, its freshwater reserves, its ecosphere, and the existing planetary systems for nutrient recycling. This distorting process, slowly and imperceptibly at first, gathered momentum with the passage of time and has now reached alarming levels in this late Modern Era.

By 55 AP, humans had appropriated nearly 40 percent of their planet's land area for agriculture, with about 10 percent assigned to crop cultivation and the remaining 30 percent to pasture; probably an additional 10 percent of land is utilized to build cities and urban agglomerations. Some estimates indicate that currently humans are harvesting, or effectively controlling, nearly 35 percent of the biomass produced by their planet's terrestrial plants. Rapidly developing anthropogenic, or human-induced, ocean acidification is wrecking the building of coral reefs and dissolving the shells of marine mollusks. Other alarming changes to the hydrosphere, including the damming and diversion of rivers, the ferocious extraction of groundwater from depleting aquifers, hydraulic fracking for natural gas, and the creation of dead, oxygen-depleted river estuaries all over their planet, are baleful portents for humanity's future. Melting ice and rising sea levels pose mortal dangers to coastal communities.

Viewed from space, humans have illuminated the night side of their planet with a glow of artificial lighting not seen by extraterrestrials even 50 years ago. This feature is indeed remarkable. It is a striking expression of massive planetary energy metabolism beginning with their Industrial Revolution, and a symbol of the countless changes these sapient lifeforms have imposed on their fragile and vulnerable habitat. Some of their scientists have accordingly suggested re-naming geologic time, starting with the Industrial Age, from the currently recognized Holocene Epoch to a newly designated Anthropocene Epoch—the Age of Humans.

CHAPTER XIV:
DEPARTURE

Bellwether portends direction, a predictor of the future. Now, this elegant word "bellwether" has a most unusual origin. A wether is a castrated male sheep whose testicles were removed before the onset of puberty. The absence of testosterone makes the sheep mature into a docile and non-rebellious adult faithfully following the shepherd's directions, instead of rutting the ewes. A tinkling bell hanging from the wether's neck serves as a sound source for the ewes and their young to follow the wether on the path set by the good shepherd for the flock. Hence bellwether has come to signify the direction of future events.

Alarming bellwethers sound for *Homo sapiens* during this extraordinary period in their evolutionary history.

Humans are a vigorous young species at the moment, just past adolescence and into early adulthood. Species, much like individuals themselves, have lifecycles. They are first born or speciate from their ancestors, continue evolving by genetic variation and natural selection, birth new species in their turn, and finally perish or become extinct. This species lifecycle lasts roughly about one million years for most typical mammals on Earth, and humans are typical mammals themselves. Credible estimates indicate that the human species is now approximately 200,000 years old. That figure allows them up to another 800,000 years of possible presence on their planet before natural extinction would "statistically" remove these hominans from the scene. Viewed relative to the lifetime of a centenarian, that would make this species just 20 years old.

Humans have indeed come a long way in so short a time. Measuring along the arrow of time as humans are wont to do, that interval has certainly been extraordinarily brief. Compressing all 4.56 billion years of Earth's history thus far into a single year of 365 days would roundly allocate visible life a solid footing of 301 days in that year. For that same year though, *Homo sapiens* as a species would have been on Earth for just 23 minutes, at the very end of the year. In that tiny fraction of time they hurtled from itinerant hunter-gatherers to settled modern humans able to split the atom and travel to their Moon. What more marvels would they accomplish in another few minutes if only they were still around?

For readers inhabiting regions outside Earth who may not be familiar with this extraordinary species, a quick recapitulation of their lifecycle may be of some interest here. Multicellular organisms, which include humans, have predictable lifecycles. This lifecycle is encoded into their genetic structure. The lifecycle of a butterfly on my host planet, for instance, goes from fertilized ovum, to caterpillar, to chrysalis, and finally the imago or adult insect. Though not always so clear-cut and discontinuous, all multicellular organisms have lifecycles.

The human lifespan may be roughly divided into seven

stages, each one lasting approximately ten years, or a decade—
the seven decades of life proverbially described as "three score
years and ten." The first decade, from conception to age ten,
is devoted to explosive physical and mental growth. From the
microscopic size of a single fertilized cell called the zygote, the
individual quickly attains a mass of about 80 pounds by the end
of that decade, accumulating over 50% of eventual body weight
for males, more than that for females. Cognitive development
is phenomenal during this first decade of life. Comprehendible
speech appears very rapidly in the first two years after birth,
new learning is prodigious, and memory functions are substantially established by age four, setting the groundwork for
primary education to begin. The second decade of life is dominated by sexual maturation, both physical and psychological,
heralded by the onset of puberty. Secondary sexual characteristics such as enlargement of breasts in girls and penis in boys,
voice changes, pubic and underarm hair growth, facial and
body hair in males, and menstruation in females, all appear at
this time. Gender based psychological factors compel females
to want to physically reproduce and to seek pair bonds with
compliant males who will assist them in this goal. Secondary
education is completed by the end of this second decade and
the individual attains formal majority or adulthood. In the third
decade, families are actively formed and this period represents
the peak for reproduction in humans. It is devoted primarily to
females birthing offspring and parents toiling long and hard to
provide for their children, just as their own parents did for them.
Selected individuals from this decade are sponsored to pursue
costly tertiary or higher education during this third decade of
life. Full personality maturation arrives in the fourth decade as
the individual approaches maximum productivity and begins

to assume important leadership positions. In the fifth decade the individual has reached the summit of productivity, wealth, and social status they will ever attain in their lives. They are now the undisputed leaders and pacesetters of society. Their kids are all grown by then, leaving them free to pursue their own interests. Divorce peaks in this decade as children no longer need married parents. In the sixth decade these humans begin to transfer their pivotal roles to those who will succeed them, devoting more of their energies now to supervision and instruction, thus sharing their knowledge and experience with those behind them. The seventh decade starts retirement from work and the progressive onset of death. All decades thereafter are bonus ones. A few humans may live to reach 80 and beyond. Most do not.

The sequence of stages in life for humans is memorably described by William Shakespeare (386 BP–334 BP) in his play, *As You Like It*. In this play, Shakespeare puts his words into the mouth of a rather gloomy and cynical character called Jaques. Shakespeare himself was only 52 years old when he died at Stratford-upon-Avon in Warwickshire, England. He is undoubtedly one of the most gifted humans ever to have lived on Earth at any time or place in its history. Writing in English which was his native tongue, the great bard of Avon is revered by people everywhere on my host planet as the most evocative poet and playwright in any terrestrial language. Shakespeare single-handedly re-made the English language and coined many new words in use today. His works are saturated with profound insights into the fundamental nature and character of his species. Shakespeare's truths are so self-evident that humans have carefully transmitted his works verbatim down to their children for over twenty generations. On Galymon, we carefully scrutinized Shakespeare's works before electing to send a mission to explore Earth.

The character Jaques in *As You Like It* (Act II, Scene VII), a nobleman living with the exiled Duke Senior in England's Arden Forest, addressing his Grace the Duke, observes:

All the world's a stage,
And all the men and women merely players;
They have their exits and their entrances,
And one man in his time plays many parts,
His acts being seven ages. At first, the infant,
Mewling and puking in the nurse's arms.
Then the whining schoolboy, with his satchel
And shining morning face, creeping like snail
Unwillingly to school. And then the lover,
Sighing like furnace, with a woeful ballad
Made to his mistress' eyebrow. Then a soldier,
Full of strange oaths and bearded like the pard,
Jealous in honor, sudden and quick in quarrel,
Seeking the bubble reputation
Even in the cannon's mouth. And then the justice,
In fair round belly with good capon lined,
With eyes severe and beard of formal cut,
Full of wise saws and modern instances;
And so he plays his part. The sixth age shifts
Into the lean and slipper'd pantaloon,
With spectacles on nose and pouch on side;
His youthful hose, well saved, a world too wide
For his shrunk shank, and his big manly voice,
Turning again toward childish treble, pipes
And whistles in his sound. Last scene of all,

That ends this strange eventful history,
Is second childishness and mere oblivion,
Sans teeth, sans eyes, sans taste, sans everything.

In principle, individual lifecycles that advance inexorably from birth to death are not at all required for life to exist. Death is not a necessary precondition for living. Death was only a phenomenon multicellular life adopted on Earth to amplify individual variation and thus augment natural selection in stable populations, just as gender was adopted for the same purpose. Death is simply another biological device that many lifeforms on this planet chose over immortality in order to increase genetic diversity in a population to aid natural selection. As old organisms die and are replaced by new ones, there will obviously be greater genetic variation in the resulting population. Unicellular prokaryotes never need to perish in their individual capacity unless by accident—they just divide by binary fission[70] into daughter cells that in turn do likewise, potentially forever. Unicellular eukaryotes such as amoebas employ asexual reproduction by mitosis to divide into daughter cells which do the same, thus living possibly forever—they were once called "immortal animalcules." For that matter, even multicellular organisms on Earth, like hydras and jellyfish that reproduce by budding, need never die a natural death and are therefore potentially immortal.

Three special bellwethers of extraordinary importance to

---

70 Prokaryotes use conjugation to directly swap genes with each other to heighten genetic variation.

humans were discussed at a recent doppelgänger conference in our beloved Collegium of Pansophy on Galymon. Mac will summarize those discussions here in the order they were presented at our Collegium meeting, for the benefit of my esteemed readers, especially those living on Earth.

The first bellwether of special consequence for the future of *Homo sapiens* is their stewardship of Earth's biosphere. Humans have now become the sole arbiters in this matter. And so far, their record has been dismal.

Earth ecologists have reliably concluded that a sixth major planetary mass extinction is now well underway on their planet, brought about principally through the agency of humans. As was noted earlier in this narrative, there have been five such Big Ones already since the Great Cambrian Explosion half a billion years ago when Metazoans or multicellular lifeforms first abruptly appeared and proliferated on my host planet. Although the Cretaceous-Paleogene or K-P mass extinction is best known among humans because it wiped out the fabulous dinosaurs, four other metazoan mass extinctions have also occurred in Earth's history, where enormous numbers of species died out simultaneously or within a limited time frame. The most severe on record occurred at the end of the Permian Period 248 million years ago, when 96% of all species on my host planet perished. Each of these five major mass extinctions eliminated at least 50% or more of all species existing on this planet when those events occurred. Taken in this context, the disappearance of numerous animals and plants at the hands of *Homo sapiens* will eventually show up in the fossil record as another major metazoan extinction, the Great Anthropogenic Mass Extinction.

Metazoans are animals with a body made of cells differentiated into tissues and organs; they usually possess a digestive cavity lined with specialized cells. Metazoans make up the vast bulk of the animal kingdom. Humans distinguish five major metazoan mass extinctions on their planet in the past 500 million years—that is, since the Cambrian Explosion when metazoans became firmly established on my host planet. These five major metazoan extinctions were the Ordovician-Silurian (440–438 million BP), Late Devonian (370–360 million BP), Permian (248 million BP), Triassic-Jurassic (210–208 million BP), and the Cretaceous-Paleogene (66 million BP). Before the evolution of multicellular eukaryotic organisms and the first metazoans, there may have been four other mass extinctions on Earth, when unknown numbers of prokaryotic and unicellular eukaryotic species were wiped out expeditiously after visible life first appeared on this planet 3.6 billion years ago in the Archean. Because of their microscopic size, no fossil record was left behind of those Precambrian extinctions. Those four Precambrian mass extinctions have been designated as Paleoproterozoic (2.3–1.8 billion BP), Sturtian (725–670 million BP), Marinoan-Gaskiers (640–580 million BP), and Ediacaran (540 million BP). With the exception of the Ediacaran event, these pre-metazoan mass extinctions were related to periods of intense climate change and prolonged glaciation developing over millions of years across the planet. Snowball Earths occurred at that time.

The present human-induced mass extinction is the sixth major metazoan mass extinction since multicellular life developed on Earth. Depending on whether resource utilization by humans continues at the current pace, their scientists predict the disappearance of up to two-thirds of all existing species on their planet by the time this terrible catastrophe comes to an end. Extinction, clearly, is a compounding process. As

anchoring species perish, many others that were dependent on
a common ecosystem will follow suit in an escalating spiral.

Honeybees in the genus *Apis* are invaluable barometers of
the environment, acting much like the proverbial canary in a
coal mine[71]. These extraordinary creatures have a close and intimate relationship with humans and are the only insect these
hominans routinely domesticate. Through widespread pollina-
tion of flowering plants, honeybees drive the plant life-cycle,
producing food for both humans and animals. The wellbeing
of these insects is a bellwether for the wholesomeness of the
environment and regrettably, this honeybee indicator has been
most alarming lately. While Mac was on their planet, well
over one-third of all domesticated honeybee colonies in North
America (*Apis mellifera*) perished each year from a pandemic
disease called Colony Collapse Disorder (CCD). Feral, or wild
honeybee colonies were virtually extinct by then. Among the
several etiologic factors identified with CCD, the widespread
use of chemical pesticides in modern agriculture by these hominans has been linked to this devastating honeybee disease. The
explosive growth in the use of Neonicotinoids, a class of in-
secticides employed in agriculture, has roughly paralleled the
rising incidence of CCD since 55 AP. Neonicotinoids, the most
widely used pesticides on Earth today, are insect neurotoxins
that are absorbed systemically by plants and then distributed
throughout their tissues. Insects that consume any part of the
tainted plant, including its nectar and pollen, are doomed to
die. Worker honeybees previously exposed to this toxin, upon

---

71 Humans once used caged canaries to warn them of lethal gas pockets inside
coal mines. They took the birds down with them into the mines, carrying the
creatures in cages as the miners proceeded deep into the mine shaft. If the
caged canary died, miners would be forewarned of pockets of lethal gas in
the area, a valuable bellwether.

leaving their hives once more to forage for food, never return home after completing their task—they become disoriented while working in the fields. Unable to find their way back to the hive, these doomed workers perish miserably on the range, far from hearth and home. The affected honeybee colonies gradually dwindle in strength and eventually perish as a result of their depleting worker honeybee population. Since honeybees serve as indispensable pollinators for countless vegetables, fruits, and nuts grown by humans, their loss is of grave concern to anyone in the area of health and nutrition.

More than half-century ago in 12 AP, Rachel Carson, an American marine biologist and conservationist, published a book called *Silent Spring* which soon became a classic in its genre. The book carefully documented how the chemical pesticide dichlorodiphenyltrichloroethane (DDT) entered the food chain and accumulated in the fatty tissues of animals—including humans—and caused genetic damage and malignancies. Carson went on to describe in her book how a single application of DDT to crops killed insects for weeks on end, and not just the targeted ones either, but countless others as well. The toxin remained in the environment for prolonged periods of time, even after dilution by rain water. Pesticides like DDT and its many relatives irrevocably harm lifeforms by poisoning the entire planet's food supply. In *Silent Spring,* Carson portrays in the most famous first chapter of her book, "A Fable for Tomorrow," an anonymous town in America where all life, from fish to apple blossoms to human children, is silenced by the toxicity of deadly DDT. Authorities banned the production and use of the chemical after Carson's book ignited public outrage, but that anger was only temporary and futile. The powerful chemical industry quickly unleashed substitute pesticides to replace DDT, some which may be even more toxic.

The toxification of the environment by modern humans for short-term profit has now become an alarming phenomenon throughout my host planet, and looms as a very inauspicious bellwether for their common future. The decline of many ecosensitive creatures such as frogs and other amphibians on Earth in just the past three decades is a very disturbing development to any concerned extraterrestrial who cares about our Universe. These population crashes and mass localized extinctions of amphibian species have been reported from all over my host planet, and are believed to be one of the most critical threats to global biodiversity ever witnessed on Earth. Credible calculations point to the current extinction rate for amphibians being more than 200 times the background extinction rate for them, and that rate swells to 25,000–45,000 times the background rate if endangered amphibian species are also included into that computation.

Reptiles fare no better. Recent studies show that 20% of all reptile species on Earth face extinction. Nearly one in five of the world's estimated 10,000 species of lizards, snakes, turtles, crocodiles and other reptilians are severely threatened today. Reptiles have an ancient and complex history on their planet ever since they first appeared about 300 million years ago. They are amongst the most ancient animals around. They play crucial roles in the world's ecosystems, both as predators and prey. Their unprecedented decline is of exceptional concern to all lifeforms.

One in eight species of birds around the world is facing global extinction according to new studies released by humans. Birds face several threats to their existence, ranging from habitat loss to climate change. Common birds such as barn swallows and purple martins are disappearing at an alarming rate, some even exceeding the rates for certifiably exotic and endangered species. Far more birds are threatened by habitat loss than ever previously contemplated or assumed before these new studies emerged. The notorious case of the North American passenger pigeon, *Ectopistes migratorius*, is an object lesson from history for humans to chew over. Hardly 200 years ago, the passenger pigeon was the most numerous bird in the world, with an estimated population of at least 3 billion of them, accounting for more than a quarter of all species of birds in North America. The famous French-American ornithologist and a fabulous painter of birds, John James Audubon in 117 BP, painted the passenger pigeon and identified the bird as the most numerous species on the continent. Audubon once described a mile-wide flock of migrating pigeons that passed over his head and "blocked the Sun." Yet by 50 BP, hardly 70 years after Audubon said that, not one single passenger pigeon was left in the wilds of America—they were all gone. The last surviving passenger pigeon on Earth died at the Cincinnati Zoo in 36 BP. Commercial exploitation of these birds on a massive scale for pigeon meat, and the clearing of forests with destruction of the pigeon's habitat by humans, did them all in.

Insects, amphibians, reptiles, and birds are not the only hapless victims of this galloping Holocene mass extinction. Mammals are smack in the middle of this holocaust as well. The complete and total disappearance during the early Holocene Epoch of once abundant megafauna such as countless mammoths, mastodons, giant beavers, and saber-toothed cats, along with numerous other smaller animals, is writ large for everyone to see. Giant camels, supersized bison, lions, and cheetahs that once lived in North America are all gone now.

Uncounted numbers of large forest mammals are ignominiously being shoved out the door by humans even as Mac narrates this horrible tragedy. The rapid growth in regional demand for bushmeat is leaving many living African species facing the dismal possibility of being eaten out of existence by surging populations of hungry humans. Chimpanzees, gorillas, monkeys, cheetahs, lions, elephants, rhinos, hippopotami, and many large mammals in Africa may be all gone in less than 300 years from now. Throughout the huge continent of Asia, surging human populations have now systematically wiped out, in hardly a few short generations, once numerous forest animals and their precious habitats in order to make room for themselves and their conspicuous agricultural practices. The Asian elephant and the fabulous tiger are only two of these imperiled species. The once widespread Asian lion is all but gone. Many species of Asian apes and monkeys, including the gentle orangutan, are hanging barely by a thread.

Numerous marine creatures are rapidly disappearing as well. Whales and dolphins, those intelligent and shapely ocean-going mammals, are now in grave and mortal danger for their very lives. Humans have overfished the Earth's oceans to exhaustion in barely a hundred years since they began using motorized fishing vessels and trawlers to assist them in their fishing operations. Fish on my host planet are classified by people into two broad categories—the bony fishes (teleosts) and the cartilaginous ones (chondrichthyans). Just counting only the chondrichthyans, it is estimated that one-quarter of all the world's sharks and rays are presently threatened with extinction; there are no real sanctuaries left for sharks today anywhere on Earth where they are safe from overfishing. Rays, including wedgefish, sawfish, stingrays, and guitarfish, are even worse off than sharks. The high value placed by humans on the fins of sharks and rays in Asian cuisine is a major contributor to this serious extinction threat for them.

Nearly 21,000 species on my host planet at this very instant, including examples of conifers, cone snails, freshwater shrimp, and the Yangtze Finless Porpoise, just to mention a few, are about to become extinct. Around the time of Mac's departure from Earth, humans had added another 4,807 species to their extinction list, bringing the total number of threatened species to 70,294, of which 20,934 are on the verge of extinction—and these are just the species that humans are aware of.

Even vegetation is not spared. Bamboo jungles are vanishing in Asia from overharvesting by teeming humans. A third of all conifers are now facing extinction. Over 200 species of them, from an already limited number of 606 known species of pine, fir, cedar and other conifers, could soon be lost forever. Conifers are some of the oldest and biggest living organisms anywhere on Earth. Some species, such as Bristlecone Pine (*Pinus longaeva*) may live for over 5,000 years, and Coast Redwood (*Sequoia sempervirens*) are enormous trees that can reach heights of 350 feet or more at maturity. Giant sequoias (*Sequoiadendron giganteum*) can attain a trunk circumference of 100 feet at the base, the tree weighing in excess of 1,300 tons. The extensive loss of coniferous forests is especially unfortunate because these forests take in more carbon dioxide per acre that tropical forests or temperate forests do.

The rapid loss of living species observed on Earth today is estimated to be between 1,000 and 10,000 times greater than the natural extinction rate, also called the background extinction rate, that would normally be expected on my host planet. And even these figures may prove to be too conservative. Such extraordinary numbers would undoubtedly place the current extinction event in the all-time-ever mass extinction league. There can be little doubt now that the Earth faces a deadly extinction and biodiversity crisis, probably one of the worst in its history so far. Regrettably for Earth based lifeforms, humans, who started this trend in the first place and could redeem and reverse it, are themselves not attuned to the crisis because of their own short lifespan. They cannot imagine, or simply do not seem to care, how this ongoing mass extinction will impact their great-grandchildren, or even if *Homo sapiens* as a species will make it till then, so expeditious are their priorities. Like Plato's prisoners in the cave, their view is confined. Out of sight is out of mind for these hominans.

Homo sapiens is not the first species to alter the biosphere through activities resulting in adverse impacts on fellow species. That distinction indubitably belongs to the photosynthetic prokaryotic blue-green cyanobacteria during the Proterozoic Eon. The mass extinction that followed accumulation of free oxygen in Earth's atmosphere due to photosynthesis in that eon, destroyed all anaerobic lifeforms existing at that time—which was everything—except those that sought refuge in oxygen-free niches deep underground or underwater. Even humans may never top that extravaganza of extinction, though the jury is still out.

The firepower for the ongoing Holocene mass extinction is the profligate orgy of human resource consumption. That misfortune is directly related to their population numbers. As was noted before in this narrative, within the short span of just 10,000 years, the human population on my host planet has swelled from barely one million persons in the early Holocene to more than 7,000 million, or 7 billion individuals in this late Modern Era. This exponential population growth was clearly propelled by the universal adoption of agriculture and animal farming by these hominans resulting in abundant food production. The great surplus of food now available for reproduction, along with the new patriarchal institution of marriage, immediately goosed baby-making into high gear. Marriage, created to secure a foundation to raise a raft of neotenous offspring, quickly set the trajectory for the surging Malthusian population explosion that followed. Today, resource consumption by humans, though gargantuan in the aggregate, is unequal among them, and is disproportionately distributed across their planet. For example, an average person living in Luxembourg today consumes 482 times as much resources than an average person living in Burundi. Therefore, as material consumption sharply escalates in the developing world and Burundians start consuming as much as Luxembourgians, the demand for global resources will go through the roof and become completely unsustainable.

The never-ending extraction and consumption of limited and finite planetary resources by this copiously proliferating species will in the end strip the planet of provisions and cast a widening circle of death across the existing biosphere. Certainly, these humans were only doing what any other species on Earth is wont to do—quickly increase their numbers and occupy every bit of territory available by infiltrating their entire planet. That is the creed for every lifeform on Earth. "Be fruitful and multiply" they said, and that is exactly what humans did, throwing every skill and resource they had into that quest. Their insatiable yen for emigration, their prolific sexuality, their cooperative ethos, their burgeoning cognition, and their economic system all came together during the Holocene to produce this extraordinary outcome. Unlike all other creatures on my host planet who have plenty of natural adversaries and competitors to keep their numbers in check, there were none left on Earth to challenge *Homo sapiens*.

In many ways, this anthropogenic extinction is related to industrialization and a capital-based economic system that shamelessly encourages massive extraction of resources from natural reservoirs merely for endless human production and consumption. This economic principle is grounded in the unsustainable premise that bigger-is-better, otherwise known as Economies of Scale. This pernicious logic espouses endlessly increasing production by unending deployment of capital and expansion of markets forever. This exploitative market system has very cleverly built into its structure a punitive mechanism for any attempts to reform it. Though it may seem quite clear to my esteemed readers that the true economic goal for humans would be to drastically reduce resource consumption, yet the exact opposite is what happens. The way the capitalist system operates makes a mockery of any economizing at all, severely penalizing those who discourage consumption, by depressing their profits—a cleverly built-in mechanism by which capital markets punish aspiring reformers. Instead, capitalism pursues the precise opposite of economic restraint—total wastefulness. This profit-motivated behavior severely threatens the future for humans, along with their doomed fellow travelers who just happen to reside on the same planet with them. Since the practice of capitalism demands increased consumption, a successful capitalist enterprise would be a growing enterprise, and that means having more customers indulging in greater consumption of ever scarcer resources. The tamasha never stops until the whole edifice implodes and disintegrates. While some may argue that capitalism will be forced to internalize costs and become ecologically sustainable, the ethos of capitalism itself unfortunately forbids that from ever happening. The rarity of a resource only makes it even more valuable in a system that commoditizes everything.

Capitalism became established in human culture in the early Holocene, soon after the Neolithic Revolution began producing surplus wealth. During all that time before this gusher of wealth appeared, *Homo sapiens* practiced an egalitarian genre of socialism or communism. In the Modern Era, the economic theory of capitalism itself was brilliantly articulated by the Scottish philosopher and political economist Adam Smith (227 BP–160 BP), in his famous exposition, *An Inquiry into the Nature and Causes of the Wealth of Nations*, first published in 174 BP. That stout volume, commonly known by its short title, *The Wealth of Nations*, is divided into five books or sections, each containing its own chapters. Adam Smith was to classical Capitalism what Karl Marx became almost a century later to classical Communism. Just as Marx overstated the case for Communism, so too did Smith overstate the case for Capitalism. In his seminal work, Smith introduces the concept of the Free Market which he believed if allowed to function unimpeded would deliver the goods in spades. Smith either naïvely or purposefully believed that when people acted in their own selfish interests they would paradoxically promote the best interests of everyone in society. He called this extraordinary genie the Invisible Hand. An extract from Book IV reveals the heart of Capitalism: "[and] by directing that industry in such a manner as its produce may be of the greatest value, he intends only his own gain, and he is in this, as in many other cases, led by an invisible hand to promote an end which was no part of his intention. . . By pursuing his own interest he frequently promotes that of the society more effectually than when he really intends to promote it."

Capitalism, by introducing the profit motive, supercharges unrestrained production and consumption. Thus more the producer sells to the consumer, the greater his profit and happier the consumer—all by courtesy of that fabulous invisible hand. The incentive of capitalism therefore is for humans to produce and consume as much as possible. Because of their burgeoning population numbers, this need is insatiable, thus directly setting the stage for the sixth major metazoan mass extinction on Earth, the great Anthropocene die-off. It is quite evident that the market-driven restructuring of human economic activity to conform to the demands of capitalism has produced the bulk of the degradation and alteration of ecosystems for numerous species threatened with extinction on this planet today. Deforestation, desertification, soil salinization, environmental poisoning, ocean acidification, dead rivers, climate change, greenhouse gases, urban sprawl, road building, housing construction, and a host of disruptive human activities now widespread on Earth will produce severe existential threats to plants and animals on this planet, most especially to its author, *Homo sapiens.*

Extinction events are followed by renewed bursts of evolutionary activity and rapid speciation through punctuated equilibrium. Life will go on, if necessary without *Homo sapiens.* Each of the five major metazoan mass extinctions so far were followed by the copious emergence of new species that in many ways only superficially resembled their ancestors. Thus birds emerged from dinosaurs after the K-P extinction event ran its course. The current Holocene extinction will also be marked by quantum leaps in evolutionary development. After most of the previous mass extinctions on record so far, there was complete recovery of the planet's biodiversity in approximately 5 to 10 million years of the extinction event. In the most severe cases of mass extinction it could take up to 15 to 30 million years for full recovery. There is no reason to believe the outcome will be any different this time.

The history of the planet Kalpa in the Ketu star system, recorded earlier in this narrative, is a case in point for resurgent evolutionary vigor. On Kalpa, though mass extinctions occur like clockwork every 42 million years, the planet's biodiversity always returns following the devastation.

The second major bellwether for humans is the inescapable impact that their own phenomenal population density will have on them.

Among mammals that have inhabited Earth, hominans are by far the most invasive ones known. Propelled by their powerful emigratory instinct and their prolific sexuality, several species of the genus *Homo* dispersed across the Old World in the last 1.8 million years since *Homo erectus* left Africa for the first time in the Early Pleistocene. *Homo sapiens*, the Big Kahuna in the mix, successfully infiltrated and occupied the whole world—both Old and New—in hardly the past 100,000 years. Most of this occupation in fact was accomplished by this animal in less than 50,000 years before the end of the Pleistocene. This global dispersal of a single large mammalian species in so short a time has never been witnessed on my host planet before or since. Because of their supremely dominant perch on the global biosphere, no other species could challenge human invasiveness.

So long as these humans lived and operated in small hunter-gather tribes, their numbers remained modest, reaching a stable peak population of about one million individuals worldwide as the Pleistocene Epoch was drawing to a close. Then everything changed fast and furiously. Beginning in the early Holocene, approximately 10,000 years ago, aided by settlement, agriculture, and marriage, their population numbers swelled exponentially as if there was no tomorrow—and that disbelief in a tomorrow may have become a self-fulfilling prophesy by now. There would indeed be no tomorrow for humans if they stay on their present course, for today they number over 7 billion, an astonishing increase of 7,000 times more than their prior referenced population, all of this in just those 10,000 years.

In pursuing a similar species goal that other lifeforms on Earth do, this proliferation of humans is not at all unusual. That is what species are expected to do in the first place—faithfully increase their numbers to occupy as much space and consume as many resources as possible. The famous Malthusian Principle ensures that all species will naturally continue to increase their total biomass until they surpass all resources available to them, at which point their populations crash and implode. Humans have been on Earth for about 200,000 years now. Yet in just the last 50 years of those 200,000 years, well within the lifetime of many people living today, their numbers have jumped from under 3 billion to over 7 billion, a more than doubling of the human population in hardly 50 years. These increases now severely tax the carrying capacity of their planet. The unending extraction of resources by people using their capitalist system to sustain this burgeoning population does indeed lethally threaten numerous other species coexisting with them. The sixth metazoan mass extinction will be a doozy.

Another looming extinction threat unleashed by population pressure is global warfare. The starkly genocidal nature of *Homo sapiens* is exceptionally well established and documented. No other known species on Earth has even remotely approached the orgy of intraspecies killing that humans routinely practice. As resources become increasingly scarce and people emigrate away from desertified or flooded regions caused by climate change, the use of military force to secure habitable space for privileged populations will become prominent. Nuclear weapons to eliminate "undesirable" populations may then turn commonplace. That would hardly be surprising, given the history of a species that counts Alexander the Great, Genghis Khan, colonial era genocides, the American, Australian and Armenian genocides, Hitler and the Nazis, Cambodia, Rwanda, Congo, and countless other genocides in its narrative. With nuclear proliferation comes the real risk that "established" and "rogue" nuclear states, and sundry terrorist organizations, will unleash nuclear weapons on their planet again, after the last time this was done back in 5 BP. It is naïve to believe that humans will not attempt to exterminate many millions of their fellows in the future in an attempt to secure resources for their own populations. Rapidly shrinking habitable space and fierce competition for clean air, fresh water, fuel, and other necessities, may in fact guarantee this outcome. It is far from unreasonable to believe that humans will one day use the nuclear weapons they have been so faithfully stockpiling. What is to stop them?

Among the many exceptional features distinguishing humans from other heterotrophic lifeforms on Earth today, a most noteworthy one is their routine manipulation of direct external sources of energy to fuel their own biologic activity. They are now even producing this energy from nuclear reactions. Apart from photosynthesis and chemosynthesis in vegetative autotrophs, no other lifeform on Earth ever does this—those others can only utilize metabolic energy from food sources to fuel their biologic activity, not raw external energy directly. Only humans do that.

Hominans first began manipulating non-metabolic external energy when their venerable ancestor *Homo habilis* began tinkering with fire more than 2 million years ago. *Homo erectus/ ergaster* then invented the controlled use of fire, and it simply took off from there. Combustion of fossil fuels such as coal, oil, and natural gas, all products of photosynthesis made from fixing atmospheric carbon dioxide over many millions of years, is now providing a vast source of external energy for behaviorally modern humans ever since the beginning of the Industrial Age. The ensuing oxidation of carbon for this energy production, and its release once more back into the atmosphere as carbon dioxide, poses an incalculable threat to all life on Earth. This carbon took hundreds of millions of years for plants to extract from the atmosphere, and is now being returned to the atmosphere in merely hundreds of years. The ambient level of atmospheric carbon dioxide recently reached new heights, measuring more than 400 parts per million (ppm), the highest on my host planet in many millions of years. Crossing the 400 ppm threshold is a fearsome signal of what may be in store for humans and their captive fellow-travelers—the numerous other species riding the planet with them.

The sine qua non of the Industrial Age was the direct coupling of external energy from carbon combustion to mass production of goods and services for billions of humans. This profligate era is quickly ending. Credible estimates now indicate that reserves of fossil fuels remaining on Earth will be exhausted in barely the next 100 years or thereabouts. Nuclear energy is often considered a substitute energy source for people, as fossil fuels are rapidly used up by them. Yet nuclear reactors today are prone to malfunction and are also susceptible to natural disasters, as memorably demonstrated by serious nuclear accidents at Three Mile Island in the United States, Chernobyl in the former Soviet Union, and Fukushima in Japan, three leading nuclear states with the best technology humans can muster. Nuclear processes, moreover, leave behind deadly residues of radioactive wastes that are difficult to dispose and could contaminate the environment for ages to come. Thus both these sources of energy—fossil fuels and nuclear reactions—will generate toxic pollutants that would ultimately poison the planet, overwhelming Earth's buffering systems and its self-cleansing mechanisms.

This second bellwether is more amenable to remedial action than the first. The initial order of business for humans is to stabilize their population to below 10 billion people which is approximately their planet's maximum carrying capacity for this species. This desirable trend is already well set in motion. Major changes in human reproductive behavior in just the last 50 years alone is starting to flatten out the population curve quite astonishingly. This prolific species reached a population of 7 billion people in 61 AP, having added approximately 3 billion more people in a little over 30 years. At the present rate of growth, Earth's human population is expected to add another 3 billion more people in the following 70 years after that, to reach about 10 billion individuals around 130 AP—a major reduction in growth rate from the previous 3 billion humans added. With the steady decline in marriage which is the main proliferator of humans, together with the emancipation of women over the past 100 years, the Earth's human population may well stabilize below 10 billion individuals even sooner than 130 AP, provided these auspicious trends continue.

The growth rate for humans has been decelerating sharply in the past few decades because of steeply plummeting birthrates in this species. This decline in birthrate is clearly more evident in the developed human populations of my host planet, although less developed populations are swiftly catching up with this trend as economic and cultural progress advance in these poorer societies as well. There appears to be a reciprocal relationship between the degree of human development and the fertility rate in a society. The higher the level of social and economic development in a society, the lower the fertility rate among that society's females. Education of girls and the liberation of women are largely responsible for this effect. As the gathering trend toward female parity among these hominans proceeds apace, a fundamental shift in their population numbers becomes clearly evident. Global human population growth is demonstrably slowing as fertility rates decline and less children are produced by each human female during her lifetime.

There is even more good news in this bailiwick. Humans are only now discovering how to collect and utilize the sustainable, abundant, and nonpolluting energy freely[72] sent their way, courtesy of their star, in the form of solar radiation. Chloroplasts have faithfully been doing this on Earth for over two billion years. Chloroplasts are modified descendants of the first photosynthetic cyanobacteria appearing over 3 billion years ago that were incorporated as endosymbionts into eukaryotic cells.

---

72 Capitalism may yet find a way to commoditize sunlight if that was possible, or for Communism to use it all up in a hurry!

They are concentrated in the green parts of plants, mostly in the leaves. Chloroplasts use the energy from incoming sunlight to bind carbon from atmospheric carbon dioxide with hydrogen and oxygen, to form glucose. A byproduct of this process, free oxygen, is released back into the atmosphere.

But chloroplasts on Earth are not very efficient at transducing energy from sunlight. Photosynthesis maxes out at roughly 10 percent of incoming sunshine; the remaining 90 percent is wasted. Humans are just learning that by modifying chloroplasts—for example, by inserting carbon nanotubes into them—they could enhance the energy absorption rate by three times as much. They have also learned to use synthetic substances like silicon, cadmium, and selenium compounds to make photovoltaic cells that can absorb sunlight and convert it to electrical energy, though not very efficiently so far. Not long after completing my mission to Earth, I learned that humans had combined solar panels, genetically modified bacteria and a synthetic catalyst to formulate a system that does exactly what a leaf does—turn sunshine into fuel—but a lot more efficiently. That system was about 10 times better at turning sunlight into biomass than even the fastest-growing plants on their own planet. It could also produce a host of useful chemical compounds: biofuels such as isobutanol for instance, or the molecule polyhydroxybutyrate which can be used to make biodegradable plastic. If the underlying technology and the overall efficiency and ease of use of these biologic and synthetic devices are significantly enhanced in the future, the Sun would instantly become an abundant and nonpolluting energy source for humans, saving them from the lethality of environmental degradation and habitat toxification. The Earth receives on average, a whopping 12.2 billion kilowatt-hours of solar energy for every square mile of its surface every year. New

York City, USA, used a grand total of about 50 billion kilowatt-hours of electricity (not counting other forms of energy) for the whole year of 50 AP. Assuming 100% efficiency in collecting the energy from sunlight, then all the electricity used by New York City that year could have come from sunshine received annually by just a bit over four square miles of Earth's surface.

Humans are only just now beginning to enter this safe and commodious path of nonpolluting and virtually limitless stellar energy. If they are successful in this effort like the now extinct Anu, or the numerous other sapient lifeforms in our Universe today, they may still dodge the bullet foretold by that second bellwether. Anus were a belligerent tribe of carbon based creatures on an Earth-like planet near a Sun-like star in the Milky Way galaxy. They were quite accomplished creatures with much potential, having already sent intergalactic probes to explore their own Virgo supercluster of galaxies like humans now probe their own solar system. Anus were an insatiably warlike race, extremely profligate and wasteful in their consumption of natural resources, thoughtlessly destroying other lifeforms on their planet, and constantly attacking and killing each other for power and hegemony in their miserable world. These wretched anus had engineered a chloroplast-like material with almost 98% efficiency in transducing energy from their star's incident rays. They fabricated this material called Kongee into ultra-thin sheets which they spread over vast areas in desertified regions of their planet. In this way, they were able to make all the energy they needed. The ultra-thin kongee sheets were less than ten "chloroplasts" thick and actively molded themselves to the surface terrain when applied. Vast areas of their planet were coated with this kongee fabric, and the stellar energy thus gathered was transformed to electricity and fed into a reticulum of superconducting[73] cables that crisscrossed their planet. By simply plugging into this network anywhere on their planet, instant access to virtually unlimited amounts of electrical power was available to them.

The anus, however, simply continued on their destructive course. After eliminating all other visible lifeforms on their planet except for one species each of vegetable and animal life they bred for food[74], and after killing the majority of their own kind as well, an elite group of anus went on to dominate their planet. Regrettably for them, they all instantly perished one day when their home planet was swallowed by a roving black hole that unexpectedly came their way. Paradoxically though, the black hole may have done the anus a favor by painlessly removing them from the scene, given they were clearly heading for an agonizing extinction. Numerous such black holes exist in space. Enormous ones, each with a mass of several thousand or million Suns inhabit galaxies, ready to devour anything that comes their way. These giants are the supermassive black holes of galaxies that merged with other galaxies such as the Milky Way to form even larger ones. As these monster black holes migrate toward the center of the merged galaxy, they voraciously devour legions of stars, planets, and gas along their way. In addition to these supermassive black holes, there are innumerable smaller, stellar black holes floating inside indi-

---

73 A superconductor is an element, alloy, or compound that will conduct electricity with no loss of power due to resistance. Resistance of course is undesirable as it causes attenuation and decrease of the electrical energy flowing through the conductor.

74 Humans, too, have lately begun growing genetically uniform crops for enhanced yields and resistance to drought and certain diseases. This type of monoculture carries the inherent risk of an entire biome of agricultural crops being wiped out simultaneously by an unexpected agent.

vidual galaxies. These stellar black holes are the carcasses of dead stars of appropriate mass that expired in supernova explosions in the past.

The third bellwether for *Homo sapiens* that we deliberated during our doppelgänger conference on Galymon was rather more nuanced than the other two mentioned here. Professor Tao himself led the discussion on this one. It dealt with the rapidly changing calculus of gender among humans. A sharp decline in baby-making by females as human populations plateau around the world has much to do with this change. This transformation in gender relationships will undoubtedly play a major role in the future of these hominans on my host planet.

Men and women, as described in this narrative, have clearly differing biologic agendas. The primary species task of female *Homo sapiens* is to physically produce offspring to maintain population numbers. This function is no different from that of any other female lifeform on their planet. The male animal is only incidental to this overarching species requirement to proliferate. In males, the instinct to physically reproduce is not rooted in their natures. For female humans, however, it is an irresistible biologic drive that preoccupies their priorities during the reproductive phase of their lives lasting for about thirty years, beginning with menarche and ending in menopause. This indispensable function of reproduction is clearly necessary to the continuation of humans as a species, as it is for any other two-gender species on Earth. Be fruitful and multiply is the stated goal.

Before the Holocene and the population bomb that

accompanied it, human females, like other anthropoids and mammals in general, usually produced offspring at a rate necessary for maintaining existing population numbers, balancing that population with available food resources. As with primates generally, and the great apes in particular, human females raised this appropriate number of offspring virtually on their own, without measurable participation by the biologic father. They thus remained independent in their personal autonomy and lifestyle, not seeking parenting assistance that subjected them to patriarchal control and domination by male partners. Gender parity therefore prevailed for most of the evolutionary history of this species. Certainly, gender-based division of labor had developed as these hominans became more proficient hunters and gatherers. Hunting animals instead of scavenging their carcasses for food, required more physical effort for which males were better adapted. Females were more suited to gathering vegetables, fruit, and tubers for the tribe. At times these roles were shared. Nevertheless, as food was equally valuable for the group regardless of the source, status was equally held by both men and women.

This egalitarian ancestral model then shifted dramatically in the Holocene. The cornucopia of food produced by the agricultural revolution starting 10,000 years ago led to a reproductive frenzy in this species. Human females, the sole maker of babies, rather than having just a few offspring to comfortably maintain population balance in line with a formerly restricted food supply, now embarked on a reproductive spree since food was no longer a limiting factor in their calculus. They began birthing six to ten children each, spurred on by the exponential increase in food availability. These multiple children, coupled with the extended neoteny they required, far exceeded the ability of these human females to handle their babies on their own. This compelled them into dependent alliances with males to provide succor for their prolific brood, thus creating both the institutions of marriage and patriarchy.

Gender parity, the norm for these hominans before the agricultural revolution, quickly went out the window. In exchange for needed male collaboration to raise their numerous offspring, females got consigned to an inferior status. They were stripped of economic, social, and political parity with men, and relegated to subservient roles in their societies. Propelled by the insatiable urge to proliferate in the presence of unlimited food supplies, these females turned into virtual birthing machines. Human populations exploded in the Holocene, reaching the mind-boggling figure of over 7 billion people on Earth today. This population explosion is directly accountable for the ongoing major metazoan mass extinction taking place on Earth right now, as well as for the unsustainable extraction and consumption of natural resources by *Homo sapiens*, thus joining all three bellwethers together.

The loss of female status and disappearance of gender parity between the sexes that began in the early Holocene became deeply entrenched in human societies for the next 10,000 years to come. That scenario only started changing after the Industrial Revolution, hardly 200 years ago. Though several European and North American societies have since come a long way toward female emancipation and gender parity after the Industrial Revolution, many Asian, African, and South American cultures continue to tolerate and actively practice prejudice and discrimination against women. In many severely patriarchal and underdeveloped regions of their planet, female education is ridiculed and frowned upon, the female role being primarily associated with reproduction. They seem not to realize that their underdevelopment is a direct result of this prejudice, and that the liberation and education of girls and women would instantly double their productivity. Lamentably, the women themselves in these toxic patriarchal societies, trapped by ignorance and powerlessness, seem to passively collude with the status quo and go along with the program. In human psychology, that phenomenon is called identification with the aggressor, and is regarded as an ego-defense mechanism. In many of these outmoded societies, human females are handled much like chattel or property by their male cohorts, who isolate and guard their females in segregated clades kept apart from other males and their overall society. Therefore such cultures still function as in Neolithic times, even in this late Modern Era. Some females even perversely approve and defend the discrimination and abuse against them, sighting culture and religion as justifications.

The political emancipation of women commenced at a glacial pace during the Industrial Revolution and gathered speed as it went along, though there is still much distance to be traveled. Women were only first ever allowed to vote in a national political election on Earth in 57 BP in New Zealand. Women's suffrage slowly spread across their planet over the next several decades and now includes most nations on Earth. Yet, there still remain anachronistic societies on my host planet where women are prohibited from voting in elections, either by law or by custom and tradition. In the advanced industrial world on the other hand, with political emancipation came economic emancipation for women, though that feature remains uneven across individual industrialized countries. Japan, for instance, is different in this respect from Sweden.

Female education is the key to gender parity among humans. So long as women were kept ignorant and perpetually pregnant, they remained helpless and vulnerable to control and domination by males. Education for girls is therefore fiercely resisted in noxiously patriarchal cultures. In the Hindu Kush region of Asia, and in northern Nigeria, schoolgirls are fatally attacked and their schools burnt to the ground in an ongoing campaign to prevent female education. The Kamlari system in Nepal encourages poor parents to literally sell their young daughters, some as little as six, in exchange for money from rich landowners; these girls then serve the landowners as virtual slaves. They never go to school.

When girls are afforded equal educational opportunity with boys, they often excel over their males counterparts. More girls graduate high school when secondary education is made compulsory for all individuals. In the United States of America, the majority—in fact almost 60 percent—of college and university students are women today. Women were once banned from the so-called learned professions. They were not allowed to study medicine or surgery and become physicians until relatively recently. The first female physician to ever graduate from a medical school was Elizabeth Blackwell in 101 BP. She graduated, ranked first in her class, from Geneva Medical College in Geneva, New York State. Before her, all registered medical practitioners in the country were exclusively men. Since Dr. Blackwell's time, women have come a long way as doctors of medicine. Today they are about equally represented in medical schools in the United States, sometimes beating out men in enrollment numbers.

The bulk of the boost in the status of females after their early Holocene subjugation by males, happened in less than

the last 100 years of human history. That would be just
five generations of humans, and most remarkably, much
of this change occurred within the memories of people
still alive today. That is truly astonishing. At the beginning
of this current century in 1 AP, practically all elected officials, government bureaucrats, soldiers, laborers, judges,
clergy, bankers, doctors, engineers, lawyers, accountants,
postal-workers, policemen, and most remunerated societal
roles—except for schoolteachers, nurses, and cooks—were
all filled by men. It was accepted without doubt or question
by human society then that only men needed employment
in order to support their hapless and dependent wives at
home and their children. Now, in only a few short generations, ancient history has been firmly set aside. In advanced
post-industrial societies, women are competing with men in
every field of human endeavor and besting them time and
again at their own game. Yet billions of unfortunate girls
and women on Earth today, living in überpatriarchal and
underdeveloped regions of Earth, continue to experience
and suffer the ignominy and violence of female gender discrimination. If only as a symbol of this discrimination if
nothing else, there are way too many societies still existing
on my host planet where females are entombed in hideous
sack-like garments shrouding their entire body and face,
forced to wear such humiliating costumes in public from
puberty to death. But as female education expands and cultural prejudices shrink, these regions, too, will eventually
fall into step with the revised paradigm for gender relations
that contemporary *Homo sapiens* prefer. Abhorrence for the
old Neolithic social norms is now virtually universal.

Two pharmacological developments and a legal one, all in

the span of barely fifty years, actively facilitated female gender emancipation. The pharmacologic ones as noted before were the introduction of birth-control pills for females in 7 AP, and access to the early-abortion pill in 38 AP. This permitted girls and women to reliably decouple their sexuality from reproduction. That measure allowed these females to independently limit the number of offspring they produced, thereby empowering them to forgo any parenting role by the inseminating male if they wished, thus avoiding control by patriarchal men over their lives. They no longer needed these males to raise their now limited number of offspring—a reversion to their pre-Neolithic style and consistent with the existing norms of primate reproductive behavior. Furthermore, as the human population is now fast approaching the carrying capacity of their planet, it is no longer necessary, and imprudent as well, for humans to continue the profligate reproductive strategy they once adopted in the early Holocene. This new trend is clearly visible today. The worldwide population growth of this species is measurably decelerating as females are opting to postpone pregnancy, and have less children as well. In many countries on Earth now, the average number of offspring per female is approaching 2.2, which is the magic number 2 for a stable population equally divided between females and males, and a small allowance of 0.2 thrown in to make up for those offspring who perish before they reproduce. Since men make no babies, the 2 offspring per female are necessary to replace herself and one other man when they die, so that new genetic variation can be introduced into the population for natural selection to do its thing. For the world as a whole in 59 AP, that figure was astonishingly down to 2.55 children per woman, a sharp drop from 4.95 children per woman in 5 AP, hardly half of what it was about 50 years earlier. This represented a decline by half in the number of people added to the existing human population during that period. The People's Republic of China, the world's most populous country, introduced a one-child per woman policy in 29 AP. That brought the fertility rate in China to just 1.55 children per woman today. In fact, many other countries on their planet, besides China, have birthrates less than 2 which is below the replacement level. The high birthrate countries are rapidly heading in a downward direction[75] as well. Furthermore, increasing numbers of these babies are now birthed and raised by single mothers, the usual model for mammals in general, and great apes in particular.

Given these fundamental demographic changes now seizing this species, the institution of marriage that was structured by them in the early Holocene to supercharge reproduction is no longer sustainable. And that is exactly what is happening to marriage in the late Modern Era. The Neolithic constructs that enforced this institution of marriage have begun to visibly crumble and traditional marriage is falling apart. In advanced secular societies, divorce is statistically the rule now rather than the exception. The number of families headed by single females is skyrocketing, particularly in the developed parts of the world, and this meme will spread globally over the next few generations. The very definition of marriage itself has been disabled. Once advertised as a supremely sacrosanct and indissoluble union between male and female for the sole purpose of procreation and mass reproduction, marriage is now routinely subject to divorce and other arrangements.

---

75 The small but wealthy island country of Singapore located in southeast Asia has the lowest fertility rate on Earth today, with just 0.8 births per woman. Niger, a poor, landlocked country in northwest Africa has the highest fertility rate with 6.89 births per woman.

The legal development that literally transformed the institution of marriage came along in the year 51 AP. In that year, the country of Netherlands in Europe passed legislation that allowed people belonging to the same gender to be formally married to each other, thus demolishing the very meaning of marriage itself that had been enforced by these hominans since the early Holocene. Many influential jurisdictions on my host planet have since followed this example set by Netherlands. With the demise of marriage will come the death of patriarchy and the complete emancipation of human females. This process, first begun during the Industrial Revolution, will finally reestablish full gender parity in humans as practiced by them before the Neolithic Revolution.

The sagacious Professor Tao closed out this doppelgänger conference by revisiting the relatedness among the three bellwethers discussed here. Clearly, the central hub connecting them all is the astronomical proliferation of humans in the brief interval separating their Neolithic and Industrial Revolutions. The subjugation and miscasting of women as just reproductive machines, the relentless extraction and consumption of Earth's finite resources to service this burgeoning human population, and the resulting sixth major metazoan mass extinction on my host planet even as the wise Professor spoke, was much food for thought for the participants at the conference. We exited that meeting in deep thought. Tao has this effect.

It is time to head home now. My mission to Earth was done. Mac's personal observations regarding this terrestrial planet and its lifeforms that I was most fortunate and privileged to explore, particularly its now dominant species *Homo sapiens*, have all been duly recorded, collated, and faithfully transmitted to Alka, our quantum supercomputer on my home planet. This narrative is a summary of that transmission. Nine appendices are included in my official report to the High Tribunal. Those desirous of perusing the full report and the attached appendices should obtain access to this information through our Collegium of Pansophy on Galymon.

As I depart this world, I submit to the attention of my dear readers the words of the incomparable William Shakespeare regarding humans. This is from his play *Measure for Measure* (Act 2, Scene 2). The words here are spoken by Isabella, a novice at the local convent, who is pleading with the puritanical Angelo to spare her brother's life. Angelo, Vienna's temporary chief executive, having zealously decided to enforce a long ignored law prescribing the death penalty for adultery, has made Isabella's brother the first victim of his new crusade against fornicators. As Angelo icily rejects Isabella's pleas, Isabella grows more desperate, comparing heaven's merciful dispensation of its own powers, to the cruel literalism of Angelo's unnatural justice:

Merciful heaven,
Thou rather with thy sharp and sulphurous bolt
Splits the unwedgeable and gnarlèd oak
Than the soft myrtle; but man, proud man,
Dress'd in a little brief authority,
Most ignorant of what he's most assur'd—
His glassy essence—like an angry ape
Plays such fantastic tricks before high heaven
As makes the angels weep; who, with our spleens,
Would all themselves laugh mortal.

I returned to the Sargasso Sea off the coast of Bermuda where I first entered the territory of Earth. Stepping into the designated wormhole, I stepped out again on Galymon.

It is good to be home. I will soon conjugate with Rupa at the Welcome-Back-Saloon on Cherry. As humans on my former host planet are wont to say, "There is no place on Earth like home!" I bid my dear readers adieu.

EPILOGUE

Zeitgeist is a German loanword literally meaning "Time-Spirit" or the Spirit of the Age. It is emblematic of that general trend of thought and feeling distinctive to a particular time and space. It heralds the efflorescing of a novel paradigm—a revised world-view—representing the ethos of a period and the resolution of the prevailing dialectic of the era. Zeitgeists dependably appear at crucial junctures in the history of life on Earth, as elsewhere. They fuse the prevailing discordant notes into a new synthesis for the future. The shift from a geocentric Ptolemaic worldview to a heliocentric Copernican one, or the transition in viewpoint from divine creation to the Darwinian evolution of lifeforms on Earth, are examples of these zeitgeists at work. Humans have encountered these time-spirits on many occasions. Most are rather unremarkable, but occasionally one comes along that has monumental importance to the future and destiny of their species. Such a time is now. The outcome of the present zeitgeist will surely set the path for *Homo sapiens*. I wish my friends every good fortune.

Mac, 64 AP.

Lightning Source UK Ltd.
Milton Keynes UK
UKOW03f0630220217
295026UK00001B/28/P

9 780578 143330